The Artist

Norman Garbo

The Artist

W·W·NORTON & COMPANY·INC · *New York*

Library of Congress Cataloging in Publication Data
Garbo, Norman.
The artist.

I. Title.
PZ4.G2153Ar [PS3557.A65] 813'.5'4
77–15027
ISBN 0–393–08790–5
1 2 3 4 5 6 7 8 9 0

*For Rhoda, who has
shared it all and, happily,
never wanted it
any different.*

The Artist

ONE

1945: Amagansett, Long Island

The light was bad and getting worse, and the painting had not been going well anyway, so Duvid Karlinsky put down his brushes and went out to look at the ocean.

The waves were high and there was about a quarter-mile of foam ripping between the shore and the whitecaps of the open Atlantic. The beach was deserted, left to the angry water, as though the day were a public disaster that everyone was wisely avoiding by staying inside their houses. Duvid picked up a stick, shook it free of sand and seaweed, and started to walk along the tideline. He walked slowly and with a slight limp, a tall, wide-shouldered man with big hands, whose long, irregular face, though scarred high across one cheek, looked far younger than it had any reasonable right to look.

After a while, he sat down and rested on a piece of driftwood. The beach had remained empty, but now a young couple appeared over a dune . . . a soldier and a girl, paced by a small black dog. Seeing Duvid, the dog came over, grabbed his stick, and tried to tug it away. Duvid tugged back. The dog growled and Duvid grunted, "Get your own stick, you little *momzer.*" The dog looked at him, shifted his glance, and let go. A small-type victory, Duvid guessed, but some days you took what you could get.

As the boy and girl went by, he said, "Your dog tried to steal my stick."

He had addressed them both, but was looking at the girl, who

The Artist

· was blonde and lovely, with golden-brown, summer-colored skin. She smiled, a Viking gift to the new continent. "It's Sammy's big problem," she said. "He can't seem to understand the whole concept of personal property."

Her eyes, wide and clear, stared into Duvid's for a moment. Then she walked on, the perfect, full, long body moving with confidence and a kind of classic grace. Miss Aphrodite, Miss Rose Festival, Miss Chamber of Commerce. Beside her, the soldier was almost unseen. Duvid watched her go, feeling just a little better than he had before she appeared. An unexpected patch of brightness in an otherwise drab day. Not his, a stranger, but enough that she was there, alive and visible, a tall, beautiful animal of his own species.

She did not go far. About a hundred yards down the beach, the couple stopped at the base of a dune and Duvid saw them kiss. Sammy reconnoitered the area, then settled down, head on paws. Duvid turned and stared at the ocean, at the tideline marked by seaweed on the wet sand. He wished he knew the girl. He wished he knew her well enough to walk along the edge of the water with her and listen to her tell him how it felt to be young, beautiful, and in love on the east coast of America in the early summer of 1945.

When he looked again, they were embracing in the sand. At that age, he thought, there was no waiting. You clutched when and where you could. He remembered. What a wonderful, hungry innocence. Except that suddenly, as he watched, it became less than innocent, more than clutching. Shocked, but unable to turn away, feeling his eyes locked in place, Duvid saw it all, in sequence, saw the exposure, saw the mounting, saw, finally, that total, convulsive flailing of flesh which, so exquisite in experience, remains so ridiculous in sight. Then it was over and they lay quietly between the patches of blowing dune grass. A few feet away, Sammy dozed.

Duvid stood up and walked back to his house.

It stayed with him the rest of the day and into the evening. He felt dirty, soiled, unaccountably angry. There was no need, no need. The beach had been empty in both directions. There was no need to perform *there*, within his sight. Were they two animals? A pair of dogs in heat? My God, the girl had spoken with him just moments before. Never mind the boy. The boy was a soldier and he knew about soldiers. The uniform itself was dehumanizing. That was its purpose. It was woven into the cloth. But what was the girl's excuse? The war? The mood of the times? Hell! Half the world was at war, subjected to the same strains. Did that mean there had to be wholesale humping in the streets? He pushed the episode from his mind, but a faint, bitter residue remained, blotting out entirely that small patch of earlier brightness.

When the sky darkened, he poured himself a long whisky and water. The drink helped put off eating a while longer. He was still unaccustomed to preparing his own meals or eating alone, but guessed he would get used to it. You could get used to anything in time. And what about getting used to your wife being dead? If you tried hard enough, that too. Though at this particular point, he still half-reached for her in the night.

He sat hunched over a small radio, twisting the dial, hearing a variety of mellow, ingratiating voices saying, "Use Lifebuoy to get rid of unpleasant body odors," and "One teaspoon after meals will relieve your excess acidity," and "The Pacific High Command has announced the capture of Shuri, on the island of Okinawa, by the First Marine Division. Marine casualties were reported to be heavy, but the victory was described as an important one . . ."

Another important victory. The dead marines would be happy to hear they had won. Duvid switched off the radio. The war in the Pacific seemed remote, like someone else's. *His* war had ended with the fighting in Europe. Even the fact that he had a son somewhere out in that vast collection of alien islands with unpronounceable names, failed to bring it any closer. The Germans had milked him dry of the necessary hate. He had nothing left over for the Japanese.

He went to a window and looked out. Between high dunes, the water was black and no light was visible in any direction. There was only the evening darkness of dune grass and scrub pine, exactly the seclusion he had wanted when he and his wife had chosen the cottage, but which now, increasingly, just made it seem lonely. It would be nice, he thought, to be able to look out and see at least *one* light. Still, he could think of no other place he preferred to be, and he did require a certain amount of solitude for his work. *Artist, thy strength lies in solitude . . .* who had said that? Da Vinci? But what

11

did *he* know about Karlinsky's needs. *Grief and mourning, sir, are a species of idleness.* And what great Renaissance mind had conceived *that?*

When his drink was finished, he started to pour another, then changed his mind and had dinner instead. He had never cared especially about food, and now cared even less. Tonight he was satisfied to open a can of soup and scramble a couple of eggs. He ate directly from the pot and pan to avoid having to wash dishes. Finishing, he felt a mild stir of satisfaction at how he had conquered another meal. He rinsed, dried, and put away what was necessary, hearing the cupboard door slam shut and wincing at the brutal loudness of the sound. Almost apologetically, he touched the knob, which had a curious warmth for metal, as though a hand had been held against it for a long time.

From the center of the kitchen, he considered the possible directions he could take. The refrigerator hummed efficiently and the pilot light of the stove gleamed its small, blue flame. He stood there for several moments, feeling the silence of the house about him, picturing its separate parts. It was a rambling, weathered beach cottage, not large, never intended for more than just the three of them and perhaps an occasional guest. Mostly, it had been a place for him to work undisturbed. A few pine-walled rooms attached to a huge, high-ceilinged, skylighted studio, so perfect for a painter it had at first embarrassed him, had made him feel he was playing an artist's role in a carefully constructed stage setting. He was not used to such faultless conditions. Four walls and a window were all he had ever required. Often, he had made do with less. The real estate agent had oozed pride. "An *atelier,* Mr. Karlinsky, worthy of an artist of your stature." Grinning, his wife had caught his eye. *Hoo-hah!* Never mind. Progress had been made. No more *schmeering* in a corner of the bedroom. He was to be an artist with an *atelier.*

Switching off the light, he left the kitchen without particular destination. He walked more heavily than necessary, taking some small comfort in the sound of the floor yielding to his weight and the house carrying at least that human sign. Past the living room, with its stone fireplace and big, naked mirror over the mantle, making him remember the old Jewish ritual, far behind him now, of covering all mirrors in time of mourning. Past the bedroom that had once been his son's, but which had been turned into a kind of spare-room catchall for the past few years, with nothing of his son remaining except his successive height measurements on a door and an enlarged photograph of a grinning, towheaded boy in a bathing suit, holding a small, dead fish by the tail. Richard . . . frozen forever at the age of nine. So past his own bedroom, with the big, brass double bed, unmade and sagging slightly in the middle. Then through the kitchen and the living room again, until he was into his unlighted studio at the side of the house and could go no farther.

In the darkness, the smell of paint and turpentine slipped over him like an old shirt, familiar, warming, and he embraced it. Here, at least, were things he knew about, that he was prepared for, that he had spent thirty-seven years of his life learning to handle. Each man had his own batch of poems to recite and this was where he told his and these were the tools he used to tell them. He picked up a handful of brushes from a work table, and felt the stiff spring of hog bristles against his palm, touched the softness of the sables, knowing precisely what to expect from each. With these he was in control, a purveyor of three-dimensional illusions on two-dimensional surfaces, a master of sleight-of-hand, a magician. "All right, all right," he said. "You're a magician. So why are you standing here in the dark, like a *schmuck?*"

With something like courage, he forced himself over to a light and turned it on. The studio leaped out in nightmare reality and he saw the big canvas still on his easel, saw it exactly as he had abandoned it that afternoon, and was afraid that even in this, he knew very little, that even here he was in deep trouble. He had seen things he needed to explain, that he needed to make a statement about, yet could come up with no satisfactory way of doing it. He was an artist and an artist was supposed to be an explaining creature . . . the roots of this, the causes of that, the sources of events, the structure and reasons why. Yet for what he had seen this past year, for what a nation of alleged human beings had somehow managed to do to the human soul, he had no explanation. And if the soul had its own natural knowledge of such things, it had so far refused to share this insight with him. So that thinking about it, all he felt was a constriction, an ache at the base of the skull where the nerves, muscles, and blood vessels were bunched. This, along with the cold breath of remembering that passed over the damaged tissues.

The painting itself, all dark umbers and blues and greens, was a black pit, a cesspool, a nest of hibernating snakes. And it was wrong, of course. This was not how you portrayed evil. He had learned that much. True evil bore no monstrous spirit of genius, carried no flashing sword, breathed no fire. Most often, it came in some quite ordinary form. The Nazis were really very ordinary people . . . lower-class, not especially well-educated administrators and small bureaucrats. A mass, industrial society produced no royalty among criminals. Everything was broken down into piecework, free of general responsibility. You just took care of your own small part and didn't worry about the rest. It was all very commonplace. Commonplace Germans doing a commonplace thing like murdering ten million people. Or was its seeming banality actually its genius? What better way to take the curse out of murder, to disguise it, to make it almost palatable, than to reduce it to trivia? What magnificent political insight! People simply did not understand. They got their ideas about things like this from books and movies. They expected obvious and bona fide villains for their murderers, not ordinary clerks and administrators. It made what happened impossible to believe. Even the victims had not believed it. Until the last, they thought they were simply being given showers. Duvid had seen the showers, walked across the tile floors, touched the immaculately clean walls. Impossible to believe. Then he had seen the results and believed it.

Slowly, tiredly, he took the painting off the easel and leaned it, face against the wall, with the others. He just didn't know enough, he thought. Nothing he had learned had prepared him for this. Yet how could you prepare? Where could you learn? When had this ever happened before?

He turned his head from side to side, trying to fool himself into thinking he was looking for something specific. Actually, he was locked in a small island of light, held fast by the echoless emptiness of the house. As if smothering in the silence, he breathed deeply and felt his lungs fill to the point of dizziness. Garbage, he thought, he would take out and burn the day's garbage. Spurred by the prospect of so positive an act, he returned to the kitchen and lifted the bag of rubbish from its pail. Then he carried it through the back door and out into the yard. There was no moon or stars, but the sand gave off a misty light. An empty clothesline creaked in the breeze and the ocean added its rolling sound. Duvid walked along a narrow duckboard path to the burner, dropped the bag in, and lighted it. He stood watching it burn, smelling the smoke and the salty dampness of the air. Not until it was finished, not until the last small spark had died, did he go back to the house.

Convincing himself he was tired, he prepared for bed. He showered, then toweled himself dry with almost brutal roughness. In the mirror over the sink, his face stared back at him through a film of steam. He smiled, as though testing the muscles, then shrugged and turned away. There still seemed to be a clinging scent of perfume, a distinctly feminine fragrance in the air. Insanely, he felt himself begin to tremble in the bright room, and finished up quickly and left.

He put on fresh underwear and lay down stiffly on the bed. He did not own pajamas or slippers or a robe. These were for sickness or lounging, and he was never sick and never lounged. The moment he was up, he put on pants and shoes, put on his man's responsibilities and dignity. His wife had teased him about not knowing how to relax, but had understood his needs better than he. The bed felt damp and haunted with lumps he had never noticed before, and his body stayed rigid. He forced a yawn to fool himself into believing he was ready for sleep, but it failed to work and he lay for a long time with his eyes closed, listening to the waves.

Slowly, he began to swear. He swore carefully, almost fastidiously, in a low, even voice, not directing it at anyone or anything in particular, but keeping it coldly impersonal. When he had exhausted every vile word he knew in English, he dug back for a few in Yiddish and added these, reciting his bitter, bilingual litany with as much sincerity as he could muster in the damp, solitary dark of the quiet room.

The Artist

Duvid swam easily, letting his body roll with each stroke, feeling strong, loose, and tireless in the ocean's early morning calm. Occasionally there was a gentle swell and he could feel himself lifted in a long, slow glide. But mostly, the water held him steady. Squinting toward the horizon, he sensed the long, sleeping bulk of the shore behind him. The beach was far off now and fading and he was quite alone.

Stupid, he thought, Cramp out here and you were fish-food. So? Fish had to eat too. But he was not amused. Nor did he turn back. Compulsively, as though gripped by an implacable current, he kept swimming. He swam in a silence that had no air left. A deep vacuum. Yet he felt wonderfully free of waste and guilt and gutting of the earth, felt that if there were mermaids around somewhere and they could speak, he would have no trouble understanding them. Pushed farther, he had the sensation that something of him was passing through a corridor and a hot breath came up over his face as if he had blundered through an unseen barrier. Then the breath turned suddenly cold, a wind off a glacier, an offer of death that was as loud and ringing about his head as the bells of a giant carillon. Or was that just the clanging of his heart? Either way, he was caught. And knowing this, all he wanted was to escape, to be some sort of rational, producing man again, nailed tight to details, reasonable, blind to the pull of the dark. But he could not turn back and a fear broke loose in him like the trembling that comes when you are forced into a fight you do not want.

"Hey!"

At first he thought it was just one of the echoes in his head. Then he heard it again and looked around and saw a head breaking the water a hundred yards back.

"Hey, wait!"

A female voice. There *were* mermaids. Treading water, he watched her pull toward him with fast, strong strokes. Annoyed, he felt the vague impatience of a terminal patient disturbed in his final sleep by the probing of a doctor's needle. To the last, they had to *nudge* you.

Her face came out of the water a few feet away. "You . . . crazy . . . or something?" The words were breathless, angry.

16

The Artist

Duvid recognized her then, recognized the long blonde hair, the classic nose, the sun-ripened flesh supporting it. Of course, Miss Aphrodite, with her clean, small-town girl's look. Alias Miss Public Fornication of 1945.

"It's dumb to go this far out alone."

They treaded water a few feet apart, the sun pink and low over the windless surface. "You're right," Duvid said and started to swim back. He tired on the way in and slowed, but the girl stayed with him. When he at last trudged out of the water, his knees felt weak, his legs hollow, and there was a sick feeling deep in his gut that might or might not have come from exertion.

Sammy was waiting on the beach. He sniffed suspiciously at Duvid, who picked up a stick and offered it to him. The dog hesitated, searching his face, then grabbed it between his jaws and trotted off. "I owed him that," Duvid said.

The girl stood dripping in the early sun. Duvid had a good, long look at her now and she was older than he had expected. She was not eighteen or nineteen as he had thought the day before, but twenty-four, perhaps, or twenty-five, and there were gray circles beneath the blue of her eyes. But even soaking wet she was lovely, with an elusive, silvery air as if she had once known a huge disappointment and now a delicate, translucent brightness had formed to cover the pain.

"Thanks," he told her, although he was not entirely certain why he was thanking her or even whether he should be thanking her at all. Still, effort and risk had been involved, and these were not commodities to be taken lightly. Not many would have bothered about an anonymous figure in the water. "Is that what you do?" he said. "Go around bringing in foolish swimmers with sublimated death wishes?" That is, he thought, when she wasn't busy humping soldiers on the beach.

"I know what can happen in this water. Sometimes there's a bad undertow."

"There was no undertow today," he said irrelevantly.

"No, but it's crazy to be out that far anyway. What a waste if anything happened to someone like you."

Duvid looked at her hair, hanging straight, wet and sleek over

her ears, small soft ears, pale chips of eggshell. "You know me?"
She laughed.

"What's so funny?"

"Everyone in Amagansett knows you. You're our big attraction.
The first thing real estate agents tell prospective buyers is that
Duvid Karlinsky has a studio here."

"You mean I'm good for land values?"

"Very good."

"I'm glad I'm good for *something.*"

The girl laughed again and Duvid wondered why it was that
when he spoke what he believed to be the absolute truth, people
invariably thought he was joking. He said, "But I don't know *you.*"

"Laurie Wallace."

"Well, Laurie, I'm sure you must be something of an attraction
out here yourself."

She turned slightly and the pink champagne light of the sun,
moving across her face, gave her a different look than she'd had just
an instant before, gave her a sober, little-girl-next-door look, a clean
tough decent little-American-girl look that gave charm to the tilt of
her nose and a touch of stubbornness to her mouth. "You're talking
about what you saw yesterday, aren't you?"

"You did put on quite a show."

"I know."

No embarrassment. No apology. Just a simple statement. *I know.*
Hell, *of course* she knew. She was tough, all right. Still, a nest of
separate personalities, not just one. But her bottom, Duvid felt, held
the key. It was a very practical ass, pleased with itself and what it
knew it could do, driven entirely by its own rhythms, just a shade
too broad and round for the waist above it. It said . . . this behind
is built for service, mister. Her face, having nothing to do with her
butt, gazed at him with complete innocence.

She said, "Did I shock you very much?"

"Go to hell," he told her, but mildly.

"Were you angry with me?"

"I didn't even know you."

"Yes, but weren't you angry anyway?"

"Are you taking some kind of poll?"

The Artist

She laughed, a warm, fluid sound in the still air. "You *were* angry."

"Of course I was angry," he said and again found, standing next to her, not one presence in her, but several, among them a deeply curious young woman of cool, green shadows and nameless ghosts . . . and then another girl, sun-browned and healthy, an athlete, a stronger swimmer than most men, the kind who looked to lovemaking for exercise. "You made me feel dirty."

"You didn't have to watch."

"Oh, yes I did."

"Of course." She looked at him, her eyes full of pepper in the glow of the sun, glints of gold and pink in the blue. In this light she was pure cat, cat's eyes, cat's poise, cat's knowing mouth. "I'm sorry."

"No you're not."

She gave him the full smile, the total treatment, the Miss Chamber of Commerce and all the rest. "Anyway, since I just practically saved your life, you *have* to forgive me."

He shook his head. Not in rejection, but in continuing wonder. "All right."

"All right, what?"

"All right, I forgive you."

"Enough to give me some coffee. I'm freezing to death in this wet suit."

Her arms and shoulders were, indeed, goose-bumped. "Come on." He led her across the sand toward his house. Sammy bounded after them. "I'll even give you some eggs."

"No, thanks. Just coffee. When I can, I try not to eat."

"Why?"

"It's such a loathsome act. Don't you think?"

"It's necessary."

"Yes, but so ugly. People should really take their food in private. The same way they eliminate it. Instead, they turn it into a whole social thing, invite their friends, do it en masse. There should be laws against it."

"Like the laws against fornicating on public beaches?"

She smiled her beatific, choir-girl smile. "Exactly."

The Artist

With the girl at his side, something returned the strength to his legs. He took the porch steps easily and pushed open the door. Laurie went in, but Sammy balked at the threshold. "Go on," Duvid told him. "Don't be such a coward." Sniffing, lifting his paws delicately, as if walking on a hot, fragile surface, the dog eased into the house, a tiny, overly cautious black mop. Duvid followed. For the first time since his wife died, he had company.

Shivering, Laurie hugged herself for warmth. "Any chance of scrounging a robe?"

"I don't own one. But my wife's things are still in the bedroom closet. If you don't mind that?"

"Mind what?"

"Wearing the clothes of the dead."

"Should I mind?"

"Some people do."

"That's dumb."

She went where Duvid showed her. He took clothes for himself and changed in the kitchen. The coffee was up and he was busy scrambling eggs when she returned in a pink terry robe that ended three inches above her knees and wrists. For the first time, she appeared a little self-conscious.

"I'm afraid I'm not as petite as your wife."

He thought it rather a nice way to put it. But when you had her kind of looks, it was easy to be generous.

They sat opposite one another at the kitchen table. Even here, in the sharp crosslight of the windows, her face had something shadowy and elusive about it, something prematurely aged or yet to be formed. No matter. She might have looked like anything at this moment. It was enough that he wasn't eating alone. Sammy looked up at him expectantly and he leaned down and shared some of the eggs.

"What happened to your soldier?" he asked.

"What happens to all soldiers. Shipped out."

"Then yesterday was his going-away present?"

She shrugged. "For a kid off to some bloody hole in the jungle, it beats doughnuts and coffee."

Duvid was silent.

20

The Artist

"I mean it," she said. "I spent a couple of years overseas with the USO. You know. A little singing, a little dancing, stuff like that. It was enough to make you sick. They dangle you half-naked in front of those poor sex-starved kids, then send them to bed with doughnuts and coffee. Talk about teasing."

"So you came home to run your own USO? Nonteasing variety?"

"Something like that." She smiled wryly, mocking herself. "On a very limited scale, of course."

He ate his eggs with care, his first tolerable food in weeks. "Where were you overseas?"

"Almost everywhere. England, France, Belgium, Germany. Mostly, we followed the advance. Camp-followers, American-style."

"You must have seen a lot."

"I saw *you.*"

"Where?"

"A lot of places. Once, in Piccadilly. Twice, in the lobby of the Dorchester. You were also passing in a jeep near Sainte Mère Eglise, in Normandy. And in Paris, I even saw you with a three-star general on the rue Saint Denis." She sipped her coffee. "What were you doing on the rue Saint Denis?"

Duvid smiled. "Not what you think. Three-star generals don't have to chase whores."

"Of course not. They get their sex shoving little colored pins into battle maps."

"Stop being so superior. Generals are people too."

"No they're not. They're loaded pistols. Anyway, I didn't like seeing you with a general that day. I remember. It bothered me, made me afraid you were like all the rest of them."

"All the rest of whom?"

"The moguls. Those in high places. I liked it better when I saw news-pictures of you slogging along hedgerows, or sharing foxholes with muddy, beat-up dogfaces. The shots with captions that said things like, FAMED ARTIST SHARES DANGERS AND HARDSHIPS OF COMMON FOOT SOLDIER. Or, KARLINSKY LIVES AND PAINTS WAR AT LOWEST LEVEL. *That* was how I enjoyed seeing you."

"You're making fun of me."

"Of course."

"Why?"

"To keep from being awe-struck in your presence."

He laughed.

"No, really," she said. "Wouldn't you rather have me make fun of you, than make an utter ass of myself?"

"Couldn't you manage something more in the middle?"

"I don't think I've managed anything more in the middle in my life."

Duvid believed her.

Finishing her coffee, she asked, "May I look at your studio?"

"There's nothing there."

"May I look anyway?"

"No." It came out more harshly than he had intended. "Maybe some other time. If you still want to."

The robe parted slightly as she stood up and Duvid saw she had removed her wet suit. Annoyed at what he felt, he turned and cleared the table.

"I'm sorry," she said.

"For what?"

"I'm not a tease."

"So you told me."

"I meant it."

"So?"

"So if you'd like to make love to me, you may."

At the sink, he did not look at her.

She was silent behind him.

"Aren't I a little overage for your USO kiddie program?"

"I didn't mean it that way."

"No? Then you took just one look at me and felt instant desire?"

"It was more than just one look."

"Oh, yes. There was London, Normandy, and Paris."

"And yesterday afternoon," she added.

The way she said it made him turn. She had the clear, cool eye of a fair lawyer who has missed an exceptional career in surgery. "Are you trying to say that was for *me?*"

She gave him her wry smile. "You *did* notice me."

"I'd have noticed you without *that!*"

The Artist

"You never did before."

The eggs squawked in Duvid's stomach. He did not like what he suddenly saw in her face, did not like that look of a practical, planning woman who has the time to get the kids off to school, buy the groceries, put the house in order, and screw the neighbor next door before she prepares dinner. "Let me tell you something," he said, feeling himself part of some sort of childish, sexual round-robin. "I haven't had a woman since my wife died and I probably need one. And I'm sure I'll never get a better, more attractive offer than this. But I'm going to turn it down."

"Why? Because I didn't waste enough time on preliminaries? Because I didn't stick to the proper mating ritual and let *you* be the aggressor?"

Duvid said nothing, but watched her expression soften from that of a tough female with velvet to sell, to that of a beautiful golden child, sweet fruit, national treasure.

"Well, let me tell *you* something," she said. "I can't paint as you can, and I can't write or compose music, and I can't even sing and dance as well as I'd like to. You've got to understand it. When I offer myself to a man, and I may offer myself for a lot of reasons, behind the whole thing is the feeling that this is when *I'm* creating, that this is when *I'm* making something really fine, that this is when *I* can do something better than any other woman. I've enjoyed *your* paintings for a long time. All I'm asking now is that you give yourself the chance to enjoy mine." She looked at him with a soft, child's look. "Is that so terribly wrong?"

It took him a moment. He was finding it hard to keep up with the changes in himself as well as in her. "Not if it's what you really believe."

"Don't you think I believe it?"

"I don't know. I don't know you."

"But what do you *think?*"

"I think this is something I never expected to have to be coping with again." He smiled dimly. "And I also think I'd be a terrible fool not to *stop* thinking."

He pulled back the terry robe and let it slip from her shoulders. Pale, untanned breasts with pink eyes gave him an unblinking stare.

23

The Artist

Below, a flat, childless belly and dainty, amber mane. She stood unmoving, letting him look. Being naked elongated her neck and added ripeness to her hips. It also seemed to make her more serious, a grave, oval-faced animal, contemplating, sniffing out her new lair. And she was naked in the morning sunlight of this kitchen, *his* kitchen. This strange, eager, too-trusting creature. She was an arm's length from him, waiting.

"Now you," she said.

"I'm not very pretty."

"No one wants you to be."

He undressed and let her see him, scars and all. She stared. "Are they from the war?"

"Not this war; the last." Then he added, "Most of them, anyway." He had almost forgotten the new ones. They were not yet properly part of him.

"But you have such a young body. It looks more twenty-six than fifty-six."

"How did you know how old I was?"

"I looked you up in *Who's Who.*"

He laughed, then kissed her mouth, tasting the faint remains of coffee and something else that carried the flavor of distant army camps and recently shelled towns and frightened young men far from home, carried too, the heat of summer sun and beaches and blonde, seventeen-year-old *shiksa* cheerleaders getting their pants pulled down in the back seats of parked cars. It was not the best kiss he had ever had, but it was certainly one of the strongest and, perhaps, one of the most welcome.

There was a couch in his studio and he led her there rather than to the bed he had shared with his wife. He had never believed in any mystic loyalty to the dead, nor even, for that matter, any total fidelity to the living, but he somehow avoided his bedroom now, for this. If Laurie noticed, she said nothing.

Her flesh was indeed a prize. With his hands on her, life came back to him again from a long way off. The past months had left him all but dead. He had felt, at times, without mind, heart, or pride. It was as if a vast collection of ashes, of burned-out aches and terrors, had formed a clot in his throat and made it impossible for him to

24

breathe. But he did breathe now, taking the air from her lungs into his, feeling the separate parts of her body and life gather to match the weight of his own. Less than half his age, she was, unaccountably, his equal . . . good to good, bad to bad. He did not understand it, nor did he even try. Eyes sealed against the morning light, he traveled through a private dark, aware of nothing but the soft circle of warmth that held him.

"Well . . ." he said when he was able to speak, "you're more than just a good painter. You're a painter of masterpieces. A genius."

"I told you I was creative."

It came out with happy immodesty, but without smugness. She had learned to bake her pies in the kitchens of the devil and they were good pies and she knew it. The same way she knew she was not a good singer and dancer.

She said, "You do feel better now, don't you?"

"Much better. That would cure anything."

She was sitting up, studying him gravely, the doctor gauging the latest condition of her patient. "You look better. I didn't like the way you looked before."

"How did I look?"

"I think," she said slowly, "suicidal."

"Great."

"No, I mean it. There's a way a person looks then. I can't describe it exactly, but I know it." She lit a cigarette and the dusty circles beneath her eyes stared out with sudden fatigue. "I've seen it on myself in the mirror."

"You?"

"Don't you think there are moments when everyone gets the feeling?"

"I've never thought about it that much," he lied.

"I have, I even think there might be a right time to do it, a time when if you didn't, you could be sorry for the rest of your life."

"You'll have to explain that to me."

"That's funny."

"What?"

"*Your* asking *me* to explain it. I always felt if I ever met you, that *you'd* be the one to do the explaining, that *you'd* be the true expert.

The Artist

I mean, everything I've ever seen that you've painted screamed with it."

"Screamed with a wish for death?"

"If not that, then the kind of loneliness that leads to it. All your people seem so terribly alone. In crowds, each person you paint is alone. In bed, in small rooms, even your lovers are miles apart. And they're all so sad. Why do you paint everyone so sad?"

He smiled. "I don't know. That's just how they seem to turn out. I don't plan it."

"I thought all artists planned what they did."

"I don't know about all artists. I'm lucky if I sometimes get to know about myself." He sat up beside her on the couch and touched her shoulder, flesh so smooth it seared his palm. Surprisingly, it was good talking to her. With so much else thrown in, it seemed an undeserved bonus. "If I put too much planning in a painting, it ends up forced, a lie, something I might like it to be, but which it really isn't. I've got to let it paint itself. So if my people turn out sad, I guess it's because that's the way they are. All faces are sad anyway. A smile is a passing thing. So is a laugh. Neither stays long. I paint whatever happens to be left when they go away."

"Hey! . . ." she said, suddenly girlish. "I'm in your studio after all."

"I told you there's nothing here."

Not entirely accurate. There was a tall studio easel, a worktable and palette, some sketches tacked to the knotty-pine walls, and the recent failures.

She gazed about, finally fixed on the backs of the canvases. "Are these what you're working on now?"

"Yes."

"Why are they turned to the wall?"

"So I don't have to look at them."

"Are they that terrible?"

The blues and greens and dark umbers rose in memory like the mutilated corpses of a battlefield. But the girl's soft circle of warmth still enclosed him, and he said, "Why don't you look at them and tell me what you think?"

She seemed startled. "I don't really know much about painting."

26

"Neither does anybody else. All we've got are reactions and opinions. And yours are probably more honest than most."

She sat staring at the backs of the canvases. "Do you know? I'm suddenly scared."

"Of what?"

"I don't know."

"You didn't feel that way when you asked to see my studio."

"No. But I feel that way now. Isn't that *dumb?*"

He did not say anything.

"But there's no *reason.* I'm really *dying* to see what you're doing." She shook her head impatiently. "Oh, to hell with it," she said, and went to the wall. There were three canvases. "Which shall I look at?"

"It doesn't matter."

"Which were you working on last?"

Duvid pointed to a canvas on the far right.

"I'll look at that one now," she said, "and save the others."

Curiously, Duvid felt himself affected, as though she had somehow passed on this sense that his current work was a spiked fence between them that had to be climbed over with some danger. Or, more than a fence, it was the entrance to some private place she might stumble into before it was ready to receive her, and so spoil everything.

She turned the canvas and stepped back to look, standing naked on the studio floor, her flesh all brown, gold, and pink, all life and warmth against the coldness and terror of the painting. She looked for a long time, then returned to the couch. "I don't know what to say."

"You don't have to say anything."

Her eyes were still frightened. "I feel as though I've been told something terrible, as if a message had come to me from the end of the world, that I was close to the end of the world. Does that sound crazy?"

Maybe he hadn't failed as badly as he had thought. "No."

"You went into those camps, didn't you?"

"Yes."

Sitting beside him, she continued to stare at the painting, dark,

27

desolate, and unpeopled except for some frightened eyes, afloat among the snakes. "I've read about them and seen pictures, but none of it seemed real."

"It was real. If nothing else convinces you, the smell does."

"What happened to God?" Her voice was small, a child's.

"I don't know. I've never met Him."

She lay back and reached for Duvid. "When I was a little girl I used to think I could see Him."

"What did He look like?"

"Different things at different times. Once I thought I saw Him in the glass iris of a one-eyed doll I had. Another time He came shining out of a rain puddle. But mostly I saw Him in the fires we used to have right out here on the beach at night. Those times were the best, with the whole family there, huddled close together against the chill off the water and all that blackness outside. Then I'd stare hard into a particular flame and He'd be right there, staring back at me, His voice kind of crackling and happy and the smell of Him all spicy, like tar burning off the driftwood. One of my brothers used to say he saw Him too, but I never believed him."

"Do you have a big family?"

"I did have. Two brothers and two sisters and a mother and father," she recited. "They're gone, though."

He looked at her.

"Everyone," she said in a bright voice. "A gasoline truck smacked into them in a fog near Secaucus, New Jersey." She laughed. "Imagine buying it in a town named *Secaucus,* of all places. Pig farms and swamps and burning garbage and six-sevenths of the Wallace family going up with the stink. But Daddy always did say we had a kind of offbeat way of doing things."

Duvid felt as if he had broken the seal on a vault. "How long ago?"

"It'll be six years next Christmas. They were driving up to see me at school for the holidays. I'd been sick and couldn't get home so they were surprising me. Some surprise, huh?"

He said nothing.

"I got through it all right." She pursed her mouth as though adding up a very expensive bill. Then she smiled, "I think."

28

The Artist

"You're fine."

"Except maybe for Christmas. I still have to be a little careful around Christmas. It's a terrible time anyway. You Jews are lucky not to have it."

"We Jews have other things."

"I guess you do," she said, and her eyes were drawn once more to the painting, although this was not what he had meant. The grayness, the exhaustion under her eyes was deeper now, fighting the rosy tints beneath, and she got up suddenly and turned the painting to the wall once more. Then she came back to him. "Ah, Mister Karlinsky. Is it too soon to love me again?"

"What time is it?"

She laughed. "I lost my watch three years ago."

"Well," he said, "we can always try, can't we?"

They did. And somewhere in the middle, afloat in this fair, silver girl with the bright hair and golden warmth, that new life began in him again, sweet and hard to follow, and he went up with it and flew out over the same waters he had been lost in a few hours before and felt them wash over him without threat.

Yet near the end, some dim continent of dread opened and spread wide in him, rising like a dragon, as if he knew that nothing had changed, and that regardless of what he felt now, nothing would ever really change. He heard it in the small sounds of love they made, in their mixed liquids, and imagined, in the unseen spaces of her, a darkness clouded by things he knew nothing about. Still, the threads of something, carefully spinning, joined them together in her belly until he felt a wetness on her cheeks, and he whispered, "Why are you crying?"

"Why are you?" she asked, which was as much of a surprise as any of the rest, because he had not even been aware of it.

"I don't know."

"I hope it's a good sign," she said. "I hope it means you're going to care about me a little."

"Well," he considered, "why not?"

TWO

1895: Trevyenka, Russia

When Duvid was six, he had already heard most of the stories about the pogroms. Sometimes he even dreamed about them and would cry out in his sleep until his mother or father came to wake him. In his dreams it was always night when the Cossacks rode into the *shtetl*, torches bloodying the dark, sabers high. But when they finally did come, when their arrival was no longer a nightmare from which Duvid could be awakened, they came out of the yellow haze of a summer afternoon.

At first there was only a distant rumble, which Duvid thought was thunder until, watching from a wooded rise beyond the village, he was able to see a faint curtain of dust. Even so, there seemed little reason for fear. The day was just another lazy summer day, different only in that Duvid's parents had gone off to Odessa that morning and left him in the care of his aunt and uncle. Duvid had wanted to go along, had been eager to see the sights of the fabled seaport, but this was business, not a pleasure trip. His father's work had to be delivered and sold. There would be time enough, declared his mother, for him to see whatever there was to see of the city. At best, it was a bad place for Jews. She kissed his eyes. And city *goyim* liked nothing better than to eat little Jewish boys for breakfast.

The rumble grew louder, the curtain of dust larger. Visitors to the *shtetl*. Wagonloads of travelers often passed through on their way to and from Odessa, and to Duvid this was always an event. New faces and voices, different styles of dress, sometimes even gypsies with dancing bears. "Come, Yitzl." Duvid picked up his pet rabbit from a hassock of weeds upon which he was feeding. "Let's go see who's coming."

Leaving the wooded knoll, Duvid ran through the high grass that surrounded his village like a yellow green sea. His father had a name for the grass. He called it Russia. "Our *shtetl,*" he would say, "is a tiny island surrounded by Russia. One strong wind, one good ripple and poof. No more island." Duvid did not understand much of what his father said, but always enjoyed listening to him. His father's voice was deep and booming, a great drum, and something happened in Duvid's chest when he heard it. He also liked to watch his father's hands, which were big and very strong and had thick calluses from his tools. Avrum Karlinsky worked with wood, but refused to call himself a carpenter. He was simply a man who worked with wood. No difference? To Avrum Karlinsky there was a difference. "There are those," he told Duvid, "who think a man who works with his hands is common. But they're wrong. A man's hands are what lift him above the animals. Remember that." Duvid remembered, but wasn't sure what his father meant. Did he mean that if Yitzl had hands instead of paws, the rabbit might have had *him,* Duvid, for a pet? He had wanted to ask, but was afraid his father would think him stupid.

A dark-uddered cow lifted her head to watch Duvid approach, and he patted her flank in passing. "Visitors, Rella. Maybe gypsies." Rella flicked her tail and drifted after him in an aura of flies. Duvid hoped the travelers were indeed gypsies. If they were, his Aunt Tybie was sure to give him a few kopecks to have his fortune told. His mother said Aunt Tybie would give him her teeth, if he asked. Young and without children of her own, Aunt Tybie had fair hair and blue eyes and when she hugged Duvid, she smelled of flowers. Uncle Herschel was a butcher and although he always washed carefully when he came home, Duvid was sure that no amount of water could cleanse him of his work. Sometimes he was even afraid Aunt Tybie might start smelling like her husband, but she never did.

Duvid passed the cemetery where two of his grandparents were buried, taking care to keep his eyes averted from the tombstones.

The Artist

Grandma Karlinsky had died only the year before and Duvid had attended her burial, standing between his mother and father as the wooden box was lowered into the grave, then hearing the first shovelful of dirt hit his grandma in the face. For the next few weeks, he had gone back every day to look at the raw earth over the grave, picking up handfuls and pressing the soil to his cheek. He did not know what he expected to see or feel, but did expect *something*.

Pausing for breath, Duvid stroked Yitzl's ears and squinted into the sun. Half a *verst* away, a domed synagogue rose above shops and cottages, and beyond these the road to Odessa stretched in a thin, straight line. There had been little rain for the past month and the road dust was heavy and obscured all beneath it. But judging from the length, movement, and sound of the approaching column, Duvid could tell they were not gypsies. "Too many horses, Yitzl. Gypsies don't have so many horses. And they don't go so fast."

Duvid continued toward the village, but no longer ran. He was disappointed at not being able to have his fortune told. Once, a gypsy had looked at his hand and told him he would grow to be a big, strong man, enjoy a long life, and live in a faraway land. His father had laughed and said never to believe anything that came from a gypsy's mouth, that they were all liars, beggars, and thieves, and that he could tell Duvid the same things better than any gypsy. Besides, declared Avrum Karlinsky, the only sensible way to live was one day at a time. To know the future would be more curse than blessing. Though to Karlinsky, the idea of living in a faraway land sounded good enough. *What* land? It didn't matter. A Jew in any land had no great bargains offered. But what place could be worse than the moldering prison of a Russian *shtetl*, with dirty peasants stinking up the earth and drunken Cossacks plaguing them with their sabers? May they live to swallow their own steel, point first.

Palestine and America were the two faraway places Duvid heard his father mention most. Palestine, Avrum felt, suffered under the Turkish heel, but at least a Jew could look at Jewish fields and breathe Jewish air. And to be buried in the sacred soil of Jerusalem would keep one's flesh forever free of worms. And America, of course, was America. Maybe no gold in the streets, but no Cossacks or ignorant, filthy peasants either. Duvid's mother became upset when her husband spoke of leaving the *shtetl.* The village had been home to her, to her mother, and to her mother's mother. Its troubles were many, but at least they were familiar. And they had learned to live with them. Who knew what might happen in a foreign land, where language, people, and customs were strange? If God had wanted them to live in Palestine or America, if such was His will, that was where He would have placed them. Avrum Karlinsky threw up his massive hands at his wife's mention of God's will. He was tired of the whole dialogue. The more God spit on the Jews, the more they kissed His feet and begged forgiveness. It was too one-sided a relationship. All God did was take. When was He going to start giving a little? Would it hurt so much for Him to once in a while make life a bit easier for the Jews? What would it cost him?

What Duvid heard of these discussions worried him. How could his father speak of God in such a way? It was a serious sin, and he imagined all sorts of terrible consequences. Would God smite his father with fire, sword, and pestilence as threatened in the Bible? After each new transgression, Duvid watched his father fearfully for some sign of the inevitable punishment. At the same time he begged God's forgiveness with his own prayers. Single-handedly, he fought off God's vengeance. At every possible moment . . . eating, running, playing, studying, he took the time to intercede for his father, listing his virtues and good deeds (a kind and honest man, a loving husband and father, a fine worker with wood, a charitable giver to the poor and to the *shul*), pleading that if God would only be kind enough to spare him, he, Duvid, would pray morning and night and perform a lifetime of good deeds. And it worked. God heard him and did as he asked. His father remained untouched, going about his daily work, continuing his blasphemy, never knowing it was only his son's prayers that stood between him and eternal damnation.

A breeze came up, making a whispering sound in the tall grass and partially lifting the veil of dust from the road. For the first time, Duvid saw the horsemen. Strung out in loose formation, there were perhaps a hundred of them riding toward the village. Duvid stopped where he was. Stroking Yitzl's head, his hand trembled against the soft fur. Cossacks. There were the tall hats, the sabers, the slung rifles. He must warn Aunt Tybie and Uncle Herschel. He started to run once more, too panicked to realize the soldiers had to reach the village long before him. His heart pumped with his legs, his mind groped. Why was he so afraid? He had seen Cossacks before. They had ridden through town many times and all they ever did was steal from the shops and pull a few beards. Not so terrible. But what of the pogroms? What of the stories? What of the dreams? He tried to imagine what his mother would say. *Nightmares. Gossip. Old wives' tales. Don't even think such thoughts, Duvidal. Momma and Poppa are here. Nothing bad can happen.* Yes, but Momma and Poppa were *not* here. They were far off. They were in the city of Odessa.

Still, a golden haze hung low over the fields and village, and with the sun warm and bright, Duvid's fears eased. The sun became his talisman. As long as it shone, he, the *shtetl,* and all in it would be safe. Needing to hear a voice, he spoke to Yitzl and kept up the chatter as he ran. It helped cover the growing rumble of hoofs. He did not want to hear the horses. How different they sounded now that he knew what they were. When he thought they might be gypsy horses, their beat had been a happy promise. But no more.

Duvid passed the first of the thatched cottages and ran toward his uncle's house. The horsemen had reached the marketplace and there was confusion throughout the village. People hurried in all directions, closing doors and barring windows, shouting to children and one another. Duvid saw an elder in his black hat and long caftan, carrying some books and scurrying like a frightened duck. The elder looked at Duvid but did not say hello or even seem to see him. No one seemed to see him, although he himself recognized and greeted several of his parents' friends. His stomach felt cold and he clutched Yitzl more tightly. A horse and cart bolted from an alley and almost ran him down. The driver swore and whipped the animal. Chickens scattered, squawking, but one was caught by a wheel and flattened. Duvid willed himself to run faster, but his legs were unable to obey. What was happening? What was wrong with everyone? He knew, but was afraid to know. Yet the sun still shone.

Aunt Tybie was not in her house. Duvid ran from room to room, calling. There was no answer. A mirror threw a white face and wide, dark eyes back at him. Breathing heavily, he stood staring. He recognized Yitzl in his arms. Nothing else. "Momma!" he cried.

Stumbling out of the house, he started for his uncle's butcher shop. Black smoke rose at the far end of the village. It spread and darkened the sky. Muttel the tailor, gray-bearded and lame, limped crookedly toward his hut. "Have you seen my Aunt Tybie?" Duvid asked.

"Go home! Go home!" Muttel cried hoarsely.

"I have to find my aunt."

"Never mind your aunt, *boychik.* Find a cellar and hide."

Duvid ran on. If he could find Aunt Tybie, everything would be all right. The streets were nearly empty now, but shouts and screams came from every part of the *shtetl.* A sweating horse and rider loomed. The rider's uniform was unbuttoned to the waist, his skin glistened brown, and he was drinking from a bottle. Duvid squatted behind some barrels. He had never been this close to a Cossack. The man had a wide, dark face, black eyes, and a thick moustache. His fur cap was pushed back, revealing a red scar high across his forehead. Duvid could have reached out and touched his boot and saber as he swayed by. Emptying his bottle, he sent it crashing through a nearby window.

A girl's voice screamed. The Cossack laughed, got off his horse, and climbed through the shattered window. The girl ran out the front door, but the Cossack caught her and threw her to the ground. It was Fagel, daughter of the dairyman, a slender, pale-skinned girl with large, sad eyes. She screamed and struggled, but the soldier held her with one hand and tore off her clothes with the other. He was still laughing. Duvid wanted to cry out, wanted to help Fagel, wanted to run away. He wanted to do all these things, but was afraid to do anything except huddle behind the barrels and press Yitzl to his chest.

Fagel lay naked and struggling beneath the strangely moving body of the Cossack. What was he *doing* to her? Duvid had never seen a naked woman before. Overhead, the smoke thickened, darkening the sun. Where was everyone? Why didn't someone come to help? Duvid tried a brief, silent prayer, a plea directly to God. Please. Let someone come.

Someone came. Gripping a long-handled ax, his face smoke-blackened above his beard, Fagel's father came stumbling toward his house. He saw his daughter under the Cossack and his mouth became a dark hole. He swung the ax with both hands and the Cossack never knew he was there. Duvid shut his eyes. When he opened them, there was blood all over and the dairyman was carrying his daughter into the house. Then Duvid looked at what had been the Cossack and vomited.

When he was able, he left his hiding place. He saw soldiers everywhere, drinking from bottles and breaking into houses and shops. Some carried torches and were setting fires. Duvid heard the screams of women and girls and guessed the same thing was happening to them that had happened to Fagel. He was sobbing as he ran, but did not know it. A horse galloped past, dragging two men at the end of ropes, and the men's heads bounced against the dirt like large balls. There was a fire in front of Ruvin the peddler's house and Duvid saw it was the peddler himself burning. Small flames made bright orange shapes in his beard and his eyes stared without seeing. His wife lay naked a few feet away, her wig half off her shaven head. There was blood on her belly and between her legs. Duvid remembered his mother saying she was going to have a baby by Purim and wondered what would happen to the baby now.

In front of the bath house, Jews with axes, clubs, and knives were fighting Cossacks, and bodies lay bleeding in the dirt. Duvid slid close along the bath house wall, feeling the steam through the cracks. Why? Why did the Cossacks come to do this? What had the Jews ever done to *them?* Nothing. Jews never hurt anybody. Everyone knew that. And if they didn't know it, why didn't God *tell* them? Why did He let such things happen? Was He too busy to pay attention? With so much to take care of, how *could* he know about everything? Then fearful of his thoughts, afraid of even greater vengeance from above (*what* greater?), Duvid silently begged forgiveness.

The air was filled with cries and screams and Duvid wanted to cover his ears, but his hands were taken with Yitzl. He wanted to close his eyes, but had to find his aunt and uncle. He no longer felt the coldness in his stomach. He no longer felt anything. His brain still recorded, but dully, without conscious belief. Was it *really* happening? Duvid understood little of it anyway. Everywhere he looked, the Cossacks seemed to be dragging naked girls and women out of houses. Many of the Cossacks were also naked, except for boots and sabers. Sometimes three or four of them held a single struggling woman on the ground, while the others took turns doing things to her. The women screamed and the Cossacks laughed and drank from their bottles. Shots were fired and a man ran in circles, bleeding from the head. A Cossack galloped after him, swung his saber, and left him lying in the dirt.

Duvid saw soldiers hammering at the doors of the synagogue and smoke rising from its roof and windows. Then the doors opened and the rabbi appeared. He was wearing his striped prayer shawl and carrying the Holy Scrolls of the Torah. A tall, gray-haired, sepulchral figure, he held the Scrolls before him with both hands and the Cossacks stepped back, momentarily startled. The rabbi was followed by a small procession of his congregation, also in prayer shawls, and carrying books and religious objects rescued from the flames. As they came out, they chanted a psalm, the ancient Hebrew dirge rising above cries and screams, above clattering hoofs, above drunken laughter. The rabbi's face was as gray as his beard, his eyes dark caves. Some of the Cossacks crossed themselves, others spat through two fingers. Appearing confused and frightened, they parted for the procession. Then one soldier swung a long whip across the rabbi's legs and he stumbled and fell, and dropped the sacred writ beside him into the dirt.

Duvid's breath whistled in his throat. The rabbi and the Holy Torah. What more terrible desecration? *Now! Now* God would have to punish the Cossacks. Peering from behind a broken cart, Duvid awaited divine intervention. God might indeed be busy elsewhere, might indeed have many other things on His mind, but surely this was too much. He *had* to pay attention to *this.*

Yet, somehow, He did not. He must have still been off somewhere. For when the rabbi's followers tried to help him, they too were attacked and knocked to the ground. The Cossacks romped like children among the fallen religious things, unwinding the Scrolls into great streamers and running drunken patterns through the streets. Those who tried to stop them were cut down. Duvid saw the *shammus* of the synagogue sitting in the dust among torn fragments of the Torah. He was holding the bleeding stump of his right arm and rocking gently as he prayed. But to whom was he praying? Didn't he know that God had gone away?

Smoke now hid the sun entirely and the air was filled with burning thatch. Suddenly the air was also filled with the rabbi. He floated over Duvid's head in a high arc . . . first in one direction, then the other. Using blankets as catapults, the Cossacks were playing catch with the *shtetl*'s spiritual leader. The rabbi sailed gracefully, caftan, shawl, and beard flowing, abruptly gifted with the miracle of flight. Duvid stared. Up, over, down . . . up, over, down. An aerial ballet to the tune of Russian laughter. Each time the rabbi rose, Duvid hoped he would just keep going and never come down. Why not? Why couldn't God just let him fly up to heaven? Maybe He would. Maybe that was part of His plan. Duvid remembered his mother saying that God moved in mysterious ways. Couldn't this be one of the ways, a scheme to get the rabbi to heaven so that the Cossacks would see and be afraid and go away?

Convinced of the logic of such a Divine plan, Duvid half expected to see the rabbi cut all earthly ties and soar from sight. But God evidently had other plans for the rabbi's heavenly ascent. For at last tiring of their sport, the Cossacks set fire to the rabbi's caftan and beard, sent him flying like a flaming comet, and watched him make his final landing upon a cluster of sabers. Spitted and aflame, the old man sizzled merrily. Duvid crawled brokenly away.

The marketplace was a big, open square with wooden houses and shops on two sides and food carts grouped in the center. Uncle Herschel's butcher shop stood between a dry-goods store and a grocery at the far end of the square. The carts were overturned and some of the shops were burning. An ant in a windstorm, Duvid inched through a chaos of men, women, and horses, of ringing steel and exploding guns, of shrill cries and wild laughter. *Aunt Tybie and Uncle Herschel.* The thought of reaching them had replaced the sun as Duvid's talisman, and he clung to it as he clung to the warmth of his rabbit. The power of love and trust. With it, he would find the Cossacks gone, the wounded healed, the dead restored to life. And, of course, God would once more be paying proper attention to His duties.

Crossing the square blindly, his eyes fixed on the butcher shop,

The Artist

Duvid never saw the horse that leaped a grain cart and sent him sprawling. Stunned, but unhurt, he slowly pushed himself up. *Yitzl!* His rabbit lay close by and Duvid carefully lifted the small, still form. Aunt Tybie would make him better. She could make anything better. Duvid had seen her. "Don't worry," he told the rabbit.

The door of the shop sagged from a broken hinge as Duvid carried Yitzl past. "I'm here!" But except for some plucked chickens and a floor full of feathers, the front of the store was empty. Duvid stared at the smashed door, then went into the back room. There was little light, but he could see large slabs of meat hanging from hooks. When his eyes became used to the half-darkness, he saw that one of the slabs was his Uncle Herschel. His uncle's eyes were open and he seemed to be looking at him. "Uncle Herschel?" There was no answer and Duvid did not speak to him again.

Then he saw his Aunt Tybie. She lay on the floor with her head pressed against a wall, and her arms and legs spread wide. She had no clothes on and her skin looked very white against the dark floor. Duvid went over and knelt beside her. "Aunt Tybie?" he whispered, not knowing why he was whispering, but afraid that if he spoke too loudly he might somehow disturb her. "Aunt Tybie, it's me, Duvid."

Her head turned slightly in the direction of his voice and her lips moved. That was all. Duvid placed Yitzl on the floor next to her. He did not know it, but the rabbit had stopped breathing. He bent and kissed his aunt's cheek. She no longer smelled of flowers, but of something strange and unpleasant. She smelled of Cossacks. There were sounds in the front of the shop and Duvid was afraid the soldiers were coming back. But no one came and when he looked, the front of the store was in flames.

"Fire, Aunt Tybie!"

She did not seem to understand. She was looking at Uncle Herschel. Duvid yelled. "We'll all get burned!" What was the matter with her? Why did she just lie there? Yitzl was lying there too. And Uncle Herschel was hanging like a piece of meat. Where were his mother and father? Why didn't they come back from Odessa and take care of him? Didn't they know about the Cossacks, about what was happening in the *shtetl?* He was suddenly furious with them. They had left him behind to *this.*

Smoke and flame broke through from the front of the shop.

The Artist

Duvid remembered a door at the back of the storeroom and groped along a wall until he found it. "Come, Aunt Tybie." This time he took his aunt's hand and pulled her. She looked at him, then rose like an obedient child. Duvid picked up Yitzl's body and led his mute, naked aunt past Uncle Herschel and out the door. The shop's backyard reached to the edge of a wooded ravine that Duvid knew well. This was where they would go.

The village burned behind them, its cries growing fainter as they entered the forest. Duvid still held his aunt's hand, understanding quickly that she was different than she had been, that she was no longer the Aunt Tybie he had known. He did not understand why she was different, other than that it was because of what the Cossacks had done to her and to Uncle Herschel. But it was clear that she would do nothing now unless he told her. Just as it was also clear that she was somehow no longer able to speak, or else, did not want to speak. Duvid was not sure which it was. Sometimes he did not feel like speaking either.

He no longer heard any sounds from his village, but, looking back through the trees, could still see smoke in the sky. Then the smoke, too, was gone. Reaching a stream, he followed it until it cut between high banks. One of the banks formed a cover under which Duvid had once taken shelter from a storm, and this was where he led his aunt.

"Sit down, Aunt Tybie."

She looked at him with wide, glazed eyes until Duvid sat down and tugged at her hand. Then she sat down beside him. Yitzl had grown stiff and Duvid laid him on a sandy shelf. He had known for a while that the rabbi was dead, but did not want to leave him behind. How he hated the Cossacks. They hurt and killed everything. And Yitzl wasn't even Jewish.

Duvid scooped out a hole beside the stream, buried Yitzl, and recited the Hebrew prayer for the dead he had heard said for his grandparents. He did not know what the words meant, but hoped that saying them would in some way make things better for Yitzl. Then he said the same thing for his Uncle Herschel and for the rabbi and Ruvin the peddler and for all those others, dead and dying, back in the *shtetl.* He was glad now that his mother and father had gone to Odessa. If they hadn't gone the Cossacks would have killed his father and done to his mother what they had done to Aunt Tybie. The thought of it turned Duvid cold and he began to shiver and to hug his aunt, nuzzling into soft, bare flesh, burrowing deep, seeking warmth and comfort. His aunt sat unmoving, her eyes off somewhere.

"Aunt Tybie!"

Something in her was reached and they rocked together in their place beside the stream. But her eyes stayed dead.

Duvid grew freshly aware of her nakedness. The female body was a mystery unveiled to him only during the past few hours. Now he saw, even touched, yet its parts remained strange, its secrets unexplained. Why did the Cossacks want to do all those things to it? And why did the women scream and cry when the things were done? It must hurt very much. Some of the women had even been bleeding. Duvid looked to see if perhaps his aunt was bleeding from that same darkly alien place, but could find no blood. Then it suddenly seemed wrong for her to be sitting there without any clothes on and for him to be looking at her this way. He took off his shirt and tied it about her, covering what he judged to be the most important places.

When it grew dark, Duvid huddled against his aunt and listened to the night noises. He had never been in the woods at night and its sounds were strange and frightening. He kept thinking he heard the Cossacks galloping through the brush and conjured up dreadful images of what they would do to his aunt and him if they were found. He remembered the terrible things he had seen, and the sights were even more terrible in the remembering.

With nowhere else to go, his mind again groped for understanding. The rabbi had always said the Jews were God's chosen people and that He loved them more than anyone else and would always take care of them. But the rabbi must be wrong. The *Cossacks* were God's chosen people. They *had* to be. Recalling his last sight of the rabbi, Duvid guessed the rabbi must have known then that he was wrong. But Duvid was still confused. He could understand God's choosing the Jews as His people, since the Jews were good and never hurt anyone and were always praying and studying the Torah.

But why the *Cossacks?* Why would He possibly choose the Cossacks, when everyone knew they got drunk and burned and stabbed and shot people, and did things to women, and neither studied the Talmud nor prayed from the Torah. Duvid finally decided that either the Jews weren't as good as he thought, or God wasn't as smart.

Still holding on to his aunt, Duvid slept. When he awoke, the sun flashed through the trees, the stream babbled, and a thousand birds sang. It took him a moment to realize where he was and why. When it did break through, none of it seemed real. But seeing his aunt beside him, his shirt covering so little of her nakedness, the cold came back to his stomach. It was real.

"Let's go see if the Cossacks have gone away, Aunt Tybie."

Duvid spoke to her now as to a younger child, as he had once spoken to his rabbit. He took her hand and led and she silently followed. He watched the sky for signs of smoke, but saw only a clear, flat blue. Listening for shouts and cries, he heard only the birds. Later, nearing the *shtetl,* there was the sound of the wind in the high grass. Closer still, came the whisper of weeping. Most of the houses and shops were gutted. Those still standing were black skeletons. Duvid led his aunt toward the place where his own house had been and found a pile of ashes and rubble. He saw one of the brass candlesticks his mother had kept on the kitchen table and used on Friday nights. He picked it up, feeling the weight in his hand and remembering the way his mother had polished it before holidays. When he led his aunt away from the house, he carried the candlestick with him.

Dark, searching figures moved among the ruins. Others lay in the dirt. Some of those on the ground were covered with blankets, but many lay as they had fallen. Duvid tried not to look at their faces. Finding a charred prayer shawl in front of what had been the *shul,* he pressed it to his lips and put it over his aunt's shoulders. He was not sure if it was a sin to put a prayer shawl on a woman, but at that moment he was worried more about his aunt's nakedness than about God. Nearer the marketplace, the wailing grew louder. Duvid barely heard it. He was looking for his mother and father. He shuttled slowly among the survivors, one hand leading his aunt, the other gripping his mother's candlestick. No one paid attention to him. When he was sure his mother and father were not yet there, Duvid took his aunt outside the *shtetl* to the road on which they would return. Then he sat her down beside him to wait.

They came hours later in a puff of dust that Duvid saw miles off and watched grow larger. When he was sure it was them, when he recognized first the wagon, then the sway-backed horse, and finally the two figures sitting together on the high, tilted seat, he drew his aunt to her feet and led her toward them. The horse stopped and Duvid's mother and father came running. His mother reached him first and hugged him so hard he couldn't breathe. She was crying and saying, "Thank God, thank God," over and over again, and Duvid cried also and wondered why, for what *possible* reason, she should be thanking *Him*.

THREE

1896: S. S. Katrina

The ship had been battling a violent storm for two days and nights and the stench below decks was a horned beast in Duvid's chest. Each time he breathed it gored him. Vomit, unwashed bodies, and dysentery. There were no separate smells anymore, only a single, bitter assault on the senses. Whatever Duvid did or thought, it was there . . . this and the constant thumping of engines and pounding of waves. And there was no relief. Gale winds and mountains of water had locked them deep in steerage without even the hope of a few minutes on deck. (A Cossack storm, using salt water like steel sabers.) So that along with his mother, father, Aunt Tybie, and hundreds of others, Duvid was held prisoner in the stinking, rat-infested slime of a floating sewer that was carrying them to a new and better life in America.

It was the middle of the night but there was no way of telling. From where Duvid lay, he saw only the same feebly lighted hold, the same bulkheads closing in, the same rows of bunks and massed bodies he saw at any other time of night and day. He also heard the same wailing of children, the same moans, sighs, and retching, the same harsh mélange of Yiddish, Russian, Polish, and German. He had been asleep but had been awakened by recurring stomach cramps. Dreading the prospect of another visit to the toilet, of having to expose himself again to the reeking filth, Duvid tried to fight down the pain. He would not give in to it this time. He would just lie quietly and wait and it would go away. It always did. He knew about it by now, knew how it behaved. The pain was bad, but it was always the worst just before it got better. Yes, but it had never been as bad as this. Not so. He had just forgotten. It was hard to remember exactly how much something hurt. Then Duvid drew his knees up against his chest, the spasm passed, and he felt about as happy as he could ever remember feeling.

The sensation was so pure, so instantly euphoric, that he wanted to share it, wanted to tell someone how it was. But everyone in the family was asleep . . . Aunt Tybie beside him in the next bunk, his mother and father directly below. So he savored it alone, letting the feeling spread and brighten all it touched. With it, Duvid was able to believe the storm would pass by morning, that America would be safely reached, that the baby his mother was going to have would be a brother and not a sister, that his father would make beautiful things of wood and sell them in their new land, and that a smart American doctor would know what was wrong with Aunt Tybie and be able to fix her. Instant magic. A moment's freedom from pain and it was all possible.

Not always so. More often, in the months since leaving the *shtetl,* Duvid had been certain that nothing good was ever going to happen to them again. And during the long overland struggle across unfriendly stretches of Russia, Poland, and Germany, little had happened to change his feeling. Every turn in the road hid its own peculiar dangers . . . wrong information, blunders, cheats, thieves, corrupt and cruel officials. The world outside the *shtetl* was a dark forest, alive with wolves. Given a choice, Duvid would have gladly crawled back to the remains of his own village and risked living with the hope the Cossacks might never return. But the choice had been his father's, not his. And Avrum Karlinsky had spat upon the bloodied Russian earth that day and sworn that neither he nor his would spend a minute more than they had to on it. He had cursed the land, the people, the Czar, and every drunken, murdering Cossack who had ever lived to poison the air. He had even cursed Jehovah Himself. When his wife had protested the blasphemy, claiming it was only His divine mercy that had spared their son, Avrum had spat again and roared, "Woman, it wasn't his *mercy* that spared Duvid.

The Artist

It was His damned blindness. That bastard up there just didn't *see* him!"

But they had finally reached Germany, the port of Hamburg, the edge of the sea itself, and Duvid allowed himself one of his rare moments of hope. There at last was the ocean. And they were about to cross it to where everything would be new, where there were no Cossacks, and where it was said that Jews were the same as everyone else. The size of the ship was also reassuring. Huge smokestacks, soaring deck houses, and great iron hull. In such a ship, what could happen? It was as big as their entire *shtetl,* a fortress safe from attack, a land in itself.

Duvid had waited with the others on the crowded pier that morning, throat dry with excitement, hands clutching one of the meager assortment of packages that held all of the Karlinsky's worldly goods. Little had been saved from the ashes . . . some scraps of clothing, the candlesticks, a samovar, a few of Avrum's tools. Not yet on the ship, they were part of a thronging, expectant crowd that pushed this way and that, its families shoving to keep sight of their members, its ears deafened by its own impatient noises and by the cries of peddlers hawking wares and extra provisions for the voyage. Some, having come so far and waited so long, could wait no more and tried to clamber up dangling ropes not intended for boarding. But most stayed anxiously still and when the moment came, shuffled and jostled along the gangway until they stood upon the ship. And when Duvid, too, was there, when the land was no longer under his feet, he sensed the sea in uneasy motion and did not know how he felt. Looking at his mother, he saw that she was crying. His father gazed at the shore with narrowed eyes, a hand heavily on Duvid's shoulder. Aunt Tybie just stood as she always did, waiting. "We're safe on the ship, Aunt Tybie," Duvid told her, and she looked at him and smiled. He thought this a good sign because she did not smile often.

Once at sea, however, the ship became less of the sanctuary it had at first seemed, and more of what it actually was . . . an ancient, rusted hulk, with crumbling engines, an undisciplined, polyglot crew, and space enough for no more than a third of the passengers its owners had crammed between its decks. From the very first day, when an old Polish Jew was somehow lost overboard, the trip was an unending series of large and small disasters. Bad weather was almost constant, engine trouble more than doubled the expected time at sea, the food was inadequate and often rotten, the steerage a cesspool of sickness, frustration, and anger. And for many, there was the final splash of burial under a dark sky, without even the consolation of a rabbi or priest.

Duvid heard women cry and men rage. Ah, we thought we couldn't be worse off than we were. But we are. Whatever we had before—pogroms, starvation, pain—it was still not dying like rotten sheep thrown into a hole; the instant the breath is out of our bodies, dropped into the sea to be eaten by the fish.

A red fury took hold of the sufferers, of their survivors, and they paced about in their damp, sticky passages. They clenched fists, but against whom should they raise them? The crew? The shipowners? The agents who had sold them their passage? They were helpless. In the end, they drifted into meaningless arguments among themselves. Violent blows were struck by furious, driven men in narrow spaces . . . until, spent and beaten, they fell back, ashamed, and picked up the pitiful belongings kicked loose, broken, soiled, soaked from the putrid ooze into which they had fallen.

It was then that for the first time, Duvid saw his father strike a man, a red-bearded Pole, without family, who slept in the top bunk of an adjoining aisle. The Pole had reached over one night and kissed and touched Aunt Tybie and Avrum Karlinsky had caught his arm with one fist and punched him in the face with the other. The man had tried to fight back, but Avrum kept punching him until he fell, bleeding from the nose. Then Avrum picked up the Pole, carried him to his own bunk, and left him with blood all over his beard and shirt. The incident frightened Duvid.

"Why did you do that?" he asked his father. "Why did you hit him?"

Avrum Karlinsky looked at Duvid, then at his hands. There was blood on his knuckles and he wiped them on his trousers. "That dumb Polack." His wife was fussing over him, but he impatiently motioned her aside.

"Did you hit him because he's dumb?" Duvid asked.

47

"I hit him because he touched Aunt Tybie. Now that Uncle Herschel is gone, we have to look after her. If you ever see any man try to touch her, you must tell me."

"Is it because of what the Cossacks did to her?"

"Yes."

"But the Polack was only kissing and hugging her. He wasn't doing any of those other things. He wasn't hurting her. And maybe Aunt Tybie wanted him to kiss her."

"Aunt Tybie is like a little girl now," said Avrum Karlinsky. "In many ways, she doesn't really know or understand what she wants. And until she does, we have to understand for her."

Duvid watched the red-bearded Pole closely after that, but he did not come near his aunt again. Nor did any of the other men. Sometimes Duvid saw men looking at his aunt and whispering together and laughing and wondered what it was that was so funny. When he asked his father about it, his father said not to pay any attention to them, that some men were the kind of fools who would laugh while watching their own mothers buried.

But foolish laughter was the least of the problems in the festering holds of the *S.S. Katrina.* Generally, Duvid heard no laughter at all, only the sounds of pain, anger, and despair, growing louder as the weeks went by. He listened carefully to these sounds because there was little else for him to do after the dysentery came. And listening, he began to notice his mother and father speaking in hushed whispers when they were close by. Duvid recognized this as an especially bad sign. It meant they were hiding some terrible worry from him. Yet what could be more terrible than the worries he already knew about? Had they learned something new? Was there a hole somewhere in the ship? Was it going to sink? Did the cramps in his stomach and his always having to go to the toilet mean he was very sick? Was he going to die? Others had already died around him. He had seen their bodies shrouded in gray blankets and carried up on deck to be thrown overboard. Most of those who had died were old, but there were young ones too. One of these had been little Jussel Relnikov, a Ukrainian boy close to Duvid's own age with whom he had sometimes played and hunted rats. Jussel had complained of stomach cramps one day, and a week later lay dead in a gray blanket. The more Duvid thought about it, the more certain he became that this was the reason for his parents' hushed conferences. He was dying.

He kept his discovery to himself. His mother and father didn't have to know that he knew. They had enough to worry about. Yet it was hard to believe that he, Duvid Karlinsky, was dying and would never see America and would be thrown into the water to be eaten by the fish. Awash in a warm tide of self-pity, he lay tight-lipped and pale in his bunk. With each cramp, with each spasm of pain, he prepared himself for his passing. He said all the prayers he knew and thought only good, pure thoughts. But what was dying like? What would happen afterward? There were things he had to know. Duvid decided to ask. He decided to ask his mother, rather than his father, since she was by far the more friendly with God. Duvid spoke to her while she was feeding him his tea.

"What happens when you die, Momma?"

Rifka Karlinsky braced herself against the *Katrina*'s pitching and stirred her son's tea. She had been a slender, pretty woman, but the months of travel had ravaged her face as the late stages of pregnancy had inflated her figure.

"Who's dying?"

Duvid swallowed hard. It was never easy to fool his mother. "Nobody. I was just wondering."

"That's all little boys have to wonder about these days? Dying? Anyway, you know what happens. You go to heaven if you're good."

"Am I good?"

Rifka's eyes flooded and she had to hide them from her son. Ah, what was wrong with her? A word, a thought, and the tears came like rain. She had to take hold. "You're very good. No momma could want a better boy."

Poor Momma. How she would miss him. "Maybe the new baby will be even better. Maybe you'll love him even more."

"A momma loves all her children the same. There's no difference. Love is love."

"What happens in heaven? Who feeds and takes care of you?"

"God takes care of everything."

"But there are so many people. Won't he be too busy? Won't he forget some?"

"God is never too busy. He never forgets anyone."

Duvid's throat closed against the tea. "Sometimes he forgets. He forgot all those in the *shtetl* the day the Cossacks came."

"You mustn't say things like that. It is a sin."

"It's true, Momma. He *did* forget." The threat of a sin would ordinarily have been enough to shut Duvid up, but not now, not when he was about to hand himself over to an eternity of Divine care. Answers were needed. Confidence had to be restored. "I was there and saw."

"You mustn't question God. He has His reasons."

"What reasons?"

"Drink your tea and stop asking foolish questions."

"What reasons?"

Rifka sighed. She was in no mood for a theological discussions with her son. She had more immediate and practical problems on her mind. If the floundering *Katrina* did not get them to port very soon, she would have to birth her child at sea. The thought sickened her and had inspired the whispered discussions that Duvid had believed concerned *him.* Besides, her belief in God was purely emotional, a deep-rooted concept with which she had been raised. She had no background of Torah to give voice or logic to her feelings. She knew only that her belief must be held. Without it, what was left?

"God never told me his reasons," she said. "Do you think He tells your mother all His secrets?"

"But I *have* to know."

"You don't *have* to know anything. You're only a boy. You have time to know. When you're older, a man, when you study the Talmud you'll learn and know the reasons then."

Duvid's voice rose in panic. "But I *don't* have time. I *won't* be older. I'll *never* study the Talmud."

"What kind of crazy talk is that?"

"You know! Why do you make believe you don't know?"

"What do I know?"

It was suddenly too much. Duvid could hold it no longer. As a fresh seizure of cramps hit him, he blurted, "That I'm going to die and be wrapped in a gray blanket and thrown into the water with the fish."

The Artist

Rifka reached for him. "Who said you're going to die? Tell Momma where you heard such a silly thing."

"You and Poppa were whispering. You were looking worried."

"Aaah," signed Rifka and told him then about the baby and how because the trip was taking so long it might not be born in America after all. And although Duvid thought this was too bad, it was certainly much better than his dying.

The storm had since come up and Duvid lay still with pain, but the weight of the gray blanket had at least been lifted. He was not, after all, about to have to deal with God and His lapses. And perhaps it would be as his mother said . . . that when he grew older and studied the Talmud, he would learn the reasons. But now, in his swaying bunk in the stench of the *Katrina*'s steerage, with angry seas hammering the rusted hulk around him, Duvid was less concerned with God than with keeping his bleeding bowels intact and free of pain. Cramps permitting, he might even sleep.

He had, in fact, briefly dozed, when a giant force seemed to suddenly lift the *Katrina* clear of the water, hang her suspended with shuddering screws, then plunge her back into the sea.

It happened and was over in an instant, but in the steerage it was an earthquake. People and baggage flew, partitions buckled, lights went out, and there was total darkness. Thrown from his bunk, Duvid landed in a tangle of bodies and flailing limbs, of shrill shouts and cries. He tried to shout too, but salty bilge ran into his mouth. He reached out with his hands, felt flesh, and clung to it. Other hands groped at him, tearing, scratching. He could see nothing. He was blind. A crushing weight was on him, squeezing his breath. The ship was sinking, going straight to the bottom of the ocean and taking them all with it. Where were his mother, father, and Aunt Tybie? He called their names and was unable to hear his own voice. Was this how it was to die? Maybe he was already dead. Maybe he was. But was this how it was going to be? Everyone together, all that screaming, the smell, the bitter taste, the blindness, the hands pulling and scratching? Could this be heaven?

Then lights came on from somewhere, bodies slowly untangled and rose from the spaces between the bunks. The weight on Duvid eased and he turned and saw his mother lying in the bilge. She was breathing heavily and a tiny trickle of blood ran from her mouth. "Duvidal, you're all right?" she whispered. David took her hand and tried to pull her up. Then his father was there and lifted her as though she were a child and placed her in a bunk.

"How is it?" he asked.

Rifka closed her eyes. Both hands clasped her swollen stomach. "Avrum, something is happening."

"You're sure?"

"Get someone quickly."

"Stay with Momma," Avrum told his son and disappeared into the confusion of the hold. Duvid automatically looked for Aunt Tybie and saw that she was close by and all right. Then he stood holding his mother's hand until his father came back with two women.

"What's wrong?" Duvid asked. "Did something happen to the baby?"

"Go to sleep," said Avrum and boosted Duvid into his bunk.

But how could he sleep? The steerage was wild. Its passengers shrieked, chattered, wept, offered a variety of prayers to a diversity of Gods, and cursed the *Katrina,* her captain, and crew, along with the sea for wanting to kill them. And Duvid listened to all this and to his mother's cries and wished they had never left the *shtetl.* How good it had been before the Cossacks came, how happily each day had followed the one before. So many things. And among the best, his first day at *chaider.* Five years old and his father had wrapped him in his prayer shawl and carried him to school as his own father had once carried him. The *melamed* had taken Duvid in and held the Hebrew alphabet in front of him on a big chart. But before beginning to learn the first letter, Duvid was given a taste of honey. When he swallowed and said it was sweet, the *melamed* told him the study of the Holy Law was even sweeter. Later, Duvid saw a coin fall from the ceiling and the *melamed* said an angel had dropped it from heaven as a reward for learning his first lesson. Miracles in *chaider.* They came each day, from morning to afternoon, with the *melamed* and the other children, then home to tell what he had learned. But no school on Friday afternoons when he helped his mother prepare for *Shabbes,* with the cooking smells all around and the sample tastes and his mother asking whether more spice or sugar should be added to the pot. His father stopped work early before the Sabbath and took him to the village bath house where they sat in the thick steam, slapping their soaped bodies with twig brushes while water was poured over their heads. All the Jews came to the bath house every *Shabbes* and the big, wooden building beside the stream was filled with the sound of men talking and laughing. Duvid loved being there with his father and the other men and seeing how they looked with the hair all over their bodies and their big, hanging parts. Someday, he would look like that too.

At sunset, they dressed in clean clothes and went to *shul,* where Duvid watched his father read from the Bible and pray like everyone else. Duvid would hope then that God was noticing and letting his father's prayers make up for all the things he said at other times. Then he and his father walked home in the dark, past the houses with *Shabbes* candles shining in their windows. Duvid's mother would be waiting, all dressed up, to kiss them good *Shabbes.* Before the meal, a cup of wine was passed from one to the other and each drank, Duvid too. After dinner they sang *Shabbes* songs and said grace and Duvid told about what he had studied of the Holy Law that week. On some Fridays, Aunt Tybie and Uncle Herschel came to eat dinner with them, and for Duvid this was always a special treat. The bigger the family, the more of a holiday it seemed. Which was one of the reasons Duvid was glad his mother was going to have a baby. The new baby would make the family bigger, which was good because Uncle Herschel wasn't there anymore and Aunt Tybie couldn't say anything or sing the *Shabbes* songs the way she used to. Of course it would be a while before the baby could do any of these things, but at least he would be there (in Duvid's thoughts the new baby was always "he") to look at and to play with and that counted for something.

On *Shabbes* afternoons, after they had come from *shul* and had eaten, Duvid and his father went for a walk together. They always walked the same way, through the village and past the poorhouse and windmills to a hill where there were rocks and trees. Then Duvid's father would sit down on the biggest of the rocks and Duvid would sit beside him, imitating the way his father sat, elbows on

The Artist

knees, hands hanging loosely between. Neither of them said anything, but would gaze through the trees at the way the *shtetl* looked
in the distance, gray and small and as though the houses weren't real
houses at all, but only toys. Duvid was careful at these times not to
speak unless his father spoke first. Sometimes his father would hum
a song and Duvid would hum along with him. Duvid didn't mind
about not speaking. The quiet and the two of them there was
enough. Maybe it was even better than speaking. After a while
Duvid's father would take out some tobacco, roll a cigarette, and sit
silently smoking. Duvid knew it was a sin to smoke on the Sabbath,
but never said anything about it, nor did he ever tell his mother. His
father never told him not to speak of it, but Duvid knew it was to
be kept between them.

They had been to the hill on the *Shabbes* before the Cossacks
came. It was a clear afternoon and the houses of the *shtetl* appeared
closer than they ever had before. Duvid's father just sat smoking and
looking out over the sea of grass toward the village. There was no
sound but that of the wind in the trees, and he had looked up into
the leaves and past the leaves into the wide, blue sky, not smiling,
but with his face as pleased and young as Duvid had ever seen it.
And as he watched his father's face, Duvid felt his hand on his head.
It pushed the hair back from his forehead and smoothed it while
Duvid pressed his head backward against the big hand until, in reply
to pressure, it slipped over the side of Duvid's face and drew his
head down against the rough cloth of his father's *Shabbes* suit. Duvid
could feel the beating heart. He heard his father sigh once, then the
hand lifted from him and they both stood up. Walking back to the
shtetl, Duvid held his father's hand but they still did not speak, nor
did Duvid want to.

The last time on the hill. Would there ever be a hill like that in
America? Or a *chaider?* Or a new *melamed* to teach him the Holy
Law? (His last remembered sight of his old one had been with
Cossack steel in his throat . . . and what was sweeter than honey
now, dear teacher?) Or *Shabbes* candles? Or a warm kitchen on
Friday afternoons with his mother cooking? Would there ever re-
ally be anything but cramps in his stomach, and the smell of vomit
and leaking, bloody bowels, and the tossing of the ship, and now,

finally, the most terrible of all, the sound of his mother's pain in the bunk below.

Duvid pulled a blanket over his head and covered his ears with his hands, but his mother's voice cut through cloth, flesh, and bone to reach deep inside. Yet it was not really his mother's voice. It was different. He would not have known it. The cries he heard had nothing to do with his mother's voice, which was soft and shining brown like her eyes, a voice that sang. One of the first sounds Duvid remembered was that of his mother singing, "Sleep my baby sleep, Poppa brings good things to eat." And he would imagine his father carrying platters of little cakes and pitchers of milk. His mother sang when she worked, and Duvid loved the sound as well as any he knew. Even when she spoke it was as soft as singing. But not now. Never had Duvid heard her voice as he heard it now.

He lifted the blanket from his head. The two women his father had brought were busy with his mother, but he could not see what they were doing. Nor did he see his father. Where had his father gone? Why had he left his mother with these two old women she didn't even know? Duvid wondered if there wasn't something he could do to help. His mother always helped him when *he* was sick. Shouldn't he at least *try* to help her? He didn't know what he could do, but maybe she would feel better if she just saw him. It worked that way when *he* was sick and saw her. Fighting the rolling ship, he climbed down from the false sanctuary of his bunk.

The two women were leaning over his mother and all Duvid could see were heavy backs and arms. In surrounding bunks, all heads were turned away. No one was even looking at his mother. No one seemed to know she was there or to hear her screaming. Only the two women were paying attention to her. Then Duvid saw his father. He stood a short distance away with his face pressed against a bulkhead. His hands gripped an overhead beam and his body swayed with the ship as if he were dancing. Duvid started toward him, then stopped. Without knowing why, he was afraid to go any closer to his father. He did not know where to look or to go. There was suddenly no place for him anywhere. His mother cried out and he turned and shoved against the two women blocking his way. But they were a wall and he stumbled and fell and was too weak to get up.

He was lying on a soft patch of grass behind his house and his mother was on one side of him and his father on the other and they were all touching hands. It was early evening, with the first stars wide and alive and very near and each seeming like a smile of great sweetness. People and things passed in front of the house, not too far away, but they passed gently. A horse drawing a wagon, hoofs and wheels softened by the dirt road, men and women in pairs, not in a hurry, their voices a murmur. A cowbell sounded faintly in the dark, died, then rose and died again. Duvid held tightly to the hands on either side of him. His mother and father. The three of them. By some chance all here in this night together, and who could ever tell exactly the way it was in this sweet, summer darkness. After a time, Duvid was taken in and put to bed. Sleep touched him, treating him as one familiar and loved in the house where he had been born and which he had never left for even a night.

May God bless my people . . . my mother and father, my aunt and my uncle, oh, treat them kindly in their days of trouble and in the hours of their leaving.

"Duvid?" said Avrum Karlinsky and kissed his son's cheek to measure the fever.

Duvid opened his eyes. He was back in his bunk but it was not the same as before. Something was different. It took him a minute to know what it was. He no longer heard his mother's voice. His mother had died.

He shut his eyes quickly. No. He was still asleep and dreaming. *Schma yisroyail adonai elohaynu adonai echud . . .* Bless my mother, O God, and keep her well. Nothing must happen to her. Not to her. All right. To all the others, but not to her. No questions asked . . . not about Uncle Herschel or Aunt Tybie, not about the rabbi and the *melamed,* not about any of those others in the *shtetl.* No questions or asking for reasons. Just let her not be dead. You're fine and smart and full of mercy and everything you do is for a good reason and I'm sorry about the terrible things I thought and said and I never will again. Only let her be all right.

"Duvidal? You're up?" said his father.

The Artist

No. Not yet. He wasn't ready yet. More time was needed. Even God's miracles took time. If he opened his eyes too soon, his mother might still be dead and then it would be too late to ever save her. He lay very still, carefully not moving.

"Avrum, how is Duvid?"

The voice from the lower bunk was faint, but unmistakably his mother's. Duvid's lids parted and he looked at his father through misty eyes. They had saved his mother . . . God and he together. A new partnership. Miracles when needed.

"Momma . . ." Duvid whispered to his father, ". . . Momma is all right?"

Avrum Karlinsky wiped his son's sweated face with a moist towel. He nodded. His cheeks were sunken and haggard, his dark beard matted, and the hand holding the towel trembled.

Duvid looked for the two old women, but did not see them. Then for the first time, he remembered the baby. He had completely forgotten about him. His new little brother had been getting born and he had been so busy saving his mother that he hadn't even thought of or said a single prayer for him. But why wasn't he crying? Didn't new babies always cry? Something pressed Duvid's chest.

"Where's the baby?"

Duvid's father looked at him with haunted eyes. His tongue flicked at his lips, but he did not say anything. Duvid had asked, but did not really need an answer. He knew. The baby was dead. He was dead and wrapped in a gray blanket and floating somewhere in the ocean. And all because he, Duvid, had forgotten about him.

"Duvid . . ." began his father.

Duvid rolled over and hid his face. He did not want his father to look at him. *Dmai ochichoi.* The blood of thy brother. Thy brother's blood cries out to me from the sea. He had killed his brother and would carry the mark of Cain with him to America.

FOUR

1899: New York, N. Y.

They called it "Follow the Leader" and said it was a game, but Duvid had never been fooled by what they said it was. Nor did he think that he was only playing. Although he laughed, ran, leaped, and cried out with the others, although he was as bold, stealthy, capricious, and daring as the leader's acts demanded, he never at any time truly believed it to be a game.

There were five of them in the loose, twisting column that wound through the tangle of East Side streets known as the "Typhus Ward." And of the five, Duvid was last . . . his usual position. For he was not only the youngest of the group, but also the most recently arrived in the country—the greenhorn. This automatically made him subject to the ridicule, contempt, and rejection of any who had preceded him across the water by as much as a day. But Duvid was tall for his age, had learned to speak with barely a trace of an accent, and, most important of all, had a firm friend and sponsor in Zelig Zaikewitch . . . the leader.

His friend, Zelig. Duvid gave him special mention in his nightly prayers. It was hard to believe now that there had been a time when he didn't know Zelig, a time when he had felt friendless, frightened, and alone in the strange city streets. Zelig was two years older than Duvid, but smaller, with a lean, dark, close-cropped head, nervous hands, and the swift, graceful movements of an expensive animal. And he could pour out an endless stream of vaudeville jokes ("This

guy ain't got an enemy in the world, but all his friends hate him.")
which made Duvid laugh until his stomach hurt. Also, Zelig was
afraid of nothing. Coming from *chaider* one evening, Duvid was
attacked and knocked down by a couple of Irishers when Zelig
appeared like a genie out of a bottle, tore into the toughs with only
his fists, and sent them running. Zelig. What kind of a Jewish boy
was this, who looked like a black Italian, fought like a crazy Irisher,
and always seemed to do exactly as he pleased? No *chaider*. No *shul*
on Friday nights or *Shabbes*. No regular meals or bedtime. Zelig
seemed to live in the streets. Yet to Duvid, he was almost like the
phantom friend lonely children invent for themselves in the long,
empty stretches of the night. And strangely, Zelig seemed to like
and want him for a friend also. Duvid was sure that Zelig had just
felt sorry for him at first, a *greenhorn* in funny Russian clothes, knowing only a few words of English, uncertain and afraid. But whatever
the reason, Duvid was grateful that Zelig had chosen to become his
first American friend.

Run, run . . . from gutter, to curb, to cellar, to street. Zelig in
the lead, the others following after . . . Yankel, Menchen, Jacob,
Duvid, a carnival of feet and hands, of testing and matching. A fence
was leaped, its spikes reaching. Duvid soared free. *My country 'tis of
thee, sweet land of liberty* . . . It was all there, all of it possible. The
things waiting to be done. Never mind the spikes. If the others could
fly, so could he. In and out of the crowds on Avenue A. Masses of
people everywhere . . . in streets and windows, on stoops and fire
escapes. They hunted bits of breeze as if they were diamonds.

It was night, but the day's heat still rose from concrete, brick,
and stone. A horsecar clanged by; Zelig caught its tail and hung on
and the others did the same. Duvid whooped as they swung around
a corner. His mother and father should see him now. They should
see *half* the things he did. Duvid could imagine the looks on their
faces. He wished he didn't have to hide so much from them, but it
was the only way. There were things he did, things he *had* to do, that
they could never understand. Duvid had not always known this, but
he knew it now. It had taken him nearly three years to learn.

Zelig dropped off the horsecar at Chrystie Street and led the way
between two red-lamped tenements into a dark hole of an alley

littered with refuse. Duvid followed Jacob's rounded back, hoping those in front had scared away any rats. Jacob's back was all he could see. When it climbed an iron ladder and flattened against a second-floor fire escape, Duvid went after it. He had never been here before, but Zelig was always taking them to new places. He knew things that no one else knew. Duvid was sure there was nothing in the city of New York that Zelig had not seen or experienced or did not know about. (Joke . . . "Hear about the *chasan* who had such a terrible voice that every time he sang in *shul*, fifty Jews ran to be *goyim?*")

Two lighted windows faced the fire escape and Duvid looked through them with the others. A naked man and woman lay on the rumpled sheets of a big brass bed. The man lurched and heaved, the woman's legs flailed the air, and they both cried out and squeezed one another's flesh. Duvid turned away. He had seen enough of that when the Cossacks burned the *shtetl.* Now, of course, he understood what was being done, but could take no pleeasure in watching it.

Jacob saw him. "Whatsa matter? Don't ya wanna' watch da whore?"

Duvid said nothing. The others were too absorbed to pay attention to him. He just wished they would finish watching and move on. Then it was finally over and Zelig led them back down the fire escape and over the fence. They huddled, laughing and gloating over wonders beheld.

"Duvid didn't even watch."

Jacob, the accuser. A real blabbermouth. Why couldn't he keep his big mouth shut? Duvid liked Jacob the least, with his soft, fleshy body, rasping voice, and smell of soiled underwear.

"Why didn't ya watch?" asked Yonkel.

"I don't see any fun in it."

"You're crazy," said Menchen. "You just ain't got enough of a *petzel* to enjoy it."

"Ah, leave him alone," ordered Zelig. "I got a real big one on and I ain't standin' here wastin' it." He opened his pants. "Last one off's a rotten egg."

Unhappily, knowing in advance he was doomed to failure, Duvid nevertheless went through the ritual with the others. He could perform up to a certain point, could share in the wondrous rites of growth, but was still too young for the true miracle of the finale. This, he knew, would not come for at least another two years. Zelig, as always, erupted first (ah, a geyser to shake the stars), followed in lesser splendor by Yankel and Menchen. Jacob, Duvid was pleased to see, was having trouble. The other s cheered him on, which only made it worse. When Jacob failed entirely, shriveling to defeat under his own frantic hand, Duvid joined in the catcalls and laughter. Fat Jacob was twelve. At that age, Duvid was sure he would never fail, but would erupt with as much speed and power as Zelig.

They moved on, dancing through the rancid night, through rotten, toylike streets. There was P.S. 23, closed now for summer vacation, its big play yard dark and empty. They climbed its gates and Duvid offered silent greeting: *His* school. He loved every part of it . . . the neat rows of desks, the white, lined sheets of paper marked with his own writing, the books read and waiting to be read, the calm, straight-backed teachers, so sure of what they knew and where it led. Which was the way it had been from the beginning, from those first days when he had jumped straight from the *Katrina*'s steerage into the foreign class and sat with all those others who spoke no word of English either. Many of them had dirty faces and hands and snarled, uncombed hair and ragged clothes that made Duvid ashamed for them and for their mothers for letting them go to school like that. He himself always took great pride in the way he looked and would no more think of going to school dirty than he would to synagogue. And he was proud too of the way his mother looked whenever she came to visit . . . slender and pretty and dressed as nicely as any of the teachers. And although his mother spoke very little English, she never seemed much like a greenhorn. Only once could Duvid remember being ashamed of her. And even then, he supposed it wasn't really her fault, but had to be blamed mostly on all those other greenhorn women who must have thought they were still in Russia.

It had happened one afternoon in June, when the Health Board doctors were in school giving vaccinations against summer epidemics. Duvid had been given his vaccinations and was back in the classroom when a mob of women surrounded the school, stoned its windows, and began screaming for their children, screaming they were being murdered and buried in the schoolyard. When they refused to leave, the teachers had to march line after line of children out of the building to show that their throats had not been cut (as rumored) by the doctors in an American pogrom. Duvid marched out with his class and there was his mother, hair flying, dress and apron torn, screaming with the others. "Duvidal!" She pounced on him. A wild woman. And in front of Miss Adams, his serene, blue-eyed, beloved teacher. "Duvidal, you're all right?" The Yiddish rasped at his ears, offending him. Learn to speak English, Momma, we're in America. Who *was* this woman? He wanted to turn and run back into the school. He didn't want to know her. She clutched him, hands searching for wounds, for broken bones. Her eyes hunted blood. She tried to lift him, to carry him away, but he was too big. Screaming women were all around and doing the same thing, but Duvid saw and heard only his mother. He shriveled with shame. What must Miss Adams think? What good now all the nice visits, with the neatly combed hair, pretty clothes, and quiet American manner? "Momma, we only got *vaccinations.* So we don't get sick this summer." He tried to show her the spot, high on his arm. *"Nobody hurt us!"* Like whispering to the wind. His mother neither saw nor heard. She dragged him off, safe from throat-cutting, Jew-hating doctors, safe from mass burials in the schoolyard. She trusted nothing but her own arms. She was beyond reason. Her heart blocked all messages to the brain. No more school. What Duvid had to learn, he would learn at home or in *chaider.* Duvid wept. "It's against the *law,* Momma. You *have* to let me go to school." What law? A mother's *heart* was the only law. And how did you argue with a mother's heart? What logic could break through such a cast-iron barrier? It took two days of pleading for reason to return. Later, she too was ashamed. "I'm sorry," she told him. "I'm older than you. I remember more and learn less quickly." But that had been during their first months in the country, when the pogroms were still fresh in everyone's minds. Nothing like it had happened since. This was America. Sometimes crazy Irishers or Italians came at you with fists, clubs, and knives, but there were no pogroms, no burning or killing —then an instinctive caution—not yet, anyway.

The Artist

Away from the gates and brick towers of P.S. 23, away from the promise of quiet orderly days, of *Uncle Tom's Cabin* and *David Copperfield* and how many other magic tales? All those shelves filled with books. Perhaps, Duvid thought, he would write a book himself someday. What better than that? What better than to be able to put down something you know is true and have others read and know the same thing? Sometimes Duvid talked about this with Zelig and although Zelig cared nothing for books or school, he listened and never laughed. Zelig didn't think at all as Duvid thought about these things. He just wanted to do whatever he felt like doing and have as much fun as he could. So far, he was doing all right. Duvid knew of no one who had as much fun as his friend or told as many jokes or laughed as much. Zelig was always laughing. Even when he was angry, he seemed to be laughing. He went to all the vaudeville shows on Grand Street, the Bowery, and up on Fourteenth Street and remembered the jokes he heard and did wonderful imitations of the actors who told them ("Some Yids are so cheap they go on a honeymoon alone to save money, ha-ha. And what about those others, who save their toys for their second childhood?"). Duvid thought he might be a famous actor some day, but Zelig said if he had to tell jokes as a job, he couldn't do it. "I got to *feel* like tellin' a joke," he said. "I can't just tell it cause someone says I *got* to." Yet it seemed to Duvid it would be easier to do something if it was your job and someone was giving you money for it. How else did you get money for food, clothes, rent? Money was important. Duvid knew of no way to live without it. More than anything else, it was what everyone in America talked and argued about and tried to get. Even the kids. Everyone, that is, but Zelig. Worrying about how Zelig was going to live without money when he grew up, Duvid decided he would share with him any money he made from writing books. Then Zelig could tell all the jokes he wanted without having to get paid for it.

At the corner of Orchard and Rivington Streets, Zelig led them up to a preacher wagon surrounded by jeering and shouting Jews. The wagon was a familiar sight in the ghetto streets, where it hunted converts several nights a week. Two big Irish policemen stood in front to protect the preacher, a tall, stoop-shouldered former Jew, from possible crowd violence. David saw a sign on the side of the wagon that read, "Jesus Christ is Lord Jehovah."

Above the mocking of the crowd, the preacher shouted, "Our Redeemer, the Lord of Hosts is his name . . . the Holy One of Israel! Dear friends, there is a mistaken belief among you that we preach that there is more than one God in existence."

Duvid followed Zelig and the others closer to the wagon. They and everyone else in the crowd were waiting for the first mention of the name of Jesus. They had dug banana peels out of a garbage can and held them ready.

"There is only one God," declared the preacher, "and that God is the God of the Jews . . ."

Derisive laughter. The words had been heard before. And they came from the crooked mouth of an apostate.

"There is only one God, I say, The God of the Jews. And this God gave to our exalted teacher, Moses, these never-to-be-forgotten words, 'Hear, O Israel, the Lord thy God is one God.' I know that. Nevertheless, you think we believe that Jesus Christ is . . ."

There were shrill cries from the crowd and Duvid saw Zelig throw his banana peel at the preacher. Then Yussel, Menchen, and Jacob threw theirs and it was finally Duvid's turn to follow the leader. On his toes, he let go the slippery peel and saw it strike the preacher's cheek.

"Christ, the Fatherless Liar!" someone yelled.

The preacher stood tall and went on through the uproar. "This is true, dear friends . . ."

"You're no friend of ours!" cried Zelig, followed, in chorus, by the others, although Duvid had nothing against the preacher personally and, in fact, could not help feeling a little sorry for him. He was trying so hard and nobody would listen.

"This is true, dear friends," the renegade Jew said again. "Jesus is the son of God. If you knew more of the truth, you would believe with me. I believe in God, who gave to Moses and the prophets His will. And, believing in Moses and the prophets, I believe them when they spoke of Jesus as God-Man. I can't help believing in Christ. If I didn't, I'd be calling God a liar. God was not always Jesus, but Jesus was, is, and always will be God . . ."

The Artist

More shouts, more banana peels flying (another direct hit), and Duvid saw one of the policemen moving toward him.

"Run!" called Zelig and Duvid turned and dodged through the crowd with the huge helmeted Irish Cossack in pursuit. Ah, now he was going to get it. Now he would be thrown in jail, beaten, left to rot forever. His poor mother and father. Poor Aunt Tybie. The disgrace. And all because of a stupid banana peel.

Duvid was out of the crowd now and whipping down Orchard Street, but still heard heavy, official feet close behind. A vague hope. Maybe he could save himself by converting. Maybe he could go to the preacher, call Jesus God, and the preacher would save him from jail. The conversion of Duvid Karlinsky. He wouldn't have to really *believe* Jesus was God, he just had to say it. An important difference. It was what you *believed* that counted, not what you *said*. His mother and father might not like it, but it was better than jail. He just hoped he didn't have to do any kneeling or cross-kissing. That might be too much even for him. *Vay iz mir.* Turned into a Christian by a banana peel.

There was a crash behind him and Duvid turned and saw the big Cossack rolling in the gutter where Zelig had tripped him. Duvid sailed around the corner, feet suddenly weightless, lighter than air. Zelig and the others followed. Aaaah Zelig. He might not go to *chaider* or *shul,* he might never pray, but he had a fine religious heart. Who else in New York had saved a Jew for Jehovah tonight?

Follow the leader, follow Zelig. Where? Anywhere. A clock tolled nine. Duvid knew his mother liked him home at that hour, but who could end such a night? Who could leave behind such magic? On such a night, you flew. On Zelig's wings. (Joke . . . "Girls who eat sweets, take up two seats.")

But on Hester Street, passing the light in his father's cellar workroom, seeing through the tiny window, seeing down there the familiar bent back, Duvid's flight faltered. A cutting edge of guilt. He danced on his father's sweat. He chased small joys while his father's labors never ended. Up in the predawn dark, his father carried his sack of tools to building sites all over the city, to wherever carpenters were needed. Avrum Karlinsky had made a small surrender. All right. Let them call him carpenter. Let them call him

The Artist

pisher. Let them call him anything, as long as they gave him work. Four stomachs were not filled with words or titles. Pay envelopes were needed. At night, over his own cellar bench, he was still a man who worked with wood. Chairs, cabinets, taborets, tables of princely design, carved chests that caught the light. Only an occasional piece sold, almost given away, while the real money to buy lay in unknown places north of Fourteenth Street. The four rooms where they lived were fast filling with what could not be sold, but Avrum worked far into the night producing more. Rifka despaired. "Enough already, Avrum. You'll work yourself into the grave. Nobody works day and night."

"I'm no carpenter."

"So who said?"

"A man *is* what he *does.* During the day I work as a carpenter. If I did not become what I truly am at night, I would *be* a carpenter."

Rifka shook her head. "A man should need a piece of wood to tell him who and what he is?"

Duvid tried to help his father by taking odd jobs after school and during vacations. If he earned enough, maybe his father could stop going on the building jobs with the Irishers and Italians, could stop having to work on the high scaffolds from which men fell and were killed. Duvid often read about such accidents in the newspapers and once saw a picture of an Italian who had fallen thirteen floors into a barrel of wet cement. The Italian didn't look like a man anymore, but like a broken statue. Duvid never told his father why he was so anxious to earn money. What was the use? He saw very quickly he could never earn enough to really do any good. All he could earn were pennies, when dollars were needed. But some nights he stayed and kept his father company in the cellar and helped with the rougher, less-skilled work. His father rarely spoke at such times and Duvid was never sure whether he really wanted him there. Once, when his father's silence seemed to have shut him out entirely, he started to leave.

Avrum Karlinsky straightened and looked at his son. "Where are you going?"

Duvid shrugged.

"Then why go?"

"You haven't said anything to me all night."

"So?"

"So I thought you might not want me here."

"Does my not talking mean I don't want you?"

"I don't know."

Avrum rolled a cigarette. "Do you remember back in the *shtetl,* when we went for a walk on *Shabbes* and sat together out on the hill?"

"Yes."

"Did we talk a lot then?"

Duvid shook his head, remembering.

"Did you ever think then that I didn't want you with me because I was quiet?"

"No," said Duvid, "but it's different now."

Avrum nodded slowly. He had shaved off his beard and cut his hair since coming to America and did not look much like himself or like a Jew to Duvid anymore. "You're right. It *is* different. In the *shtetl,* we were one, you and I. We breathed and felt as one. The same lungs and heart. The same world from morning to night. Words were not needed." He dropped into a chair and sighed. "Aaach. You're right. In this country, the son is smarter than the father. Here, we must talk more or we grow apart. I have locked myself up. I'm glad you told me. I must talk more to your mother too."

So in those evenings deep in the cellar, working with his wood, Avrum talked to Duvid. He spoke in Yiddish because his English was still rough and he was uncomfortable with it. The talk was self-conscious at first, but grew easier, more natural. Duvid listened. The things that poured from his father . . . the days with the Irishers and Italians on the scaffolds, the miracles worked halfway to the sky. No, no miracles. Avrum Karlinsky did not believe in miracles. He believed in what he had to do, and with his own two hands he made his own miracles. He took reasonable chances because he had to take them, and hoped for reasonable victories. And what was a reasonable victory? A week in which he had squeezed through another sixty hours on the scaffold plus thirty more in the cellar, in which he had found scattered moments of peace in his four rooms facing a wash-hung tenement courtyard, in which he could look at his wife, son, and mute sister-in-law across glowing *Shabbes* candles and feel that whatever may have come before, what lay ahead was sure to be better. Victory too, was being able to accept and live with defeats. He was a Jew and a greenhorn. Demands were made. When an Irish foreman extended his hand, it was not in friendship. The palm was up and empty and it had to be filled. It it were not filled, things happened. You could have strong hands and be willing to fight, but jobs were not kept with fists. A family's empty stomachs were held for ransom. So Avrum learned to accept and pay. Bargains had to be made with the unbargainable. "They squeeze you from all sides," Avrum told his son in the cellar, not in complaint, but in explanation. "They won't let you live." Survival. You found out what you had to do to get from one day to the next and you did it. It was not always easy. Sometimes it was impossible. There were limits. When a limit was reached, Avrum came home bruised, bloody, and jobless. "A little accident on the job," he would tell his wife. But to Duvid, at night, in the cellar, "I gave that Irisher today. I gave him good." Dark eyes glowed through the puffiness. The cost was high—sometimes weeks without a pay envelope—but worth it. The stomach and brain were not everything. The heart had to live too.

His father. Duvid turned away from the accusing cellar light, erased the guilt of his pleasure, and followed Zelig. Tomorrow we'll talk again, Poppa. Tonight is for flying. Where next, dear leader?

Another country. The sounds of the street were far below. It was black all around and the tar was soft underfoot. But Duvid could still see his friends and this changed everything. The thing was, he was not alone. He had once explored the roofs alone at night and had been afraid. There were threats in the dark, in the unseen height, in knowing the edge was there and waiting. Yet how different during the day, when the sun shone and the clean wash snapped and blew in the wind off the river and you could see east across to Brooklyn and west to the Hudson where the Palisades rose high and gray in the distance. Fine during the day. So that Duvid often took his Aunt Tybie up while it was light and showed her the sights, pointing out the Statue of Liberty in the harbor and the lacy webbing of the

The Artist

Brooklyn Bridge. He could never be sure of exactly how much his aunt understood, but she always seemed to listen carefully when he spoke and sometimes smiled and pointed as if she understood everything.

Tybie had been afraid of the excitement of the streets at the beginning, and the tenement roof had been the only place to take her for sun and air. Later, with Duvid holding her hand, she allowed herself to be led through the crowds and pushcarts, but still liked the roof best. Sometimes, sitting there talking to his aunt, the two of them alone, Duvid was able to forget the way she was, and imagine she could speak and understand again. When he began learning English, he spoke to her in the new language instead of Yiddish. If Tybie ever did speak again, Duvid wanted her to speak in the words of their adopted country. Although doctors offered little hope of this happening, Duvid still liked to dream of the way it would be, with the first words out of his aunt's mouth enunciated in perfectly structured paragraphs of accent-free English. No ugly, greenhorn guttural from his Aunt Tybie. When she spoke, she would sound as pretty as she looked.

Pretty Aunt Tybie. Maybe too pretty, Duvid sometimes thought, making men look at and whisper about her. Able to understand more now, he had begun to view the entire male population of the East Side as united against his aunt in a grand conspiracy of lust. His father had said she must be protected and Duvid was doing it, but it was not always easy. And the way his aunt looked made it no easier. Because besides her fair complexion and pretty face, she also had breasts. All women, Duvid knew, had breasts, but not like his Aunt Tybie's. Hers were bigger, more fully extended than anyone else's and they were a great trial and embarrassment to Duvid. Wherever he took his aunt, there they were, leading the way. *Everyone* looked. Duvid wanted to hide them under a blanket. And because there was a child's mind in control of this very womanly body, additional problems were created. In time, Duvid had to face and deal with them all. He had been forced to deal with the most difficult earlier that summer.

Duvid was his aunt's favorite. She followed and obeyed him with the blind devotion of a puppy. She was sad when he left and joyous when he returned. Warmly affectionate, she liked nothing more than to kiss and embrace him. Duvid enjoyed it too. A little love game. They had played it for as long as Duvid could remember. Then on the roof one day, it was suddenly different. Tybie's soft, baby kisses became stronger and she held him against her in a way she had never held him before. She kissed his lips and pressed his head between her breasts. The front of her dress seemed to have magically opened and Duvid felt and tasted flesh and was frightened. He knew what was happening now and that it was wrong, that it was exactly what he was supposed to protect his aunt against. Yet he felt helpless to stop it. And why *should* he stop it? If it was what his poor aunt wanted, if it was making her happy after all she had suffered, what harm could there be in it? Maybe if he were older, really a man like Zelig . . . maybe then it would be wrong. But surely not now.

The womanly body took over entirely from the little-girl brain above it. Duvid did not know what he should do, but found he did not have to do anything. Whatever had to be done was being done for him. He felt himself rocked and tossed as though he were back in his bunk in the hold of the *Katrina*. Except that now there was no pain, only a sweet, flooding warmth from the flesh that held him.

When it seemed to be over, when Tybie's body had quieted and the little-girl brain had taken charge once more, Duvid carefully arranged her clothing and led her down from the roof. He felt as though he had somehow managed to give her a present that he had never even known he was able to give. He waited to feel that he had done something terrible, but the feeling never came and he wondered if perhaps there was something wrong with him. Because all he felt was good. He wished there were someone he could talk to, someone who might tell him more than the little he knew. His father or the rabbi? Impossible. But what about Zelig? His friend was, after all, a mine of information about such things. If anyone knew, it would be Zelig. Yet the idea of sharing what had happened with anyone at all, even with someone as trustworthy and close as his friend, seemed too forbidding. Unless, of course, he could do it in a way that did not actually tell how it had been. Maybe then, if he were careful, it could be managed. Duvid decided to wait for the right moment and try.

The Artist

The right moment arrived one night when the two sat alone on a fire escape of an abandoned tenement. The street noises were far away, the sound of a violin drifted from an open window somewhere, and Duvid felt there was nothing in the world he could not share with his friend.

"Zel, you know my Aunt Tybie."

"Jesus, what a pair!"

It was not the precise response Duvid would have chosen to start off with, but knew it was just his friend's way.

"She's like a little baby."

"*Vay iz mir,*" moaned Zelig, clutching himself and rocking. "Some little baby."

"I mean in her mind. She can't understand much. She can feed and dress herself and go to the bathroom and all that, but she can't think about much else. The doctor says she's like three years old in her mind."

"With a pair like that, who needs a mind?"

"That's just the thing," Duvid pushed on. "She's a grown-up woman everyplace but in her head. And that's what makes the problems."

"What problems?"

Duvid moistened his lips. "You know."

"Ya mean gettin' a *petzel* in her grown-up *knish?*"

Duvid nodded, relieved that it was out. He knew Zelig would understand.

Zelig said consideringly, "I never even thought'a that. A grown-up woman and no *petzel,* and a little baby upstairs in the head. She must need it bad too."

Ah. Exactly as Duvid had thought. The need was great.

"She must need it *very* bad," declared the expert gravely.

"What are you supposed to do?"

"Who?"

"Anyone," said Duvid. "I mean, you can see what sort of problem this can be. What happens to a woman inside if she needs it so bad? Does it hurt?"

"Sure. Sometimes it hurts so bad it can make a woman scream and yell."

Duvid heard women screaming and yelling all the time. In how many cases was this the cause?

71

The Artist

"Listen," said the expert, "I know how ya feel about your aunt. It's a very sad case. When ya like someone like that, it makes ya feel bad when they got problems."

"Yes."

"Ya want I should help Aunt Tybie out?"

Duvid looked at his friend in the darkness.

Zelig said, "I don't mean no insult. But if it would help her out . . . if it would keep ya aunt from all that hurt inside, I got a *petzel* that ain't doin' much mosta' the time."

"No," said Duvid.

"It wouldn't be no trouble. I got more *jism* than I know what to do with anyway."

"It wouldn't be right."

"Why not? It would just be helpin' the poor lady out. And no one but us has to know about it. It would be a real *mitzvah.*" Zelig grinned. "Ask the rabbi. God'll thank us both."

Duvid had no wish to involve God in this in any way. The less He knew about it, the better. But Zelig had already given him exactly what he had hoped for. Now he knew. A woman needed certain things. If she didn't get them, she hurt. What he had done was right. There was nothing wrong with him after all. He had done nothing to be ashamed of. A real *mitzvah*, Zelig had called it. A truly good deed. Poor Aunt Tybie. It was the least he could do for her. And if Uncle Herschel was watching from whatever place in heaven murdered Jewish butchers watched from, Duvid was sure he would be happy to see that his wife's needs were being cared for within the family, by one of their own.

The roof, dark now under the stars, was not the roof of Duvid and Tybie during the day. This one was strange, a place of moving shadows, of bodies sprawled and twitching in far corners. (Womanly needs being cared for?) Wash lines reached for the throat and you ducked in time or were hanged. Yussel went down first, coughing and choking, followed by fat Jacob. Watch out, watch out! There were hidden dangers. But Zelig led and held the key. The ultimate rites of manhood. Six floors above the streets and it might have been Mount Everest. They moved silently, eyes straining, alert. No jokes now, no teasing or laughing. That time was past. The roof joined with another, a brick wall at the joining, and they climbed over. Duvid followed the pale, stumbling blur of Jacob's shirt. There was comfort in being behind Jacob. What Jacob could do, Duvid knew he could do also. Which was important. Sometimes you failed, but how much worse if you had to fail alone. As long as Jacob was there, Duvid at least felt safe from solitary failure.

The line buckled and stopped and Duvid went into Jacob's back.

"We're here," said Zelig.

"Where?" asked Menchen.

"Da great divide," declared the leader.

Duvid pressed forward with the others to look. The roof they were on had ended, separated from the adjoining one by a narrow airshaft. Peering down, Duvid saw the spaced lights of windows and heard a woman's voice yelling something in Yiddish. More unsatisfied needs. There was nothing to see at the bottom of the shaft. It was just black.

"So what?" said Yussel.

No immediate reply. Zelig had not haunted a thousand shows for nothing. Timing, a sense of the dramatic had invaded his blood. The Yiddish Arts Theatre ran like rain from his pores. He stood confronting those clustered about him . . . Boris Thomashevsky, stage center, before the final third-act curtain.

"So what?" said Jacob.

"So we go over." There it was . . . simply, quietly spoken, letting the words themselves carry the full, dramatic impact.

"Over?" echoed Menchen dumbly.

"Over."

They all looked again. The airshaft was actually no more than four or five feet wide, under ordinary conditions an easy jump. But the conditions were not ordinary. There was no room for a run, the jump was to and from narrow parapets, and the ground was six stories away.

"You're nuts," said Yussel.

"A person could get killed," wheezed Jacob.

Menchen howled, *"Oy vay!"*

Duvid said nothing. He was as shocked as the others, but as the junior and greenhorn of the group could not afford to react honestly. Besides, Zelig had said they were going over. And what Zelig said they would do, they usually did. He took a deep breath, wrestled his stomach down from his throat, and waited to see how his friend would handle it.

Style. At the age of thirteen and half-illiterate, the Yiddish David Garrick had more pure style than most men achieve in a lifetime. Without a wasted glance or motion, Zelig stepped to the parapet, launched himself into space, and landed easily on the far side of the airshaft. Then before anyone could react, he flew back with the grace and dignity of an angel returning from one of the Lord's missions.

"Jesus Christ!" whispered Yussel.

"No," modestly corrected the leader, "Zelig." He grinned. "Hey, hear about the sleepy whore who couldn't stay awake for a second?"

Duvid wanted to jump up and down and cheer. Was that a Zelig? Who else in all the world? He would dare and do anything. *Anything!* And following his friend, touched with so free and soaring a spirit, Duvid felt himself capable of as much. Lead, Zelig, lead. Lead anywhere. He, Duvid Karlinsky, would follow.

"See?" said Zelig. "Easy. Nothing to it. Just look at the other side and forget what's down there."

No one moved. Duvid was ready, but there were rules. He was last in line. He had to wait for the others. If and when they refused to jump, he would be free to act. But not before. He began to hope no one else would go. A great chance for him. He would then be second in line, just behind Zelig. His feet danced on the warm tar. Hurry, Zelig. Rule them out. Your friend, Duvid, is ready.

But the leader was in no hurry to rule anybody out. It was too good a moment to rush. Such moments were rare and valuable and not to be squandered. The thing to do with such moments was to stretch them, make them last.

"Whatsa matter?" Zelig addressed himself to Yussel and Menchen, respectively first and second in the hierarchy. "Still scared?"

Where was there to look? They looked at the black space separating the parapets. They judged and measured. The short hairs

The Artist

(but recently achieved) crawled between their legs. What hung there, each tight in its sac, hung in the balance. It was unfair. They were too young to make such decisions. They were just boys and their mothers and fathers loved them and worried about them. They went to *chaider* and had only begun to learn. What did they know about choices like this? About living or dying? Unfair. They looked at the black, terrible space and said nothing.

"All right," said the leader. "Ya want I should show ya again how easy? I'll show ya again."

The quick hands made small, deprecating movements. It was nothing. He would show them. Benevolence glowed from the narrow, intelligent face. It was all so clear, simple, and possible, so easy to see. Why couldn't others see it as he did? Zelig felt heavy, weighted with knowledge. He was an old man obliged to lead children. Ah, look at them. Yussel and Menchen . . . about to wet their pants with fright. Poor Jacob . . . frozen, a fat Yiddish statue. Duvid . . . ah, Duvid. Duvid was ready. A *mensch.* Ten years old and already a man. The lousy Cossacks. If the bastards didn't kill you, they made you a man quickly. A little more time and Duvid could lead. In the blue light of the stars, Zelig smiled pure love into his friend, turned, and climbed onto the parapet. Style. Sidney Carton going to meet the waiting blade could have done no better. A simple act. On this, his third flight, the leader soared, faltered briefly as a bit of tar on one shoe clung to the parapet edge, then glided, with silent grace, through the darkness below.

It was a neat fall. Zelig managed even this. Nothing visibly broken to shock or offend the sensitive eye. Zelig's mother was dead and his father worked nights and could not be reached, so helpful neighbors plugged Zelig's nostrils with cotton, combed his hair, and sat him on cakes of ice placed in a washtub in his living room.

Duvid stayed with his friend all night. His father came for him twice, but he refused to go home and his father finally left him there.

The Artist

A few neighbors stayed part of the time, but toward morning Duvid was alone with Zelig in the living room. The lights were on and all the mirrors covered with sheets so the ghosts should stay away. There were rules for this too. Duvid sat quietly opposite the leader, hands folded in his lap. Zelig had been propped up nice and straight on the blocks of ice, but started to slip over as the ice melted under him. He was a little crooked now in his ice-chair, looking like a child sleeping off his first binge. His mouth hung slightly open, as if to tell a joke in the bare, sparsely furnished room ("Hey, my cousin's so bow-legged we hung him over the door for good luck."), with the crates and boxes all around, brought up and left there by neighbors for sitting *shivah.* Duvid sat on one of the crates, feeling the slats cut into his bottom, but refusing to make himself more comfortable. Zelig didn't look comfortable. What right had *he* to worry about his behind. Follow the leader. *Lead, Zelig, lead. Lead anywhere. He, Duvid Karlinsky, would follow.*

Well, Zelig had led and he hadn't followed. Nor had any of the others. Zelig had fooled them all. Always something new. Duvid felt vaguely resentful, as if he had somehow been tricked by his friend. What right? What right? He wanted to be angry, but who was there to be angry at? What he should really do was cry. His friend was dead, on a pile of ice in a tin basin, and all he could do was sit here. No tears. They refused to come. He felt dry, inside and out.

Duvid closed his eyes and thought of Zelig as he had been, quick and graceful and sure, always telling jokes ("Italian opera is where a guy gets stabbed and instead of bleedin', he sings."), afraid of nothing, rescuing him from the Irishers and becoming his first American friend, saving him from Cossacks at his back, forcing his acceptance by the others. . . . Zelig, leaping fences and hanging from the backs of horsecars, his manhood held with firm pride and exploding in a high, shining arc, never interested in books or school, speaking English in his own rough, careless way, but listening to whatever Duvid told him and never laughing. And Zelig at the end, looking at him in the darkness up on the roof, then turning and stepping up on the ledge and disappearing without sign of fear or trouble, without shout, cry, or scream, but just going down as if he were some sort of hurt bird and only that soft sound, far below, afterward.

The Artist

Duvid opened his eyes and stared, dry-eyed, at his friend. The ice was melting into the washtub with the steady drip of a light rain and Zelig had slid even more crookedly in his seat. He looked awkward and foolish leaning over like that and not like Zelig at all. Zelig had never looked awkward or foolish in his life. It didn't seem right. Duvid jumped up, crossed the room, and tried to straighten his friend. Zelig's body felt stiff and heavy under his hands and when Duvid moved him, he slid right back. Duvid tried again and again to straighten Zelig in his chair of ice, but each time he got him into an upright position and took his hands away, Zelig slid crooked. Duvid braced himself against the washtub with his knees to give himself more leverage and tried once more. But Zelig, who had always done pretty much as he pleased with his parents, his teachers, his friends, and anyone else who ever had anything to do with him, was not going to be changed now. If he chose to lean crookedly, he would lean.

Duvid dropped back weakly into his chair. Zelig still leaned far to one side on the melting ice, his face pitiful and pale under the dark, close-cropped hair, under the stubborn, closed lids. Looking at him, now, Duvid finally wept.

Zelig's father arrived with the first gray light, a thin, worried-looking man in a worker's cap who seemed to have been put together with sticks and pieces of string. He made night deliveries for a drayage company and word of his son had not reached him until he stabled his horses. He said nothing to Duvid, but just stood rocking gently and praying. Once, he went over and touched Zelig's cheek with the back of a bony hand, as though to see if he had a fever. Duvid watched him, thinking how different he was from Zelig. Even dead, Zelig seemed more alive than his father.

Mr. Zaikewitch suddenly stopped praying and looked at Duvid. "You were with my son?" he said in Yiddish.

"Yes."

"They said he fell off the roof."

"No."

"What no?"

"Zelig didn't fall," said Duvid heavily. Certain facts had to be kept straight. They were important. "He jumped."

The narrow, rheumy eyes widened.

"We were doing "Follow the Leader" and Zelig was the leader."

"A game?"

It was more than a game and Duvid knew it was more, but how to describe it? And if he did try to explain, would this sad old man, who seemed so wholly unconnected with Zelig, with all Zelig knew and was, be able to understand?

"My son died playing a game?"

"Zelig was the leader," Duvid said again, refusing to acknowledge it as a game. "What he did, we had to do also. He jumped from one roof to another. Over an airshaft. He did it fine. Twice. But when he tried to do it again, something happened."

"Something happened?"

"There was tar on his shoe. He slipped."

"Aaah. He slipped."

"Yes."

The drayman nodded slowly, consideringly, his small, frail head in its worker's cap going up and down, up and down, as if once started it was unable to stop. "And you? You followed my Zelig? You jumped, too, from the roof?"

And there it was. As suddenly and clear as that. His failure. His treachery. Yet he *had* intended to jump. He had just been waiting his turn. Still, there was only one true answer to the question. "No."

"You were not so crazy as my son."

"Zelig wasn't crazy."

"You were not so crazy as my son." The same words, cutting into him again.

"I was going to jump. I was just waiting for my turn."

But who heard or cared? Zelig's father had turned away and was praying once more, rocking gently back and forth before his drunken-looking son on the melting ice.

Duvid sat watching. Then he stood up and quietly left. He ran down the tenement steps and through empty, early morning streets, turning, doubling back, and searching until he found the building and hurried to its roof. When he reached the parapet, he paused briefly to catch his breath, not looking down, but remembering what Zelig had said and keeping his eyes fixed on the far side. It was going to be another hot day and the morning mists were still low, rolling in off the oily waters of the harbor and cutting off the tops of the tenements. Duvid stared through the gray fog and breathed deeply, feeling his throat ache with the running and the dampness and with something else that he could not name but that he knew was there and would continue to be there for a long time to come. (Joke . . . "Hey listen, my teacher's so ugly she leaves a bad taste in my eyes," ha-ha.) Then Duvid bent his knees, jumped across the air-shaft, and slowly walked home.

FIVE

1904: New York, N. Y.

Duvid felt the first touch of moisture on his face as he turned into Rivington Street, and thought it was rain. Then he saw the snow-flakes against a streetlight, stared up at them for a moment, and stopped walking. He had not thought about snow. He had thought about everything else, about time schedules, places, routes, people, equipment, all carefully figured out, all finely planned weeks in advance, but he had completely failed to think about snow. Now, standing on the East Side street corner, he thought about it. There were just two questions to be considered. Would the snow affect anything? And if it did, would it be worth cancelling out because of it? When the answer twice came up no, Duvid took a deep breath and started to walk once more.

How did he feel now that the time was finally here? Excited, he thought, but not really nervous. Then he caught his hands sliding through his pockets over and over again, touching cord, tape, knife, and leaded billy, checking and rechecking them all in a small, con-tinuing ritual of reassurance. All right. So he was nervous. He'd have to be an idiot *not* to be nervous. But he was annoyed with himself anyway and forced his hands from his pockets and examined them. They were steady. And big. Even bigger than his father's. Size had come fast to him and was still a surprise. At fifteen, he was four inches taller than his father and still growing. It took time to accept.

Duvid tried to avoid standing near his father, as if his being taller diminished the older man in some way. A mark of disrespect. Although his father took wild pride in his growth. "Stand, stand. Show Momma. Apples he can eat off my head. A giant we're raising." He was an American dream, his size a product of their adopted land, of the new, free soil. *What* soil? The concrete and cobbles of East Side streets? Duvid had seen the grass of Central Park exactly twice. Uptown was another land. But never mind the reason. They loved his height. A six-foot Jewish boy. A Maccabee warrior. His father looked at him and saw victory. Duvid looked at his father and saw only defeat.

The snowflakes became larger, heavier. There was no wind and they drifted slowly. Late shoppers rushed from pushcart to store to pushcart. Workers rushed homeward, heads bent under the day. Duvid found himself rushing too and had to shorten his stride. He did not want to reach Location One too soon. Everything was to be timed with the precision of a military operation. Duvid Karlinsky's war. Rivington Street, 6:20 . . . Avenue A, 6:31 . . . Delancey, 6:39 . . . Location One, 6:47. Duvid took out his watch and checked it . . . 6:25. On schedule. The silver watch felt solid, smooth, pleasantly familiar in his hand. His *bar mitzvah* watch. His father must have squeezed himself dry to pay for it. How many hours on the scaffolds? How many nights in the cellar workshop? Listen, Poppa. Who needs a silver watch? Who needs *any* watch? I already know what time it is. It's time to get America off your back. It's time to get angry and shake your fist at the Land of Opportunity. *What* opportunity? They're tossing crap in your face and calling it opportunity. It's time to throw some of it back. Tonight, Poppa, we start throwing.

He returned the watch to its protective metal case and slid it back into his pocket. The watch was having a special airing tonight. Duvid usually kept it at home, in a bureau drawer, along with his prayer shawl, Bible, and phylacteries. His Jewish cemetery. What he buried there was resurrected only on holidays and special occasions. No more afternoon *chaider*, no more Friday nights in *shul*, no more Torah. What had happened to the honey, to the sweetness of learning? When had it turned sour? It was still inside him. He could feel the juices sloshing around. But the sweetness was gone and he did not expect it back. His mother mourned its passing, her eyes confused. She blamed her husband. (Who else?) Avrum, you should *make* him go to *chaider*. You should *drag* him to *shul*. You should *stop* him from becoming a *goy*. Avrum Karlinsky shrugged off his wife's attacks. When Duvid became a *bar mitzvah*, he was technically a man. How could he then force on his son, the man, what he did not believe himself? And he was not worried about Duvid's becoming a *goy*. Even without *chaider* and *shul*, Duvid (the giant) was as much a Jew as any pale, psalm-singing *yeshiva-bucher* in the city of New York. Maybe even more of a Jew. Jewishness was not measured by Torah reading. It was measured by what took place in the heart. And in the heart, declared Avrum Karlinsky, his son was a Samson of a Jew.

Duvid passed Avenue A on schedule and crossed Delancey at precisely 6:39. The streets were almost deserted here. There were no shops and pushcarts, only factories and warehouses—all closed at this hour. Duvid turned into a cobbled alley, followed it a short distance, made two sharp turns, and came out beside a low, flat warehouse. Light from an office window yellowed the snow. Everything else was dark. The nearest street lantern was a hundred yards away. Duvid looked around and saw no one, then stepped back into the alley to wait. He was at Location One.

The snow was melting as it touched the ground. A few flakes went down Duvid's neck and he shivered and pulled his collar tighter. He pressed against a wall, but the snow was falling straight and the wall offered no shelter. He would have about ten minutes to wait . . . maybe longer if Hymie felt like having a little fun along the way. Fun, to Hymie, was scaring his customers half to death. No real hurt or damage. They were, after all, paying good money each month just to avoid anything like that. But what harm in reminding them of what might happen if they grew tired of paying? What harm in a brief glimpse of knife, club, or gun? . . . or in a little playful pushing and shoving? It might even be doing them a favor, remove the need for real hurt or damage sometime in the future. Hymie's favors.

Duvid sought and found the leather-covered handle in his pocket. Things to remember. Stay out of sight, move quickly, hit hard. But not too hard. He was stronger than he sometimes realized

82

The Artist

and did not want to break any skulls. Not that these particular skulls did not deserve breaking. But that part was not his business. Vengeance was the Lord's, thundered the rabbis. Let *Him* take care of that part. All Duvid wanted tonight were the collections. God was welcome to the rest.

He heard the quick footsteps an instant before he saw Hymie turn the corner and pass under the streetlight. The collector was hurrying along the empty street, head down, shoulders hunched against the snow. Duvid watched from the alley, seeing the dark bowler hat and expensive well-fitting coat. Hymie loved clothes and always wore the latest styles. It was said he had more than twenty pairs of shoes at home, which he arranged in neat rows and spent hours lovingly polishing. Duvid had once seen what the toe of one of Hymie's lovingly polished shoes could do to a stubborn customer's face, and he remembered it. Hymie knew his business. People were very careful not to step on or dirty his shoes. Respect. Duvid's father claimed that people had more respect for Hymie Zaretsky's shoes than they did for Chief Rabbi Heitsfeldt's *tallis*.

The hard bowler hat could have been a problem, but Hymie always wore bowlers and Duvid was ready for it. As the collector passed the alley, Duvid gently lifted the hat with his left hand and swung the billy with his right. Hymie went down without knowing what hit him. Moving fast, Duvid pulled him into the alley, tied his hands and feet, gagged him, and taped his eyes. Then he took the billfold with the collection money from a breast pocket. The wages of sin bulged . . . the monthly payments of twenty-three customers, just one short of Hymie's full route. Murphy's warehouse, next door, would have been his last stop. Murphy was going to be in his office late tonight, waiting for the collector. Duvid put the money in his pocket and dragged Hymie deeper into the alley. The collector lay on his back, toes pointing at the falling snow. Duvid looked at the respected shoes, wet now with slush and not about to convince anyone of anything. It was said that Hymie was good to his mother and never missed a *Shabbes* in *shul*. So Duvid rolled him under a ledge and out of the snow as he left the alley.

Location Two was nearer the river, just to the right of Fishman's Junkyard . . . the recessed doorway of a burned-out loft building.

The Artist

Duvid reached it with seven minutes to spare. All right, Poppa, we're started. Hymie's shoes are without respect or polish. Things are twenty-five percent better. Soon, they'll be a hundred percent better. Your son, the Jewish giant, is taking care of it. And with his own two hands. You said it yourself, Poppa . . . *a man's hands are what lift him above the animals.* Well, Samson Karlinsky was lifting.

The money swelled against Duvid's chest and he felt a crazy compulsion to pull it out and count it. How much was there? Twenty-three monthly payments (insurance dues, they called it) from twenty-three storekeepers, manufacturers, junk dealers, stable owners, warehouse men, and assorted other members of the Lower East Side business community. The payments were based on ability to pay. An apogee of fairness. Avrum Karlinsky's tiny cellar shop was allowed the grace of the fifty-dollar minimum. But most would go far higher. And in an hour, there would be three more route collections to add to Hymie's. In weeks of planning, Duvid had been able to figure everything but the size of the take. He had no idea what the bigger customers were paying. He just knew that the final total of all four of the Association's routes had to be huge. Until now, enough to know. But now, with the billfold thick and heavy and actually in his pocket, it was hard to keep from wanting to know more. Easy, Duvid thought. It's only money.

Only money, hell! It was *life!* His father's. Without it, memorial candles would burn in the kitchen for Avrum Karlinsky. Who was he fooling? Tonight was a last desperate chance, a dangerous gamble. He could be dead himself by morning. These *momzers* didn't fool around. Bodies were fished from the river. Men looked up at the sky through holes in their skulls. Blood dripped like honey from fire escapes. He was strong and had thought it all out carefully and had plans, but *they* also had plans. It had to be kept straight in his mind. It was no game. But he had chosen to do it because there was nothing else he could think of to do and he couldn't just sit and watch what was happening to his father. The things that could happen to a man. Fifty dollars. You don't bury a man for a lousy fifty dollars a month. But that was just what they were doing. Every day they buried him a little deeper. Duvid watched him sink, saw the light go from his eyes, the color fade like old paint from his cheeks. A hunch came into his shoulders and he walked with a shuffle. Only

The Artist

money? Avrum Karlinsky was a Jew, and Jews had been taught for five thousand years, with fire and sword, that there was no freedom without money. Even in America, money was a nipple and you fought to suckle. The streets weren't really paved with gold. They were just paved. And you called yourself lucky to finally get your feet out of the mud and the chance to take it from there.

Warmed by the billfold, Duvid waited in the doorway of Location Two for Joey Mantucci. He had gone to school for a while with Joey, but had never really talked to him. Joey was a few years older and never went in much for talking. What he went in for mostly was showing his knife. He found this better than talking . . . at least until someone with a bigger knife left him on Mulberry Street one night with an open throat. From then on, he was unable to talk at all, but had to use a pad and pencil to write down everything he wanted to say, which, Duvid was sure, wasn't much. As a collector for the Association, very little talking was necessary. A blessing on America. It offered work even to the handicapped.

Duvid saw Mantucci approaching and this time remembered to tie a handkerchief across the lower part of his face. He had forgotten about it before. Hymie hadn't seen him, so it was all right . . . but just to forget was frightening. In this, you didn't forget. There was no second chance.

Mantucci walked splay-footed, with an easy, rolling swagger. The confidence of the knife. Duvid wondered how many men the collector had killed and how much he had been paid for each. What, exactly, was the cash value of a life on the Lower East Side of New York in the year 1902? It was said you could have a man killed for a flat fifty and even that price was negotiable. Only money. But where did life end and the dollar begin? Hey, Joey! How much for *me?* How much to slip a blade into Duvid Karlinsky, the shivering little sheeny who sat two rows in front of you in Miss Pomerantz's class? Any special prices for old classmates? Remember me, Joey? Once, in the schoolyard, you cut my suspenders and pulled down my pants to show all the little blue-eyed *shiksas* what a circumsised Yid looked like. Remember how I stood there, crying? How my poor, shriveled *petzel* drooped in the sun? Sure you remember, you murdering bastard.

The collector half-turned as Duvid came out of the doorway

behind him. He saw dark eyes above the handkerchief. Then he saw nothing.

Duvid dragged Mantucci into the gutted building, took the collection money out of his pocket, and bound and gagged him. Very quick, very smooth. A man could earn a good living at this. Why sweat making and selling furniture? Poppa, I'm quitting the business. It's easier to knock *gonifs* on the head and steal what they stole. Duvid bent over his old classmate, seeing the jagged line that ran across his throat, ear to ear, like a single railroad track. He dug for and found the knife, switched open the blade, and flicked its cutting edge with his thumb. The honed steel sang. Well, it would sing no more. Duvid broke the blade against a wall, dropped the pieces beside Mantucci, and left them there together in the rubble.

It was going too perfectly. Duvid worried all the way to Location Three. He was not used to things going this well. It wasn't normal. Something had to go wrong very soon. Didn't it always? Duvid came by such worry naturally. It was inherited from his mother. Rifka Karlinsky didn't exactly believe in the evil eye, but neither did she see any point in challenging it. What did it hurt to knock wood? Why take risks with too much hope? Why raise yourself to heights, when it hurt enough to fall from the low places? She put off questions with, "If we'll live and be well . . ." or, "We'll see . . ." or, "Only a fool speaks today for tomorrow." So that Duvid learned to go to his father when a definite yes or no was needed. An answer was a risk. It might have to be changed later. Rifka wanted no such risks.

Location Three . . . a cluster of shipping crates on an East River pier, and Duvid crouched in their shadow and considered (of all things) his mother.

What did he really know about her? All Jewish boys carried their mothers in pouches and he supposed he was no different, but what real knowledge did he have of her? She was just Momma. With a steady gaze of loneliness in the lidded, cautious eyes, she sat in his pouch like an unused coat in a closet. She never complained, never spoke of her disappointments, but Duvid heard the words nevertheless . . . Was a time you let me love you. Was a time my arms kept you from the cold. From my own mouth, I fed you. Now you shut me out. You grow away from me. You give me nothing of yourself.

The Artist

What am I, an old toy to be put away with your diapers? Because you've grown tall and strong, become a man, a smart American, am I to live in exile until I die? Listen to me, Duvidal. A day will come when horses play violins on fire escapes and your hands turn red before your eyes. Then you'll feel what I feel. Then you'll know how you need me. Then you'll come calling in the dark like when you were a little boy. And I'll come and kiss and make it all better.

Duvid saw no horses playing violins on or off fire escapes, but his hands, in the reflected glow of a ship's lantern, were indeed red. Poor Momma. Disappointments, one after the other. He was nothing she had hoped he would be . . . no great *lamden*, no scholar, no student of the Torah, not even (God help him) to finish an American high school. And such a prize student. Such books read. Such stories written. A talent like few had. And to give it all up for what? To work twelve hours a day with his hands? To bury himself in a cellar with his father?

Yet what could he tell her? That there really was no talent, but only a cheap, easy knack? That he hadn't the dedication or patience to be a true scholar? That he simply wasn't able to sit, hiding behind books, soaking in ideas and words, while his father quietly drowned? That he kept an angry kike deep inside his chest, far from where anyone could see, who carried a club in each fist and a knife between his teeth? And if he did tell her, could she understand? His mother breathed the air of a different world. She walked a landscape of interiors . . . of kitchens, bedrooms, and closets, of washtubs and stoves, of something she called a mother's heart. What did she know of the world outside? Her experience stopped at the locked front door. Outside was where she shopped and where her husband and son worked, faced trials, suffered hurt. Outside was unreal and only temporary. The real, continuing world was that of her tenement rooms. All that was genuine . . . love, schoolwork, sickness, aggravation, religious, personal, and financial problems, even old age and death, took place in her kitchen and bedroom. Here was where the important battles were fought, where they were lost or won. But it was *her* field of battle, not Duvid's.

And Duvid's field of battle? Location Three was his latest. Lochinvar, awaiting his Black Knight. Literally black. Frank Lincoln was

The Artist

a Negro. Huge and wide-shouldered, but with a soft, fluid voice, deceptive gentleness, and easy smile, Lincoln needed no overt violence to keep assigned customers paying. They just had to look at him. *Ayee.* Menace. A dark, alien skin. From such as this, God only knew what to expect. You didn't argue or look for trouble. You just paid and were grateful you had it to give. Duvid knew Lincoln (he was called Link . . . some swore, the missing one) differently. He was the first Negro he had ever seen, a wondrous ebony illusion in a beautiful, white suit. Smiling, he showed a gold tooth. Splendor. At the age of eight, Duvid had followed him through the streets. Sometimes he had picked Duvid up and let him see the gold tooth from very close, laughing, the gold shining in the sun. Duvid's mother had warned him to keep away from the *schvartzer.* An evil man. Dangerous. All *schvartzers* were dangerous, but this one was the worst. She had heard stories. She never told Duvid what the stories were, only that they were bad. Duvid had since heard the stories himself and they were, indeed, bad. But whenever he saw Frank Lincoln in the streets through the years, he still waved and said hello and the solid gold tooth continued to shine brightly back at him.

The snow was falling more heavily now, and foghorns moaned from the river. Duvid shifted position behind the piled crates. Link was about ten minutes behind schedule, but he had a longer route, a bigger list of customers than the others and there were usually delays. Old, big, black Link. Not really old, but to Duvid, a long-remembered part of the scene. He would give it to him nice and easy, a sure, gentle hit. He had almost considered passing Link up entirely, but could not afford the sentiment. There was too much money at stake. And money was why he was there.

Lincoln came then, tall and unbending, even against the snow. No white suit tonight, but a pale tan coat with hat to match. Link had as many hats as Hymie had pairs of shoes. Duvid lifted the handkerchief over his face and waited. When he went for the back of Link's head, he was thinking, regretfully, of the clean coat stretched out in the slush.

The Negro went down like a great tree and Duvid eased him behind the wall of crates. He tied his hands and feet as he had the others and took the collection money. Then he rolled Link onto his back to put on the blindfold and gag and stared, disbelievingly, into his eyes.

"Gotta hit big Link harder'n that, boy."

Duvid's hand shot to his handkerchief and found it down around his chin. He felt suddenly sick.

"Got youself a little problem, huh Duvid?" He pronounced it Doe-veed.

The deep voice was quiet, almost sympathetic. Duvid kneeled, as if praying. He had held back for a childish sentiment and the small kindness was about to destroy everything. What did he do now? If he just walked away from it, he would end up in the river. Maybe his father, too. Yet the alternative was not something he was able to face.

"What you gonna do now, boy?" Link watched Duvid wrestle with it. Feet and hands tied, on his back in the snow, he might have been at home, at his ease, an interested and mildly curious spectator.

Duvid said nothing.

"You get any of the others?"

"Hymie and Mantucci."

"They never saw you?"

"No."

"What about Finkelbaum?"

"He's next. After you."

"Yo' daddy know what you doin'?"

"No."

Link laughed, the sound oddly warm in the wet night. "Damn! You doin' pretty good for a kid. Why didn't you hit me harder? You'd done that, you be fine now. You sure big'nuf to hit harder."

"I didn't want to hurt you."

"I thank you for that." The gold tooth flashed. "But you didn't do me no favor. Cause now you gotta kill me."

Duvid felt his skin tighten.

"It's real easy. You just drag me to the edge of the pier there and shove me over."

Almost reflexively, Duvid glanced in the direction of the river. The edge of the pier was less than fifty yards away, there was no one in sight, and the falling snow offered a thick curtain of secrecy. It could be done. That part was not in doubt. But good God! To even *think* of it!

"Killin' ain't hard," purred Link. "It jus' the *idea* of killin'. *That's* what takes some doin'. But only with the firs' one. After that, it ain't nothin'. After that, you can do it and hardly think 'bout it at all."

Duvid stared at the dark face above the wet planking. It looked smooth and even, like black velvet.

"Of course," Link went on, "some don't never get used to it. Some don't stop thinkin' 'bout it. They kill one man and maybe for the rest of their natural days they ain't never the same. I mean, they just brood and feel bad. They can't hardly eat or sleep or laugh or enjoy anythin'." Link's eyes glowed in the dark. "Maybe, Doe-veed, you're one of these. An' if you are, I'm afraid you gonna be in real trouble when you kill me."

"I don't want to kill you, Link." Duvid's voice came out hoarse.

"I know you don't, Doe-veed. You a real nice Jewish boy. You not like Hymie or that murderin' Finkelbaum. I mean they *enjoy* hurtin' people. That's why I thought of a way that maybe you don't *have* to kill me."

Duvid leaned forward. "How?"

"Lift me up a bit, boy. Never could think or talk so good on my back. A back's for sleepin' or fuckin'. Besides, it gettin' awful wet down here." Duvid propped him against a crate. "That's better. Now let's look at this real hard. Your big problem is keepin' me from talkin' and you got just two ways fo' that. One way is t' kill me, which you don' wanna do and which I don't want ya' t' do neither, 'cause I ain't really ready t' go yet. The other way is t' just make sure I keep my mouth shut."

"How do I do that?"

"By makin' me a partner."

Duvid kneeled there.

"Listen, Doe-veed. The Association ain't my God or my religion. They pay me pretty good, but all I am is a messenger boy. I jus' collect the money for them. They ain't makin' me rich. So if there's a way I can pick up somethin' extra without gettin' my throat cut, I'd be real stupid not to grab it. And with you hittin' all four collectors, there ain't no reason in the world for them to suspicion me."

"How much do you want?"

"Well, boy," Link said slowly. "I ain't aimin' to be hoggish. I wanna do us both right. But if yo' smart, you'll give me nuf' to make sure I don't talk."

"If I threw you in the river, I wouldn't have to give you anything." Duvid's fear had passed. The thing was bargainable. He felt strong, in control once more.

Link grinned. "You learnin' fast. I swear, you gonna' be a big success in this here world. How's about puttin' aside my own collection?"

"How much is in it?"

" 'Bout eight thousand."

It hit Duvid's throat like a club. *That* much! "I'll give you half. Four thousand."

"Five thousand and ya' don't have to kill *nobody.* "

"You've got it."

"Good boy."

With thick fingers, Duvid counted out fifty hundred-dollar bills. "Where should I put it for you?"

Link thought. "You know that empty lot, corner Delancey and Essex? There's a billboard there, advertisin' the Bowery Vaudeville Show?"

Duvid nodded.

"Ya' jus' bury the money behind that billboard, next to the right-hand post. I'll pick it up t'morra night."

Duvid stuffed the bills back into his pocket. He checked his watch. "Damn! I'm late for Finkelbaum."

"Where ya' plannin' t' get him?"

"Near Mulberry."

"Ya' ain't too late. I saw him leavin' his woman's house no more'n half an hour ago."

Duvid was surprised. "He never goes there on collection night."

"Well he sho' went tonight. He said she been foolin' around some and needed to be put straight. That Finkelbaum's mean. When ya' hit him, boy, you make sure ya' hit him hard."

A sign of good faith, thought Duvid. His new partner was already proving valuable. A stream of warmth flowed from him to the black man sitting in the snow. "I have to gag and blindfold you like the others. It'll only be for about an hour. When I finish with Finkelbaum, I'll let the Association know where everyone is."

"Don't ya' worry none 'bout me. I'll be fine here." The gold tooth glowed. "An' be careful with that Finkelbaum. Ya' don' need no more partners."

Duvid put the gag and blindfold in place. Then he left Frank Lincoln propped behind the crates and hurried toward Location Four. A lesson. Five thousand dollars worth. And he had gotten off cheap. But what if Link turned greedy? What if he decides he wanted more? Duvid considered it through the wet, dark streets. He would have to protect himself. But how? He foraged for ideas. Maybe a letter. He could tell Link he had left a letter with a friend, accusing him of planning the whole thing. If Link started trouble, if anything happened to Duvid or his father, the letter would be mailed to the Association. He didn't actually have to write the letter. Just the threat should be enough. The idea took root, grew, flowered. It would be good insurance. Link was right. He was learning fast.

And now, finally Finkelbaum. Whoever it was that said fat men were good-natured, had never met this fat man. It was hard for Duvid to even think of Finkelbaum as a Jew. To be a Jew meant having at least a small core of feeling. Finkelbaum had a core of snake's tails. All Jews were supposed to ride the same beast, but this one rode his own. It was Finkelbaum, more than anyone else, who had lessened Duvid's father.

The breaking of Avrum Karlinsky. Duvid had watched it happening. He had not wanted to look, but there was no way to cover his eyes. And if he did cover them, he would have seen anyway. His father was stamped deep into his brain. Indelibly. Once big, now smaller . . . A. KARLINSKY***FINE WOOD FURNITURE. The three stars in the sign had been important. They would one day raise A. Karlinsky out of his cellar and into the sun. That, at least, had been the hope. Duvid had watched his father carve each star himself, the big hands moving with swift skill. His father did everything quickly, neatly, with graceful European flourishes . . . dressing, buttoning his shirt, shaving, sharpening his tools on the whetstone, sawing, planing, cutting, jotting numbers in his account book. Ah, the numbers. Few enough, but at least a living without swinging from scaffolds like a monkey in the wind. Avrum created, put together, and sold chairs, tables, and cabinets—a man of pride and dignity, pleased to put small pieces of himself into wood. Duvid helped in the shop as well as outside with the selling. A few places uptown were learning about Avrum Karlinsky. They were beginning to buy. There were dreams of a street-level shop. Out of the cellar at last. Avrum remembered how to laugh. Then. one day, *Finkelbaum!*

A messenger from the devil, Finkelbaum spit sulphur and ashes into the greening of Avrum Karlinsky. Fine furniture he declared, needed insurance. Insurance from what? . . . asked Avrum. From accidents. Who had accidents? The message rang clear. Without insurance, Karlinsky would have accidents. Karlinsky had his own message . . . *two* of them . . . one in each fist. *Momzers! Jewish Cossacks. He would give them accidents!*

Finkelbaum had the gift of prophecy. He could read the future. Suddenly, there were accidents. Not just one or two, but a plague of disasters . . . fires, floods, broken wagons, smashed cabinets, exploding tables and chairs. A biblical pestilence. Duvid waited for the sores to appear on his father's face. Snakes? No snakes, but one morning a swarm of rats squealing and scurrying through the shop. And after the rats, Finkelbaum again. A cold day, but Finkelbaum sweating, glistening in the doorway. He was dipped in chicken fat. Puffed cheeks glowed with the devil's own fires. "Well, Karlinsky?" Duvid watched his father's face. Things were happening beneath it. He was dark under the eyes and there were tight lines around the mouth. His arms hung loose, blue veins crawling through the black, curly hair. The blood shrieked like eagles in his ears. A sour sickness drained into his mouth. Job and Noah had patience and endured, yet even Job was allowed his anger. And Avrum was no Job. He was only a Karlinsky. He knew nothing of heavenly rewards. He knew no other place for passion and justice except here on earth. He started toward Finkelbaum who, with the instinctive wisdom, with the true genius for survival of his profession, looked once at his face and ran.

A small, last victory. Two nights later, Avrum did not return from a late delivery. Duvid knew the route and went looking for him. He found the horse and wagon outside a First Avenue warehouse. Avrum Karlinsky lay in back of the wagon, bloody, half-buried beneath his splintered furniture. Alive! But God, look at his hands!

Duvid took his father home and entered another level of his apprenticeship in grief. He was learning about the cries of the soul. They lie in the chest and in the throat. The mouth wants to open wide and let them out, but they refuse to go. Duvid looked at his father in bed with his two smashed hands, felt needles behind his eyelids, and wanted to scream. His mother wept loudly. Aunt Tybie, understanding little, but able to smell calamity, dripped silent tears. Avrum's face was swollen and black, his body kicked raw, but it was only his hands that Duvid saw. It was more than he could bear that anyone could have done this to him . . . his father, a sacred being, a king. His heart was suffocated by it. Whom could he ever love as he loved this man?

Avrum Karlinsky's voice came strange and thick between cracked teeth. "The *momzers* were waiting for me. They had the road blocked. They smashed everything. Two months' work. Everything."

"They might have killed you," wept his wife. "Who? Who?"

"They had handkerchiefs over their faces, but nothing could hide that lousy, fat Finkelbaum."

Rifka was disbelieving. "Finkelbaum? A Jew? No Jew could do this to another Jew."

"No?" Blood bubbled from Avrum's lips and he spat into a pot. "Why not? There are no Jewish pigs? Listen, Rifka, we got our share."

"No more!" cried Rifka. "I can't stand any more. You must give up the shop."

"What should I do then? Go back on the scaffolds? Hammer nails in planking the rest of my life? Let the earth open first and swallow me!"

"No!" said Duvid. "The shop stays open."

They looked at him.

"We'll pay the insurance. I'll work alone till Poppa's hands get better. But we won't close the shop." Duvid stood tall above the iron bedstead in the small, gray room, a slave to his father's pain. In all the world, there were only those two broken hands. "No matter what, the shop stays open."

And it did. But at a price. Fifty dollars in cash each month, and a daily draining of Avrum Karlinsky's blood. Duvid worked while his father sat staring at his great monster's claws in their splints and bandages. Four mouths to feed, doctor bills, extortion money, and back rent to pay and Avrum was a crippled foreigner in a still-strange land, with bad English, no friends, no influence, no protection (the police abused, never helped), no assets but those now frozen in his crippled fingers . . . no help anywhere in all the world. Except from his Duvid. *Ah, his Duvidal.* Yet there was pain, a further draining of pride even in this. A son grows strong, becomes a man, and the father shrivels to less. There was reason to it. A law of nature. Still, reason was no help. Avrum was unconsoled by it. Reason did not help when he lost everything, a way of life to a herd of drunken Cossacks. Reason did not help when he lost his unborn son to an Atlantic storm, along with all hope of ever having another. Reason was only a way of trying to make the insane logical and disaster bearable, and it never did the whole job. It washed over pain, but left the pain where it was. It shrunk defeat to a tiny lump of cement in the belly, but it left its weight intact and was never quite able to move the defeat and shame from where they lay.

Avrum's hands healed, but not what lay in his belly. More than his hands, more than his body, his life had been assaulted and beaten. He was nothing. What he did was nothing. He worked again with wood, but without joy. He looked at his finished pieces, smooth, graceful, useful works of art every one, but saw only Finkelbaum. He lost weight and the bones of his face threatened to break skin. "Eat," ordered a worried Rifka. "Look how you look." And Avrum ate, thrusting in the food with his usual swift, pendulum motion. But the food seemed to pass straight through him. Nothing stayed. Finkelbaum walked in his stomach . . . swollen, leering, sweating. How could there be room for anything else?

Duvid talked to his father, hoping to break holes in the darkness with words. But Avrum listened and did not hear. What he did hear, he rejected. He went through the motions of working, of daily living, but without hope. What was there to hope? They would never get out of their cellar hole, never escape, never save enough to see daylight. A slow death. They would be cave-dwellers forever. The more they worked, the more they earned, the more they would be bled. No hope, no hope. Duvid should leave, get out while he still could. He should do as his mother said . . . go back and finish school, study, read books. Avrum had been wrong about a man's hands. They were out of date, useless, of no help anymore. To stay here and work with them was to be buried.

And Duvid had thought, if we're really being buried, then what I must do now is find a shovel and start digging. It had taken long to get ready, but tonight the digging had begun.

Duvid was in position and waiting as Finkelbaum appeared through the snow. A Jewish devil rising. *What devil?* Only a mean, fat man, waddling like a duck along a dark city street. My God, look how he walks! Look, Poppa! Here comes your Finkelbaum, your *dybbuk.* You should be here to see. *This* is what lives in your stomach? *This* is what's eating you up? . . . burying you? Watch, Poppa, and you'll see what hands can still do.

Duvid swung hard, hearing the dull, flat sound that weighted leather makes when it strikes bone. Finkelbaum melted like the snow. Lying face down in the slush, he seemed smaller than Duvid remembered him. A greasy little *gonif* who belched up sour and broke the hands of good men. Duvid rolled him over with his foot and saw the loose jowls, the round, potato nose. He felt a crazy instant of regret that Finkelbaum was unable to see him, was unable to know whose hands were responsible for his lying there. Then he did what he had to do—took the collection money and left Finkelbaum lying, a plump, trussed-up pig, in a cellar stairwell.

It was done.

Duvid walked, trotted, ran, then made himself walk once more. Grown men did not run through city streets. And he was a grown man. That much had been proven. He had gone into the arena and had not been carried out. Yet how did you hold your feet to the ground when you felt like flying? He felt as he had when he was ten years old and soaring behind Zelig. Yet he had not come naked of experience and training to this night. He had been preparing for it

The Artist

from the moment he had climbed out of the damp, rotting *Katrina.*
Maybe even before. He had escaped from the *shtetl,* but preserved
its Talmud in his nightmares, in the games he and his friends had
played in the streets of another country. Games? No. Rituals of
soft-core brutality. In these streets you learned to make violence
work for you. If you failed to learn, punishment was handed out
according to a rigid set of rules. There was a certain magic in it, the
magic of a working system. The streets were a free-fire zone. The
first blows were always aimed at the most recent arrival. If he got
through it, it was his turn to swing at someone else. If he didn't get
through it, if he ran away or cried, he was condemned to isolation.
Duvid had gotten through it, a scarred veteran of the pushcart wars.
It had prepared him for Finkelbaum & Co. Its rules were the same
as the Association's. A man must be violated and must violate in
return.

You have visions, fantasies, imagined moments of such transcen-
dent joy that you know they can never be. Duvid's moment was the
one in which he found his father sitting alone in a dark corner of
his shop. "Poppa," he would say to him, and as his father looked
up with old, faded eyes, Duvid would raise his arms and loose a
shower of currency in a green storm. In the fantasy, all movements
were slow, silent, dreamy, a ballet without music, in which all the
bills floated, and he and his father embraced and sailed along with
them. Then the only sound was that of his father laughing, and
when Duvid looked at him, his eyes were no longer old and faded
but were young and laughing too.

No fantasy.

Avrum Karlinsky was, indeed, sitting in a corner of the shop.
Duvid closed and locked the door behind him, and drew the shades.

"Poppa?"

And the eyes were, indeed, old and faded. Old? Avrum was
thirty-six. But there was a faint, automatic smile. Avrum always
smiled when he saw his son. It was the only time he did smile.

"*Nu?* So how was the show?"

Duvid had told him he was going to a Fourteenth Street theater.
As if he could sit and look and laugh at six acts of vaudeville.

"I didn't go to any show."

97

"No show?"

Duvid shook his head. Insanely, he found himself trembling. He sat down, but instead of getting better it seemed to get worse. Arms, legs, his entire body shivered with a monstrous chill.

"What's the matter? You don't feel well?"

"I'll be all right in a minute."

"You're wet through. Look at your coat. Your shoes are soaked. You been walking all night in the snow?" Bugles blew somewhere in Avrum's head. His son, his baby boy. He stood up. "Come. We'll go home. Momma will make some hot tea. You'll go to bed."

"No."

"What no?"

"Sit down, Poppa." What was wrong with him? What was he waiting for? His pockets were bulging with money, a fortune, his father's life, and all he could do was sit and shake.

"What sit down? You're shaking like a leaf."

"I have something to tell you."

Avrum Karlinsky sat down. He could sniff out disaster in advance. He sighed, the sound that of escaping steam. He lowered his head to take the latest blow. "So what's now?"

Duvid pressed his hands together to quiet the trembling. "Everything's going to be all right, Poppa. From now on, everything's going to be fine."

Avrum stared at him.

"We've got money. Enough to pay Finkelbaum, enough for a new shop, enough to do whatever has to be done."

"You're sick, You're talking out of your head. *Meshuggener.* You've got a fever already. Come home to bed."

"I'm not sick. Look Poppa."

Hands fluttering like birds, Duvid took the billfolds from his pockets and carefully laid them on a workbench. Then, one at a time, he shook them empty. When he had finished, the bench was green with bills. Some were twenties, but most were fifties and hundreds.

Avrum's face had gone red, then white. His lips worked, strained, finally managed a hoarse whisper. "You *stole?*"

"No. I *took.* I took from thieves. To take from thieves isn't stealing. Hymie, Mantucci, Link, Finkelbaum. I took from them all. A month's collection."

"The *collectors?*" Avrum's voice went high, preadolescent with fear. "You took from *them? Vay iz mir.* They'll kill you. They'll cut you in little pieces and throw you in the river. You went crazy? What happened to you, Duvidal? You lost all your senses?"

He was on his feet, frantically gathering the money into piles. "Come. We must give it back. We must explain. A mistake. A terrible mistake has been made. We must give it back right now. We must apologize. There's still time. Come, Duvidal. Help me. We must get the money together."

"They didn't see me, Poppa. No one knows it was me." No point in explaining now about Link. There would be time enough for that later.

Avrum stopped his wild harvest of cash and slumped into a chair. He closed his eyes. To shut out sight of the money was to shut out its existence. He had been dreaming. When he opened his eyes again, the money would be gone. He opened his eyes. The money was not gone. "What are you talking? They're all blind? They couldn't see your face?"

"I hit them from behind." Duvid showed his father the blackjack. "With this."

"*Oy vay!*"

"It's all right. I told you. No one saw me."

It began to soak through. "You're sure? *No one?* Somebody passing, maybe?"

"No one passed. I picked the places carefully."

"You picked the places carefully." Avrum repeated the words as though mesmerized. He looked at his son's face, at the money covering the workbench, at the blackjack, then once more at Duvid's face. How and where had this boy learned such things? What was happening around him? What kind of world? Avrum felt old and doddering, confused, baffled. His Duvidal had done *this?* While he, his father, had been doing what? Sitting and dreaming of death? He was unfit, unprepared. He had brought his family out of a cemetery and into a jungle. Wild beasts roamed loose in the streets. Yet somehow, incredibly, he had raised a tiger. Avrum felt a stirring

99

among the tombstones in his chest. He breathed heavily. "So tell me," he said, "tell me what you did."

Duvid told him. He told him from the beginning, from first vague plans to detailed action. He left nothing out. A son telling a father a bedtime story, a fairy tale, a dream of a magic landscape peopled by dragons and a heroic giant. And some parts Avrum, like an enraptured child, had Duvid repeat.

"Again. Tell me again how it was with Finkelbaum."

Duvid described it once more.

Avrum nodded slowly, savoring it, picturing it all, seeing the fat villain go down in the snow, his son standing over him. "Only one knock in the head?"

"One knock."

"And he never knew who? What? Where?"

"All he saw was his own *tsatske.*"

Avrum laughed, the first time in months. The laugh came from somewhere deep, far away, from across oceans, from places and scenes long gone. He stood up. Was he taller now than before? . . . wasted neck fuller? . . . shoulders straighter? He went to the workbench and saw the money for what it was. He touched it, felt the quality of paper, breathed the smell. "We mustn't tell Momma." Ha! He fooled no one. He would tell her ten minutes after he arrived home. Could he leave such a thing unshared? She had to know what a son they had carved out, what a tiger.

Having enjoyed the sound before, Avrum laughed again. "Insurance. Now we'll give the *momzers* their insurance. Every month, we'll give. As much as they want. Their own *vershtunkeneh* money. Feh! They should only choke on it." It had appeal, a certain delicious irony, a quality of high poetic justice that only a Jew with his own angry God of vengeance could fully appreciate.

"Listen, Duvidal," Avrum's voice lowered to a whisper, dark, conspiratorial. "We must be careful. We must think and be smart. The money should be put in a vault. No one should ever know it's there. We must act like before. No different."

"Yes, Poppa."

Avrum's voice changed, took on weight. "Still we can plan. It doesn't hurt to look ahead. I passed last week with the wagon a place

100

The Artist

for rent. Uptown. Thirteenth Street by Second Avenue. For our work, a perfect location. Street level. No cellar. No hole in the ground. No grave dug in cement. Daylight can be seen."

His eyes were suddenly off somewhere, misty, threatening to flood. "You know? You know what this means? You *know*, Duvidal?"

Did Duvid know? He knew. He had laid his head on a chopping block for the knowing. Still, he would have had it no different. If he had it to do again, he would willingly do it again. This man was his father, he, Duvid, was his son, and there was love. It was as simple as that. Perhaps a time would come when it would not seem nearly so simple, when he might weigh, judge, question, measure differently. But right now, in this dismal little shop below the sidewalk, with its single bulb burning like the *ner tamid*, the vigil light in the synagogue, this was the way it was.

SIX

1945: Amagansett, Long Island

Duvid was trying another and different approach, this time working wet in wet, the whole of the canvas brushed in and flowing. The skeletal forms were barely discernible, an amorphous rising of ghosts. Gently, he dragged them with a dry sable, feeling the tug of swampy oil on soft hair, seeing the forms merge and fade even more. But not too much, he thought, not so much that they'd be lost entirely. No falling into the abstract. Although here, in this, the temptation was great. How much simpler to just let it all melt together, and let everyone see what they wanted. Everyone a partner. Except that he wanted no partners. *He* was the one who had done the seeing and feeling. *He* was the one who knew. And if any of it was to come out, it had to come through *him.* No sharing. It couldn't be done. You might as well try sharing an orgasm.

He smiled at the sexual analogy and, caressing the paint, caressed her, the silky sable brush, an extension of his hand, the moist canvas, that sweetly remembered place. Painting as an act of love. What a sensuous thing it could be. The movement, the touch, the blending of odors all added to the illusion. Or was it just the thought of *her?* Wondering, his body turned tense as a harp, but not unpleasantly so. A welcome surprise. The girl, herself, another surprise. He had expected nothing. Still didn't, really. No reason to. They were locked rooms to each other. Yet voices could be heard behind doors.

The Artist

He had walked home with her, seen where she lived, a sprawling barn of a place, big even for a family, in which she and Sammy rattled around alone. There were family photographs everywhere, on tables and walls, on bookshelves, sideboards, and cabinets. She had not put away a single one. Duvid had gone over them, studying mother and father, sisters and brothers . . . all fair, all slender, all classically Nordic, and all looking, he thought, eternally prosperous, healthy, happy, and beautiful.

"What are you trying to prove?" he had asked.

"About what?"

"The pictures."

"They were there, I just never touched them."

"Why not?"

"Why haven't you gotten rid of your wife's things?"

"I will. I haven't had a chance."

"You haven't had half an hour?"

A bird wept hoarsely outside. A cat screamed. Twice, he had started to clean house, and both times had stopped and put it off.

"I'm not being morbid," she said. "I've found it's better for me to see them around like this. It keeps me from glorifying them too much."

Duvid gazed again at the photographs. "They look pretty glorified just as they were."

"Oh, they were fine enough to look at. Dazzling, in fact. They called us the Golden Wallaces. Seeing us all lined up in church on Sunday was enough to make you believe in God. Only we weren't nearly so pretty on the inside. Inside, we were mostly lizards and toads." She studied him, taking silent measurements. Her face said they had a decent profit riding from their earlier time together, so she could afford to spend some of it on the truth. And if she couldn't . . . if it proved too much for him? Then they didn't deserve the profit, and to hell with it. "We really should be written up in genealogy books. It took two hundred years of selective inbreeding to produce this last batch. My mother was a whining, self-pitying lush, my father an embezzler and womanizer, my younger brother preferred boys, my older brother preferred himself, and the most fun my two little sisters could think up was taking cats out on the

103

beach and burying them alive. As for me, until I was seventeen, my greatest ambition was to go to bed with my father. I never did, but it wasn't because I didn't try. Poor daddy. I used to parade naked in front of him, until he finally slapped me silly and sent me away to school. It was the only moral strength he ever showed. Or maybe it was just that I didn't appeal to him."

She smiled, but it was fragile. "The thing was, I loved every damned one of them. With it all, they were the beginning and end. Everything. And time just makes it worse. It just makes me forget what terrible creeps they really were. So I keep the pictures around to remind me. I guess that sounds kind of weird, doesn't it?"

"Not if it works."

"It doesn't always. Do you miss your wife very much?"

He nodded slowly. "So much, it surprises me. I never really thought of myself as needing anyone. Neither did my wife. She used to say all I really needed was a brush, a bit of food, and an occasional lay. It turns out we were both wrong."

"I'm glad you miss her."

"Why?"

"It makes you human."

"Did you think I wasn't?"

Her eyes were enormous and stared at him with a clear, luminous look, a young animal's fright, some nameless creature with great orbs, estimating her danger. "I told you I was in awe of you."

"You don't have to worry. I'm as human as most."

And she said gravely, "I know."

But she knew nothing. She knew only what he wanted her to know. Which was as good as nothing.

There was no love in the brush now, no caress, no sweeping softness. He stabbed with a broad bristle, letting the paint roll and twist, and an angry red suddenly exploded the dark. Easy, he thought, and cooled it with blues and greens. But the violence was still there, was still in the stroke, a bomb blast that scattered the ghosts and set them screaming their toneless wail right out of the canvas and into the room.

Something made him turn and he saw her peering through the studio window. A waif. A strayed animal seeking shelter. How long had she been there? The glass was moist with her breath, and her nose, when she saw she had been seen, suddenly pressed shapeless against the pane. A child's game. Her hair was pulled back and tied with a ribbon, her forehead shining, her eyes fresh, clear water. Then she picked up Sammy and pressed his face to the window also, the two faces side by side, and Duvid looked at them and thought, my God, I'm glad to see them.

"I brought you a present," she said when they were in, and handed him a large pot. "I made them myself."

He lifted the cover and stared at a mass of pale, lumpy balls. "Beautiful. What are they?"

"Can't you *see?* They're knishes."

He stood dumbly.

"Potato knishes," she said. "Jewish people are supposed to be crazy about them. It says so in the book."

He felt bubbles in his stomach, a faint tickling in his throat. "What book?"

"Secrets of Ethnic Cooking. It also says 'the warm heart of Jewish passion lies in the core of a well-baked knish.' "

"You made that up."

She lifted her right hand. "So help me."

The bubbles and tickling broke as laughter. He choked, "What else did it say?"

"That no male Jew can resist blonde, blue-eyed *shiksas* bearing knishes."

"That is an absolute, poetic truth." He put down the pot and reached for her.

"Why are Jews so wonderful?" she whispered against his neck. "Why are they so brilliant, so passionate, so warm, so sensitive, so creative."

He nibbled an ear. "You mustn't judge all Jews by me."

"I want to be Jewish too."

"You've got to be chosen."

"Then please choose me."

"Sorry. No conversions today."

"Give me back my knishes!"

He considered. "Well, we do have a little something for emer-

gencies. The conversion would be only temporary, but the ceremony itself is rather pleasant."

"And I'd really be Jewish?"

"To the *core.*"

"I hate to interrupt your work."

"You already have."

Her face, aglow in the studio light, became beatific. "I'm ready."
She closed her eyes. "Convert me."

He put his arm under her thighs and lifted her. She kissed him
on the mouth. "What's it called?" she said. "The ceremony. Does
it have a name?"

"The Benediction of the *Petzel* and the *Knish.*"

They tumbled, laughing, to the couch. Then they stopped laughing. But the tickling remained in his throat and the bubbles came
back to his stomach and put him off.

She was surprised. "What's wrong?"

"I guess I can't laugh and love."

"I'll fix it."

Crouching like a golden animal drinking water, she kissed his
lips, his neck, his chest, his stomach, went farther down and stayed.
Her mouth nibbled feverishly, but her hair, released from its ribbon,
tickled his belly and merged with the tickling in his throat, so that
she was working for nothing.

"I'm sorry," he said. "I'm afraid we'll have to convert you some
other time."

She looked up at him, eyes stricken, looked across the flat plain
of his stomach, up between the twin slopes of his chest. "No. Wait.
It'll be all right." Then she was down and at it again.

He tried, gently, to free himself, tried to ease her away, but she
held on and he finally lay back. Strange girl. He could feel her body
harden, sense hidden tensions and fears. Apart now, he watched her
apply what she knew, and she knew a great deal. Another expert. In
bed, he seemed to have known only virtuosos. Every one a master.
And he? Eternally the student. Albeit a willing one. Where did they
learn so much? Or did it come with the glands? He stared at walls,
at ceiling, at high, naked beams, finally found sunlight trapped in
cobwebs. The place needed dusting. It was neglected. His wife
would be mortified. *Duvid, how could you let someone see the house like*

this? Don't worry, my darling. She isn't looking at the dust. She doesn't care how the place looks. She has other things on her mind. His glance moved to the easel, to the painting, to the screaming ghosts. He stared and the ghosts stared back. What did he want from them? Why couldn't he let them rest in peace? *What* peace? Who knew about peace? The whole species was crazy. The evidence was all around. A mixture of heroes and madmen. If you had the strength to do what you had to do every day, you belonged with the heroes. If not, there was only the other.

Because he was thinking of the wrong things, he was of no help to her. Then he did concentrate properly. But seeing her laboring so hard, so desperately now, struck him as terribly sad and washed out all hope. Poor girl. He drew her up, finally, and held her. "It doesn't have to be now."

Her face blurred, dissolved against his. Her body tensed. Her fingers clutched his chest, dug deep.

"Hey, it's no tragedy," he said.

"It *is.*"

"You mustn't get so desperate about it."

She lay heavily, flesh turned to lead. "I guess I just hate the idea of failing."

"If anyone failed, it was me. Not you."

"When a woman can't arouse a man, it's *her* failure."

"A male *bubba meise.*"

"What's a *bubba meise?*"

"An old wives' tale."

She was silent. A cluster of sea gulls passed overhead, crying to one another as though lost, their voices high, brassy, childlike. "It's just never happened to me before."

Duvid glimpsed erotic images of her successful arousals. They stretched to infinity. "I'm sorry I had to spoil your record."

"I didn't mean it that way."

He knew, of course. Yet some odd perversity, some faint aroma of humiliation, of singed pride, prodded him. "How old were you when you first opened your ledgers?"

"You don't have to punish me about that, Duvid. I punish myself enough."

It turned him right around, snatched the bludgeon from his

107

hand. And he thought, I must remember how finely tuned she is. It would be a sad mistake to forget.

She stayed to watch him work, huddled silent and still, with her Sammy, in a corner. Gravely, she tried to soak it all in. Important lessons were to be learned here, deep secrets were about to be revealed. She had the layman's reverence for the act of creation, felt an immutable awe in its presence. Pure wonder. A brush moved, paint swirled, and what had been nothing, became something. Typically, too, she was impressed most by what she understood least. And Duvid's screaming ghosts, those vague, skeletal images floating out of their red mists, were cryptic enough to overwhelm. In a spiritually confused age, Duvid thought, the artist had been anointed high priest and prophet. But it was a mistake, a misplaced honor. Because the century's true oracles weren't its artists at all, but its auto dealers and junkmen.

He stopped work only when the last of the light had gone, as if to quit even an instant sooner would have been an unforgivable breach of contract. He had hoped, as he grew older, that age might ease the compulsiveness of his rigid work ethic, but just the reverse had happened. He had become a greater time-miser than ever. With fewer hours left, he hoarded them more. And for what? He had long ago given up any illusions of leaving behind indelible marks. He cherished no visions of immortality. Nor did he care the slightest about such things. Museums were just caretakers for the dead. And in the end, dust. Still, he labored as though his soul hung on each stroke, as though hell would be payment for each squandered minute, as though any good he may have done before would be canceled out if he could not do more today and tomorrow.

Why? He asked the question but had no answer. And when his wife and son had asked, he'd had no answer for them either. And they deserved one. It was from *them* he had stolen the time. A minute here, an hour there. Bits and pieces that had finally added up to years. His wife had been a woman of understanding and patience, yet once, driven beyond both, she had called him the most selfish man she knew. She later recanted, but was probably right. Denying it then, he admitted it now. Self-indulgence came with the territory. It was as essential to the calling as paints and brushes. On his fiftieth birthday, in reply to an interviewer who had asked why he painted, he said, "When I was twenty, I painted to convince myself of how brilliant, compassionate, and perceptive I was. Now that I'm fifty and have lived and worked for the better part of a lifetime, I find that I still paint to convince myself of how brilliant, compassionate, and perceptive I am." Joke. Yet probably the only true change was that at fifty, the convincing came exactly thirty years harder.

Laurie permitted herself speech only when he was finally cleaning up. "Does the gift run in the Karlinsky blood?"

"What gift?"

"Painting."

"It's no gift. No one gives it. It's a craft you learn like any other. Though my father did pass on his feeling about hands. He makes furniture with his, I make pictures with mine. The only difference is, *his* stuff can be *used.*"

"What about your son?"

Duvid looked up from scraping his palette. "How did you know I had a son?"

"*Who's Who.* It said, 'one child, Richard, born 1919.'"

"You got a lot from that book."

"Does Richard use his hands too?"

"Only on a machine gun." He went back to his paint scraping, bending the thin, flexible blade against the wood of his palette, absorbing its sound, relaxing, indulging himself in this small, end-of-day ritual. "But even before the war, he never did show any interest in painting."

"Weren't you disappointed? Wouldn't you have liked him to follow you?"

"Jesus, no. I'm not one of *those.* I don't have to feed my ego with my kid. Besides, there are easier ways to get through life than stripping naked and starting all over again every morning." He paused. "Richard is adopted anyway. So the whole question of Karlinsky blood doesn't even come into it."

She stared silently out of her corner and he thought, now why did I tell her that? Why, at this moment, should I have found it necessary to tell this girl, whom I barely know, what I have never told *anyone?*

"I kind of wondered why you had only one child."

The Artist

"No one knows he's adopted."

"You don't have to worry. I won't say anything."

"I'm not worried."

"Was your wife the one who couldn't have children?"

"What man would admit it was *him?*"

"*Was* it you?"

"No."

"Did you have children with any other woman?"

"Not that I know of."

"Did you ever try?"

He laughed. "No."

"Then how do you know you can?"

"We went to doctors. They said I was all right."

"What a shame," she said sadly. "I mean, what marvelous babies you could have made."

"I might have produced a bunch of cretins."

"Not you. I *know* they'd be lovely. I'm rather witchlike when it comes to babies. I can *tell* how they'll turn out."

"Even before they're conceived?"

"Preconception happens to be my specialty."

"Well, we'll never know, will we?"

"Haven't you ever wondered? Haven't you ever tried to imagine what a child of your own might have been like?"

"Years ago, I suppose." *He supposed?* Had he forgotten the times, with Richard at his worst, when he had conjured up all those images of perfect progeny, all those lovely little carbon copies of himself? . . . with only the best of him, of course, being passed on. And if his imaginary brood was, somehow, faulted, it would be in so familiar a way, so completely his own unique blemishes, as to make them even more dear. Oh, he had wondered, all right, but each time with guilt, each time as if the thought itself were a gun aimed at his son's heart. How sad, how strange. We make children out of air and love them, yet hurt those whose flesh we touch.

"You don't think of it anymore?"

He laughed. "I'm long past that. My involvement now is with endings, not beginnings."

"That sounds terrible."

110

The Artist

"But true." He waved a hand at the ghostly images of the dead on his easel. "There's my new métier. I'm becoming an expert at it." He smiled. "Like you and your preconception babies."

"I like my specialty better." She offered a long, slow look that opened its arms to him, but he was still cleaning up and his back was turned and he did not see. "Duvid?"

"Mmm?"

"Why don't we make a baby?"

"Later. I'm busy right now."

She let several moments pass and the room and the beach outside and even the ocean beyond was quiet. "I mean it."

He turned then and saw the way she looked. She does mean it, he thought, and a gust of something hot went through him like a blast from a suddenly opened furnace. "You're talking crazy."

"No, I'm not. "Maybe I do sometimes, but not now. Now I'm being very sensible."

"Of course."

"I am. Think about it."

"I don't have to think about it."

"Yes, you do," she said. "Then you'd see it isn't so crazy at all, that it could be just what we both need."

He had to laugh.

"It's not funny," she said.

"Oh, yes it is. I may need an awful lot of things in my life right now, but the thought of a baby as one of them is really funny."

Her face remained patiently sober, stayed all cool Georgia peach, all sweet, ripe American fruit. "You wouldn't have any obligations. I mean, I wouldn't expect you to marry me or pay for support or anything like that. I have plenty of money. More than I can ever use. And you could see as much or as little of him as you wanted."

"*Him?* You're that sure of a boy?"

"Of course." Something flowed from her to him, then flowed back again, the kind of righteous insanity that you can feel most strongly in the early morning dark or late on certain gray Sunday afternoons. "I wouldn't have it any other way."

"All right," he said, deciding to play the game because it would

111

probably be simplest this way. "A boy it is."

"With *your* eyes and hands."

"And *your* coloring."

"And *your* shoulders."

"And *your* hair."

"And *your* bones."

"And *your* crazy honesty."

"And *your* Yiddish passion and talent."

"And *your* Presbyterian coolness."

"And *your* feeling," she sang.

He considered. "Let's spare him some of that."

"No. That's the best of it."

"It gets a little heavy to carry."

"He'll be strong enough."

Then they were quiet and apart, as when someone new comes into a room and people suddenly become self-conscious. The game, Duvid saw, was over.

"It would be a sin not to pass on what you have," she said.

"I don't believe in sins."

"What do you believe in?"

"Very little."

"This might give you something."

"I don't want anything."

A small cloud darkened each eye, hung there, slipped down, and tugged at her mouth. "I guess it's me."

"It has nothing to do with you."

"I'm hardly the people's choice for mother of the year."

"That's not it at all. But why in God's name should I have to explain not wanting to have a child with a girl young enough to be my daughter, whom I've known exactly three days?"

Her face was pure innocence. "Would it be better for you to have one with some old crow you've known for thirty years?"

"It would be better for me to have one with *nobody.*"

"It can't be done alone. Not even by you."

He grinned and went over and kissed her. "You're really a very funny girl."

"I don't feel funny. I feel tragic."

The Artist

"It's the same thing," he said and led her to the kitchen to heat her knishes, while he mixed a decent amount of scotch with a suitable measure of water. He'd had enough of this particular conversation. *Too* much. He knew it had gone too far when, for an instant, he had stared past her head at an early star and felt something in its pale light, some not-so-innocent radiance out from the depths of the dead, leap through space and into him. And suddenly her whole idea had not seemed nearly so insane, and a feeling passed through him that the only true path of reason was from the depth of one being to the heart of another, and that compared to this, all the usual brands of logic meant nothing.

So where he could, he did his best to avoid looking again at that distant, mystic light. Although with the passage of time and scotch and water, its threat did seem gradually to lessen. He was, after all, the one in control. He had never yet abandoned himself to any wild, emotional pull. Restraint had been his watchword, his lifelong philosophy. He was diligent in its practice. He worked at it unendingly and showed steady improvement. With luck, he expected to be in really great shape on his deathbed.

When they loved later, the last of the threat had gone. Drink and fatigue and something else he could not name had freed him. Yet he felt doubly alive in some warm dream where effort was separated at last from price. And she stayed with him all the way. Through a grotto of curious lights, through the darkness of the night outside and the silence of his house and all that was gone from it and would never be back, through all the endings past and present. Lying soft beneath him, he held her across a distance shrouded with his wife's drying bones, and those of ghosts screaming from his easel, held her too, across the distant flesh of his son, which he loved as well as any he had ever touched, but which was still not truly his own.

He opened his eyes and she was golden in the half-light. A child's whisper came up, so faint he could hardly hear, not hers, surely, because her lips were closed, but a sigh from some passing prayer. "Ah, love, why not?" To which he had no answer, nor did he try to think of one, but chose instead, for at least this once, to cut all restraints, *damn it,* and not think at all. So that he slipped free of her and reached down and did what had to be done, did it quickly

113

before he could change his mind, did it as she waited quietly for him to return. Then back in, like going into a warm pool on a winter day, without anything false between them now, and he thought, maybe it won't happen, because it doesn't always happen exactly how and when you want it, but if it does, that will be all right too, and what the hell, anyway. I've had enough of controls and good sense, enough of endings. If there's one last beginning left somewhere in me, let it be used now.

She held him hard and floods washed over him like balm for every remembered hurt, and for some long forgotten. And it was her voice now, unmistakably, that said, "Ah, love, sure," and his that added its own rush of sound as, for the first time ever, an iron shield melted and he came from somewhere inside his chest rather than from his brain.

SEVEN

1908: New York, N. Y.

At first Duvid thought he was alone when he entered the studio. Then she coughed and he saw her sitting in front of the screen that served as a dressing room for the models. She sat on a high painting stool, her back very straight, her hands folded in her lap. She wore a faded pink robe and frayed slippers.

She said, "I was afraid no one was coming. I've been waiting here forever."

"The class doesn't start until seven," Duvid told her.

"Oh. I thought they said six."

He took a paint-stained smock from a wall hook and tied the sleeves about his waist. It was hot and his shirt clung moistly to his back. He moved an easel into position, set up a fresh canvas, and busied himself mixing paints. The studio was quiet except for the scraping of his knife on the palette. Occasionally a horsecar went by outside, the sound of its wheels rushed and metallic and losing itself quickly in the heavy summer air. Duvid liked arriving early for the class. He liked the particular quiet of the empty loft, the pale stillness of the antique casts, the smell of old and new paint. He liked just being there, as if the air itself might in some way soak through his pores and help turn him into an artist.

"That looks like fun."

The girl had left her stool and was standing beside him. Up close she was younger than he had thought. There was a softness to her

115

flesh, a vulnerability that time had not yet been able to cover over. She was not especially pretty, but if you bothered to look, there was something even better there.

"Like making little colored mud pies," Duvid said. He mixed a small pile of flesh color and placed it neatly under the cadmium red on his palette.

"Have you been an artist long?"

"Long? I'm not even an artist *yet."*

She looked at him.

"I'm in the furniture business. In between chunks of wood, I come up here and try to learn to be an artist."

"Oh, I see. Well, then I guess I'm not really a model either."

"No?"

"I'm an actress. I just do this when things are quiet in the theater. And summer is always a very quiet time for us."

Duvid studied the bright yellow ochre of her hair, then mixed some of the same color.

"Besides," she smiled, "posing is supposed to be good experience for an actress. They say it helps develop muscular control."

Then the model who was not a model at all, but an actress, returned to her stool and sat down once more.

The other students began to straggle in, faces moist, breath quickened by the three flights of steps. There were usually twelve in the class, but this evening only eight showed up. The Professor arrived last, mopping his face with a damp handkerchief and cursing stairs, heat, and general nature of the universe. But his swearing was rendered gently and without malice, in a soft, lyric Italian that made it sound like a paean of praise. He arched a graying brow at Duvid, who grinned, taking pleasure in the small, shared intimacy. Professor Santino Venturi, keeper of the flame. What *kind* of professor? It was vague, He was simply, *The Professor.* More than that. He was a conjurer, a wizard of effects. Maybe no sleight of hand or rabbits turned into pigeons, but something even more wondrous. He was turning Duvid Karlinsky into an artist.

At exactly seven o'clock, Duvid called, "Pose please!" and the girl climbed onto the model's stand and removed her robe. Duvid had the job of posing and timing the models, and tonight decided

116

on a standing position because the girl showed good, long, well-proportioned legs. It was a simple, classic pose, weight on the right leg, one hand resting easily on a stool. She stood under a single, shaded bulb, and the light flooded her hair and shoulders and spilled down over her breasts, which were small, but high and elegantly formed and tipped with the delicate pink nipples of the true blonde.

"Does it feel all right?" Duvid asked.

"Fine."

He glanced at the Professor, received a nod of approval, and went back to his easel. The girl was facing him, eyes shadowed, cheeks drawn and hollow, lips set in a determined pleasantness. Looking at her, Duvid decided to paint only her face rather than the full pose. He did not know why. He did not think it an especially beautiful face. The mouth was too wide, the teeth slightly buck, the chin much too square. He knew only that painting this particular face was something he wanted to do.

He made a rough sketch, then brushed in the masses of shadow with an umber wash. He did not work easily. He labored . . . adding, taking off, changing. He envied the ease, the facility of line and stroke, the quick brilliance of some of the others in the class, the Italians especially, but knew this was something he would never have. Not his style. He was a plodder. Less than brilliant. But stubborn. Also, he was a Jew, a traditional fugitive from the rendering of graven images. Who ever heard of a famous Jewish artist? Name *one.* They were a people of the spirit, who for five thousand years had steadfastly refused to put the heart of their life into external forms. Allowances had to be made for the adjustment. He was, after all, five millennia late in starting.

Considering it, he was still surprised, still felt himself an imposter with a brush in his hand. What was he doing here with these others? He was no artist. He and his father made, sold, and delivered furniture . . . A. KARLINSKY & SON*** FINE WOOD FURNITURE. The "son" had been added to the sign when they moved uptown to Thirteenth Street. And this was what he was. You didn't just wake up one morning, pick up a paintbrush, raise your right hand to Jehovah, and proclaim yourself an artist, It was not that simple or miraculous. There had to be something in the blood, some background, some show of talent and desire from early childhood. He possessed none. Looking back, it had all been a crazy accident. The whole thing had started three years ago with the flu and somehow infected him right along with the disease. On his back for weeks, bored, restless, his hands groping for something to do, he had, in desperation, finally picked up a pencil, scribbled a few lines on a pad, and there it was. The sense of wonder was immediate. You made marks on a clean sheet of paper and suddenly something was there to see. Maybe crude, primitive, but *something.* And it stayed. It never faded, never disappeared. You could look at it afterward and know, that for at least that moment, this was the way it had been.

In that first flush of excitement, he had sketched everything in sight, everything he could see from his window . . . tenements, washlines, people in the street, pushcarts and wagons—the world. There was suddenly so much there that it dizzied him. It mixed with his fever, produced dreams and visions, sent him soaring to uncharted places. Had he been a believer, any kind of mystic, this would have been the moment he saw the lightning flash, the heavens open, and his path revealed. As it was, he remained mired in reality, practical. Drawing pictures was pleasant enough, fine as a bed-toy for the sick, but nothing more. When he became well, he returned to the making and selling of furniture. This was the expected order. Things had to return to the way they had been. And they did . . . except that nights, holidays, and all spare moments in between, Duvid *did* go on drawing, he *did* grow a new pair of eyes, and his father *did* become convinced his hands had turned to gold.

"Golden handt!" cried Avrum Karlinsky. "These hands can do anything!" In an age devoid of miracles, here, suddenly, was a miracle. And under his own roof. Each crude sketch was snatched up, nailed to a wall and exalted. The artist in Avrum, imprisoned for a lifetime in wood, found new release in Duvid's drawings. And if Duvid made light of his own efforts, if he claimed to have no real ability but only an unexceptional knack, Avrum became furious. "It is a gift of God!" he thundered (suddenly, thought Duvid, his father had taken notice of God's existence). "A great talent. It must be treated with respect. Nourished." His mother's judgment was more

reserved. Duvid wanted to draw pictures? Why not? Draw. Enjoy. Only make sure not to neglect the work. Make sure not to neglect what was *really* important. The furniture.

Duvid neglected nothing. He did his work as usual. But a small piece of him remained apart, peering through his new eyes. He stripped familiar ghetto streets and saw them naked. *His* slum. As though for the first time, he looked at those who lived and worked there, at the bearded old men in black bowlers, at the workers in their massman caps with the American Dream in the brim instead of a ribbon. Wear this cap, *landsleit,* and you will be carried from the misery of the *shtetl* to the joys of Hester Street in the summertime. Sights. Fat babies wearing what looked like tents with sleeves. Old ladies bundled against a winter six months away, the cold of Russia still in their bones. The air was fried on both sides, yet they shivered. And the faces! Duvid stared, a blind man gifted with sudden sight. Had all those eyes and noses always been there? All those separate lips? All those curving cheeks and jowls? Where had he been looking, that he had never seen? He found it worked two ways. You learned to see as you became an artist, and you became an artist as you learned to see. In between, a wasteland of frustrations. Your eyes saw, your brain knew what it wanted, but your hand went its own way. Your hand, finally, was the traitor. It had to be taught to obey. All right, Duvid decided, he would have it taught. And he did. Four nights a week, he climbed the three flights of rotting steps that led to the Michelangelo Academy of Art. A hand-lettered sign over the loft entrance proclaimed, HE WHO HESITATES IN ART IS LOST, and Duvid had laughed when he first read it. That was almost three years ago. The sign was still there and Duvid still read it, but he no longer laughed.

After twenty minutes, Duvid called a rest and the girl broke the pose. She put on her robe and walked about the studio, looking at each canvas, not saying anything, just looking and walking on to the next. When she came to Duvid's easel, she stopped, surprised by what she saw.

"But you're painting only my *face.*"

Duvid wiped his brushes on a rag and squinted at the canvas. He said nothing.

The Artist

She studied the masses of dark and light that were the beginnings of the portrait. "You're good. You're really very good."

"You mean for a furniture peddler?"

She looked at him curiously. "I mean for an artist."

During the second pose, she perspired a great deal. The windows were open, but they faced a narrow court and no breeze entered. Duvid watched the moisture form into beads on her forehead, roll down her cheeks like tears, and drip from her chin. Her eyes blinked in the shadows, but she did not move, nor did the pleasantness about her mouth waver. And if the leg that took her full weight was beginning to tremble, it was barely noticeable. It was a good leg . . . lean, strong, shapely, and true. But there were still some things that were beyond it.

She fell suddenly and heavily, dropping to her knees, and would have toppled from the stand if Duvid had not lunged forward to catch her. He lifted her into a chair and someone quickly covered her with her robe, as though her nakedness had all at once become a thing of shame. Her face was very flushed.

"I'm sorry," she bent to rub the failed leg. "I'm really awfully sorry. I'll be all right in a minute."

"It's a mean pose." Duvid felt a rush of guilt. The hottest night of the year and he had to make her stand. "Maybe we'd better change it to a sitting position."

"Oh, no! Not in the middle. It was my fault. I'm fine now."

She got to her feet and walked slowly about the studio to show just how fine she was. Her face was no longer flushed, but very pale. Duvid looked at the Professor to see how he felt about it, but the old man shrugged and threw it back at him.

"All right," he said. "If you think you can."

The girl managed to make it through the third pose, although the leg was still shaky. She did not walk at all during the next rest period. She sat very straight in her chair and smilingly assured everyone that she was fine, absolutely fine. Five minutes before the final pose was due to end and with her smile still intact, she fainted, dropping quietly and undramatically, seeming only to fold in upon herself.

Duvid stayed behind with her afterward, assuring the Professor he would see that she got home all right. She was dressed now and sitting with a glass of water held tightly in both hands. Every once in a while she would sip from it. Whenever she saw Duvid look at her, she smiled.

"How do you feel?" he asked for the fifth time, wishing she would not feel it necessary to smile every time he looked at her.

"Oh, much better. Really. Except I feel like such a fool. I don't know what came over me. I'm actually very strong."

Then for a while they did not say anything and she sipped from the glass of water and smiled at Duvid each time he looked at her. So that finally, he was careful not to look at her at all.

"Whenever you feel all right," he said, "I'll take you home."

"That's very kind of you, but you really don't have to bother." She spoke with a studied, almost archaic politeness, as though she had once learned the words for a part in a play. "I live only a few blocks from here."

"It's no bother."

"But I hate to keep you."

Duvid felt suddenly and unreasonably angry. "Look! It's no bother and you're not keeping me from a single damn thing."

"All right." This time she forgot entirely to smile at him.

He went over to his painting, still on the easel, and the girl followed and stood beside him. It was a boldly painted portrait, with the brush strokes showing sure and strong. The girl's eyes burned darkly from hidden places and her cheeks shone, pale and gaunt above ridges of bone. Her mouth was a full-lipped, scarlet smear, bent into a fiercely determined smile, and the painting seemed touched, all of it, with an incandescent kind of joy.

"Is that the way I look?"

"It's the way you look to *me.*"

"It's very exciting. But I don't know whether I understand it."

Duvid shrugged. "I'm not sure I understand it either. I just know there was something here I wanted to paint."

"I'm glad. I mean I'm glad you like the way I look." Her fingers went to her face, exploring, trying to feel what Duvid saw. "But I'm afraid there are an awful lot of prettier, better faces around."

Studying her, Duvid thought, maybe prettier, but not better.

The Artist

He closed the studio and they walked down the three flights of stairs and out into the warm darkness of lower Manhattan, quiet now, with the special quiet of factories and lofts with their day's work done. Duvid carried the portrait with him, holding it carefully away from his body so as not to smear the wet paint. He always carried his paintings home wet. His father was too eager to see what he had done to wait a week for the paint to dry. All right, Poppa. This one, I admit, *might* have something.

They walked slowly between the blank walls of buildings, not talking much, occasionally passing people sitting on tenement stoops. At Canal Street, Duvid stopped in front of one of the small Russian cafés that dotted the area. He suddenly did not want to let go of this girl. He felt an insane fear that if he took her home at this moment and said goodnight, she would be gone and he would have lost something important. He looked at her, then at the painting of her in his hand, then at her once more.

"Would you like some coffee?" The words almost jammed in his throat. She nodded and they went inside. The place was crowded and noisy with talk, but they found an empty table and Duvid stood the portrait on a chair beside her. He wanted to be able to see them both at the same time. It was not until fifteen minutes later that he asked her name.

"Rachel Renard." She smiled at him over her coffee. "At least that's the name I use."

"What's your real name?"

"I was born Rachel Rabinowitz."

My God! Duvid thought. *Jewish.*

It must have showed in his face because she laughed. "I know. A Jewish girl standing naked in front of all those men. Even you, an artist, can still be shocked by it."

"I didn't say I was shocked."

"You don't have to. The reaction is in the blood. But I wouldn't call Rachel Rabinowitz my real name. It's not how I think of myself anymore. That girl was just an accident of birth. The real me, the me I chose for myself, is Rachel Renard. Actress. Which actually makes my stage name my real name."

"When did you last have a part in a play?"

The Artist

She thought. "About nine months ago. It's been a bad year for the theater."

"How long did the play run?"

"Ten days. It wasn't a very good play."

"And when did you work before that?"

"I had a week up in Yonkers last summer."

"Then in the last year, you've worked just seventeen days as an actress?"

There was the smile again. "I'm hoping next year will be better."

"What do you do in between?"

"Go to producers' offices. Pose when I can. But mostly, run a sewing machine for the Premier Waist Company."

Duvid signaled a waiter for two more coffees, then stared across the table at the pale, moist, haggard, but oddly compelling face.

He said carefully, "Isn't it time you stopped fooling yourself?"

"How am I fooling myself?"

"By making believe you're an actress."

"But I *am* an actress."

"No. What you are, *really,* is a sewing-machine operator. Just as what I am, *really,* is a furniture peddler. There's no such thing as a part-time actress or artist. My father always says, a man is what he does. I guess a woman too. And what *you* do is run a sewing machine."

"Wrong. I'm whatever I feel myself to be. I don't care *what* I have to do to support myself. And what I feel myself to be is an actress."

"Even if you work seventeen days a year at it?"

"Even if I work seventeen *minutes* a year."

Duvid sipped broodingly at his coffee. She was a rock. How did she get that way? What great secret did she hold that *he* didn't? What odd mixture of juices bubbled beneath that pale flesh to create such certainty, such confidence?

"Why is money so important to you?" she asked.

Duvid looked at her.

"All you keep talking about is how you earn your money, about how you peddle furniture. Why don't you ever talk about how you paint?"

He said nothing. The whole thing had somehow gotten turned

123

around. She was not as simple as he had thought. Of course not. She was Jewish.

"*Do* you ever talk about your painting?"

"No."

"Why not?"

"I guess because I'm not sure I'm any good."

She looked at the painting on the chair beside her. "If you could do that, you're good."

"That's about the best thing I've ever done. But I have a strange feeling it's more you than me."

"What do you mean?"

"I'm not sure. But there must have been *something* I saw in your face that made me want to paint it." Duvid grinned. "Maybe I thought if I could get some of it down on canvas and carry it home like some kind of secret magic, a little might rub off on me."

"Now you're making fun of me."

"No. It may sound crazy, but I mean it."

She did not say anything and for a moment they just sat there, looking at each other like a pair of jewelers who have unexpectedly come upon a rare gem and are busy trying to figure out the best way to share it. Then without thinking, Duvid leaned forward and kissed her lips. He breathed the sweetness that came off them and spoke of what she knew, not in any language that Duvid had ever heard before or that he could understand, but that he could nevertheless feel. He closed his eyes afraid to do or say anything, afraid to make a move, afraid something vital might be disturbed.

"That was nice," she said.

Duvid opened his eyes. "You felt it too?"

She nodded.

"I'm glad. It would be a terrible thing to have to feel all by yourself."

"Have you ever?"

"What?"

"Felt it all by yourself?"

"No. And not with anyone else either. What about you?"

"I've felt it before."

He was sorry he had asked. Idiot! What did he expect from a girl like this? Her flesh was young, but not her eyes. Meeting them, he felt like a child.

"How often?"

"Every other Tuesday." She laughed. "No. Only once, and that was a long time ago."

"What happened to him?"

She seemed startled. "Why should you think something happened?"

"I don't know." Of course he knew. Who would leave her unless *carried* away? *"Did* something happen?"

"Yes." She offered nothing more and Duvid left it.

Afterward, they walked side by side along a street that ran close to the river. There were no other walkers. Once, a wagon went by, its wheels clattering on the cobbles, making the following silence even more intimate. Duvid savored it.

"I live on this block," Rachel said, "near the corner."

Everything ends.

The building was one of a row of identical tenements, its stoop littered and chalk-marked, its fire escapes bearing wash, bedding, and those too hot, too desperate for air to sleep inside. They kissed again on the stoop, Duvid with one hand pressing her close, the other still clutching her portrait. And in the middle of it, came the sound.

It was soft, vaguely musical, a voice lifted in melancholy song. Unearthly. But not the heavenly host. Duvid heard it first, then Rachel. It seemed to rise from somewhere below.

"What is it?" he asked.

"Oh," she said, softly, only that, and left him, going down the steps and disappearing into a passage that ran beneath the stoop. Duvid followed.

"What is it?"

"My father."

He lay in a corner of the cellar, in the dark, in his own wetness. Weeping, his voice broken, choked with drunken passion, he sang in a deep, mournful Yiddish . . .

The Artist

I lift mine eyes against the sky,
The clouds are weeping, so am I:
I lift mine eyes again on high,
The sun is smiling, so am I.
Why do I smile? Why do I weep?
I do not know. It lies too deep.

Rachel was bending, trying to lift him. Duvid went to help and found the painting still in his hand. He gave it to the girl. "Hold this. I'll take care of him."

Duvid carried him easily, a packet of bones, wrapped in rags. He was a small man. He could not have weighed over a hundred pounds. He nestled against Duvid's chest and clung—safe, protected, a child come home. Rachel led the way out of the cellar, into the tenement hallway, and up flight after flight of steps, past sweet, bruised, rotting-wood odors, past dirty light bulbs covered by wire cages and dripping threads of dust. The garbage was out on the landings, the heavy smell of stale cooking, the stink of garlic, onions, and cabbage—a teeming misery. At the top of each flight, the door to the latrine was open and moisture seeped off the floor along with the stench of slum plumbing. It carried the terror of disease, of villainous old bowels. And going up those stairs, old Rabinowitz, drunken, weeping, and gurgling, carried like an infant in grown-up arms, sang his grief . . .

I hear the winds of autumn sigh,
They break my heart, they make me cry;
I hear the birds of lovely spring,
My hopes revive, I help them sing.
Why do I sing? Why do I cry?
It lies so deep, I know not why.

"Shhh, Poppa. You'll wake everyone up," said his daughter.

Carrying Rabinowitz, breathing his odors, listening to his tragic wailing-weeping, Duvid studied the old man in the yellow light of a soiled bulb. He was not actually old. His beard was more black than gray. And although there were great ridged patches of dark under his eyes, the eyes themselves gave off a brightness. Above a straight, drunken nose Rabinowitz wore a battered bowler that pressed the veins of his forehead and made him look, Duvid thought, like an actor of the Yiddish stage, a tragedian, a heartbroken, Orthodox father who has just discovered his only daughter has run off with a Polish pig farmer.

Doors opened along the way, sleep-ridden heads appeared, voices swore and shouted for quiet in three languages. They knew him.

"Rabinowitz again!"

"Who else?"

"Dreckische shikker!"

"He should be thrown out of the building, locked up."

"A disgrace. A *landsman*. A Jew!"

There it was *A Jew!* Duvid grinned beneath his burden. Who ever heard of a drunken Jew? Not part of the tradition. Diabetes, yes. Alcohol, no. The Rabinowitzes had somehow managed to escape the mold. The daughter exposed her flesh to the eyes of men, and the father was a drunk. Duvid wondered what the others in the family were like. Surely not like the daughter. There could be only one like that. Look at her! He wanted to break into cheers. Head high, she marched up the steps as though leading a parade up Fifth Avenue. Delacroix could have used her for his *Liberty Leading the People*. Breast bared, she could have looked no more valiant charging the barricades than she did at this moment. Proud, untouched, supreme, she yielded nothing. And Duvid, after having known the girl for something less than six hours, was absolutely certain he loved her.

They lived in two rooms on the fourth floor, alone, no other Rabinowitzes with them. Rachel's older brother, Duvid learned later, was off somewhere in the Oregon woods; her mother had been committed six months before to Bellevue's mental ward. Naturally, thought Duvid.

Rabinowitz inquired about him only once. "Who is this man," he demanded in his rolling, actorish, oratorical voice, "that dares lay hands upon my person?"

"His name is Duvid, Poppa. He's a friend."

"What friend? I am barren of friends, I am alone in the camp of my enemies." Rabinowitz closed his bloodshot eyes. "Make haste, make haste, O Lord, to deliver me. Make haste to help me, O Lord."

Yanking off Rabinowitz's befouled trousers, Duvid wondered where he had learned to speak English like a Hebrew king on an embassy to the East Side of New York.

"Deliver me, O my God, out of the hands of the wicked, the unrighteous, and the cruel."

"Would you put him in the washtub for me, please?" asked Rachel.

Duvid lifted the old man's matchstick body and placed it in the galvanized tub his daughter had partially filled with water. He sat naked as she scrubbed him, shivering slightly in the cold water, his bowler still firmly, implacably set upon his rolling head. "Flesh of my flesh," he intoned deeply from under his hat, "bone of my bone, you are being punished for the sins of your soul."

Duvid grinned. There was something insanely funny in the sight of this cluster of bones in a bowler, sitting naked in a basin of water and emoting like a shepherd giving dictation in blank verse to a secretary on a hill in Judea.

"Do not smile!" Rabinowitz was suddenly peering at Duvid, his eyes surprisingly sharp and knowing in the hollows of his face. "Do not smile, my son. My flesh is bleeding for us all. For you too."

"I'm not smiling, Mr. Rabinowitz."

Rabinowitz's mouth twisted in oratorical scorn. "You think I do not know? You think I cannot see you standing there in your American clothes and thinking, "What has this foolish, drunken old man to do with me? He is a stranger to me. I have never seen him before and if he suffers and dies in these cold, stone streets that are America, in this crude world of finery and excrement, what of it? How does this in any way affect me? Well my son, I am not a stranger to you. I am a Jew and the world is hunting me. And *you* are a Jew and the world is hunting *you*."

He closed his eyes in exhaustion and Duvid glanced inquiringly at Rachel. But her washcloth was busy at the moment with her father's genitals and she seemed unaware of anything else.

"Let me tell you," Rabinowitz went on, without opening his eyes. "This is a grasping, bourgeois land in which we live, a land that worships its own boorishness. But beaten and bloody though I may be, I will never kneel before their fat gods. Let them have their gold. Let them die with it. At the edge of doom, beside the final grave, they will still be counting their paper, they will still be praying over their balance sheets."

Rabinowitz took a deep breath and sat in silence while his daughter scrubbed him as though he were a child. In the mean kitchen light, he looked forlorn and in pain. Then his eyes opened. But when he spoke again, his voice had changed. Suddenly it was small and without timbre and no longer carried the ring of the orator.

"Perhaps our trouble is that we wish life to end. We have befouled it. Beauty, honor, friendship, love, all made filthy. So that we despise ourselves, despise even the bread that extends our lives. We are sad, pathetic creatures. If I were Death, I would by now be tired of us. If I were Death, I would seek out Jehovah and tell him I wanted to resign. I would tell him there was no longer any pride or dignity in being Death, I would beg Him to release me from the meanness to which my work has fallen."

Rabinowitz looked at Duvid, seemed to be speaking directly to him, yet no longer saw him. His eyes were glazed, racked, lost in a secret anguish of their own. "My Ruth. My bride. They have taken her from me. They have put her away. The big important men. The bosses. They have imprisoned her. As if to go on loving someone like me was proof she was mad. A pure soul who understood only pure things. She, too, would not kneel before their fat gods. We had nothing but each other, yet they were jealous even of this. They could not bend *me,* so they broke *her.* They wanted only to part us and they did. It was a sweet and holy thing we had and we made the fat gods envious. So back of it all is this terrible land to which we came with such great hope and which finally betrayed us . . ." He sighed. Under his eyes, the skin was yellow. "Betrayed us . . ." His voice was even weaker now, querulous, that of an old man, his head slipping forward and falling at last onto the frail bones of his chest.

When the washing was finished, Rabinowitz was asleep in the tub. Duvid carried him to his bed and covered him with a sheet. He lay as though dead, splinters of light falling on his face, on the veins of his nose, the rigid, deep eye sockets.

The Artist

"Poor Poppa." Rachel sagged into a chair. "Each day another knife between his ribs. An unlucky poet." She smiled tiredly. "To be unlucky is bad enough, but to be an unlucky poet is terrible. It sharpens the blades, makes them cut deeper. And when Momma was put away, they cut out his heart entirely."

Heart? Whose heart? Duvid felt a deep pity for Rabinowitz's heart, but was having too much trouble with his own just then to concentrate properly on anyone else's. His chest felt swollen, an expanding balloon. Soon it would explode. The pressure was too great. It had to be released. He had to tell her. "I love you," he whispered, fearful of waking the sleeping poet, fearful of any distraction that might delay his message. "I love you."

She studied his face. She touched it with the tips of her fingers, silent searching. Duvid held his breath. What would she discover? What could she possibly find that held more truth, that was of greater importance than what he had just told her? If he knew her for six years, could he possibly love her more than he did now, after six hours?

She kissed him. "You'd better go home. It's very late."

"Yes," he mumbled numbly. "Very late."

Only when he had reached the door of his own house nearly half an hour later did he realize he had never before, in all his nineteen years, actually said "I love you" to anyone.

Avrum Karlinsky sat smoking in his usual kitchen chair when Duvid came in. Regardless of the hour, Duvid knew his father would be there, waiting, unwilling to sleep until he had seen what he had brought home . . . or on a night when there might be no new painting, waiting to hear the Professor's latest comments about his work. After three years, it was an accepted rite. Sometimes Duvid invented praise from Venturi so as not to disappoint his father. What harm if it gave him pleasure?

"Poppa, you shouldn't have waited up." The old flash of guilt.

The Artist

He had forgotten all about him, had been busy falling in love while his father was sitting here, waiting.

"So who's waiting up?" Avrum was already straining for his first glimpse of the canvas in Duvid's hand. "You think I can sleep with your mother's snoring?"

"I know. You haven't slept in twenty years." Duvid deliberately kept the painting turned away from his father. He yawned. "Well, I'll see you in the morning, Poppa."

Avrum was out of his chair with a roar. *"Tuyvil!* With two swollen eyes, you'll see *nothing* in the morning." He snatched the canvas from Duvid's hand, propped it against a wall, and stepped back to study it. He was silent for several minutes. He looked at his son once, then turned again to the portrait as if trying to establish some connection between the two.

"This is how she looked?"

"It's a good likeness."

"Prettier, I've seen."

"Yes."

"She was posing *nacheteh?* For the figure?"

Duvid nodded.

"But you painted only her face?"

It was obviously not a question, just a simple statement intended to set certain things straight. Nevertheless, Duvid nodded once more.

"So if she's so skinny, if she's got such bones showing in her face, why is she so happy?"

"I don't know, Poppa. I guess she's just a happy girl."

Avrum Karlinsky peered closely at his son. "And this is why you're so late coming home? Because she's so happy?"

Duvid laughed. "Something like that."

Avrum again studied the painting, moving forward, back, then forward once more on the creaking kitchen floor, shading his eyes against the glare of a bulb, squinting, as Duvid had taught him, to eliminate detail and see only masses of light and shade. He was the expert, probing for fine points of form, tone, brushwork, and color, the distinguished connoisseur, seeking subtle judgments within the broader contexts of history. Several times, he glanced up at the other canvases, all painted by Duvid, that covered nearly every inch of wall in the kitchen. Comparisons were being made. Time was being taken. Only when he was ready would a decision be rendered. And he would not be rushed.

At last, Avrum straightened. "The best," he announced. "It is the best you have ever done."

Almost every new painting received pretty much the same praise, yet to Avrum, there was nothing either illogical or insincere in any one of such judgments. He not only meant every word but considered it merely natural that each of his son's paintings should be progressively better than the one before. Had it been otherwise, he would have been disappointed. Duvid was learning more every day, was growing older, wiser. Why *shouldn't* each new work be better than the last?

"You really think so, Poppa?" For the first time, Duvid was ready, even eager to accept his father's prejudiced judgment at face value.

"Absolutely. Never have I seen this girl, yet I look at this painting and I feel I know her. Everything important, you have already told me about her."

"What have I told you?"

"A *shiksa* she looks like," Avrum said slowly, consideringly, "with the yellow hair and pale skin, but the eyes say Jewish. Only Jewish, such eyes. Also, she does what she wants, this girl. She is strong where it is right to be strong. Stubborn, she is too. Ah, that is some chin you have hammered to her face. Of iron. Yet her mouth is soft. A sweetness there. A lower lip to break a man's heart. With such a lower lip, I am surprised only at one thing."

"What's that, Poppa?"

"Why you should have come home at *all* tonight."

Rachel posed for three more nights and Duvid completed three more paintings. One was another portrait, the others figure studies.

The Artist

He made love to her body with his brush, to all those lovely, gentle curves, to the cool hints of lavender and silver in the shadows, to the soft pinks that were the lights. Each stroke, a caress; each blending, a promise of what was to come. But he also became jealous. He fretted over the others in the class. He resented having to share her with them. How dare they gaze upon this beloved secret flesh. He wanted to cover her with a blanket, hide her from all eyes but his own. He almost hit a student for saying she had delicious thighs. Illogical. Insane. He knew it, yet he suffered. Was this what love did? When the last pose ended, Duvid went weak with relief. No more. He would never let her pose nude again. She could work longer at her sewing machine if she needed money. The sight of her flesh would be his alone.

But when he told her, she laughed. "That's silly, Duvid."

"Maybe. But it's how I feel."

"Yes. But it's not how *I* feel," she said quietly, and that ended it.

He was to learn about her. The sharp edge of strength he had so admired at first meeting, could cut in two directions. Her stubbornness could be a spiked wall. But the learning was to take time. The loving came more quickly. Yet even in this, it was she who led. It was she who took them, finally, out of the furtive embraces in doorways, away from the hurried kisses on rooftops and stoops, and into a proper bed.

"I have a surprise for you," was all she told him one evening, then mysteriously walked him to a tenement on Eighth Street, up two flights of steps and into a neatly furnished apartment, whose door she opened with her own key.

Duvid stared. "What is it?"

"A place with a door that we can lock and be alone in."

"But whose?"

"It belongs to a girl I know."

"She let you have it?"

"No. I hit her over the head and stole the key."

Duvid did not even smile. "For how long?"

"Until midnight, when I turn into a white mouse."

He stood there, still dazed, still struggling to accept what it meant. When he did accept it, there were other confusions. He had taken girls to bed before . . . five, in all (he kept careful count), but two had been whores and the other three were sluts who laid for half the neighborhood. Never anyone decent, never anyone he cared anything about, never anyone he *loved*. Thinking about it now, there was a coldness in his stomach. He felt weak, frightened, ridiculous. He was not religious, but certain concepts ran through his veins like blood. It was simple and clear-cut. There were those you laid and those you loved. And the only time they became the same was after you were married.

He looked at her.

"Are you going to just stand here in the middle of this room until midnight?"

"Do you know how much I love you?"

"Of course. And I love you. Which is exactly why we're here."

She kissed him and he tried to respond, but it was no good. She drew back. "Duvid, I don't expect you to marry me. I don't *want* you to marry me. I don't want *anyone* to marry me. Do you understand that?"

Not understanding at all, he nodded anyway.

"And you needn't worry about deflowering me. That particular problem was taken care of a long time ago."

Duvid was sure the entire English language had clotted inside his throat. He tried to swallow and couldn't. Baffled and lost, he felt himself adrift on an endless, irrational female sea from which he would never be rescued.

"Now listen to me," she said carefully, reasonably, a seasoned debater stating her case in terms simple enough for anyone to understand. "We're not children. If we love each other, we should make love. I'm sick of the medieval stupidity that dirties the whole thing. I'm not a tramp and I don't know if I'm ever going to want to be a wife and mother. Does that mean I've got to go on kissing and clutching on stairways for the rest of my life? And if I did, would that make me any purer than I am?"

It was a question, but Duvid was unable to answer. All he could do was stare at her and ache.

"Don't you want me, Duvid?"

The Artist

"*Want* you?" The clot in his throat broke and the words came out like tears and blood. Enough. What was she trying to do to him? He was up half the night with wanting her. He found escape in anger. "Yes, damn you!"

"All right. Then stop acting like an old rabbi and take me."

She turned and walked into the next room, the bedroom, suddenly as angry as he, the humiliation seeming to have just caught up with her. Duvid followed, the executioner trailing his eager, lunatic victim to the block. And this was the mood in which they moved into it.

They undressed separately, without speaking, and what was in the air at that moment was not love, but something quiet the opposite. Deliberately, they left a light burning, a beaded lamp that threw a glaze of amber over walls, ceiling, and flesh, and this added to it. When they met in bed, it was less like lovers than animals in a quiet mood who have come through the forest to meet and join in a clearing. Nothing was loving in either of them. Only the act itself was tender and this they were unable to destroy. So that Duvid looked into her face where it lay beneath his and found it more desirable than he had ever seen it, with her eyes golden in the light and so filled with him that it was like looking into a mirror. When it was over, when they lay at least holding to one another to keep from flying off the edge of the earth, the anger, too, was over.

"Why am I so stupid?" he asked.

"You're not stupid. You're just you."

"The same thing."

"No." She trailed her lips along the line of his jaw. "You just need a little educating."

The education of Duvid Karlinsky. A private joke between them, although not really a joke. There were things Rachel was sure she could teach him. She had ideas, thoughts, opinions on everything . . . on books, acting, politics, on the position of women in America, on religion, prejudice, and money. Whatever the subject, she had a theory. And she especially had judgments to offer on Duvid's art.

"What do you want to do with your painting?" she asked one Sunday. "I mean, what do you want to *say* with it?"

Duvid shrugged. He was busy sketching a derelict tug tied to the East River pier on which they sat. Beyond the tug, the river lay flat and quiet and empty except for two men fishing from a skiff. "I'm not sure there's *anything* I want to say."

"Of course you do. All artists want to say something or they wouldn't be artists."

"But I'm no artist." Squinting at his sketch, Duvid angled the line of the tug's stack. "I keep telling you. I'm a furniture peddler."

"Can't you be serious for once? This is important."

Duvid looked up at the morning light on her hair. A nimbus of gold. You could reach out and touch it. "All right. I'm *seriously* not sure there's anything I want to say. All I care about right now is learning to paint."

"You've already learned that. You're able to put down what you see. You have a good enough technique. Now it's time to decide what interests you."

"Everything interests me." Duvid dropped his pad and pressed his lips to the soft place at the base of her throat, enjoying teasing her, enjoying her instant response. She was mercurial, ever-changing. Each time they met she was someone else, yet never anyone but herself. He spoke while nibbling: "On summer, Sunday mornings, I'm interested mostly in old tugboats and your flesh. In that order. Is that very bad for a Jewish artist?"

She would not be distracted, "What's bad for a Jewish artist is to forget he *is* a Jewish artist."

"Well, your flesh is Jewish and that old tug there has a really Jewish look around the nose. Anyway, I think I'd rather be more of a universal-type artist. Isn't that what art is supposed to be all about?" A kind of universal truth?"

"There's no universal anything. That's just a lot of nonsense. That's for critics, writers, and schoolbooks. You can only see and feel for yourself, from what *you* are. And what you happen to be is a Russian-born, progrom-driven Jew, raised in an East Side, New

136

The Artist

York ghetto. So if anything good is ever going to come from you, this is what it has to come out of."

Rachel gazed at Duvid with partially abstracted eyes. She was speaking only half to him. The rest was for herself, for areas that Duvid still knew very little about but was slowly discovering. She seemed to come to him in small sections, in assorted bits and pieces. Her father, in the few times Duvid had seen him, had continued to contribute his own unique fragments, never seeming to remember Duvid from one meeting to the next, yet unfailingly greeting him as an old friend. The poet, sober, appeared little different from when he was drunk. "Feh!" was Avrum Karlinsky's instant response to Rabinowitz, whom he knew by sight and reputation. "A socialist intellectual. The worst kind. Every night speeches in the cafés. In jail, he'll end. Or worse." Duvid's mother was more worried about Rachel herself. A girl who stood naked in front of men, whose father was a *schikker,* who's mother was in a *meshuggeneh* house and who *(vay iz mir)* tempted her son with God only knew what corruptions of the flesh. Aunt Tybie's reaction, though necessarily silent and limited, was at least positive. To her, Rachel was simply a series of beautiful pictures that Duvid brought home and for which she seemed to feel a strangely intense attachment. From the very first portrait, Tybie took Rachel as her own, carrying the fiercely joyous face off to her room and adding to her collection with each canvas that followed. Alone, she spent hours staring at them. Sometimes Duvid would join her. "Some face. Huh, Aunt Tybie?" And the two of them would sit together on Tybie's sagging bed and share their separate devotions.

Rachel focused more fully on Duvid. "But what you've got to be most careful of," she said, "is turning into a trivial stylist who paints without direction or purpose. Because this is the hardest country in the world for real art to get a hearing in. Americans just want to be amused by their artists. They treat them like their actors and actresses, as public servants whose job is to amuse them when they're tired. They make a big fuss over style. They cheer technique. They shout, 'Ha! Here's a man with a new and fine style. A great artist!' But he's no artist. He's just a decorator. Trivial and empty. He doesn't grab a chunk of life and scream the truth about it. A *scream.*

That's what art is all about. Scream and attention will be paid."

"Is that what you do on the stage? Scream?"

"I try. When I get the chance. I do try."

"I'd like to see you act sometime."

"I'd like you to."

"I'll bet you're very good." How could she be otherwise? Who could stop her?

Rachel's face seemed to blur in the sun. "I *think* I'm good. I *feel* I'm good. But in acting, it's hard to know. What you feel inside doesn't always come out that way. And there's nothing to look back at and judge afterwards. There's nothing to see and touch. You scream into air and not even an echo is left. You're lucky. All painters are lucky. You can do your work anytime, anywhere, and have something to show when you're through. Without lines to speak, without a stage to speak them on, you can't even exist as an actress."

An instant's vulnerability. It showed in the tiny crease between her eyes, in the pulling in of her chin. Duvid ached to hurl himself into the breach, longed to seal the crack with his flesh. It didn't belong there. He waited anxiously for it to leave.

Then she said, "I have an audition in two weeks," and it left. "It's an unbelievable chance. Wish me luck."

"You don't need luck."

"Everyone needs luck."

"All right. I wish you luck," he said, although he did not really believe in it. Luck was like praying. He did not believe in that either.

"What you should paint," Rachel continued, not letting go, ". . . what you should do your screaming about, is our East Side. We haven't had any real Jewish art come out of this place yet. It's time. Never mind the classics. Never mind the epic grandeur of nature. The truth for an East Side Jew isn't in nature. That's for the upstate *goyim*, for the old Hudson River crowd. The truth for you is right here in your own streets. You're no Winslow Homer. Don't try to be one. You're Duvid Karlinsky." She smiled and passed something sweet to him. "And from what I've seen so far, that's good enough."

The men in the skiff had pulled in their lines and were rowing for the pier. Duvid watched the wake ripple and trail behind, silver threads unraveling in the sun.

The Artist

"I know I'm no Winslow Homer," he said. "But neither am I a Rachel Renard."

"What's that supposed to mean?"

"That I'm not you. That I don't have your kind of belief. Listen." He hesitated. "I'm not even that sure I *want* to be an artist."

"Of *course* you do!" She almost shouted it. "My God! What nonsense!"

Duvid laughed.

"Don't laugh. You're just afraid. *That's* what you are. Just the idea scares you silly. You're afraid you might not be good enough, afraid you might fail. So you make jokes about it. You laugh. You mock yourself as a furniture peddler. Yet you hang onto your father and his furniture business for dear life. Well, it's time to cut loose. If you fail, you fail. So what? It's no shame to fail. *Everybody* fails. It doesn't make you any less of a man. But being afraid to reach for what you want *does.*"

Right. Duvid had to nail his eyes to the approaching skiff to keep her from seeing exactly how right she was. Not that she needed further proof. She knew. Still, you don't want to sit bleeding in front of someone you love. So you look off at a boat. Something dark lay in the bottom between the two men and Duvid focused hard on this, wondering, dimly, at the pleasure men took in such things as hunting and fishing. Sport. A strange joy in the act of killing, of taking life. Christian pleasures, his mother called it. Maybe a little unfair, yet who could deny the gentile needed a greater diet of blood than the Jew?

Collected, but still not looking at her, he said, "It's just that I can't seem to think of myself as an artist. I can't seem to feel or even believe it."

She nodded.

"So what am I supposed to do? How do I get to feel differently? Do I mumble some sort of painter's incantation? An artist's prayer? Do I baptize myself with a holy mixture of linseed oil and turpentine? *What do I do?*"

"I've already told you," she said. "You have to cut the cord. Leave the furniture business, leave your father. Leave your father's house. You have to stop feeling so comfortable. You have to stop thinking of painting as something you do in your spare time, and start thinking of it as *all* you do. You said it yourself the night we met. There's no such thing as a part-time artist.

"And you disagreed."

"Yes, but only for myself. You were right before. You can't believe as I believe. The only way you're ever going to think of yourself as an artist is by living and working as one. And until you do, you'll never feel like anything but a cabinetmaker. Not that there's anything wrong with spending your life making furniture. It's just that I don't think it's what you want."

"No," Duvid said. "It isn't." His first conscious admission of the fact. A small victory even in this.

She touched his hair, fingers working through the rough thickness to his scalp and, for the moment, holding there, reaching, feeling for the bone beneath. "Ah, Duvid. Of course not."

There was a soft thump as the returning skiff hit against the pilings below. One of the fishermen called, "Hey, up there!"

Duvid rose from the stringpiece and walked to the ladder at the end of the pier. He looked down at the two men in the boat. Red-faced Irishers. A rope was tossed up and Duvid grabbed it.

"How's about a hand? We got us a big catch."

Duvid saw it then in the bottom of the boat. Some big catch. A few fish and the swollen, darkened remains of what had once been a man. The body lay in the stiff, unnatural posture of a store dummy, arms and legs spread, hands reaching for nothing. It was naked, the skin shredded in places by nibbling fish and hanging in small streamers. Confetti. Duvid's stomach flipped. The men had a rope looped around its middle and were preparing to lift it to the pier.

"What is it?" Rachel called.

"Stay there. They've fished a body out of the water. Don't look."

One of the fishermen laughed. "Better listen to him, lady."

Duvid pulled on the rope as the men in the boat lifted and shoved. The body rolled onto the pier with a moist, spongy sound. It lay on its back, self-fringed, in a spreading puddle, Duvid kept his eyes averted. He had already seen too much. His throat filled with sand, he stumbled backward, reflexively, invisible hands against his chest.

The Artist

"Here's your sketch pad."

Rachel had come up behind him. She put the pad in his hand and he took it without thinking. Her eyes were on the body . . . wide, unflinching. She might have been looking at a big fish. It was that kind of look. "Sketch it," she said.

Duvid stared at her.

"Sketch it. You might never see anything like it again."

The two men had climbed onto the dock and were gazing at Rachel in much the same way as Duvid. She seemed unaware of them. She was staring at the body, the brightness of her cheeks drawn into her eyes. Duvid forced himself to look with her. What did she see that he couldn't? What mysteries revealed? What more here than ravaged carrion? The eyes were gone, the nose fragmented, the mouth agape in an idiot's grin, the stomach bloated and shapeless. While down below, in those dark roots between the legs, the fish had dined well, leaving only some shriveled scraps for a later dessert.

"Ya like lookin' at dat, lady?"

It was the taller of the two fishermen, thick-shouldered in a collarless shirt unbuttoned at the chest. Matted hair crawled free, a nest of worms seeking light. He grinned obscenely. "If ya' want, I can show ya' somethin' better."

Duvid clutched at the distraction. "Shut up, you big slob." He took Rachel's arm in his free hand. "Come on. Let's get away from here."

She shook loose. "Do a sketch first. You have to look at this thing and put it down the way it is. It's important."

"What's important? Sketching a half-rotted corpse?"

"If you're an artist, yes. In this business you don't run from the truth just because it's unpleasant." She stabbed a finger at the object on the dock. "And finally, that's about as true as you can get."

Her voice was quiet, but charged, crackling. As if immobilized by the current, Duvid stood frozen in place, hesitant, without decision. His sketch pad hung limply from his hand. A flag of defeat. Then he saw the tall Irishman studying him, measuring, taking quick inventory, adding up the big hands and chest, the height that reached almost to his own, the wide, sloping shoulders, adding up

141

the square, tight lines of mouth and jaw, the hawkish nose, the deep, shadowed eyes. *Ah, the eyes.* The rest, solid and hard enough, but the eyes a soft, liquid brown, a warm gentle dark. The rest a possible anything, but the eyes unmistakably, unalterably Jewish. No problems. Duvid watched the doubt vanish, fascinated by the easy readability of such things for him, having grown expert at it. Once they recognized the eyes as Jewish, all fear died. The eyes of a perennial victim. A lamb awaiting the knife. Not easily achieved. It had taken the sustained effort of two thousand years of talmudic cheek-turning. Relieved at having escaped all need for decision, Duvid awaited what he knew was coming.

"Hey, kike! Who you telling to shut up?"

Duvid wanted to lean over and kiss the broad Irish face, beefy above its great moustache, aglow with what lay ahead. He grinned. He could not stop himself. It was that kind of feeling. *"You!* I'm telling *you* to shut up, you dumb, dirty-mouthed mick." He let his sketch pad drop.

The grin should have given warning, but the fisherman was already on his way. He swung heavily at Duvid's head, careless in his confidence. He'd finish the sheeny fast and show his blonde whore what a real man was like. He never quite knew what happened. Later, his friend would tell him, but even then he refused to believe it. Jews didn't fight like that. Except that this Jew did. This Jew stepped easily inside his clumsy haymaker, doubled him over with a straight left six inches into his belly, and put him away with a solid right hand, a whistling hook, to the lower jaw. The sound of the second blow was that of a wooden mallet striking cement. The fisherman fell beside his rotting catch and lay still. Duvid looked at his companion, but the man just stood with his eyes wide and his mouth partly open. Duvid picked up his pad and for the second time took Rachel's arm. "All right. Let's go." This time, she went.

"You didn't need to do that," she said.

"Oh, yes I did. You're a very smart girl and you know an awful lot, but you don't know how much I needed to do that."

"I didn't expect that kind of violence from you. I didn't think you were capable of it."

"That's another kind of unpleasant truth."

The Artist

There was a coldness inside him, a chill wind between his bones that came off the river water, that came off the shredded flesh of what had been a man. He saw it again, all of it, as it had been, knowing he did not have to sketch it to remember, that he would not forget. Just as he was not likely to forget her standing there and staring, unflinching, everything drawn into her eyes and wedding her to it. Don't look, he had warned, hoping to spare her the shock. Yet there had been no shock. And what part of his chill had come off of this?

She took him to see her mother at Bellevue Hospital that afternoon. They went alone. Rabinowitz could not visit his wife on most Sundays, which was the time when he earned his few dollars as a wedding poet. His part of the ceremony was to address the bride and groom in verse so solemn it would bring tears to their eyes, and then entertain the guests with burlesque lines. Sober, he mocked himself and his efforts. Drunk, he reviled the world. Both ways, he mourned his wife.

In the hospital, the women in gray cotton dresses wandered the corridors on soft shoes, murmuring. Some sat in wheelchairs above puddles of urine. Mrs. Rabinowitz had bandaged wrists. Rachel had told Duvid it was her third suicide attempt. She sat in a corner, a pale, slender woman with a ruined version of Rachel's face, holding her breasts in her arms and gently rocking.

"Hello, Momma." Rachel kissed her cheek. "How do you feel?"

Mrs. Rabinowitz just looked at her.

"I've brought a friend to meet you. This is Duvid. Duvid Karlinsky. He is an artist."

Mrs. Rabinowitz slowly turned to Duvid. Her flesh was yellow parchment, but a patch of deep pink marked each cheek like poorly applied rouge. She started at Duvid, still rocking, her eyes pecking at his. Then without change of expression, she spit at his feet. Her saliva sprayed the floor and the tops of his shoes with drops ringed by tiny bubbles. She studied them intently for a moment, as if trying to glean an important message from the pattern. Then she glanced once more at Duvid's face.

"That is my opinion of artists, Mr. Karlinsky. Does it disgust you?"

Not knowing what to say, Duvid remained silent.

"It was *meant* to disgust you, Mr. Karlinsky. Because artists disgust *me*. Tit for tat." Her voice was surprisingly young, precise, genteel, almost girlish in its lilt. "Tell me. Exactly what kind of artist are you?"

"I paint."

"I see. *That* kind of an artist. Well it is not only painters who disgust me, but all kinds of artists. And by that I include writers, poets, musicians, actors, and . . ." with a brief glance at Rachel, " . . . actresses. Do you know why they disgust me?"

Duvid felt as if hurled into a play in which no one had bothered to assign him any dialogue. "No."

"Then I will tell you. They disgust me because they are the cruelest, most self-centered people on God's earth. They believe all that matters is themselves and what they are doing. They suffer from the sick notion that a book or a poem or a painting or a piece of music or a part in a play is of greater importance than people, than even the act of living itself. They will hurt, sacrifice, or destroy anyone and anything that happens to stand in the way of their own narcissistic ambitions. They know only one song and it has only one word and they sing it day after day. 'Me . . . me . . . me . . . me.' I am an authority on that song, Mr. Karlinsky. I have been listening to it for more than twenty years. First my husband sang it to me, then my daughter. Do you have any idea how tired one can get of listening to such a song?"

She paused as though awaiting an answer, then went on without it, her tone even, her manner that of a lecturer addressing a large, attentive audience. "Blood, Mr. Karlinsky . . . life. That is what *really* matters. One drop of blood, one breath of life is of greater value than all the art, all the culture in the world. Believe me. I know what I am saying. Do not think me mad merely because I am sitting here in this madhouse. I am speaking the absolute truth. Artists are the ones who belong in this place. They are the ones obsessed, the ones haunted by visions, the ones convinced they are the bearers of celestial messages, of divine secrets revealed only to them. If that is sanity, Mr. Karlinsky, then I prefer the company of those here with me now."

Mrs. Rabinowitz rocked in silence, her eyes suddenly off somewhere. She seemed to have forgotten her visitors. Rachel unwrapped a small package she had brought and handed her mother a slice of buttered bread with smoked salmon on it. "Lox and *challeh*, Momma. Fresh from Epstein's."

Mrs. Rabinowitz took the offering without glancing at her daughter. She ate hungrily, gripping the bread with both hands, as if fearful Rachel might change her mind and snatch it away. Duvid found it hard not to stare at her bandaged wrists. He had never known anyone who had tried suicide. The whole idea was alien, beyond comprehension. It happened, of course, but to reach such a point? So final, so completely over. Tomorrow would *not* be better. Next month would *not* improve. No more chances. What did you say to someone like this? Once they had decided, once they looked at all they had, added it up, and chosen to leave it forever, how did you tell them it was a mistake? Unless they already knew. Maybe those who *really* wanted to kill themselves did kill themselves. Maybe those who tried and failed wanted to fail. Or were they all, at that moment of trying, just plain crazy? Mrs. Rabinowitz didn't speak as if she were crazy. But how was a crazy woman supposed to speak?

"Where's Poppa?" Mrs Rabinowitz said, addressing her daughter directly for the first time. "Lying drunk in the cellar?"

"A wedding, Momma. He's reciting at a wedding."

"Lovely. My husband, the high priest of love, the poet of the *chuppah*. He has made such a shining success of his own marriage that he goes about sanctifying others. What he should do is use himself as an example, hire himself out as a warning to bride and groom. He should say, 'Listen to me. Everything I have recited, everything I have told you is a lie. I know nothing of love and loving. I know nothing of marriage. I have led a miserable life, blind to all but myself. I have betrayed every vow to love and to cherish. I have driven my wife into a crazy house, my son has run three thousand

145

miles to escape me, and my daughter, . . ." Mrs. Rabinowitz intoned, her voice growing low and toneless and losing itself quickly in the murmur of sane and insane, ". . . my daughter is a monster without a heart, a *golem* that I have fashioned in my own image and who will finally destroy whomever she touches."

She turned to Duvid and he caught a glimpse, in a passing flash of brightness, of what she had once been. "You seem young, Mr. Karlinsky. How old are you?"

"Nineteen."

"My daughter's age. She is also nineteen." With a graceful, almost coquettish gesture, her hand swept toward her ear to smooth down a stray lock of hair. "But do not be deceived by her age. She is not as young as you. She has never been young. *Golems* are born full-grown. Sometimes I think she is older than I am. Be warned. She can eat you whole. She has done it before. Artists, actors, are her favorites. She finished her last one in a single bite. Or has she told you?"

Duvid said nothing.

"No? I'm surprised. Rachel does not usually try to hide things. She prides herself on her honesty. An exceptionally honest person. Believe me. She will tell you the truth if it tears your heart." Mrs. Rabinowitz looked at her daughter. "Why didn't you tell Mr. Karlinsky?"

"There was no reason. It was a long time ago."

"Oh? I thought you might have forgotten."

"No, Momma. I didn't forget."

Mrs. Rabinowitz smiled dimly, her teeth like the awkward second teeth of an eight-year-old child. "Perhaps you would like *me* to tell him."

"It doesn't matter, Momma."

"It doesn't matter, Momma!" Mrs. Rabinowitz mimicked in a thin, bitter falsetto. "My daughter manages to kill a man at the age of seventeen and she says it doesn't matter. My daughter the *golem.* Will someone on this God's earth please tell me what I ever did to deserve such a blessing? Whom did I ever hurt? What terrible sins did I commit?" Her face collapsed and she began to weep, tears streaming down her cheeks and straining the gray of her hospital

dress, hands tearing at her breasts through the bracelets of bandages. "Why . . ." she wept, her voice broken and hoarse and unrecognizable. "Why . . . didn't . . . they . . . just . . . let . . . me . . . die?"

Rachel was on her knees on the cement floor, clutching the weeping woman, the two of them, mother and daughter, rocking back and forth together like a pair of old Jews on the Day of Atonement. And sitting there, Duvid did not know where to look.

Rachel had the key to her friend's apartment and this was where they went afterward. On the way, they said nothing of the hospital visit. Leaving, they had stood across from the great brick building, seeing the crowd of ghosts in their gray uniforms watching the visitors depart. At one of the grilled windows, Mrs. Rabinowitz raised her bandaged wrist, a limp hand. Good-by, her mouth silently said. Good-by, good-by. A slender female figure, straight, still with dignity. And they stood waving back until she disappeared.

An instant clutching in the apartment. Duvid reached for her with his back still against the door, holding hard, pressing, trying, in that first moment, to shut out all else. He did not know exactly what he was trying to shut out, but he knew it was there, could, in fact, feel it between them. In bed later, he still felt it, dark and chill, lapping at their flesh like the low, sullen waters in a midnight swamp. So that finally, what he was sure could never be spoiled was spoiled.

"I'm sorry," she said. "It was my fault."

"No."

"We should have talked about it. We should have gotten it out of the way first."

Duvid lay staring at the amber-lighted ceiling. "Why did you take me to see her?"

"She's my mother."

"Did you know how it would be?"

"Just about. It was an average visit. She rips me. I sit with bowed head. She cries. I hold her and she holds me. She has what she needs. I leave."

"What's going to happen to her?"

"They'll let her out in five or six weeks. She'll come home, be miserable, make my father and me miserable. We'll have wild, screaming scenes. She'll accuse us of ruining her life, of driving her into the grave. Then in a few months she'll be ready to cut her wrists again." Rachel spoke in a monotone, wearing the look of naked relaxation that often follows sex, grief, or great physical exertion. "Or maybe this time she'll really finish it and go out the window. Poor Momma. She married the wrong man and had the wrong daughter. We're too much for her. I guess we'd be too much for anybody." She forced a thin smile. "Though I didn't actually kill a man at seventeen."

"Why did she say that?"

"Because someone did die and she blames me."

Duvid touched the flesh of her throat, touched her breast, then looked down across the rest of her, across all the subtle shades of gold and lavender. She was taking him some place, and at that instant he began to know where. "Who died?"

Her body tensed under Duvid's hand, then went slack. "That first night. You asked what happened to him. Remember?"

"Yes."

"He was an actor. I met him in my first bit part. A twenty-seven-year-old Italian with a smile as wide as all Sicily and the worst actor I ever saw. My God, he was awful! But beautiful. And in love with the whole world. And from the minute I saw him, he never had a chance. Even his having a wife couldn't stop me." There was sour self-mockery, disgust in her voice. "Not little Rachel. Although he did try holding off for a while. But he had a fatal weakness. A big heart. He couldn't stand hurting anyone. If I was so hungry for him, how could he deny me? So he knelt before his Blessed Virgin, crossed himself, and let me nibble around the edges. Until his wife walked in one day while I was nibbling.

"Italian wives." She laughed suddenly, the laugh shrill, gasping, slightly out of control. "Let me tell you about Italian wives. They're very jealous, they've got terrible tempers, and when they go off, they'll come at you with anything that happens to be around. And what happened to be around that day was a great big kitchen knife. But I'll tell you something about seventeen-year-old Jewish girls. They're quick. Especially when they see great big kitchen knives coming at them. You have no idea how quick they can be. Much quicker than lousy Italian actors. Duvid, I rolled clear of that knife so fast, that even when it was sticking in Ricci, his wife still thought she'd stuck it in me. Until she saw the blood."

Rachel stared vacantly at the ceiling. A guilty grief expanded her lungs, clouded her eyes. "He lay pumping blood. I never knew there was that much blood in a person. I kept trying to stop it. I kept trying to scoop it up and put it back. And all he cared about, all he kept saying to everyone, was how it was an accident, how he had tripped and fallen on the knife. He was good. Even the police believed him. It was the only good acting job I ever saw him do. You never saw such a scene. All the screaming and wailing, all the running around, all the blood. Like a third-act finale in an Italian opera. Except that the blood was real and there was no fat tenor dying. Only Ricci." She pursed her mouth as though adding a bill. "Sometimes I forget. When I do, Momma helps me remember. Maybe it's better that way. I shouldn't forget. Not that I'm sentimental. I know how it was. You don't really force a man into that. He decides for himself. And if it wasn't me, it would have been someone else. But the thing is . . . it *was* me."

She was silent then, her body carefully apart from Duvid's. His move. He knew it, knew she was waiting. Tell her, he thought. What? *Putz!* Tell her you love her. This is the time. But he didn't. He couldn't. He just lay there, listening to a child crying somewhere on the other side of the wall. To punish her, he waited for her to speak first. There was a blankness in him and he had no idea what would come to fill it up.

She said harshly, "Well, what did you expect? A bedtime story?"

"I don't know what I expected." And he didn't. She was a long, dark, twisting corridor that he was walking blindly.

"You think I killed him, too?"

Too? He and her poor, crazy mother. "I wasn't even thinking of that."

"What then?"

"For Christ's sake! What do you think it feels like lying here next to you hearing about another man? Do you think it's nothing?"

"It was two years ago," she said quietly. "And he's dead."

"I know."

"Would you rather I hadn't told you?"

"Of course not. It was great fun. Let's hear some others."

"There are no others." Her voice was small, barely audible. "I told you. There was only that one. And I thought it was better that you heard about it now."

"I could have waited."

"I guess you could have." She had a careful, very delicately put together expression on her face. "But did you ever think, maybe *I* couldn't?"

When he looked at her, the fine, expensive expression had slipped and let go the tears. They began in some tight, hidden, long-buried pit of grief, flooded her eyes, flowed down her shattered face, dripped between her breasts and collected in the groove. A tiny puddle full of two years' sorrow.

"Rachel . . . don't." He closed the space between them and held her. She shook in his arms, sobbing, the ancient bed creaking in the small, borrowed room.

"Duvid . . . Duvid . . ."

"It's all right," he said senselessly. "It's all right."

"What's wrong with me?" she whispered.

"Nothing's wrong. You're wonderful. I love you and you're wonderful."

"No. I'm *not* wonderful. And *don't* love me. Don't have anything to do with me. Run. Run as fast as you can. Momma's right. I'm some kind of monster. I'll eat you."

"Eat, eat! . . ." Joyously, he offered himself. Sustenance for his love. Let her bite, chew, swallow. He was big. Fresh. Strictly kosher meat. None of that Italian *trayf.* "Please! . . . Eat as much as you want."

The Artist

She should get the part just from the way she sits, Duvid thought. He watched her from the rear of the darkened theater, from across forty rows of empty seats. She sat on-stage with the others, but might have been alone. There was that quality about her. Something inside him shouted. *Hey! That's mine up there. Attention must be paid.*

He had rushed through his shop work and deliveries, left his wagon on West Forty-third Street, and slipped in through a side door. He had not told her he was coming. He had a wild notion this might throw off some fine point of balance, some delicate tuning of creative emotion. She had been preparing herself for more than two weeks, had thought of nothing else. There was only the audition. The rest of life hung suspended. Yet waiting now, she appeared untouched, almost indifferent. *There* was acting. Duvid's own palms were sweaty, the tip of his nose cold. A girl stood reading in a high, thin voice and he tried to listen, but the words passed through him. Poor girl. Poor Rachel. Poor all of them. Cruel and unusual punishment. There should be laws. Or maybe the laws should be against wanting anything this badly.

The theater was awesome, huge, all soaring columns, cupids, frolicking nymphs. Duvid felt swallowed. A whale's belly. Its aroma was of dust, of crowds long gone, of deep plush and polished wood. On-stage, two work lights caught and held those waiting to read. Alone at sixth-row center, solitary in judgment and power, sat the great man himself.

Duvid stared at the back of the producer's head, a shining melon on a stick. Richard Cragan. Rachel had been astonished that Duvid didn't know the name. *What? You've never heard of God?* She herself had studied Cragan with the intensity of a novitiate preparing for ordination. She could have written a monograph on him . . . likes, dislikes, foibles, weaknesses, strengths . . . a complete and detailed life history. Even the dress she now wore, of a white, clinging material that somehow combined the virginal and obscene, had been chosen only after a careful assessment of the gowns worn in his last five plays. Her hair style, different today than Duvid had ever seen it, had been created solely for the occasion. Nothing that might be of help was left undone. No effort was too great. Not for such a prize.

The Artist

She had called it an unbelievable chance, a once-in-a-lifetime opportunity. A new play by a new playwright and Cragan wanted a new face in the lead. A professional, but an unknown. Titled *Wild Woman,* the play had as its central character an idiot girl, a pathetic, fragile creature filled with the mysterious wonderings of an incapable mind. Her shadow terrifies and interests her, she is puzzled and worried by everything, the slightest sound preys on her. Physically alert, her senses only trouble and frighten a mind that cannot interpret what they present. She begins to feel love, but does not know what it is, cannot understand it. When she tries to describe this new feeling she finds she does not have the words for it. She is finally forced into a desperate half-pantomime and must construct, gropingly, a complicated symbolism to express what she does not know. It was this scene that Cragan had chosen for his audition.

Rachel had let Duvid read the script. "Does the girl remind you of anyone?" she asked.

He shook his head.

"I thought of your Aunt Tybie right away." He had told her all about Tybie, and she had seen her in the street.

"Tybie is no idiot." He was indignant. "And she can't speak a word."

"I know. But I feel they're the same in a lot of ways. Expressions, mannerisms. That's why I want to spend some time with her. I want to watch the way she moves, study everything about her. I don't want to have to imagine the way this girl is. I want to *know.*"

Duvid was reluctant at first. He felt it a kind of betrayal. Yet why? What harm to Tybie? No ridicule was intended. If anything, it would create a greater understanding. And equally important, it could help Rachel.

He arranged it and Tybie was joyous. The face she had loved in the paintings was suddenly alive. It moved, it laughed, it could be touched. Rachel spoke and Tybie clapped her hands in delight. Duvid watched happily. He brought them together every evening. When he had to take Tybie home, she brooded over each parting. "She really loves you," he told Rachel.

"She's like a sweet child. What a sad thing."

"Yes. But sometimes I almost think she's better off this way."

The Artist

"No. Don't say that."

"The things she saw . . . the things that were done to her . . ."

"I don't care. You can shut it out. The mind can be strong."

"Maybe *yours* can."

"Yours too. You were in the same pogrom."

Even in this she had to have things as they were. There wasn't a message in the world she would refuse to read.

A different girl was standing stage-center. Her voice dipped and soared, flew erratically. Another portrait of an idiot girl. A dozen versions so far. Be patient, Cragan. You'll soon see the true one. Watch the girl in the white dress. She's going to stand up, step forward, and bring you just about the truest idiot girl you've ever seen. Take my word.

What word? How could he promise what he'd never seen? Rachel had refused to show him a thing. If she got the part, she said, he would see then. She was afraid of draining something, of losing some piece of it in advance. But he didn't have to see. She *breathed truth*. She knew no other way. And a little was starting to rub off on him. He had to be careful. There were times he caught himself sounding just like her. His father understood, but not his mother. What was happening? He was behaving strangely. And where was he taking Aunt Tybie every night? He finally tried to explain. It wasn't easy. When he had gone through it all, his mother shook her head.

"*Meshuggeneh.*" The single word described it all. He was crazy. Or Rachel was crazy. Which was beginning to mean the same thing. "They should let her mother out from Bellevue and take her in."

"She's an actress, Momma. You don't understand."

"*I* don't understand? Since when have *you* become such an expert on actresses? You give a girl a tickle and suddenly you're an expert. Let me tell you, Duvidal, I know about actresses more than you think. I know they have to be a little strange in the head to want to be one in the first place. I know they have this thing inside them that can't be trusted, that is so rotten it smells. You haven't smelled it yet? Wait. You will. They can hold it in only so long. Sooner or later it comes out."

His mother's view. When it came like that, Duvid just listened.

His father also listened. They exchanged glances. A conspiracy of understanding. They were men of the world. They knew things a wife and mother could never know. They worked together, dealt with customers, with competition, with gangsters and thieves. Life revealed its secrets and the secrets were slowly getting better. The struggle was less desperate. They now had two men working in the shop. Disaster no longer lurked around every corner. They dared look for the sun. But not Rifka Karlinsky. Her eyes still saw only clouds beyond her kitchen door. And Rachel was just part of the outside darkness.

Rachel stood up and Duvid leaned forward. The naked work light was good for her, a fine light for a pale blonde. It gave an edge of silver to the shadows of her face and deepened the green circles beneath her eyes to magic hollows. She stood unmoving in the light, not rushing to start as some of the others had done, not worried about squandering a few extra seconds of the great man's time, but letting the mood build, letting the silence stretch flat and thin and tight. When she did finally start, it came so gently, so softly that the sound seemed to have drifted in from outside.

Duvid knew nothing about acting, knew nothing of technique or style or timing. But he didn't have to know. From the first of it she was simply Tybie. Tybie, if she had suddenly found her voice, Tybie in movement and expression, Tybie even in appearance. What black magic *here?* How could she *look* like her? Yet somehow she did. He stared and blinked and saw it still, saw it in the wide, childish eyes and hesitant smile, saw it in the hollow cheeks, in that particular lift to the nose with its constant searching and sniffing out, saw it in the uncertain line of chin and trembling lower lip. Rachel was gone. Some unseen devil had spirited her away. What remained in her place was Tybie.

Something else. The burlesque was there too, that slightly grotesque image of the clown that made you want to laugh and thereby increased the horror. Something the others had not known, that had not been written into the part. An idiot could be funny. An extra bonus. Laugh and have your soul wrung at the same time.

And Cragan laughed. It was the first reaction of any kind the producer had shown. A good sign. Duvid grabbed for it like a gold nugget. He felt a sudden and deep affection for the back of that anonymous head and the frail neck supporting it. An invisible line had been crossed. Cragan was no longer an omnipotent threat. He had been beatified, had become a force of enormous benevolence. He could nod that bald head and offer Rachel the sun on a plate. A wonderful man. An expert on acting. He *knew* she was good, *knew* she had more to offer than any of the others. See how he sat a little straighter in his seat, how he leaned forward. More nuggets. Duvid scooped them up like a miser and squirreled them away in his growing hoard of hope.

Light reflected from Rachel's face, little pearls of perspiration bright as sun on wet snow. Fingers and hands groped, danced in the sun, frail, fluttering birds free of their cage, come to speak of love. Tybie, long ago on the roof, feeling what she did not know and could not tell. Even this. Carried with it, Duvid swam further through an old mood. Tybie, dazed and naked in the woods beyond the *shtetl.* And before that, on the floor of the shop, staring at the bloody thing that was once her husband. *Tybie.* Yet here, now, and dressed in a virginal white not her own. Emotions passed through Duvid's body like ghosts. When they left, Tybie had left also and Rachel had returned. She finished as she had begun, her voice fading to silence, the mood held until it drew thin and tight once more. Then she cut it clean, turned and sat down.

Two others came after her, but Duvid watched and listened impatiently, without interest, and sensed the same reaction from Cragan. They shared a deepening bond, a tie so warm and strong that Duvid fought an impulse to climb over forty rows of seats and plant a grateful kiss in the center of that glorious, shining head.

When the last girl had finished, Cragan summoned an aide and issued whispered instructions. The announcement was made. "Mr. Cragan thanks each of you for your time and effort. He would like Miss Brian, Miss Shaw, and Miss Renard to remain and meet with him in his office immediately. Everyone else will please leave their copies of the script with me."

It was a letdown. He had been so sure she had it. Still, the odds were narrowed. She was now one of three instead of fifteen. Cragan rose and walked briskly backstage, a surprisingly small, almost gnomelike man. The three remaining auditioners followed him into the wings. Those eliminated left through a rear exit. Duvid sat alone, unable to leave. How could he go now? If there was some way for him to slip into Cragan's office, he would have done so. He decided to wait. One way or the other, he had to know.

The theater was absolutely quiet. Its plaster cupids and nymphs played silently overhead. Wherever Cragan's office was, not a sound escaped its walls. Duvid took a small sketch pad from his pocket and started to draw. He drew Rachel on stage, hands raised, groping, a blind woman seeking sight through touch. It came out Tybie. He tried again, but could still see only his aunt in the sketch. He heard footsteps and saw one of the girls leaving through a stage door. Too bad, Miss Brian. A short while later, the other girl left the same way. But what did it mean? Had they been eliminated? Or was Cragan just having each of them run through it again before he decided? Or maybe none of them would get it. Maybe a whole new group would be brought in next week. Tension settled across his back in a dull ache. Waiting, it grew worse. Maybe he should leave. If it turned out badly, it might be hard for her to face him at once. She might want time to settle with it alone. Yet he stayed.

She was taking longer than either of the two others. A good omen. If it was bad, she would have left quickly. The longer, the better. Take your time, Cragan. Study her carefully. The more you see, the more you'll like. Make no hurried judgments about this one.

But when more time had passed, he began to worry. She might have left the theater, gone out a different way. He had been waiting almost an hour. It was stupid to go on sitting here. She could be home by now. He gave it ten more minutes, then went to find out. He located a stairway backstage, climbed it to the mezzanine, and saw a door marked "private" at the far end of the corridor. His feet made no sound on the carpeting. No sound came from behind the door either. They had gone away, had left him the whole damned theater. He listened at the paneled door. Nothing. *What a fool!* He grabbed and turned the knob in an instant of anger and frustration and watched the door swing open. Smooth, well-oiled hinges. Even the door was silent. Everything silent. Except for a most delicate slipping, silvery sound, which Duvid now heard at precisely the same moment he saw what caused it.

156

The Artist

They were on a tufted couch, her bottom aimed at the ceiling and forming the top half of a valentine heart. Except that the heart was white, not red, and was rising and falling and had nothing whatever to do with love as Duvid understood it. Cragan lay underneath, his flesh blue-veined and putty-colored in the light of a beaded lamp. He seemed to be doing very little besides lying there —although his hands, each claiming its own section of the heart, did perhaps encourage some movement. His eyes were closed, two slits punched in sagging, cherubic cheeks. Duvid looked at his legs. He still wore shoes, stockings, and garters. Two naked animals being punished, one being made to stretch out and carry the other on its stomach. Duvid was unable to see her face, but did not have to. In all the world, was there another ass like *that?*

Cragan opened his eyes and saw him. He showed no change of expression, but his fingers tightened into Rachel's flesh and held her. "Who the devil are *you?*"

Rachel spun, eyes like two match burns. There was no color in them. "Duvid!" It came out a whisper. She rolled free, clutched a cushion, tried to cover herself with it, to hide. From whom? Cragan lay exposed . . . a skinned, suddenly shriveling snake in a gray, pubic patch. An old man. He did not move. Nor did Duvid. They stared at each other across forty years. Duvid stood frozen, a block of ice waiting to melt and feel something. He tried to look at Rachel, but couldn't. All he seemed able to do was stare at Cragan, who stared back, little pebbles of eyes black and knowing, secure and defiant in the aging, liver-marked face. He looked at Duvid without surprise, as though it were the most natural thing in the world for strange young men to walk into his private office and find him naked under an equally naked actress.

"Duvid." Again his name. Just that. She tried to put whatever hope she had left into it. There wasn't much.

Cragan had understood.

"A good lesson, Duvid." Tiredly amused, yellow lids drooped like parchment, hooding the pupils beneath. "Next time you'll know enough to knock."

Knock? Was that what he was supposed to know? The ice melted to blood and he was able to look at her. "Whore." His voice was soft, shaking, not his own. Someone else had spoken. He waited, as though for denial. When it didn't come, he hit her with his open hand, hit that well-loved face with its soft lips and its eyes dark with pain. His slap felt like slapping rubber. It stung his fingers and did him no good. He needed more. He grabbed her hair in one hand to hold her face steady and raised his fist.

"Not in the face!" Cragan shouted. "If you've got to hit her, for God's sake hit her where it won't show."

A blankness in Duvid answered. She must have gotten the part. Congratulations. The fist hesitated, drifted a little, hung there. It could finish it for her right now. It could end the dream before it started. Duvid knew what those knuckles could do. He was close enough to smell it. She smelled it too. And her face waited, open, unflinching. Waited.

Her eyes passed something to him. More truth. This was the way it was, they whispered. Nothing for nothing. You wanted something, you found out the price, you paid for it. No begging, no haggling. A straight business deal. Value given for value received. Yet something wept, something mourned. Sorry, my darling.

Ah, love, he thought, and buried her right there. . . . *Yisgadal, v'yiskadash, sh'meh rabbo* . . . buried her complete, with everything intact. No damage done, no visible hurt.

Ah love.

He turned then, while he could still manage it decently, and left the gravesite.

EIGHT

1945: Amagansett, Long Island

She had brought over a few things and moved in and they'd had their first nights together with the sheets smooth under them and the bed wide and comfortable and everything more leisurely. But perhaps the best was waking in the night to find the other there and the touching and holding to make sure, and the talking, which was the final proof. Things were different in the night and reassurances were needed then that would not normally be needed during the day. They slept well too, but when one woke, so did the other, so one was never alone. Duvid had never been affected by such things, but being alone in the night now was no joy to him. Nor was it to her. So that once, awake in some deep, midnight black, she confessed, "This is the first time I've ever been able to sleep in complete dark. I've always had to have a light on somewhere."

"Why didn't you tell me?"

"I was ashamed. I didn't want you to think the mother of your son-to-be was some kind of spook."

"Do you want a light now?"

He had started up, but she pulled him back. "Don't you dare leave this bed."

The night was cool and she huddled against him beneath a light blanket. Far off, the ocean made a steady, rolling sound.

She said, "With you here, I'm fine. But I'm suddenly afraid of other things." It took her a moment. "What if I can't have a baby?"

159

"You'll have a marvelous baby. You're the original baby witch, aren't you?"

"Yes. But maybe only for others. Maybe it won't work for me."

"It'll work beautifully. I feel it."

"Do you really?"

"Yes," he said, but felt nothing. Even holding her here, now, in the dark, seemed unreal.

"What else are you afraid of?"

"Nothing."

"You said you were afraid of other things."

"I've forgotten."

"Tell me."

"All right. I'm afraid you're going to send me back to my house."

"I'm not sending you back anywhere."

"I know. But I'm still afraid, and I still keep seeing that big old place standing there, waiting to swallow me up." She seemed to go off somewhere. "I never used to be like this. What's happened to me?"

"Maybe the first signs of pregnancy."

"I think it's just that I suddenly want something. I mean, *badly.*" She tried to huddle closer. "Are you ever afraid?"

"All the time."

"You know too much for that."

"I know very little. And it seems to get less by the day."

"No. You're the smartest man I ever met." She nuzzled his neck. "Are you *really* afraid?"

"Yes."

"But you were in the *war*. *Two* wars. After that, how can you be afraid of anything?"

"Compared to other things, wars are very simple. The worst that can happen to you in a war is that you die, and dying is probably the easiest thing of all to do. It has to be. Eventually, everyone manages to do it. If there were anything really hard about dying, somebody, somewhere, would have failed at it by now."

"I know about dying."

In the dark he imagined her face and wished he could see it. Instead, he touched a finger to the tip of her nose. "Yes. You do. And you're very brave."

160

The Artist

"No I'm not. It broke me a little."

"Everybody breaks a little. But when you heal, you're stronger than before."

"I *am* stronger now. I feel it. But only with you."

"You don't need me."

"Yes I do." But she must have sensed something. What? A subtle tightening of flesh? An instinctive pulling away? "If you don't want me to need you, I won't."

"I didn't mean it that way," he said, yet felt an old grave open in his stomach.

But her fears were mostly for the night. During the day, she was too busy doing what she called her motherly things, attacking all household chores with a kind of mystic joy, as though each one brought her a step closer to pregnancy. She even found joy in just getting up in the morning . . . unlike Duvid, who had to ease his way into each new day with caution, a timid thief, fearful of being caught breaking and entering. Once, watching her charge cheerfully through breakfast preparations, he said, "My God! How can you start off like that?"

She was setting a table on the porch, a glint of gold edging her hair, the sun dancing on the water behind her. "Isn't it awful? I've gotten to be a real happy idiot in the morning. And its all your fault."

"How?"

"You're too lovely to me."

"Am I lovely to you?"

"Oh, yes."

"I don't really try," he said and kissed her.

"Mmmm." She stood with her eyes closed. "Want to do a little more work on the baby?"

"Not before breakfast."

"*After* breakfast?"

"It depends on what you feed me."

"Wait till you see. You'll be able to make twins."

It proved to be lox and eggs, which she set before him with a flourish.

He laughed. "Jesus, how did you *know?*"

"*Secrets of Ethnic Cooking.* My bible." She waited for him to taste it. "How did I do?"

161

"Magnificently."

"As good as Momma?"

"Better. Momma always made the eggs too well-done."

"Why didn't you tell her?"

"You don't tell Momma about cooking."

She sat watching him eat. "Do you tell her about your blonde *shiksas?*"

"I'm afraid it's hard to tell her about anything these days. She's getting pretty senile."

"I'm sorry."

"You live long enough, it happens." He picked at the eggs. "Though you never do quite believe it. You think they're doing it on purpose. Sometimes I want to shake her and yell, 'cut it out, Ma. Enough's enough.' "

"But you don't."

"No," he said. "I don't." But each visit was affecting him more deeply than the one before. How odd to find her like that, looking no different, really, than she had for years, with her thick, iron-gray hair, and still carrying herself so straight, still with the handsome face and dark intelligent eyes. Among other things, she had gotten it into her head that her husband was running around with women, had become a *trombenik*, a tricky, undependable chaser. She pleaded with him to end the shame he was heaping on them all. Duvid had been there, had seen his mother first order, then beg his father to please stop his fickle ways, at last getting down, awkwardly, on her knees to clutch the old man's hands. "Please, Avrum. I've lost my pride. See? I'm begging on my knees. Stop this craziness." And Avrum Karlinsky, who, to Duvid's knowledge, had never, in almost sixty years of marriage, strayed once from his wife's bed, raised her from her knees and promised, "All right, Rifka. There'll be no more women."

"They're waiting for you, naked." She said it *nachade*, more and more mixing her Yiddish with her English, fifty years in America turning to stone along with her arteries.

"No, no. Not one."

"A man your age, Avrum. How does it look for the neighbors?"

The Artist

"I promise, Rifka. No more. Come. Listen to the radio. You want to hear 'The Romance of Helen Trent?' "

And Duvid had watched his father gently lead her to a chair, where this fine strong-willed old woman, who had survived more than three-quarters of a century of difficult living, sat for most of the day listening to one soap opera after another. With Duvid, she was half rational, half not. Sometimes he was a boy again to her, other times a young man foolishly leaving his father's shop to become a *meshuggeneh* artist. "You want to paint pictures, Duvidal? Paint pictures. But you must also work like a man at a man's work. You must also go in with Poppa to the shop. This, what you do with paints, is for children." Maybe not so senile at that. Often, he felt no differently himself. But it was almost worse when she was rational, with her eyes clear and melancholy, those remembered lights making her message harshly readable . . . *My son, this is the way it finally is.* Or else, holding his hand, warm in both of hers, which were already cold as the blue loam of earth, she would slowly nod her head up and down as if to say, *Yes, Duvid, you won't have to worry about me much longer.* How beautiful her face then; how splendidly it reflected her responses to the fate of being human.

Laurie asked, "And what about your father?"

"He still goes in to work every day, still loves to handle tools. As soon as someone comes to stay with my mother, he goes." Duvid smiled. "The sign over the shop still says, A. KARLINSKY & SON, FINE WOOD FURNITURE. There are three stars in the middle and I'm the son."

"Were you in the business?"

"Not since I was twenty. But he's kept me on the sign, an unseen, silent partner for thirty-six years."

"He must be very proud of you."

"To Avrum Karlinsky I was nothing less than a genius from my first sketch on. He framed everything I did and hung it in the shop. And it's still there. He refuses to part with a thing."

"I think I'd like him."

"And he'd like you."

She laughed. "I doubt *that.*"

"You'll see," Duvid said, not quite sure of what he meant, but

163

pleased at what happened to her face when he said it. The reassuring prospect of continuity. Would she ever meet his father? And if she did, what *would* he think? It was hard to tell with Avrum. At eighty, he was still changing, still moving on. Unlike most of the aged, he talked very little about the past. He was more involved with the future. Although he rarely talked about that either. *Today* was what counted. Get through today, he figured, and tomorrow would take care of itself. When disaster struck, it struck today, never tomorrow. And this was the only time you would have to deal with it.

But what he did mostly now was try to master the sense of his life. And his eightieth summer, Duvid thought, was as good a season as any for it. They still talked often. The two of them, face to face. Not on the telephone, which Avrum mistrusted. A disembodied voice over a wire meant nothing. You had to see eyes, a mouth, changing expressions. You could get a voice over a wire to say anything. *Looking* was what mattered. And looking at his son, at his Duvidal, a brilliant, childish smile would crease his cheeks. What did he see? A five-year-old little *tchotchke* in a burned-out Russian *shtetl* six thousand miles away? Better that they had moved on. Better that they had left behind the smoking ruins, along with its ancient dreams of Sabbath bread. And he was still moving on. He still liked the smell of fresh sawdust blowing through his lungs, the feel of finished wood against his hands. He never said it in so many words, but he approved of his life. At the age of eighty, he planned new ventures, envisioned new designs. He watched those he knew take sick, retire, or die, went to at least two funerals a month, but lived as though the shadow of oblivion would never darken his own flesh. Nor would he dwell on such a possibility for his wife. What was going to happen would happen. Looking ahead and worrying was as bad as looking back and regretting. Both poisoned you. And neither changed a thing.

"He'd like you," Duvid told her again, finding it important, suddenly, to commit his father to this girl in advance, as if éven so loosely imagined a tie would carry its own blessing.

"Why?"

"Because you're young and beautiful and shining and bright, and these are all things that even eighty-year-old men can appreciate. Also, you're both pretty much the same." Duvid was starting to understand it now, starting to see the link. His father had little true comprehension of the power of doing or of love, and neither did she. But they were the familiars of both. Lacking the language for them, they wore these articles as if they were personal uniforms. "You're both great believers in beginnings," he said, "and both your own brands of phoenix."

"What's a phoenix?"

"A beautiful, mythological bird which lived alone in the desert for five hundred years, consumed itself in fire, then rose from the ashes to start another life."

She considered it, a child's eyes bright with pleasure. "I think you've just said something very lovely to me."

"I meant it."

"Because I fed you lox and eggs?"

He finished the last of it and leaned back. He smiled, not because he was amused, but because at that moment it was simply impossible not to. "Probably."

"Shall I make you some more?"

"Not now. I'm a one-portion man."

"But you loved it?"

"Oh, yes."

She placed her hand on his where it lay on the table. "See? Aren't I a fine Jewish mother?"

"The best."

"And you're not going to send me back to my house?"

"You know I'm not."

"Yes. But I have to hear you say it."

"All right."

She seemed to go a long distance away without stirring or moving her hand from his. "I wish I really were a phoenix. Though I'm not sure about wanting to live five hundred years."

"It might be a little too much."

"Is your father really one?"

"At eighty, it's beginning to seem so."

"What ashes did he rise from?"

"Those of a town in Russia. Trevyenka. The Cossacks rode in

one day and burned it to rubble. To hear him tell it now, it was the best thing that could have happened to him. With nothing to go back to, he could only go ahead. And he's been going that way ever since."

She returned from wherever she had been. "Your father's a smart man too."

"He wouldn't call it that. He doesn't analyze things. Not with words, anyway. He lives in a world of do and make. He insures himself that way. What he can deal with, he doesn't leave to chance."

"I wish I were that smart."

"I told you. The two of you are the same. No different."

"I hope you're right. I must try harder, though." She nodded slowly, confirming it, and her hand tightened on his. "How about a little more insurance work on the baby?"

"You can only conceive one at a time."

"Yes, but we don't know yet. And it's kind of nice work anyway."

Automatically, he glanced at his watch.

"You bastard!" she said.

He laughed. "I'm sorry."

"Give me that thing."

He took off his watch and handed it to her, studying her face as he did so, seeing the rare mixtures that washed across it. What a flood, he thought, what a rampaging river I have tapped here.

"Now," she said, leading him inside by the hand, "your son and I are about to steal a few small drops of your precious time and immortality."

That night, he woke. He came up out of sleep like a diver, taking the climb slowly and resting at each level, his body waking as he emerged. He turned and she was half-sitting up in bed, her face soft in the dark. He touched her cheek and felt velvet. "What's wrong?" His voice was a whisper. Whom was he afraid of waking?

The Artist

"Nothing." She, too, whispered. "I was just thinking."

"What?"

"I've never said I love you."

"You don't have to say it."

"I've wanted to. But I was afraid if I did, you'd think you had to say it too." She lay down beside him. "And I didn't want you to have to lie."

"The words aren't important."

"Oh, but they are. You don't know how I've wanted to say them. I've been busting, just holding back."

He smiled, unseen. "Please, I don't want you busting."

"You won't mind if I say it?"

"God, you make me sound terrible."

"You won't mind?" she insisted.

"No."

She tightened her body to his and it felt transparent, as if he could see through her to the window beyond, starlit, opening onto the beach and ocean. In so soft a whisper it might have been only a thought he had overheard, she said, "I love you."

"And I love you," he said without examining it.

"I said you didn't have to lie."

"You're very easy to love."

"Easy?" She deliberately mocked herself with the word.

"I meant it the good way."

She was silent against him. "Sometimes I wish I could have come to you untouched. Then I think, maybe, in a way, I did. Until you, I was never really there, never really cared about anything for myself. I just wanted to give to whomever I was with. With you, it's all for me. Darling, you make me feel so wonderful. I'm afraid I'm getting terribly selfish."

"Love is supposed to be selfish."

"It isn't."

"It's the most selfish thing we have. We only love people because we *do* feel wonderful with them. When we stop feeling wonderful, we stop loving."

"That's terrible."

"It's true."

The Artist

"Then it's true and terrible." Her flesh relaxed as she sighed. "Do you feel wonderful with me?"

"Of course. That's the only reason you're here."

"I guess maybe it is," she said slowly and with such deep sadness that Duvid enclosed her head in both his hands, and held and knew its curve . . . *this sealed cup, this strangely fragile fruit.*

Still close, they fell asleep. But when he next awoke, she was gone, and the darkness shuddered and through the window, the stars were cold stones. He touched her pillow and it, too, was cold. Somewhere, a dog, howled. Sammy. Duvid's breath rushed from his throat so fast it burned. "Laurie?"

Then he was out of bed, the floor cool beneath his feet. He found Sammy whining against the front door and realized this was what had waked him. He picked up the dog. "Where did she go, Sammy? Where is she, boy?" A gentile madness. Now she had him talking to animals. What sane Jew ever asked questions of a dog?

He went back and dressed. Kneeling to put on his shoes, his stomach jammed into his throat. Then they fled the house, man and dog, across the dunes to the flat, damp sand near the water. A blue desert on the edge of a silver lake. Duvid stared. While he and Laurie had clung to their own small patch of darkness, an unsleeping world of earth and water surrounded them. The universe was an insomniac. Maybe that's what dying was. Being forever awake.

He had been running, but slowed to a trot, a lengthening distance behind Sammy. Sometimes the dog turned and came back to make sure he was still there, then ran ahead once more. Dread came up in him like a wave, then receded. She had simply gone back to her house, he decided. That was all. She was impulsive, emotional. She did things like that. *In the middle of the night?* When else?

Then looking up, he saw the glow in the sky, a dome of rose-colored air that rose ahead and slightly to his right. At about the same time, a faint wail grew into the overpowering grief of a siren. The occasional houses beyond the dunes were still dark, but suddenly held a sense of sleep disturbed, of people whispering in double beds. Frightened and confused by the new sounds, Sammy stopped, and waited for Duvid, then stayed close beside him. Other sirens joined in and the night howled with visions of red, shrieking

168

swords. He glared at the flaming sky. When those dry, old shingles went, they really went. But why should it be *hers*? It didn't *have* to be hers. Yet even then, he knew it did.

He began running again, angling inland now, away from the water. Her house faced the dunes, sprawling alone on a two-acre strip. And it was burning. Duvid grabbed Sammy and carried him the rest of the way. Clusters of people, dark, anonymous shapes, stood watching. Hoses poured arches of water, but the house was a torch. The smell was acrid, bitter, the smoke heavy and black. Duvid scanned the upstairs windows, as if expecting to find Laurie's face there, but saw only flames and charred beams. Then, circling the crowd, he saw her off to one side, talking to a policeman.

Sammy saw her too and began yelping and squirming until Duvid let him run to her. Her legs were bare under a short robe and her hair hung loose. She picked up Sammy and went right on talking to the policeman, who was writing in a notebook. Duvid watched her look past him as though he weren't there, wearing that cool, tough little-boy look she had shown at the beginning. And she was saying, "It was probably that old water heater. I thought I smelled a leak the other day and meant to call the gas company. But I never did."

The policeman sucked on a tooth as he wrote—a sun-browned, stolid man for whom the act of forming words on paper was clearly a chore. "Old gas heater, you say?"

"Must have been in there at least twenty years."

"How many persons were in residence here?"

"Just me."

"Parents' names?"

"They're dead."

"We need their names anyway."

Laurie told him, looking straight at Duvid now, but still showing no recognition. A section of roof caved in with a roar and the policeman stopped writing to watch. He shook his head. "You sure got away lucky." Reflected firelight gleamed off his face and badge. The house had become a garden, sprouting different shades of smoke and flame. Water vaulted first into the upstairs windows, then into the lower. The building was a total loss, but the firemen still played their hoses and the crowd still waited, held by a pack sense of smell. Death was in heat, but unsated. Maybe, with luck, a body would be discovered.

"Any brothers or sisters?" the policeman asked.

"They're dead."

He looked up from his pad with eyes the color of mud. "Dead?"

"That's right."

"Who's your next of kin?"

"Why should that matter?"

"We need the information."

"I have an uncle. Scott Wallace. He lives in Bangor, Maine."

The policeman took a long time writing the name. "What's his address?"

"I don't know."

"You got someplace to stay?"

She nodded. "I have friends here in town."

"You know their address?"

"Why do you need that?"

"We might have some questions later."

"Four Dune Lane," she said, giving Duvid's address.

The policeman wrote it down and closed his notepad. A great cloud of orange smoke gushed from the smothering flames. "You could have been cooked good," he said, and left to wave back some spectators who were getting in the way of the firemen.

Laurie watched him go, then came over to Duvid and stood silently beside him, holding Sammy and staring at the remains of her house. "It's funny," she said, "but I feel nothing." She spoke so softly that she was hard to hear against the sounds of the crowd and fire crackle and hissing water.

"What did you expect to feel?" There was a void where the dread had been and it was beginning to fill with anger. "Or is this your first house burning?"

She chose to ignore it. Or might not have heard. She was that far inside herself. "I was hoping you wouldn't wake up."

"Why?"

"I didn't want you to be worried."

"You're a very considerate girl."

Her shoulder touched his. "Please don't be angry with me."

The Artist

"Why should I be angry? I'm used to having people disappear from my bed in the middle of the night to burn down houses."

"Poor Duvid." She smiled, her face smeared black and gray with ash, a tomboy called in from play. "I'm afraid you've got yourself a real loony."

Which, in a sense, he already knew. Yet something extra was in the wind tonight, some break in the heavens, a siren blowing that had nothing to do with the sirens on the fire trucks, but had the long, ripping sound of a hungry wind at sea that tears off the water and snatches at your flesh with cold fingers. An attention was present that he could all but feel, telling him if he had half the sense he was born with, he would run somewhere, very quickly, alone. Except that he did not want to run anywhere, and did not want to be alone. What he wanted mostly, just then, was to beseech someone (who?) to let him share some good with this girl, and be part of another beginning, and try to do something of value with his work. Yes, since he knew nothing of prayer, he was willing to beg.

The flames died and they stood watching the firemen hose down the smoking wreckage. The crowd thinned and broke apart, their sense of tragedy frustrated. No charred flesh, no hint of blood. They would have to be content with their daily ration of war news, of accounts of far-off battles, of casualty lists, of Signal Corps photos of Japanese dead. Sorry folks. With luck, maybe next time. The sky began to pale in the east and Duvid felt the soot settling on his bones, making his eyelids heavy. He heard the air, softly pulled toward the embers, felt the dying heat. Paint and varnish smoked like incense. Ancient shingle and flooring seemed to smolder gratefully. A funeral of exhausted objects. And whatever visible past she'd had lay buried among them. All those pictures, he was thinking, all those pictures of beautiful people.

Leaning against him, she said, "I don't really expect you to understand, but it suddenly seemed right to do."

He fought a violent urge to lecture her.

"Duvid, I didn't *hurt* anyone."

"Except the insurance company."

"I won't take their money."

"You'll have to take it. Unless you want to confess the arson."

"Then I'll give the money to charity."

"Fine. You can start a scholarship fund for needy pyromaniacs."

"You shouldn't joke about it," she said, but laughed.

"It's either that or shake your teeth loose."

"All right."

They stood without speaking. A silent vigil at the bier. The firemen were collecting their equipment, winding up hoses, setting up red lanterns to warn people off. Sammy sniffed around, but seemed confused and frightened and stayed close. The air tasted sulphuric. Duvid looked at a pair of elms, scorched on the sides facing the house, leaves and branches black against a pale smoke-mist.

Then he heard her say what he had known she would finally have to say, not having known it, perhaps, consciously, but rather sensing it as one senses summer rain long before a storm. "Well, you can't send me back to my house now, can you?" She said it with a smile, because this was the only possible way, but the smile was as clear and grave as the noblest intent, a sweet, delicate presence that spoke of the meaning of love for those fearful of losing it.

"No. I guess I can't."

"And I'm a true phoenix?"

"There was never any doubt about that. You didn't have to burn down your goddamn house to prove it."

Looking at her, his head felt clear, too clear, and his body came across drunk, its nerves curiously alive, his flesh new. And the sulphuric air came into his nose with the full history of its making, with all the compromised souls of those who had once lived in the house, along with a century's worth of those who had gone before, all those golden, straight-backed *goyim* from dry New England towns, with their fine bone china and inherited sterling and dark family portraits and Sunday church meetings and, finally, their closets full of hidden lusts.

"Are you still angry with me?" she asked, unable to decipher his silence or his eyes and suddenly worried.

He shook his head, thinking that anger certainly had a way of passing through him very quickly, thinking, too, that perhaps this was the only true way to cleanse the present of the past, that without burning, the odor of death would live on like a beast in the air along with the musk of stale memories in stale furniture. This way, at least, the last anguished molecule was gone.

He took her arm and felt it warm and familiar through the fabric of her robe, but still with its own hint of fevers he knew nothing about, still with its own ghosts released. "Come on," he said. "Let's go home."

NINE

1909: New York, N. Y.

Duvid woke to silence and the old man staring at him, one-eyed, from the easel. The eye was a pale, glittering blue that caught the light of a frozen window and threw it back like chipped glass. The other eye, the blind one, gazed out of a milky pool. It had been blinded by a crippler when the old man was a boy in Russia to keep him out of the army. Better one eye than dead. A Jew never came out of the Czar's army alive. If he did come out, he was no longer a Jew. Same as dead. Some boys had index fingers lopped off, others had eardrums punctured. It was the crippler who decided what would be done to whom.

From beneath piled covers, Duvid stared back at the half-sighted face, imagining the small parade of boys and parents dragging their terror to the crippler's hut. *Momma!* Birds rose with the scream. Done. Now, seventy years later in another country, the result gazed out of a stillwet canvas in the bare, second-floor room of an East Side tenement. The old man, a ragged street peddler, had not wanted to pose. He had a Jewish horror of the image and Duvid was forced to sing to him for much of the time to banish the devil. But fifty cents was still fifty cents and he had sat for three hours under a flickering bulb, alternately dozing, mumbling into his beard, and sipping tea through a lump of sugar.

The painting had life. The old man was there. Duvid could feel him . . . all of him. Not just flesh, bones, rags, hair. The rest too.

174

The Artist

It blazed out of the one good eye and hooked across Duvid's chest. The old man hated him, hated anyone young, strong, whole, hated the little he'd had and the still less left to him. He would not go gently to his final dark. This one would fight all the way, scratching, kicking, and biting, hanging on with the last wobbling tooth in his bleeding gums. And every brush stroke screamed it. There was no other sound in the room. Duvid soaked it in, lost himself in it. Sighing under the warm blankets, he felt his body relax. A wonderful honey gathered in the deep part of his throat. This morning he was an artist. Maybe not yesterday, or the day before, or the day before that. And maybe not even tomorrow. But his morning, yes.

It was that first waking glance that told everything. Good or bad, it hit the moment you opened your eyes. There was no time to prepare defenses. The easel was placed so that whatever painting was in work would be seen instantly. Forget what you may have done before. You were no better than your last.

Duvid stretched, lengthened his body into the cool margins of the bed and took his reward . . . a few extra minutes under the covers. Had his first reaction been bad, he would have been up instantly and at the easel. But he did not close his eyes. Sleep was not included in his reward. Sleep was finished. His thoughts were already on the day ahead. Another cold one. Frost ferns sprouted from the corners of the window, snow edged the roofs across the street. Everything was frozen. Even the clotheslines seemed locked into place in the sky's purple ice. It was December and the end of his first year as a full-time working artist. Happy birthday, Karlinsky!

The first months were the worst. Suddenly no Momma and Poppa. Twenty years old and he had never passed a night apart from them. The cord finally cut. Though not really. They were just blocks away and he saw them at least once a week. Could he miss a Friday dinner? Still, there was a difference when he closed the door at night . . . a silence between the walls, a solitary plate on the table, no voice but his own. And when it came to his work, there may as well have been an ocean between them. He was alone.

He had told his father when they were getting ready to close one evening. The two helpers had gone.

"Poppa, I want to talk to you."

175

"So who's stopping?" Avrum ran a loving hand over a half-finished cabinet, reluctant to leave it.

"It's important."

A rough spot discovered. Less than perfection. Frowning, Avrum reached for the sanding block. "What's important?"

"I'm leaving the business."

Avrum turned to look at him. "What are you talking?"

"I've decided. I want to paint."

"You're painting beautiful. What's to do with the business?"

"I can't do both."

"Who says?"

Who says? Rachel says. Duvid was sure she was hiding somewhere inside him. His private *dybbuk. His* voice, her thoughts. "I took a room on Hester Street. I'm moving there next week."

Avrum Karlinsky sat down, the sanding block forgotten in his hand.

"The business is doing all right," said Duvid. "You don't need me."

"Don't need you?" Avrum was suddenly shouting. "A father don't need a son? You looked maybe at the sign lately? A. Karlinsky and *Son.* Half the business."

"It's your business, Poppa. It always was. Your wood, your tools, your feelings. I never felt like you about it. I couldn't. You know that. I thought you'd be happy."

"What happy? With a knife in my chest?"

Duvid grinned. "You keep telling me I'm such a great artist. A genius. My paintings should be in museums. It's your own fault. I'm finally believing you."

"So believe. Who says no? The paintings are fine. Beautiful. I could bust looking. You should never stop." Avrum's arms spread. Palms up. An appeal for understanding, for logic. "But who makes a living painting pictures?"

Duvid shrugged.

"You'll starve!"

"I've got some money saved."

"Vay iz mir!" Avrum clutched his head and rocked. "Wait till Momma hears. She'll die!"

The Artist

A big surprise. Momma didn't die. "What are you screaming?" she asked her husband. "What are you making such a *tummel?* You didn't see it would be like this? You didn't know? Where were you looking? What kind eyes you got in your head?"

Avrum glared. What had happened to the expected support? "And *you* saw?"

"Blind, I'm not. I can see what a person loves, he'll finally do."

"You think it's right what he's doing?"

"Right, I didn't say. Don't put words in my mouth. I said only I saw. And if you weren't so busy oohing and aahing about the pictures, maybe you'd see too."

"And in all your *frechliche* seeing," said Avrum. "did you see also your son moving out of your house into a cold room on Hester Street?"

Duvid was proud of his mother. Her face showed nothing. "So? You expected to keep him wrapped in blankets the rest of his life? It's time he got out. He's big and strong. He's done for you since sixteen. It's time he did for himself a little. And what's so terrible? Hester Street isn't the end of the world." She gave Duvid a kiss. *"Mazel tov.* I wish you luck. Make nice pictures. You're hungry, you know where to come to eat."

It was not the first surprise from Momma. Duvid was discovering things about her. She could have a sensitive touch. More so than his father. It showed when Rachel vanished from his life. Avrum spewed questions. Duvid produced lies. Rifka Karlinsky said nothing. She mentioned it only once, briefly. "Never mind, Duvidal. It'll pass. There'll be others." Only it didn't pass and there were no others. None that meant anything, anyway. You could bury the dead, but what about the ghosts? His moving was no help. They followed him to Hester Street and settled in. They flourished. It was perfect for them. They had him alone. The place was small, there was nowhere to hide. Working was his only escape. When they saw a brush in his hand, they retreated, fled into the walls.

A special magic. You started with a blank stretch of canvas, ran in some color, and presto! A new world. And it was all yours. Whatever you wanted to see, you saw. Whatever you wanted to happen, happened. Awesome. Sometimes his brush trembled, his

177

eyes blurred, his stomach knotted. Whom did he think he was?.
. . . God? If not God, then at least a sorcerer. Yet at other times, it
all seemed so logical. No great mystery of creation. Just working and
getting to know your craft. Lights, darks, proportion, perspective,
composition, color. Endless bits and pieces. Each day you picked up
a few more, put them together, and watched them turn into something. He followed Rachel's advice. He painted the ghetto. His
window looked into its heart. Double rows of pushcarts straddled
a street black with people, with peddlers and shoppers, with children running, dancing to hand organs, with draymen forcing horses
through clogged gutters. And enclosing it all like the giant walls of
a prison, rows of lofts and tenements. Life in the never-never slum
. . . men and boys stooped under the burden of their next meal,
women and girls in skirts of flowing orthodoxy. Immaculately alien.
Rubbish along the curb. Cigar-store Indians under kosher-butcher
signs. *His* Hester Street.

He read statistics . . . 3,021 people living on two acres of land
—1,603 rooms, of which 452 were totally dark and another 637
faced airshafts . . . 467 babies and one bathtub. He knew what went
on in these pits they called gardens of opportunity. It was the most
crowded slum in the world, China and India not excepted. Its shop-
ping center of pushcarts was known as the pig market. In the winter,
they died with their boots on. They called tuberculosis Jewish
asthma. In the summer, babies fell from open windows and fire
escapes. His magic landscapes . . . tenements, vaguely Venetian in
design, with brick parapets, Mooresque radiators, toilets out back
and in the hall, and fire escapes for balconies. Pad in hand, he
wandered streets and buildings, factories and sweatshops, trying to
absorb it all. The recorder. He had to show how it was. Future
generations depended upon him. Posterity peered over his shoulder. Nothing must be left out . . . not even the slaughterhouses.
Strictly kosher. The *shekhiteh* method used. Chickens and steers flew
before his eyes, feathers filled his ears. Pictures of the melting pot
. . . a magic chicken turned to Friday night soup, a gangster had his
liver chopped on a stoop, *Yortzeit* candles burned for seven days and
nights, a boy dove from a roof and rang an old bell in his stomach.

He worked alone, the only artist in the world. He met other

painters, saw what they were doing and wasn't interested. Still lifes, nudes, pastorals, flowers, dressed-up portraits. Very pretty pictures. But he didn't want to paint pretty pictures. They sat in cafés and each others' studios, arguing and talking art by the hour, and Duvid found it a waste of time. He didn't want to talk about painting. He wanted to *paint.* The endless discussions bored him. Who cared what was happening in the studios of Paris, Rome, or uptown New York? So a Frenchman was slashing paint on landscapes with a knife, an Italian was dripping glazes on his still lifes, an American rendering flesh in irridescent pinks. Arty nit-picking. What had any of it to do with *him?* . . . with life and living on Hester Street? *What?* He began to find out the first time he bundled up some canvases and took them to an art dealer.

There was no way to prepare for it. Just getting the paintings out of his room was an ordeal. Full exposure. A package under each arm, he paraded naked through the streets. The gallery was uptown on Twenty-third Street and he walked all the way. It was not a warm day, but he was wet when he arrived. A Mr. Willoughby showed him into a paneled office, sat down in a carved chair, and said, "Well, let's see what you have, young man." What he had was a dozen pieces of himself, sliced flat and thin and tied with brown cord. The knots were impossible to open. Or was he just afraid? He finally ripped the cord with his hands and cut himself.

"Please lean the paintings against the wall," said Mr. Willoughby, a polite, soft-spoken gentile in thick glasses, dark suit, and the most beautifully polished shoes Duvid had seen since Hymie the collector's.

Then there they were. It was like somebody suddenly screaming in synagogue, throwing mud in a hospital, clanging pans in Carnegie Hall. They defiled the rugs, desecrated the wall paneling. What were these ragged peddlers, these sweatshop cadavers doing in this fine room? A plague of plaintive eyes, of fierce noses, of reaching arms. Take them away before this neat, shining *goy* was infected. Duvid wiped his bleeding palm on his trousers. Please. No blood on the rug. It was enough his paintings were there.

The art dealer looked, polished his glasses, moved closer, looked again. He blew his nose and Duvid heard a rushing sound, a beating of wings. The *Angel of Death*. He would not get out of this room alive.

"Well . . ." Willoughby cleared his throat, dabbed his lips, held the handkerchief there. He frowned and bent for another look. A kind man. He knew about artists, knew the terror, the terrible vulnerability of these moments. Attack the work and you strike the man. They were one. Thirty years in the business had made it no easier. He had gotten so he could see what happened to their faces without looking. Slowly melting wax. The cheeks sagged, dripped over the chin. The eyes died. Their lights went out. This one looked big and strong, but size made the pain no less. Still, he was a Jew. A certain negative advantage in that. They were not easily destroyed. History had proven it.

"You're a new experience for me, Mr. Karlinsky. I've never had a Jewish artist bring me work before. I don't imagine there are many of you around."

"No. There aren't."

"I believe it has something to do with your religion. No graven images. That sort of thing. Is that true?"

"Yes," said Duvid, feeling less than brilliant, feeling huge, awkward, and totally out of place in the presence of this slender, cultured gentile.

"But apparently religious restrictions have not stood in your way."

"I'm not very religious."

"I see." Willoughby turned to the paintings once more. "I must say you paint with passion, Mr. Karlinsky. Your technique is still crude and undisciplined, but there is great emotion, great feeling shown."

Duvid wasn't sure whether to feel insulted or complimented.

"And I would say you have caught the flavor of these ghetto types very well."

"They're not *types*. They're *people*."

"Yes, yes. Of course. People. But to anyone who does not actually know them, does not live among them, they do tend to become types." Willoughby's pale eyes blinked lovingly behind their lenses. "And you must admit, not especially attractive ones."

"That depends on what you call attractive."

The Artist

"True enough. Standards of beauty do vary. Among certain tribes of Africa, a twelve-inch neck is considered quite exquisite. However I must make my own judgments only as what I am . . . a New York art dealer. And I know of none among my list of clients, Mr. Karlinsky, who would consider hanging these ghetto people of yours in their homes."

"Why not?"

Willoughby smiled with quiet patience. He was used to artists arguing in defense of their work. It was instinctive, if futile. The best arguments in the world couldn't do for a work of art what it failed to do for itself. Yet there they were. *Look . . . you don't understand . . . what I really mean is . . . you don't realize . . .* And the more hopeless the cause, the more intense the pleas. "I'll tell you why," he said. "Because your subjects would make my clients feel uncomfortable. Perhaps even a little guilty. When the privileged classes are busy enjoying their privileges, Mr. Karlinsky, they don't like to be reminded that it may be at someone else's expense. And looking at your crowded tenement hovels, at your sad-eyed sweatshop children and ragged street peddlers is hardly conducive to a sense of joyous well-being."

"But this is the way things *are* down there. It's the *truth*. What's the use of painting if you have to lie?"

"I'm not suggesting you lie. But the world is full of many beautiful things. They're all around us. As an artist, you should see them. There are flowers as well as garbage cans in the streets of New York. Each has its own truth. I'm merely saying that if you ever expect to sell your paintings, it would be more provident to choose your truths from among the flowers rather than from the refuse."

Duvid felt a wetness against his fingers and watched a drop of blood disappear into the rug. He hid the offending hand in his pocket, peered at Willoughby's faded blue eyes, and saw the impossibility of this watered-down Christian's ever understanding. Flowers or garbage cans. One or the other. Well, if he had to choose, the choice had already been made. It was in his blood, nestling into the rug, seeping slowly inside his pocket. He had been born to it, raised with it, had now been given a name for it. He was, clearly and unmistakably, a garbage-can painter.

"As I said," Willoughby went on, "you do paint with passion.

The Artist

This is good. Part of your Hebrew heritage. I will tell you a little secret, Mr. Karlinsky. I have always believed that if the graphic arts had not been contrary to the Hebrew religion, the Jews would be far and away the world's leading painters and sculptors. They are more intelligent than the French, more disciplined than the Italians, more industrious than the Dutch, more feeling than the English, more imaginative than the Spaniards. Once a Jew knows what he wants, there is no stopping him. He succeeds. He is the yeast of any country in which he lives. If the country is smart enough not to let him go, it must rise with him."

Duvid stared broodingly at the lined-up paintings, at his collection of improvident truths. Instead of a sale, he was getting a Christian lecture on Jewish potential. An art dealer who loved Jews, but didn't know any. The best way to love people. You could make them into anything you wanted. He didn't need that kind of love. What he needed was someone to buy a painting.

"A little friendly advice from an old man thirty years in the business, Mr. Karlinsky. Do yourself a favor. Paint the beautiful truths, not the ugly. Don't try to walk alone. It's lonely. They'll break your heart for you. You'll paint out your life's blood, and won't be able to *give* it away. You'll become angry, bitter, frustrated. You'll hate the world and make the world hate you. You're young. You can do whatever you want. Look around. Get out of the ghetto. New York is a big, beautiful city. America is a bigger, even more beautiful land. It's filled with wonders. Take advantage of them. Look for the best, not the worst. If you look for it, you'll find it. Art needs no purpose. Most of the time it is just a happy accident."

Duvid bent and slowly gathered his paintings into two bundles. His hand had stopped bleeding. He knotted the torn cord and ran it around the canvases. No purpose? A happy accident? He couldn't believe that. If he did, he might as well have stayed in the furniture business. Yet he had to admit it. The rug, the wall, the room, looked better, freed of his people. Come, my ugly *landsleit.* Back where we belong.

The art dealer gazed at him with a sad, pinched face. His shoulders drooped under the finely tailored suit jacket. "I know you're not going to pay attention to anything I've said. Nobody listens to free advice. Because it costs nothing, they think that's all it's worth. Price is very important in this world. It's our only sure measure of value. If money were ever abolished, people would go mad in a week. They wouldn't be able to tell good from bad. If I charged you a hundred dollars for my advice, perhaps then you would listen to me."

Insanely, Duvid could almost feel sorry for him, for this pleasant man sitting here with his beautiful truths, happy accidents, and no purpose. "I appreciate it."

"No you don't. You don't appreciate it at all. Not now, anyway. Perhaps in a few years."

The first. Other dealers followed. A long list. Duvid soon lost count. After a while they all seemed to blend together. Although few were as kind or gave him as much time as Willoughby. He was usually in and out very quickly and became expert at tying and untying the canvases. No more cut hands. Those dealers that did bother to talk to him said pretty much the same things as the first. But more strongly. "Primitive" . . . "ugly" . . . "crude" . . . "distasteful" . . . "indecent." Some of the variations. Duvid grew used to the words. They lost their weight, stopped hurting, stopped meaning anything.

His father swore. *"Damned Christian art dealers!* Anti-*semiten!* What do those dried-up *goyim* know about the juices of Yiddish life, about what we feel. Paint them a Jesus on a cross . . . *feh!* . . . paint them a few of their *holy* saints and a genius they'll call you. What's the matter? There's no Jewish art dealers? In the whole city of New York, you can't find even *one?"*

"I never looked."

"Then *look!"*

Why not? His father might be right. Maybe A Jewish art dealer would identify more easily with what he was doing, be able to feel what the gentiles couldn't. Maybe there would be wealthy Jews among his clients who wanted something more than pretty pictures for their walls. Looking, Duvid found. On Thirty-fourth Street and Madison Avenue. LIPSCHUTZ FRÈRES, DEALERS IN FINE ART . . . NEW YORK, PARIS, LONDON, ROME. Wonderful. International Jewry. Rothschilds, Salomons, Loebs, and Sassoons his clientele. One of the

183

The Artist

Lipschutz brothers himself saw him, a short, round man in striped trousers and morning coat. A real *gemütliche* face. Nice. One of their own. Duvid oozed a warm, amorphous potato love. He wanted to embrace him, cover them both with a great prayer shawl and chant, *"Mi pnei chatoenu golino m'artzenu.* . . . And for our sins we were exiled from our land." Lipshutz and Karlinsky. A pair of old-time Jews. Duvid unbundled his wares. Look, *landsman. Our* blood. *Our* people.

Lipschutz looked. He teetered forward on tiptoes. An unconscious quest for height, for just a bit more than the sixty-two inches allotted him. God had to be so stingy? A few more inches for Lipschutz would have upset some sort of divine plan? He turned and gazed jealously up at Duvid. Six-foot Jews. Was that any way to even things out? Better everyone should be five-foot seven.

"Just what I needed," he said.

A vein fluttered in Duvid's temple.

"Things aren't bad enough? You had to bring me a bunch of cockamamy greenhorns? What am I supposed to do with them?"

"I thought . . ."

"You thought? I know what you thought. You thought, Lipschutz is a Jew . . . Lipschutz's customers are rich Jews . . . Rich Jews will be happy to buy pictures of poor Jews." The art dealer's cherubic face blossomed a deep pink. "Well, let me tell you something about rich Jews, Mister Pushcart Artist. They wouldn't pay two cents for a picture of a poor Jew if it was painted by Leonardo Da Vinci himself. They see nothing picturesque in the dirt of Hester Street, nothing colorful in tenement prisons. They've fought most of their lives to escape them. You think you can hand them instant nostalgia on a piece of canvas? You think you can turn remembered pain into pressed roses? They left half their *kishkas* in those sweatshops and tenements. You think this is something they want to remember?"

Duvid had thought he was past reacting. He wasn't. It was still a knee in the groin. And by his own. Betrayal doubled the pain. He had not expected this from Lipschutz. He knew about rejection, but this was more. This man was making it something deeply personal. Did he know him? Had he met him somewhere before and done him an injury? Duvid looked at the round, livid face again. No. He had never seen him. The man was a stranger. Yet you never knew. He asked, "Have we ever met?"

The Artist

Lipschutz glared. "Only in my mind. In my mind I knew some day you'd walk in here. It had to happen. Finally, ʾone day, the Messiah. A Jewish artist, carrying his people on his back like a hump. One look and I knew. There were the burning eyes, the passion, the sense of mission. I should have locked the doors. Messiahs, we don't need. Jewish Daumiers, we can do without. Listen, Messiah. You want to help your people? You want to do them a big favor? Stop pointing at them. Stop putting them in pictures. Stop trying to show everyone how dirty and oppressed they are. Stop picturing them as victims. The worst thing you can do to them. Whomever the world sees as victims, they *keep* as victims. Why do you think we've been crapped on for two thousand years? Because no one *knew* we were getting it in the face? No. The reverse. We got it because they *did* know. It's become our role. The world expects it by now. We expect it ourselves. We're surprised and grateful just to be left alone for a while somewhere. We kiss the new land under our feet. Thank you, thank you. Thank you for not crapping on us, for letting us wake up in the morning, for letting us live. And now you come along, Mister Messiah, and think you're doing something good by showing us wallowing in our own ghetto filth. You know what you're doing? You're playing right into the hands of our enemies. You're singing the same song as the anti-*semiten.* You're saying, see the dirty, ugly, smelly Jew."

Anger rescued Duvid. The bastard. A blue Jew. The worst anti-Semite of all. He blamed the corpse for stopping the bullet. "You don't know what you're talking about."

"I'll show you how much I don't know." Lipschutz went to his desk, picked up a folded newspaper, and shoved it under Duvid's nose. "This morning's *New York Times.* Maybe you read it?"

"No."

"No? So where do you get your news? From the *Jewish Daily Forward?* You want to know what's going on in the *real* world, Mister Messiah, buy yourself the *New York Times.* Here, I'll read you a little of what it says about our noble East Side *landsleit.* "

Squinting, Lipschutz held the newspaper at arm's length and read in a cold, precise voice, "Pushcarts obstruct the streets in the old Seventh Ward, making Ludlow, Suffolk, Hester, and Canal Streets almost impassable for pedestrians. The carts are piled high

185

with food, but would make the average citizen turn his nose high in the air. Putrid fish, maggoty cheeses, loaves of Polish bread black as tar . . . a mass of reeking rottenness alive with worms and larvae. Yet in spite of the dirt and stench, the ragged, bewhiskered descendants of Abraham, Isaac, Judah, and Jacob put their fingers into the food and then suck them with great and evident relish."

Lipschutz shot a glance at Duvid's rendering of a similar scene, then continued, "A writer could go on for a week reciting the abominations of these people and still have much to tell. One of their greatest faults is that they have an utter disregard for law. There is a certain hour when they are required to set out their garbage and ash cans, but they pay no attention to that. The ash cart comes along and takes what is in sight, and perhaps five minutes later some of these people will empty pail after pail of household ashes and garbage into the middle of the street. If they are arrested for this or any other offense, hundreds of their compatriots and coreligionists follow them to the courts and stand ready to swear in their favor. Filthy persons and clothing reeking with vermin are seen on every side. Many of these people are afflicted with diseases of the skin. Children are covered with sores, and hundreds of them are nearly blind with sore eyes. There is hardly a person among the whole crowd of street vendors who has not sores underneath the fingernails and between the fingers."

"This neighborhood," Lipschutz read, "peopled almost entirely by the people who claim to have been driven from Poland and Russia, is one of the worst eyesores in New York and among the filthiest places on the western continent. It is impossible for any self-respecting citizen to live there because he will be driven out by the dirt and stench. Cleanliness is an unknown quantity to these people. And they will not be lifted to a higher plane until they undergo a complete change in attitude."

Lipschutz put down the newspaper. "So I don't know what I'm talking about?"

"A stinking anti-Semitic reporter."

"Maybe. But what has he said so different from what you say in pictures? The same thing."

"It's *not* the same thing! If you think it is, you're worse than that

186

reporter. You're a Jew. You should know better." Duvid thrust his face close to the art dealer's, saw sudden alarm, got a whiff of fear. "You think when they come with the knives they won't cut your *tsatskes* off because you're wearing striped pants and a fancy coat? You think your clean hands will save you? They'll slice you up right along with the dirty peddlers. I've seen how it works. I learned early. Jews are Jews. Pogroms are very democratic. No favorites. You think they need reasons? You think if we all stay quiet and clean and speak in hushed voices we'll be loved? You *schmuck* in striped pants! You think you can escape the ghetto by standing up here on Madison Avenue and Thirty-fourth Street? You'll *never* escape it. You carry it with you in your *kishkas*. New York, Paris, London, Rome. Go anywhere you like. Scrub your hands raw. Eat in the best restaurants. You'll still belch up pickles and lox. You'll still be a dirty Jew with sores under your nails."

He tied up his paintings and left. So much for Lipschutz Frères. A lesson. Expect nothing from your own. But the *Times* article bothered him. He was used to worse from the mouths of dumb Polacks, Irishers, and Dagos, but this was something else. You couldn't yell dumb at the *New York Times*. He bought a copy of the paper and read the article for himself. It was titled, EAST SIDE STREET VENDORS, and the name beneath it was Clark E. Hutchins. A fine American name. With a name like that you had to bathe at least once a day, keep your fingernails polished and pink, and never say shit out loud. On impulse, Duvid walked over to the *Times* building. He told the woman at a reception desk he wanted to see Mr. Clark E. Hutchins and was sent to another woman on the third floor.

"Your name, please?"

"Karlinsky. Duvid Karlinsky."

"Please sit down. Mr. Karlinsky. I'll tell Mr. Hutchins you're here."

Duvid wondered how many hundreds of years it would take the Jews to become as polite as *goyim.* Or was it something in the blood? He picked a chair and sat down to wait. The bundled paintings leaned against his legs. A race of peddlers. Always selling something. But what was he trying to sell Hutchins?

"Mr. Karlinsky?"

The Artist

A dark-haired man in shirt sleeves came toward him. Young, but the circled eyes, beaked nose, and rumpled, vaguely harried look made him seem older. Duvid stood up and knocked over his paintings. The reporter helped him pick them up. "I'm Clark Hutchins."

Duvid ignored the extended hand. Surprise. The Christian bastard looked more Jewish than *he* did.

Hutchins dropped his hand.

"What can I do for you, Mr. Karlinsky?"

"I read what you wrote in today's paper and I just wanted to get a look at you."

"Why?"

"I've never seen a genuine, living anti-Semitic writer up close. I wondered what you'd be like. I also wondered how it feels to be so goddamned superior."

Hutchins stood looking at him, shoulders slightly hunched, eyes, within their concentric circles, those of a tired owl. "I'm no anti-Semite, Karlinsky. I'm just anti-dirt, disease, and lawlessness."

"Sure. And all your dirty, diseased lawbreakers just happen to be Jews."

"In this case, yes. But only because I was writing about a Jewish slum. I've also written about Irish, Italian, German, and Polish slums. Have you read any of those columns?"

"No."

"Then before you come up here and start calling names, I suggest you do."

"I don't give a damn what you wrote about others. That doesn't change what you wrote today. But if you made them sound anywhere near as bad as you did the Jews, then you're even more of a son-of-a-bitch than I thought."

For a moment, Hutchins appeared unable to decide whether to swing at Duvid, answer him, or just walk away. Then, surprisingly, he grinned. "Listen, you big Jew bastard. If you came here looking for a fight, you're in the wrong place. The editorial policy of the *New York Times* is one of devout cowardliness. You got complaints? Write a letter to the editor." About to go, his eye caught the bundled paintings. "You an artist?"

"Yeah."

"What do you paint?"

The Artist

"Dirty, stinking, vermin-ridden Jews."

Hutchins laughed. It had a good sound. "Let's see."

"No," Duvid said and gathered up his bundles.

"What's the matter? Afraid?"

"Of *you?*"

"Then let's see what you can do besides run off at the mouth."

Obvious baiting. Nevertheless, Duvid hesitated. Why not? He untied the paintings and put them against a wall.

Hutchins whistled softly. "Karlinsky, I swear to Christ I can almost smell them."

"Go to hell!"

"No fooling. They're good. You don't hold back *anything.*" Owl eyes stared, blinked. "But why so angry? We see the same things."

Again? First Lipschutz, now him. Duvid felt shaken. Was he seeing only what he wanted to see? Were there things in his own work he was blind to? Look long enough and nothing stayed the same. He thought he painted his people with heart, with his hand in theirs. Hutchins wrote only of abomination, disease, filth. But was the end result really the same—accusation?

Hutchins said, "What I mean is, we're both just trying to show things as they are. That's the only way to get them changed."

"I'm not trying to change anything." He wanted no ties, no alignment with this man.

"Of course you are. Look at that one there." The reporter pointed to a family group—mother, father, three children, all huddled together over small mountains of clothing, tortuously sewing by gaslight. "A whole damned family, kids and all, having to sweat through half the night over piecework. And for pennies, for just enough to squeeze out food and rent. Don't you think *that's* a statement for change? Don't you think *that's* an appeal for a man's right to a living wage? Christ! How could I write anything clearer than that? What's wrong with you, Karlinsky? Don't you even know what you're doing while you're doing it?"

"All I'm trying to do is paint like an artist. I'm no labor reformer. I'm not any kind of reformer. I don't even think that way."

Hutchins exploded. "Then for Christ's sake, Karlinsky! *Start* thinking that way!"

More advice. Everybody had solutions, answers. Duvid was

drowning in them. Even an anti-Semitic reporter he had come to attack. Although of this particular condemnation he was no longer certain. But enough. Too much. He gathered up his assorted Jews and flew away, happy to escape the *Times* building alive.

A year.

Still, he was *painting.* He lived frugally, making his savings last. Six dollars a month paid for his room and another twenty for food and supplies. He had learned to cook for himself. Sometimes his mother sent him packages. *Eat. Look how you look.* Actually, he looked fine. Maybe a little gaunt about the cheeks and chin, maybe a little lean about the ribs, but he liked that. Ascetic. Burn away what you didn't need. Live with the basics. Be an artist. *Believe.* In what? He didn't know. It was enough he could keep painting, enough he could waken on a cold winter morning, meet the one-eyed gaze of an old Yid squatting on his easel, and feel himself an artist.

The covers were warm and soft, but his reward-time was over. "Get to it, Karlinsky. The world hangs on your brush." He grinned as he slid out of bed. Living alone he had started talking to himself. Interior dialogues . . . ideas formulated, problems worked out. He enjoyed it. Karlinsky and his Greek . . . no, his *Yiddish* chorus. Alone, too, he had taken to long hours of reading. There were lost years to make up. He liked best the realistic Russian writers—Tolstoi, Turgenev, Chekov. Among the Americans, he chose Melville and W. D. Howells, who seemed to him to write in the proper spirit. But as a group, he found the Americans hopelessly romantic and unreal. Everything had to come out happy for them. Fake. Sugar candy. You had only to look around. Who could believe a word?

He dressed, got the coal stove going, prepared his usual tea and eggs. The same every morning. His stomach was trained, had learned what to expect, was satisfied. Food was a necessary nuisance, something to be gotten out of the way, quickly forgotten. He had become a time-miser, his goal, the easel. Whatever kept him from it he resented. A fanatic. He laughed at himself. He worked as though production schedules had to be met, as though paid by the hour, as though hordes of patrons were hammering at his door. Sorry. Only one to a customer. Madame, *please!* You'll have to wait your turn with the others. While the canvases piled up against his walls, crowded his parents' apartment, overflowed to his father's shop. The pure joy of creation? Bullshit! He couldn't help himself. What else was there for him to do?

This morning he planned to work from his window. He took a fresh canvas, killed the clear white with an umber wash, and waited for the street to come alive. He shivered with a quick chill and found the stove had died. He shook the grate and raised an ashen dust. The grates grumbled and squealed, the puny shovel clinked in fresh coal, and the fire rose again. Duvid went back to his window. The snow was spoiled and rotten with urine, manure, and litter, dead rats, a dog. The morning light fought to free itself from gloom and frost. Up and down the street the brick-recessed windows were shadowed, filled with darkness. And the parade came . . . pushcarts, wagons, drays, the horses shuddering, the air drowned in leaden gray, the vendors and peddlers bundled, round, and bulky against the cold.

Mood, he thought, work from mood, and went into it, broadly, sweeping in the masses with wide bristles, squinting away color and detail until all that was left, all he could see were great chunks of light and dark, swaths of movement, abstract patches of form. Push it, push it! Keep the street flat. *Schlemiel!* No slant. They'll slide into the sewer. That's it. Clean. No scumbling. Let it flow. No thinner. Leave it heavy. Now you're working. Keep the rhythm. Swing, press, lift. . . . No sudden stops. More ochre in the snow. That's horse piss down there, not whipped cream. *Show* it! Make it *stink*. No blending. No sables. Stick with the bristles. Let's see the strokes. All of them. Now the buildings. Up, down . . . up, down. Straight, or they won't stand. They'll fall right in the damned gutter. Shadow! It's weak. *More* shadow. Darker. Darker! . . .

The light held, sunless, gray, and steady, and he worked straight through the morning and into the afternoon. He thought briefly about eating, but did nothing about it. Only his bladder, less patient than his stomach, was able to force a hurried break. Then back at the window. More slowly now, the early panic fading, that first fear of not being able to catch, to soak in everything. His glance lifted up out of the street, climbed buildings, picked up background touches. Windows glittered, chimneys smoked, factories soared.

The Artist

Eight, ten, twelve floors of brick. Smoke drifted from a window. His eye passed it, skidded to a stop, went back. *A smoking window?* It was far away and nine stories high, but unmistakably smoke. The mist came out in a long, purple plume and hung, thinning, in the frosted air. And directly beneath, stamped across the building in a ribbon of faded letters, ran the words PREMIER WAIST-COMPANY. Rachel's beginnings. Duvid read the name of her old employer as he had so often before. His daily reminder. Although he didn't really need any reminders in the sky. He carried his own in his throat. An overgrown tonsil. All he had to do was swallow to know it was there.

A tiny figure appeared at the smoking window. Doll-like in the distance, it waved its arms. It did not seem real. Another figure joined it and waved also. A silent chorus. Duvid sat watching a few seconds longer. It took that long for it to break through. Then he was up, out, and running, coatless, a clutch of brushes still in his hand. He thought he shouted, "Fire!" but wasn't sure. Was it imagined? Amidst the market noise, the clamor of peddlers and crowds, it didn't matter. No one heard or paid attention anyway. In the distance, a faint clanging of bells. Or was this also in the mind? And why the panic? She wasn't there anymore. She had not been there for over a year. Still . . . he ran. Advice from a famous philosopher. Forget what hurts, what you can't bear to remember. Good advice. But who could take it? And what of the small, special pleasures of pain? For a while he had hated her. Hatred was self-respect. How else did you live with yourself?

She had come to him soon after, had waited in the dark one night outside the studio. "Duvid?" He kept walking. He could not trust himself. He might put his hands on her, do some terrible damage. As it was, he felt spattered forever with things that bled or stank. "I love you," she said and walked beside him, her footsteps matching his on the pavement. Incredibly, she looked the same. Why was she here? What did she want from him now? Punishment? A cleansing fire? He stopped and looked at her in the light of a streetlamp. He was wrong. She didn't look the same. Her face was wild, still frozen. "Go away," he told her and walked on. She stayed with him. "It had nothing to do with you, with us. I just want you to understand. He never touched me. He couldn't. Not in any way. Not where it counts." Oh, sure. And that was enough to do it. He reached for her, felt an old warmth through the fabric of her blouse, then ripped and saw her breasts. "Get away from me, whore, or I'll leave you naked in the street." When he walked away this time, she did not follow. Small comfort. And even the hatred failed to last. The thing was, he *did* understand. He *did* believe she loved him. He *did* know she did not, in any real way, consider herself touched. She could manage that. The mentality of the whore . . . the body simply an instrument, a soulless thing, a piece of merchandise to be used. Inside, she was the same. Nothing changed for her. She believed what she had always believed, wanted what she had never stopped wanting. The actress. The change was all his. He mourned it, accepted it, managed a certain level of peace. He was even able to go into the theater one night and watch her from the balcony. The newspapers had said she was good, had called her an exciting and original talent. He had to resist starting a scrapbook. A crazy pride actually drove him to cut out and save the first few notices. A return of sanity allowed him to tear them up. Seeing her on stage, in the role, was strange. She was Aunt Tybie, not Rachel. He felt nothing. It wasn't even she. Only after he left the theater, was he able to picture her again.

Nearer the smoking building, others were also running. The clanging bells grew louder. Duvid looked up and saw smoke coming from windows on the tenth and eleventh floors as well as the ninth. More dolls waving. People in the street waved back. A cheerful game. Some dolls climbed through the windows and stood on the narrow ledges. A breeze blew smoke at them, made their hair fly. Duvid pushed through the crowds and the dolls grew larger, became girls, women, an occasional man. Screams . . . high-pitched, shrill, rose and fell with the wind. A girl leaned forward and fell, skirts billowing, hair streaming, legs walking, running, kicking through air. Duvid heard the sound as she hit the pavement, heard it above shouts and screams, above clanging bells. He arrived with the first fire wagon and watched the ladders being rigged against the building, watched the last ladder lifted and pushed into place, saw that it reached only to the seventh floor. On the ledge of a tenth-floor window, two girls also stood watching. Twice one of them

193

made a move to jump. The other held her back, almost falling herself. For the third time, the more frightened girl tried to leap. The bells of arriving fire wagons must have reached them because the other girl motioned in the direction of the sounds. But she talked to ears no longer able to hear. Without turning, her companion dived headfirst toward the ladder three stories below, hit it, bounced off, and sailed on down to the street. The other girl seemed to stand straighter. The crowds stretched their arms up at her, shouting and begging her not to leap. She made a steadying gesture with her hands, looking down as if to assure them she would hold on. But a thin tongue of flame shot out of the window at her back and licked her hair. In an instant her head was aflame. She tore at her burning hair, lost her balance, and came shooting down after her friend.

Duvid screamed with the crowd, his throat muscles rigid, his body leaden on its bones. People were black shapes all around . . . more black shapes high on ledges, at windows, flying through clouds of smoke. Hoses lay uselessly across the gutter, fat as big snakes, hissing from their joints. Fire nets appeared. Duvid ran forward, reached for a net, found his brushes still in his hand and let them go. The first body tore the net loose and exploded on the cobbles. The second body ripped a hole in the net and went straight through. A slender leg moved, jerked twice, and lay still. An instant before, a girl. Duvid stared at what was left, at the bright blonde hair slowly staining red. He groaned, a cry not freely given but torn loose. He closed his eyes. *Rachel?* For just an instant. . . . There was that about her. A pressure from behind like a blow on the back of his head suddenly pitched him forward, pushed him, propelled him toward the building. Insane. She was long gone. *Go,* something said, and he felt an awful desire to do just that. His teeth were literally grinding, his belly was a pit of snakes. He could feel them move inside. *Go,* it said again, and he had the sensation something of him was passing through stone, and a breath, a touch of clear air, came up over his face as though, finally, he had blundered through an opening. And he went.

He knew the building, had ridden its elevator, a square steel-and-wire cage, to meet her after work, had stood waiting on the tenth floor among the sewing machines, the long cutting tables, the

194

great piles of linen and silk. Three hundred girls on that floor alone and just one staircase, one elevator, one fire escape. They were bringing people out as he went in. The lucky ones; coughing, puking, smoke-blackened, singed, but alive. He went up the stairs, fighting the traffic down. Why was he going *up?* Only firemen went with him, shining black beetles in their helmets and coats. There was no sign of fire on the lower floors. It was a fireproof building, walls solidly holding. It was also other things . . . a mausoleum, a graveyard, a giant frying pan, a corpse factory. Mass production. How many on the other two burning floors? Nine hundred? A thousand? More than his whole village in Russia. Not a Cossack in sight, but they roasted you here too. And on a much grander scale, with much greater efficiency. Fewer than fifty had been locked in the *shtetl's shul.* America improved on everything. Where else could you get cooked nine, ten, eleven floors in the sky? Where else could you learn to fly? They should be grateful. Tomorrow the *New York Times* would call it a purification rite. Those who survived would be better off. Lessons would be learned. *What lessons?* Flesh burns like wood? You can't fly without wings?

It was a dream, nightmares remembered, a stumbling through roiling, smoke-filled darkness. Where was he going? What was he looking for? Rachel? She wasn't there. Yes, but she might have been, he thought, and knew then he was in a locked cage of her making and had no key.

The smoke thickened higher up. Duvid urinated into a handkerchief, masked his nose and mouth, and followed the firemen. On the ninth floor, he began to believe in hell. Most of the fire had moved upward, leaving its waste behind. Bodies were burned to bare bones. White teeth grinned in charred faces. At the single, narrow door leading to the fire escape, bodies were piled like cordwood. A limb stirred, a moan sounded. Two firemen dug something free, but Duvid had no idea what it was. He felt sick and stumbled to a window for air. Dark forms, screaming, hurtled past from above. He bent over the sill and retched. Kneeling as though in prayer, he pressed his forehead to the crisped molding. The center of the world, a voice shrilled in his brain. He was at the exact center of the world.

When he lifted his head, the firemen were gone. Only he and the dead remained. He walked slowly across the smoking floor and looked at them, at what was left . . . lying, sitting, stacked in piles. How far they had come searching for this blackened loft on the shore of the Atlantic. Out of the grimy streets and dusty roads of Russian and Polish towns, across the Baltic Sea, across the ocean, into the sweat and clangor of the East Side of New York, and up, finally, to the ninth floor of a fireproof death trap with one escape ladder. Duvid felt them all, carried them all in his chest. His chest was an empty sewer with plenty of room inside. The skeletons rattled, roasted flesh sizzled, grinning teeth clacked. Come, *landsleit,* I take you with me. There's no other way out for you now.

He joined those still streaming down the stairs. On the street outside, ambulances were lined up with the fire wagons, and bodies were being loaded like produce going to market. Cordons of police held back the crowds, held back wailing, shouting relatives and friends, held back squads of reporters. As survivors stumbled or were carried out, those watching pressed forward in search of a face; sighed, moaned, wept, fainted, or cried out with relief, depending upon what they saw. Different tints of smoke drifted over the streets and gutters. Wood, linen, silk, paint, tar, chemicals, plaster, flesh, each burned differently, each gave up its own separate parts to earth and air. Duvid saw it all through a pale gauze of shock. He felt bereaved, weak, sick with smoke, with what he had seen, with what he carried in him. Eyes smarting, he lurched away from the crackling oven, tripped over a hose, and fell to his knees on the wet cobbles. He stood up, reeling as though drunk. A hand grabbed his arm, held him steady.

"You all right, Karlinsky?"

Duvid looked dumbly at the beaked nose, the dark, owl eyes.

"Hutchins," the reporter said. *"New York Times.* Remember?"

"Oh."

"Jesus Christ! Were you *up* there?"

Duvid nodded. His face was black, his hair matted, his hands and clothing dark with soot. When he swallowed, his throat burned. And there were all those things going on in his chest. He coughed up smoke, retched, coughed again.

"You look terrible. Want me to get you out of here?"

The Artist

"No. I'm all right."

Hutchins looked at him but said nothing, and they stood together at the edge of the crowd. It was almost over by then anyway. The smoke and flames had disappeared, the ledges were empty, and except for the three stories of blackened windows at the top, it would have been hard to tell that anything had happened in the building. But the bodies were still being lowered at the rate of one a minute and the ambulances and patrol wagons were still carrying them away. The sighing and moaning was softer now. A muted respect. Hutchins got a tally from a fire official. Eight hundred and fifty men and women had been working in the three floors. An estimate of the dead ran to slightly over two hundred. Of these, seventy-two had died jumping from windows.

It grew dark and searchlights played over the final moments of the scene. Duvid stood shivering, nailed there, unable to leave, unable to turn his back on the dead. When the last body had been lowered and driven away, when the last clanging bell had drifted off, he turned and walked away, Hutchins with him. The streets were in mourning. They moved as through a cemetery, a high keening trailing after. The tenements were tombstones. Without invitation, Hutchins followed Duvid to his room, got a fire going, found a bottle, and poured them each half a glass of whisky. Duvid had to hold his glass with both hands to keep it from shaking. The door was closed, but the wailing seeped through the walls.

"What was it like up there?" the reporter said.

"Like hell. You wouldn't believe it."

"Try me."

Duvid told him, his voice clotting. He was forced to stop twice for a drink. The whiskey burned but helped.

"Could you draw it from memory for me?"

"Why?" Duvid asked flatly. "You think dead Jews make better pictures than live ones?"

"No. But I think pictures of *these* dead Jews might help keep others from dying the same way. I want to run them with my story. I want people to see what Jewish skeletons look like, dangling over sewing machines. I want to show how piles of dead Jews can stack up searching for exits that aren't there, what missing fire escapes

197

can do to Jewish flesh, what happens to a Jewish face when it hits concrete from ten stories up." Hutchins shoved his nose inches from Duvid's. "Listen, Karlinsky. I've been screaming about our lousy fire laws for years without anything happening. There's too much money at stake. Politicians get paid off. Profits suffer when three hundred girls can't be squeezed into one loft. This fire is the worst public disaster since the *General Slocum* went down. I want to raise such a stink with it that City Hall will *have* to act. And no words can do what a few of the right pictures can."

Duvid stared broodingly at his glass. "When would you need them?"

"Now. Right away. I want to make the early edition. You've got till three A.M. About six hours."

Duvid said nothing.

"Use pencil, ink, charcoal. Whatever you want. But keep it line. We can't use half tone." Hutchins indicated some pencil sketches on the wall. "That kind of thing would be all right."

Duvid held out his hand. His fingers trembled minutely. "I don't know if I can even hold a pencil."

"Bullshit! Karlinsky. You can damn well hold anything you *have* to hold." The reporter looked at him. "And what in the name of Christ were you doing up in that building anyway?"

"Getting material for your damn pictures. What else?"

He began as soon as Hutchins had left. He tried pencil first, but quickly switched to ink. The line of the pen was better . . . more dramatic in the darks, more delicate with detail. He gave it its head, let it wander freely, lightly, until the feeling came and he knew exactly where it should go. Then he leaned into it with the extra pressure. His hand was no longer shaking. At least Hutchins knew that much about him. What he had to do, he somehow did. And if dead Jews were needed for the early edition of the *New York Times,* who was better able than he to produce them? Who was more expert on the subject? Who had started learning earlier? His pen scratched and stabbed, skidded and thrust. Shoulders hunched like a boxer's, he leaned over his drawing board and swung for the gut. No graceful flourishes, no swirls, no decoration. Forget the showlines that caught the eye, amused, delighted, but said nothing. Going for the *kishka,* he crawled back to the ninth floor, saw it all again, felt it, squeezed it through the cutting edge of his pen. That wasn't ink flowing. That was *blood.* And it took him a full hour to find that not a bit of it was working.

His eyes burned passion, yet his drawings were passionless, unmoving. All that carnage, all those charred, broken, anonymous bodies. It was just too much. Where did you look first? Whom did you weep for? . . . all *two hundred* of them? *Schmuck!* There're too many. Who could believe two hundred dead Jews? The mind boggled, refused to accept. Scale them down. Pick a few. Creep into them. Lay them open.

He started again. Single bodies, single faces . . . isolated, blown up, exaggerated. Eyes wide and staring. What did they see? A mouth open to scream. What was it trying to say? No matter. It would never be said. All right. Weep for *that.*

He was at the *Times* building with almost an hour to spare. He sent in his name and Hutchins came out to meet him. Duvid handed him a manila folder. "They're the best I can do."

The reporter looked at Duvid instead of the sketches. "What do you think of them?"

"They seemed right when I finished. But I did them too fast. I don't trust myself when it goes that fast." He shrugged. "I might look at them now and think they stink."

Hutchins slipped the drawings out of the folder, scanned them quickly, then more carefully. "They're good. No. *Great."* He took Duvid's arm. "Come on. My editor wants to meet you."

Duvid held back. He felt drained, exhausted, as if he hadn't slept for days. All he wanted to do now was go to bed. "What for?"

"I've told him about you." Hutchins smiled. "Ostreich's curious. He's never met a Jewish artist."

He led Duvid through the clamor of the city room to a glassed-in office at the rear. Beneath a green eyeshade, Ostreich had the lined face and tired look of a worried chimpanzee. He acknowledged Hutchins's introduction with a nod, then sat studying the drawings. "Ever do work for a newspaper before, Karlinsky?"

"No."

"You draw with a goddamned club." He glanced at Duvid's

hands. "And with those mitts I can understand it. My God, what a pair of loppers! We pay five bucks a sketch. That all right?"

Duvid stood there. He hadn't thought about getting paid. It had never even occurred to him. Money for *this*? Profit from the *dead*? It seemed wrong, almost ghoulish. Yet how stupid to refuse. The dead would be just as dead.

"We're planning a whole series on the fire," said the editor. "Hutchins will be doing it. It'll cover working conditions in the slums and ghettos, archaic fire laws, exploitation of immigrant labor, a wide range of Lower East Side problems. It's your area. You want to do the illustrations?"

Duvid hesitated. "I'm not really an illustrator."

"No? What *are* you?"

"An artist." It had almost stuck in his throat. And once out, it sounded so pompous he wanted to pull it back in.

Ostreich frowned, deepening the monkey lines. "Well, what in hell do you think an illustrator is? A *plumber*? We run some damned good art in this paper. This stuff you've just done is good art. *Living* art. Better than a lot of that candy-box junk I've seen in galleries. And you'll have a bigger audience for it, more real people weeping over it in tomorrow's edition, than you would in twenty years of showings in those phony, satin-and-lace salons."

"He's just tired," Hutchins said. "He's not used to these crazy hours. He'll do it." The reporter hustled Duvid out of the office. "Are you out of your head?" he hissed. "Do you know how many hungry artists would hock their easels for a chance like this?"

Duvid knew. He was one of them. It was just that so much had happened so fast. God, what a day!

Riding the horsecar downtown, he tried to sort it all out, but the rocking motion of the car soon put him to sleep. He awoke half a mile past his stop and walked back through the early morning dark. The moon hung low over the rooftops, dividing the streets into blocks of light and shadow. A hushed emptiness hung over the city, broken occasionally by the sound of hoofs clattering on cobbles in the distance, the noise sudden and harsh, then drying among the forest of buildings. Somewhere in the dark Duvid thought he heard a low wailing, faint and far away, an echo of the afternoon. Shining under the moon, the East Side of New York seemed oddly frail and appealing through his mist of fatigue. He suddenly loved it. He loved the worn, snow-covered pavements and the alleys winding off the avenues like entrances into another century. He loved the tenements lined up in rows and the shops crowded together between the stoops and the streets where the pushcarts would appear in another few hours. He loved the people sleeping now behind their locked doors and those weeping silently into their pillows and those beating their breasts for the dead. He loved the dead too, all two hundred, and the fact that he and those close to him had not been among them, and that he had been up there on the ninth floor and had seen and known what it was like. And he loved his having been able to put down on paper his feelings about the way it had been, and knowing that in the early morning edition of the *New York Times*, thousands of others would be looking at his, Duvid Karlinsky's drawings and, because of them, feeling the same things.

And he loved the hour, this calm, dark moonlit hour, when he could walk home alone, unafraid, through these streets and know finally that his life was not being wasted, that he had not been born merely to burn away his days uselessly and without reason. He was of use and he had been put to use, and a man could ask no more.

TEN

1912: New York, N. Y.

The morning of the exhibition, a Sunday, Duvid began the hanging early, with Molly and some of the girls helping as the day wore on. There were more than seventy paintings and drawings in all, each carefully framed, the best of four years' production. They filled most of the lower floor, climbed the high, graceful walls of parlors and reception rooms, and set the distinguished Federalist town-house ablaze with color. The three hundred engraved invitations that had gone out several weeks before had read:

> Miss Molly Adelman
> cordially invites you to attend
> a showing of paintings and
> drawings by Duvid Karlinsky
> Sunday, November 17th, 1912
> 8:00 P.M.
> 4 Washington Square South
> New York City

Duvid had taken great pains with the wording. Everything had to be correct. It was too important an occasion to be marred by any careless breaches of form. It was, in fact, an historic double first . . . the initial public showing of his work, and the first such art show ever to be held in a New York whorehouse.

The Artist

Duvid took no credit. It had been Molly's idea, not his. He had thought she was joking when she suggested it. He laughed. She didn't.

"What's so funny?"

"Come on, Molly."

"No. Really. Why not?" Even then, she had some of his paintings hanging in her private parlor, some of his usual ghetto Jews. He had intended them as gifts, but she insisted on taking them in trade. She adored them. The old men were all her grandfather, the old women, her grandmother, the others, surely related by blood. Looking, her cheeks flushed pink with pleasure . . . middle-thirties cheeks, but still translucent, still alabaster. "Look at them!" She pointed. "Such *feeling.*"

"Sure. But not exactly the kind of feeling your customers want."

"If you don't try, you don't know!"

Her motto. She had it embroidered on samplers in the girls' rooms. She believed in it, credited it with her success. She had come off a boat alone at the age of eleven, wearing dirty underwear and a torn dress, and she remembered it. She had been born Jewish and remembered that too. She would use only Jewish girls. She had recruiters meeting the ferries from Ellis Island. In a strange, cold land, she offered food, clothing, shelter, her own brand of warmth. Nothing forced, no compulsion. A free choice. Sweatshop and servile drudgery, or riches beyond immigrant dreams. And at the end of five years, a Molly Adelman bonus . . . a husband. It was a promised part of the contract. She arranged it. Serve her well for the agreed period, and even the rabbi was paid for. Her pleasure. On *Rosh Hashanah, Yom Kippur,* greetings arrived from all over the country. A hundred godchildren bore her name. She kept an up-to-date list and never forgot a birthday.

"Are you ashamed?" she asked. "Is that it?"

Duvid knew, then, that she was serious. When she spoke of shame, she was always serious. She had elaborate theories on the subject, all founded on the premise that there was no such thing. All shame, she contended, was man-made and therefore artificial; a false feeling created solely to smother the natural impulses and set up narrow bands of repression. An indispensable line of logic,

The Artist

Duvid thought, for anyone running a whorehouse.

"No. I'm not ashamed. It's just that the whole idea is crazy."

"Why?"

"Why?" Duvid grinned. "What do we do? . . . send out engraved invitations to people requesting the honor of their presence at an evening of Fine Art & Fornication? Can you imagine the news headlines? . . . 'FUCKING GOOD ART AT MISS MOLLY ADELMAN'S.' Or maybe . . .'RECORD ERECTIONS NOTED AT MISS MOLLY'S OPENING.' My God! The possibilities are endless."

"Very funny. But it doesn't have to be that way. We'll keep it very dignified. No business upstairs that night between the hours of eight and eleven. And I can bring in as many people with as much real money to spend as you'll find in any of your fancy uptown galleries."

Duvid never doubted that part of it. The names on her roster read like a directory of New York's financial, professional, and political elite. And she pulled them in from outside the city as well— Philadelphia, Detroit, Cleveland, Chicago, Boston. Even as far west as San Francisco, they knew about Molly Adelman and her Jewish virgins. *What* virgins? An inside joke. To a Christian, all Jewish girls were virginal. Traditional racial chastity. The whole world knew their legs remained locked until marriage. And who ever heard of a Jewish whore? What wonders *here?* Molly worked the myth all the way, pushed it even further. *You want a rabbi's daughter? A plump, Chasidic dove? Look! Take!* Credentials could be furnished. Signed affidavits. Yiddish passion was famous. None of your frigid Anglo-Saxon lumps to just lie there. Light the fuse on one of these hot little Mediterranean numbers and watch her go off like a Roman candle. Molly gave personal seminars in passion to her new girls. Wild. The *goyim* stumbled out of bed dizzy, but ten feet tall.

Duvid wondered later at his own reluctance. Was it better to just let his paintings keep piling up in his room? There still wasn't a gallery in New York that would touch him. His newspaper illustrations paid for rent and food, but how long could you go on painting without being *seen?* It was like writing with invisible ink. Still . . . *a goddamned whorehouse.* He had denied it to Molly, but of *course* he was ashamed. It was a joke. And although he could laugh at it easily enough as an idea, laugh even at himself, at his own part in it, he did not want his paintings laughed at. He did not want them turned into a dirty joke.

He told Hutchins about it.

"You're kidding!" said the reporter.

"I'm not kidding."

Hutchins looked at him. "I guess you're not."

"What do you think?"

"That depends."

"On what?"

"On what you want," Hutchins said. "If it's recognition and acclaim from the art world you're after, forget it. Even if you invite the critics, they won't come. They're a tight, tough, snobbish, incestuous bunch. They feed on tradition, dignity, adherence to the established order. They may even think you're laughing at them, deliberately trying to demean their dignity and eminence. And if they do, they'll be antagonized for life. In a hundred years, they won't forgive or forget. But if you just want to get your work out where it can be seen, maybe sell a few canvases, and have some fun thumbing your nose at the stuffed shirts in the art establishment, then go ahead with it."

"Yeah. But what do *you* think?"

"You mean what would *I* do in your place?"

Duvid nodded.

"An impossible premise. In a million years, I couldn't think like a crazy, immigrant Jew painter. But if I *could*, I'd probably say screw them all and do it."

Words from the professor. What came from Hutchins's mouth could be put in the bank. Checks could be drawn against it. In the three years Duvid had known this lean, New England gentile, this alien aristocrat of the rocky Maine coast, whose bloodline included two university presidents, three governors, and a Supreme Court justice, he had gradually become glued to him with a thick paste of respect and affection. It was Hutchins who had introduced him to Molly, who had first led him up the steps of the Washington Square house with the stern warning that if he didn't get some of that juice out of him fast, if he kept working and letting it all pile up inside, he would finally explode in a cloud of semen. "Your kind of place,"

Hutchins assured him. "Every girl strictly kosher." A dedicated disciple of whorehouses, Hutchins considered them the single civilized thread running through the generally uncivilized fabric of history, the one hopeful constant in the midst of changing patterns of confusion and despair, the only place in our entire social structure where a man could be absolutely certain of where he was, what he was doing, and what it was finally going to cost him. "The importance of price in human relationships cannot be overestimated, Duvid. And it's normally impossible to gauge in advance. Only weeks, months, or years later is it possible to add up the cost in disillusionment, heartbreak, and pain. In Molly's place, all prices are reduced to a dependable, clearly visible list. No problems. Nothing hidden. There it is. You know what you have to pay and you pay it. How could you possibly do better?"

A cynical judgment from a totally uncynical man. If anyone lived constantly on an edge of hope, if anyone labored unswervingly for the positive, it was Hutchins. He accepted no evil as unchangeable, no disaster as unmanageable, no defeat as inevitable. Duvid knew. He had worked long and closely with him. How many hundred hours of anguish? How deep a capacity for pain? Duvid went with him, stayed close, saw with Hutchins's eyes as well as his own. And the things they saw . . . executions, floods, mass murders, maimings, epidemics . . . an endless plague of human catastrophe observed and transferred, in words and sketches, to the neatly spaced pages of the *New York Times*. More learning, more truths. Duvid's pen grew fat on them, bulged, spat them out. A murderer's eyes wept fear, begged forgiveness, shone with remorse. Old men's hands reached from faraway places, tried to touch, couldn't. Lost children stared without understanding. The things people did to one another. Where was the *good*? Not in the pages of any newspaper. Good news was no news. But why not once, just *once*, a special edition? . . . SOME NICE, SOME LOVELY THINGS THAT HAPPENED TODAY. Two cents a copy. Would anyone buy? Would anyone care to read about a few warm, quietly pleasant moments in the course of a decent citizen's day? Never. The edition would die, untouched, on the stands, while hungry hands grabbed for their daily diet of calamity.

But no calamity at Molly's. Here, a warm, dependable haven, a

The Artist

refuge from the world, where you could be sure of being admired when you weren't admirable, praised when you were not praiseworthy, loved when you were less than lovable. And Duvid, from his first night, was positively adored. An instant hero. Molly herself set the mood. "A *Jewish* artist! And *gevalt!* Look at the size!" Evidently a man's size, to Jewish whores, was very important. They exclaimed over his hands, touched his arms and shoulders, marveled at his chest. The Jewish male was never especially large. He may have been noted for his intelligence, sensitivity, passion, and culture, but never for his great physical stature. So that to find this towering, larger-than-life *landsleit* suddenly in their midst, to see him standing there tall as a tree, his scrubbed, twenty-three-year-old-face aglow with a mixture of embarrassment and pleasure, was as if an ancient Maccabee warrior-hero had been resurrected for their delight. They fussed over him, vied for his attention, sought his favor. But Molly had decided. "Leave him alone," she said. "He's for Annie."

Who was Annie?

Molly took him upstairs, led him to an empty room, told him to wait. Then . . . Annie. Her black eyes rose from the surface of her cheeks in the same way her breasts rose from the surface of her body. She had a small mouth that she kept open slightly, partway between a smile and the beginning of speech. "Allo. My name is Annie. Ve bathe now." It was a recitation, heavily accented, learned by rote. She unbuttoned Duvid's shirt, took off his clothes, and when she had him settled in the swirling perfumed water of the tub, she got in behind him singing what sounded to Duvid like a Yiddish nursery rhyme. Such dainty, tremulous lips. A child's. But later, abed, no child's. Everything about her was dainty, delicate, her flesh a golden cream. Touched, it kept the imprint, unwilling to let go. Her joy was in *his* joy . . . the dedication, total. Even her eyes, that last refuge of besieged truths, could look at him with only rapture. The perfect whore, she transformed a cold cash bargain into a salient act of love.

Annie was his. Never mind who or how many came in between. Once with her, his chest was an empty cage from which all the dark birds had flown. He felt free, light. Enchanted by the idea of his being an artist, she begged him to draw for her. What? Anything.

A lamp, a chair, the bed. Ah, that bed. Pure delight. A child's version of magic. "Draw *me*," she said and he drew her. "Now you. *Both* of us." How? She showed him. "Making love." Grinning, he did as she asked. "More," she begged, giggling, and he drew more until she had a whole series of the two of them, a graphic symposium on the art of love, Western-style. Wanton. Obscene. And Duvid thought . . . is this really *me*, here, doing these things? Is this really possible? Have all the days of my years, all the passions, hopes, and traditions of my life finally brought me to drawing dirty pictures in the rumpled bed of a whore? As if anyone cared what he was doing here. As if it affected the fate of the world in any way. Must there always be a high moral purpose to everything he did? For once, couldn't he just let go and *enjoy* himself? He tried.

With it all, there was an innocence to it. Often, in the slow morning hours, he would listen to Annie talk. She was a dedicated reader of the *bintel briefs,* the letters to the editor carried by the *Jewish Daily Forward,* and would offer him grave, detailed recitals of the latest list of tragedies. A young boy had died of consumption working in a sweatshop and the bereaved mother wanted to know why. A servant girl was abused by a cruel employer and was too terrified to leave. A heartbroken father had banished his daughter and chanted the prayer for the dead because she had married a Christian. An endless chain of catastrophe, and Annie would weep and cluck over each link, breathless, her small, soft body overwhelmed by the world's pain. Or taking off Duvid's miserable shoes, scrubbing him, toweling his body pink after the bath, she would describe the things that happened to her on her outings from the Washington Square house. She had seen a three-legged dog frighten a horse and make him gallop onto the sidewalk. An old beggar had pleaded for the copy of *Der Forverts* she was carrying, only the Yiddish paper, nothing more. A Negro had exposed himself in an alley. "Ooooh, Duvid! *Sehr shvartz.* So black! I didn't like. Not pretty." Duvid laughed. "To a Negro girl, it's pretty." She searched endlessly for bargains among the East Side pushcarts and proudly displayed her purchases. "Dis hat. How much you think I pay for dis hat?" Duvid made a great show of studying it. "You paid at least five dollars." She beamed. *"Nein, nein,* Duvid! I pay sevenny-fi' cents." Duvid

The Artist

shook his head in wonder. "You must be the greatest bargain hunter in all of America." She laughed and winked broadly. "Yah. I make some lucky Jew vunderful vife."

It was on her mind. Her five years were almost up. Very soon, Molly would carry out her end of the contract and arrange her marriage. Her hope chest was full, overflowing, a sweetly scented collection of satin-and-lace dreams. Once, she spent two hours taking everything out and showing it to Duvid. "Beautiful. I've never seen so many pretty things," he said, and thought, there has to be a distant garden somewhere, a place where mysterious, exotic objects grow . . . and there, in a lovely, pink haze, the heart of Annie Malruvitch hangs like a soft, clean peach.

"You vant marry me, Duvid?"

He laughed. "I'm having trouble enough paying for you once a week, Annie."

"You marry me, you have me every day and no have to pay nothing no more. You get plenny money too." She dug into her hope chest, took out a bankbook and showed it to him. "Look."

She had eighty-two hundred dollars in the bank. More than *he* had earned in the past four years. Clearly, fucking paid better than painting. Yet he was touched. She had made the offer lightly, jokingly, but he knew she meant it. And she would ask little enough from him, no great sacrifices. Only the granting of his name to transform her into a married lady, one of these wondrous, mythical creatures who peopled the dreams of whores and dwelt forever in an aura of sheltered love. He had no doubt that she would be a good wife. Weren't reformed whores *always* supposed to make the best wives? Although he had never actually known any. Still, the thought of Annie tending to him in perpetuity did offer moments of pleasant fantasy. Her English might be poor and often funny, but it was innocent. She told him no such broken truths and dirty lies as he had heard from those who handled the language better. And in her area of particular interest, her perceptions ran subtle and deep. He had never mentioned Rachel, but she had her own ways of measuring such things.

"Ah, Duvidal." She kissed the palms of his hands as they sat on the bed. Her eyes were tender, shrewd, and showed a thrifty light at times. She knew where to invest her sensuality to make his grow. "Maybe soon you vill tell me 'bout her."

"Tell you about who?"

"Who it vos sent you here to me." She smiled, a subtle showing of small, even teeth. "You think I not know? I know. Vun like you . . . big, young, nice . . . some girl alvays send. They give *klop im kup, macht* headache, then you come here to *macht* better. Vy else you pay money? You not have to pay. Plenty girls happy to make fuck with you for nothing."

Duvid grinned at her pidgin obscenity.

"Vy you smile?"

"I love the way you say, make fuck with you."

"You not love vay I *do?*"

"That too." He reached for her.

"Langsam und zeuss, Duvidal." Slow and sweet. And she turned up her eyes so that he saw only the whites.

She understood, all right. There was no standing up to the logic of whores, anyway. All the arguments were on their side. A nice, clean business arrangement, no emotional clutching, no frustration, no hurt. Just expert, professional talent when and where you needed it. Hutchins's principle. *Know your cost in advance.* He had failed to know it just once, and after four years was still making small, irregular payments. Each time he saw Rachel's name in the paper, each time he watched her in another play (would he dare miss *one?*), he paid a bit more. And when he happened to meet one of her parents, when he actually had occasion to hear them speak of her, he paid double.

Yet it was no accident when he ran into the Rabinowitzes. He knew the Canal Street cafés where the poet sipped tea sober, the bars where he could be found drunk. And between hospital confinements, Mrs. Rabinowitz shopped the same Orchard Street pushcarts month after month without change of schedule. No accident when Rabinowitz clutched his shirt to pull him close, thrust his odors into his face, and mourned the anguish of his life. No accident when his wife, scarred wrists flashing in the sun, pecked at Duvid with tortured eyes and denounced her daughter as bitterly in success as she had once denounced her in failure. No accident, this sharing of

The Artist

remembered pain. *"Yemach sh'mo,"* intoned the benighted mother, condemning not only her daughter, but any and all with whom she might convene. "Let their names be blotted out." And what did Duvid say? *Amen?* Not that it mattered what he said. *Their* need was to talk, *his* to listen.

Raw turpentine poured on the heart, the nerves. Better that his ailing parts recapture their health in a whorehouse. Pain and tension required sexual relief. Whatever your age, background, condition, knowledge, culture, or lack of it, you somehow had an erection. Molly's place was really a hospital, the girls were nurses, and his own Annie, a learned doctor-professor. Then reading Nietzsche, Duvid found the claim that semen reabsorbed was the great fuel of creativity. Of course Nietzsche was German, so allowances had to be made. But better to be careful anyway, better to keep a little something in reserve for your work. Teutonic practicality . . . a brush dipped in semen instead of linseed oil.

And now, four years of reabsorbed-semen-inspired creativity spaced over the public rooms of a whorehouse. Assembling the pieces one by one, seeing them hanging there together, Duvid felt a sense of indecent exposure. Whatever he was, whatever he may have learned, was there to be seen. And what he *hadn't* learned? That too. His personal statement. Assets and liabilities. He took silent inventory, but could find no clear marks separating good from bad. And in the realm of time, there seemed neither beginning nor end. It was all one. A little frightening. Yet certain truths remained at all levels of learning, and these he was able to see, to pick out, to list and store away. And what were they? That the wrinkles in a child's dress were full of the history of the day, spoiling the dress, but making the dress part of the child. That you had to feel the dignity of your model, not feel superior to him, because you weren't. That it was better to look at one wonderful face than the Grand Canyon. That a sense of the wonder of life was more important to a painting than the whole complicated business of making a picture. That there was no such thing as color for color's sake, that colors were beautiful only because of what they meant to us, and that the red in a young girl's cheek was lovely because it was bursting with youth, health, and the promise of life to come.

The Artist

Just a small part of the list and maybe more an accidental stumbling upon than a conscious learning; but a learning nonetheless. And all managed alone. (A pride in that?) Although for a while now, he had accepted a certain amount of help from the preserved dead hanging in the Metropolitan Museum of Art. He had taken to spending long hours feeding upon them, siphoning off whatever good he could find there. It was new for him, this business of learning and taking pleasure from the past, from what other artists had felt and done. He stood before a sketch by Rembrandt and saw him at work and in trouble and met him there. Courbet showed in every work what a man he was, what a head and heart he had. Daumier's pen and brush said, "If you want to know about people watch their gestures. The tongue is a greater liar than the body. Your enemy is never thinking of the skin on the back of his neck. Watch it. A woman may not say a word for an hour, but her body has been speaking all the time." Everybody Velasquez painted had dignity . . . from a clown to a king. In the Infanta Margarita he tied together the look of a child with that of a queen. He was a man in love with humanity, who could show equal feeling for a nobleman, a beggar, or a dwarf. What majesty in Titian. Hogarth's head of a fish girl was like a strong wind blowing in from the sea. Winslow Homer could paint more pure integrity into an oncoming wave than most artists could squeeze into a life-size portrait of the pope. Whistler's sensitivity affected every touch of his brush, from the soft silence of velvet, through air, to the screaming passion of the flesh.

And all those others.

What a brotherhood he was part of! They were of all places and of all times. And you were a member to the degree that you were able to be a member . . . no more, no less. You took what was there and gave whatever you could, added your own findings. You found moments in your day, moments in your life when you could only stare, stupid with wonder at what you saw, knowing that what you saw was far beyond the usual. These were the moments to remember, to nail to a piece of canvas, to save for all time. Another signpost on the way to what might be. Another moment in which you might paint, if you were lucky, as though you were going over the top of a hill, singing.

The Artist

Ah, what a feeling. Enough to carry you over the low places, over those gray hollows in which you saw very clearly what you were and what you had done so far and what, if you were going to be realistic, you were likely to do in the future. The feeling was no luxury, reserved for idle moments. It was bread and water. You survived on it. Without it you would swear what you were doing was pure idiocy, no way for any self-respecting Jew to go through life. No comfort either, at such moments, in even the brotherhood. All artists, past and present, were suddenly alien to him. Not a Jew in the crowd. How could they have known what he was feeling now? Always an extra cause for doubt in his Jewishness, in his lack of artistic heritage and tradition. A race of moneylenders, peddlers, students of the Talmud. Was it really possible for an artist to spring, full-blown, from such a crowd? *Chutzpah!* Did he think he had suddenly been touched by the finger of God? Traveled often enough, the circle of doubt became a rutted path. Leading where? To a showing of paintings and drawings in a Yid whorehouse on Washington Square. *Where else?*

That was it, of course. You became desperate enough and you were willing to try anything. So you established an attitude. You made a wryly amusing thing of it, a study in irony. Mockingly, you even sent an invitation to Anthony Flemming, the single most prestigious art critic in the city of New York, knowing he wouldn't come, but sending it anyway because it seemed a logical part of the game. Then to top it all off, to show how utterly scornful of everything and everyone it was, to demonstrate to yourself and anyone else who cared to notice how lightly you were taking the whole crazy affair, you sent out a final invitation . . . and this to a girl you had buried deep and dark more than four years ago.

A significant moment in the history of human relations. Because her home address seemed to be unlisted, he mailed the invitation care of the theater where her current play was running. He had toyed for a while with the idea of a handwritten postscript, a few elegantly sardonic words to demonstrate his attitude toward the exhibition and his reason for asking her. But nothing sounded right and he finally just sent the engraved invitation as it was. No comment. Let her wonder. Let her think about it. Why should he wonder

The Artist

alone? All right. It was something to wonder about. Why now, after four years, was he suddenly rescinding the prayer for the dead he had recited over her grave and digging her up? And why on such an occasion and in such a place? Or was he just grotesque, a reasonless fool? No. It was more than that. He was after something. What? Some vague form of poetic justice? *Whore . . . come see my art in this whorehouse to which you have driven me?* Justice on this earth must surely originate within each heart. *Justice?* Look who wanted justice! Most of mankind had lived and died totally without it. People by the uncounted billions and for ages past had been gypped, enslaved, tortured, bled, buried, with no more justice than animals. But Duvid Karlinsky, at the top of his voice, screaming with remembered hurt and ancient pride, had to have his allotment of justice.

Never mind. It was his right as the offended, the innocent party, his right for all he had suffered. Ah, his suffering. Naturally. Always at the true core of Hebrew belief. What was a Jew without suffering? So now his suffering had grown so great and deep, his anger so murderous, bloody, positively rapturous, that he couldn't wait to confront its cause, and had, in fact, created this entire elaborate fiction for the express purpose of getting her here and reminding her (in case she had somehow managed to forget) of exactly how much he hated her.

Good God! Would he never be able to face the truth? He had sent her the invitation for just one reason, and one reason alone. *He wanted to see her!* There! How simple. Was that really so hard to admit? And if it was, why should it be? He wanted to see her, to speak with her, to find out what, if anything, would happen when they were in the same room together. Four years was a long time. He had changed, had learned things. So, undoubtedly, had she. They might meet as strangers. If they did, he wanted to know that too. He had housed her memory long enough. He was tired of his purged body adrift in the night, tossing with dreams of her.

He turned his head to kiss her lips and she was gone. But she had wakened him. It was her presence. And through this opening in her grave a thousand details were set free . . . pale strands of hair, small twists of expression, the ways of her voice in different moods. He saw her merged with the moonlight on his bed, the features of

214

face and body, her slightly prominent teeth, the long line of her thighs, the curved smoothness of her bottom, that full, soft, lower lip. Moments returned when they had been together, the dip of waist under his hand, her two angels of arms, the soft sliding within her, the small cries as she went off. Deep glimpses into her eyes came back to hurt him. He had deadened himself against certain feelings and did not want her to call them out. He was not ready. He had taken punishment. Let the Cragans, the impressarios, the important and powerful of the world have her. His turn had come and gone. She was touching him again as he lay dreaming in that once-familiar amber light between the anonymous walls. He very gently brought up his hand to smooth her hair. Waking to find his hand reaching for nothing, he cried in the darkness. An old grief rose out of an aching chest. Remembering her hurt when he had sent her off in the streets, the poor singed eyes and ripped blouse, he blinded himself, left stains on the pillow. The stains would be gone by morning. No sign would remain. Yet she had been there.

The whole thing, thought Duvid, was like a carefully rehearsed entertainment put on by some of the better controlled inmates of a local asylum. He expected all hell to break loose any minute. The distinguished gray-haired gentleman in impeccable evening clothes, gravely studying the brushwork of a sunlit street scene, would suddenly start screaming hysterically and have to be led away. The little, plump woman sipping champagne in a corner would finish her drink, then begin chewing up the glass. The small group of men in the entrance foyer, quietly discussing the relative merits of a pair of character studies, would, at a given signal, stop talking and explode into a bloody free-for-all. And Molly's loveliest girls, looking unapproachably regal in shimmering décolletage, would abruptly strip themselves naked and dash about shouting dirty songs and clutching at men's privates. While he, Duvid Karlinsky, would crawl under a table and stay there, sucking his thumb and weeping and absolutely refusing to ever appear among people again.

Yet stiffly elegant in his rented dinner clothes, he moved among the guests in the brilliantly lighted exhibition rooms and wondered if perhaps *he* wasn't the only crazy one in the crowd. It was all too much. Too many subtleties of Western culture were beyond his limited understanding. Rooted in the rigid doctrines of the Old Testament, the idea of the continual improvement of human life on earth, he felt himself lost in the dazzle and glitter, in the consummate ridiculousness of his present position. *Lord, I ran to enlist in Thy holy and uplifting cause, but I kept tripping on the way and never quite reached the scene of the battle.* But never mind his personal responsibility for mankind's generally sorry state. He had is own problems to deal with first. Then maybe he could figure out what to do about the rest of the world.

In the meantime, he played out his required role as best he could, acknowledging introductions with a small bow and speaking with a nervous solemnity that reduced his voice to a strange animal sound he was utterly unable to recognize. Earlier, he had found it equally impossible to recognize the dressed-up store dummy staring back at him from the mirror. Wax and papier-maché. Even now, he carried his head as though he had rented it for the evening along with his clothes. Yet why the nervousness? Wasn't it all supposed to be a big joke? . . . a fine bit of irony? No one could really take art in a whorehouse seriously. Maybe not. But somehow he didn't feel the least bit like laughing. And much of it had to do with Molly.

Earlier, she had gathered Duvid and the girls together in the main reception room. "I want to say a couple of things." Resplendent in white satin, she stood beneath a crystal chandelier, surrounded by four walls of Karlinsky paintings and drawings. "In case some of you still aren't sure, I want you to know exactly how I feel about tonight . . . since this is all a little outside my regular line of business."

A few of the girls giggled and Molly waited for them to quiet. "Mostly, I feel it isn't funny. I know a lot of you think it's a big laugh. And I guess even Duvid does. But I don't. I think it's just the opposite. I think it's sad. I think it's sad enough to cry about. And if you can't see it, if you can't understand why, then something's got to be wrong with you."

The Artist

She paused, swung about, and embraced the roomful of art with the perfumed flesh of both arms. "Look! Open your eyes and *look!* You don't have to know anything about art to know what we got hanging here. Nothing has to be explained. You just have to *look!*"

They looked . . . the six Jewish whores and the Jewish artist. "What do you see?"

The girls looked to Duvid for some clue. Annie, sitting beside him on a green brocade settee, plucked at his sleeve for the answer. Surely the artist himself should know. But Duvid, baffled himself, said nothing.

"What do you see?"

Hesitantly, one of the girls ventured, "Pictures?"

"Dumbkup!" Molly's eyes blazed, nailed the girl to her chair. "I'll tell you what you see. You see *verschlepte* Jews!" Then mockingly addressing the whole of her exquisitely groomed retinue, "And in case some of you high-class whores forgot what *verschlepte* Jews are, they're those poor *schlimazels* who have to make claw marks on cement just to stay alive. They're those miserable *meshuggeners* who eat a pound of dirt a day, belch up sour, and call it *halvah*. And they're what you'd all be right now if I hadn't given you a bath, bought you clean underwear, and taught you to play men's *tsatskes* like harmonicas."

Duvid marveled at her, wondered at this tall, handsome woman giving off her mixed aroma of sweet and sour, revealing her dazzle of half pure diamond and half cheap glass. What a unique and moving force she was. And they were not strangers. He knew her. Incredible things had taken place between them. For Duvid, the courtesy of the house had been personally extended. Noblesse oblige. The queen mother actually offering herself. A strange feeling at first, like bedding down with an institution. Although she claimed to be no more than thirty-four and offered a repertoire of sensuality worthy of inclusion in scientific journals. *Ah, Molly. You gave me the best of your precious inventory and at less than wholesale, less even than cost.* And what had she asked in return? Only a few drops of his abundant seed and, she hoped, his child. Exactly that. *His child!* Duvid Karlinsky, at stud! And she was serious, had thought it all through. Consider. What possible harm to *him?* No one need ever know, he would bear no responsibility, and the child would be

217

raised clean. She had no need of a husband, just a child. Asked why, she showed a curious reticence, even a shyness. An emptiness was there, it needed filling. She was still a woman. Yes. But why him? What was so special about *him?* The answer came in three parts. He was big, he was Jewish, he was artistic. To Molly, all rare qualities. In combination, special. Go argue it. So she had a weakness for larger-than-life Yid artists. It wasn't so terrible. There were worse things a woman could want. It was all academic anyway. Nothing ever happened. Even his knowledge of what she wanted came after the fact. She told him only when the project had clearly failed. Would she have told him if he *had* taken root? Probably not. *What harm, Duvid?* He didn't know what harm. Maybe none. Yet he found it an oddly chilling thought. Good God! He might have had a son or daughter walking about. And unknowingly. The frightening thing was, how really little you had to do with the whole thing. An instant's pleasure, a random tossing of seed, and you earned that most holy of titles . . . father!

"Our own, our *eygene,*" Molly was declaring, her voice heavy with emotion. She peered at Duvid's Jews over enough bosom to power a sloop in a fair breeze. "Painted with such a full *Yiddishe* heart. And what happens to them? Shut out! All doors closed. No place for them to go. Only here are they welcome. And *this* is what's so sad. This is what's not funny. An artist should paint his heart out and no one should even *look?* A sin against God. But also a lesson. We should learn it. We should remember the world is ninety-nine parts *goyim* and only one part *Juden.* And the ninety-nine parts hate us all the way. Alive, dead, or in pictures, they spit on us. And don't you ever forget it. Not even when they're inside you and crying, my lovely, my darling, don't you forget it. Because the minute they fall out soft, you're no more lovely, no more darling. You're just a dirty, sheeny whore again."

A fierce, green, milky poison rose to her eyes. Her mouth twisted. "Ah, how I know them with their little picknose ways . . . they and those dried-up prunes they marry, those tight-assed *shiksas* hiding under their sheets for forty years with the lights out. I swear to God! They deserve each other!"

Molly's Holy War, thought Duvid, standing now in his rented

The Artist

suit. She had somehow managed to turn his paintings into a personal rebellion against the world's gentiles. Well, that was *her soft spot*. But whatever her reasons, she had managed to squeeze away most of his carefully contrived irony. *It wasn't funny.* And she was actually making sales. She had already collected for nine paintings and four drawings. Christ only knew what sort of selling tactics she and the girls were using, but there was no arguing with the results. Five hundred and fifty dollars so far. *Cash.* No checks. Her instructions were very specific on that point. Minds could be changed in the daylight. She believed in a strictly cash-and-carry business.

Anthony Flemming, senior critic of the *American Art Review*, arrived at precisely 8:30. Duvid thought at first the champagne must be affecting his eyes. Yet there was no mistaking that gaunt, craggy, monk's face. How well he knew it. All those newspaper and magazine pictures. He found Molly and excitedly grabbed her arm. "My God! He's here!"

"Who?"

"Flemming!"

"Oh, The art big shot you invited. Sure he's here."

"What do you mean, sure he's here? You *knew* he was coming?"

"Of course I knew."

"How?"

"A little rabbi told me." Her smile was positively beatific. "You want to know what else I know? I also know your Momma and Poppa are coming. I sent Arnold to bring them with the carriage. You should be ashamed you forgot to invite them."

He could only stare at her.

"What's the matter?" she said. "They can't have a little pleasure from their son on such a night?"

"You didn't!"

"Duvid!" Her eyes fluttered in mock reproach. "You're ashamed of me. You're ashamed of the girls, of all your good friends."

"Jesus Christ, Molly!"

"Don't worry, *tateleh.* They'll love us. And they'll be proud of *you.*"

They did. They came into that house on Washington Square and were held enraptured. *Aiyeee!* The heights to which their son had

219

The Artist

risen! Molly had explanations for everything. Duvid, she claimed, had deliberately kept it as a surprise for them. She herself? A devoted friend, a patroness of the arts, an obviously well-left widow. Alas, no children of her own. Rifka Karlinsky clucked sympathetically. A shame. Such a house. Such a beautiful woman. Still, she was young. The men would be around like flies. Molly's smile was so sadly wistful, Duvid didn't know where to look. The girls, introduced one by one, were her nieces. Lovely! Such beauties! Avrum Karlinsky, distinguished in his dinner clothes, patted Annie's cheek with his great artisan's hand, beamed approvingly, sipped his champagne. Alone with his son, he discussed the business end, whistled softly at news of the sales, marveled at the size and quality of the crowd. Duvid gripped his father's arm and felt warmth and pride burn through the fabric of his sleeve. While across the room there was his mother, all primped and aglow, getting cozy with Annie. A Karlinsky family triumph rising out of Molly Adelman's miracles. Duvid breathed deeply. If he was destined to be witness to miracles this night, he might as well relax and enjoy it. Belief couldn't always be based on reason. All right, Molly. I believe, I believe. *If you don't try, you don't know.*

Not without pride, he pointed out one of the evening's more exceptional miracles. "That's Anthony Flemming," he told his father. "Critic for the *American Art Review.*"

Avrum was unimpressed. "That skinny little *goy?* He looks like a real *nebechel.*"

"He's not such a *nebechel* in the art world."

"An important man?"

"Thousands of people read what he writes."

Avrum nodded slowly, consideringly. "So how is it such an important person gets all dressed up and comes to a Yiddish whorehouse on a Sunday night?"

Duvid looked at his father.

Avrum's face showed nothing. "What, Duvidal? You think maybe I'm not old enough yet to know about such things?"

"How did you know?"

"Don't worry. A customer, I'm not." A grin creased the sloping, Tatar eyes. "I got trouble enough lately to keep up the business at home. I got nothing to contract out."

The Artist

"One of the girls said something?"

Avrum shook his head. "Dolls. Perfect ladies every one. Come. I'll show you." He led Duvid to a polished walnut cabinet in the entrance foyer, tapped it, ran loving fingers over its surface. "There! You're out of the shop so long you don't know our work no more?"

Of course. A. KARLINSKY AND SON***FINE WOOD FURNITURE. And he had been the son. Departed now for artistic greatness in the fleshpots of Sodom. His father was smiling. See? . . . said the smile. We're partners again. We share, we show together even here. Never far apart, the work of these four Karlinsky hands. The story? No great mystery. The piece had simply been sold and delivered by one of the men in the shop . . . Yudel Epstein, it was. That was some Yudel, all excited, he came rushing back. Where was a Karlinsky cabinet sitting? They'd never guess. In a high-class whorehouse on Washington Square. They had laughed for weeks. A fine setting for a Karlinsky gem. *And there it was!*

Avrum's bulging shoulders shook. "Duvidal, when I came in before . . . when I saw it, I was only afraid Momma shouldn't look at my face and know something."

"Momma doesn't know?"

Avrum stared at his son. "You crazy? Right now she's busy making a *match* for you with one of the nieces. That little Annie, I think it is."

At least she'd picked the right one. Great. Next Friday night he'd walk in and find Annie in his mother's kitchen for dinner.

Molly pulled him away for further introductions. The celebrity. *His* night. More people to be met, more hands to be shaken, more words to be growled. Mostly gentiles, but fine types, all very polite. And among them, incredibly, Anthony Flemming. Duvid had to keep reminding himself none of it was real. This was *not* an art gallery, these people were *not* art patrons, and although the famed critic himself was genuine enough, he was surely *not* here because of any interest in his work. Then why *was* he here? What magic wand had Molly waved to bring about *this* particular miracle? It was time to know.

"All right." He had finally managed to follow and catch Molly alone upstairs. "How did you get Flemming here?"

221

"What's the difference? You invited him, you wanted him here, and you've got him."

"Molly, I want to know."

"You sure?"

"Yes."

"You won't like it."

"Molly, for Christ's sake! I'm a big boy now."

She shrugged. "I guess you got a right." She took an envelope from her purse and handed it to him. "I sent him one of these."

Duvid opened the envelope and removed a photograph. It was a snapshot of two men engaged in a homosexual act. Looking closely, Duvid recognized one of the men as Anthony Flemming. His hands had a hard time getting the picture back into the envelope.

"What else did you do?"

"I called and said I wanted him here tonight and that I also wanted him to write nice things about your work in his magazine. If he was a good little *fageleh* and did as he was told, he'd get the pictures and negatives and no one would ever know about it."

"And if he didn't do as he was told?"

"Then I'd send copies to every dirt peddler in the city." Looking at him, Molly's eyes softened. "I told you you wouldn't like it."

Duvid said in a whisper, "How did you know about him?"

"I didn't know. I just had someone watch and check into him for a few days." She smiled without looking amused. "Duvid, everybody's got something. *Everybody.* It hits you fast in my business. It's all in how deep you want to dig."

He stood there, the envelope still fluttering in his hand. The mind had a way of putting up fences. It took him a minute to get around them. Then he said, "Here's what I want you to do. I want you to go over to Flemming right now and tell him it was all a mistake. Tell him to forget everything you said. Tell him he can have the pictures and negative and not to worry about anyone finding out from you."

"No."

"What do you mean no?"

"I mean, no I won't tell him a goddamn thing, and no I won't

222

give him the pictures and negative." She shook her head impatiently. "You said you were a big boy, Duvid. Well, *Gott in himmel!* Start acting like one. How did you *think* I got him here? What did you *think* suddenly made this high-class, art-big shot come to a whorehouse to look at the pictures of a *schmeerer* he never even heard of?"

Molly's miracles. "I wondered."

"You wondered! And did you also wonder why the rest of this hoity-toity crowd is here?"

Duvid had no answer.

"I'll tell you why. They're here because *I* invited them. *Me.* Molly Adelman. And they didn't come because they love me. They came because they're *afraid* of me. I know about them. I know all their smelly little *yiches.* For love, people do for themselves. Make them afraid and they do for *you.*"

"Bullshit! It's dirty and it stinks. I don't need anything that bad. I won't be turned into one of your . . ."

"Whores?" Gently, she finished it for him. "Finally, it always comes to that, doesn't it? But don't worry, *tateleh.* It don't bother me. You think I don't know what I am? I know. And that's what puts me ahead of you and everyone else. Because you're all whores too, only you *don't* know. Or if you do, you make up prettier names for it. It might take different things to spread different legs, but that's just a question of price. That don't change the rest of it."

"I want the pictures and negative, Molly."

"What are you so worried about? A *fageleh* art critic? They're the worst bastards of all, these big shots. They got you and every other artist by the balls and they sing hymns while they squeeze. Well, it's your turn to do a little squeezing. And since you're too much of a *schnook* to do it for yourself, I've got to do it for you."

"Molly," he said tiredly, "you can't operate that way. Apart from the dirt and everything else, it just won't work. You don't understand the art business."

"I understand more than you think. When I got interested in you, I also got interested in this whole fancy art business. Some business! I found out things. I found out it's crazy. But mostly, I found out it's the artist who gets it in the *kishkas.* All his life he paints and starves, then watches from his grave how others, the smart ones, get rich from his work. And what suddenly makes his pictures worth fortunes when they worth *bubkes* before? I'll tell you. The styles get changed. *The styles!* Just like the dress business. No different. And who makes the styles? The experts, the *fagelehs*, the Flemmings. Why?" Molly shrugged. "Who knows why. Maybe they got their *tsatskes* tickled a special way the night before. Maybe a brother-in-law cornered the market in hot pinks. Maybe they made a deal with some *macher* who bought up job lots cheap. It could be a hundred reasons and one makes as much sense as the other. And the people who buy? Sheep. They know nothing. Less than me. I at least know what I like. *They're* afraid to like unless the experts tell them. And God forbid they should like the wrong thing. What *one* buys, they *all* buy. And when our own personal *fageleh* writes in his important magazine about Duvid Karlinsky, the sheep'll come running to you with money in their teeth."

Molly held Duvid with her eyes, smiled, kissed him lightly. "You worry too much, *tateleh*. The Lord Himself sent us our own good fairy. It would be a sin we shouldn't use him."

She left to return to her guests. Duvid felt subdued, shaken, without control. What could he do? *Beat* her into calling it off? Yet she had been right about one thing. When he agreed to the exhibition itself, when he put himself and his work in her hands, he should have known what was possible. Maybe he *had* known. A good system. Let Molly do the dirty work, while *he* carefully kept his eyes averted and stayed clean. Had he really gotten to the point where he needed *her* to show him the facts of life?

He found the critic putting on his coat in the vestibule. "Can I speak with you a minute, Mr. Flemming?"

"*Speak* with me?" Flemming smiled wryly, a short, slight man with eyes wreathed in the twisting hairs of shaggy brows. "At this point, Karlinsky, I fear you can do just about anything you want with me."

Duvid led him to an empty room and closed the door. "I didn't know about it," he said. "Not a thing. Molly just told me a few minutes ago."

Flemming lit a cigar with great care, looked at Duvid, said nothing.

"I'm sorry," Duvid said.

"About what?"

"About the whole dirty thing."

Flemming looked mildly surprised. "Does that mean you're giving me the pictures and negative?"

"I'm afraid Molly has them."

"I see. And I take it Miss Adelman doesn't quite share your own high-minded view of the matter."

"No."

Flemming showed small, regular teeth as though about to smile. But he didn't. "Then what have you come to offer me, Karlinsky? Your sympathy? Or is it absolution you're seeking? Is *that* it? The hangman needing to be forgiven by his soon-to-be victim?"

"Don't you believe me?"

Flemming drew deeply on an expensive cigar, blew smoke, and studied it. A man is born to be orphaned, to struggle and know pain, and to leave orphans after him, but a cigar like that cigar, if he can afford it, is a great comfort. "I neither believe nor disbelieve you, Karlinsky. It doesn't really matter to me whether you did or didn't have anything to do with putting this rope around my neck. All I care about right now is whether you can get it off." He paused. *"Can you?"*

Duvid shook his head.

"No. Of course not. How easy to be generous when you've nothing to give. Now why don't we stop playing games and get down to what you *really* want to know . . . what I'm going to write about your work."

Staring at the critic's drawn, illusionless face, Duvid swung between pity and annoyance. There was surely enough to feel sorry for in an aging homosexual threatened with exposure, with loss of dignity, of reputation, of everything he had worked a lifetime to achieve. Yet the man had an arrogance about him, an air of mocking superiority that seemed to defy compassion. Even his voice . . . cold, high-pitched, thoroughly drilled in its affectations, loftily held itself above sympathy.

"Or perhaps," Flemming went on, "it's my *true* opinion of your art you want. Perhaps you're wondering whether you're really worth anything as a painter, or whether you'd be better off sticking with the usury and peddling of your kike ancestors? Is *that* what you want to hear?"

Gratefully, Duvid swung all the way to anger. How much easier and simpler. Then he tried to guess the secret of this cold, deliberate belligerence. What view of things was this trapped fairy advancing? He seemed to be trying to give him punch for punch. With his baiting, with his insulting fantasy, he defied a worse reality. *Your blackmailing and my degeneracy are one and the same.* It must be something like that. Molly had declared that everyone was a whore. Of course he, Duvid Karlinsky, hadn't spread his legs literally, yet in one way or another he had done or didn't do whatever was necessary to get himself into this position. Still, he had come to this man apologetically, without accusation or malice. Flemming was the one who seemed to claim spiritual superiority. Did he really believe fellatio to be a better path to truth and honor than Judaism?

"You can keep your opinions, Flemming. I don't give a damn about them. I just wanted you to know I had no part in this."

He started for the door, but the art critic stopped him with a wiry hand. "Don't be childish. Of course you give a damn about my opinions. And well you should . . . as an artist. It was why you sent me an invitation in the first place." He looked at Duvid with pale, round eyes, smiled with a curiously empty cheerfulness. "I apologize for that stupid slur on your ancestry. And it *was* stupid. Because I happen to have a profound respect for the Jews, for their traditions and their history. And I have always been moved by the injustices they have suffered. So you see how low fear can drive a man. Oh, I'm afraid, all right. I'm scared to death. I have a lot to lose. Everything. Which is why I'm going to have to give you and Miss Adelman exactly what you want . . . the kind of review that should have the best galleries in town howling for your work."

Duvid grimaced. "The best and worst have been turning me down for four years. Every one. I never had a prayer."

"You'll find reviews a lot more effective than prayers. It's the coin of the realm in this business. I must admit it, Karlinsky. Critics function in an enormous cloud of snob appeal. Without it, we'd be nothing. We might not quite enjoy the divine rights of kings, but we do come close." Flemming blew smoke. "Thank God!"

The Artist

He laughed, the sound starting deep in his throat and rising with the cigar smoke. "As a matter of fact you should prove an excellent case in point. I've always contended that most so-called art lovers were without true taste of their own, that if I wished, I could feed them excrement and make them swear it was chocolate cream pie. Now you've given me a chance to actually watch it work."

"Thanks," said Duvid heavily.

"No, no . . ." Flemming patted Duvid's arm. A soothing gesture. Friendly. They were suddenly intimates, co-conspirators. "I didn't mean that as it sounded. I was talking purely of salability. You saw for yourself. What gallery would show your work? None. Your paintings conform to none of the established standards, none of the accepted patterns of subject matter or technique. They are crude. They are rough, unpleasant, bruising. They leap off the walls and grab you by the throat. They shake you until your teeth rattle. Who would want to live with such violence? Yet they have the power to move. They are deeply felt. You are not a polite, gentle, polished painter, Karlinsky, but you *are* a painter. And your people, as I see them on the walls, will not merely endure . . . they will *prevail.*"

That poor, trapped, wonderful fairy. Duvid felt rocked with warmth. A random net tossed and Molly had pulled in a chunk of solid gold.

"Survival . . ." said Flemming. "They know about it, these Jews you paint. They hang on and that is what it is all about. I recognize the look. I have known it intimately most of my life. I have lived with it among wolves. Let the pack see you are different and they will tear you apart." The critic's voice was empty, toneless in the small room, his eyes clouded. "Flemming, the surrogate Jew. No. That is too good, too easy. Flemming, the *leper.* Worse. A secret one. Not even part of a colony. To feel despised is bad enough. To feel *alone* and despised can be too much." He peered long and consideringly at Duvid. "I will tell you something, Karlinsky. If I hadn't been so enterprisingly blackmailed into coming here tonight, I would never have seen your paintings. That is for certain. But having once seen them, there was really no need for further blackmail. With or without it, I would have felt moved by what I saw. And any review I wrote would have had to reflect that feeling."

227

The Artist

The art critic stood studying his cigar. "We are not animals, you know. We are different, but that does not mean we are something vile. Given half a chance, we are really very much like people." He smiled, then turned and left the room.

And Duvid thought, I hope he believed me. I hope he understands it was really Molly and not me. But he saw through himself, saw through to the sharp, practical edge of his compassion. Because how nice that it *had* been Molly.

It was late and he had almost given up all hope of her coming, when he saw her. My God, he thought, and just stood staring. He had forgotten how lovely she was, how delicately made, how finely the flesh was drawn over the bones of her cheeks; as if cut to order by a precise and frugal craftsman. Not a millimeter wasted. Anything extra had gone into the modeling of her lips, which seemed a little tighter than he remembered them, less ready to smile, with perhaps more to lose than before. His instinct, crazy, was to reach out and pet her . . . do something, like touch her hair or the tip of her nose or the soft part of her arm, that you would do to a child. But he did none of these things. All he did was cross the room and say, "Hello, Rachel."

She looked up past the evening clothes, seeking his face. Finding it, her eyes rested there, lightly, ready to fly off if what she saw there frightened her, if his face had saved anything of what she had seen there last. Evidently it was all right because she smiled. "Duvid." She studied him more fully, all of him, missing nothing. "How wonderful you look."

"Don't be fooled. The clothes are rented."

"And the face?"

"That too. The cultured look goes back in the morning with the suit. I'm a complete fake."

They laughed together, but it was a little too eager, a little too loud. The joke was not that funny. Then they just stood looking at one another, awkwardly, the years pressing down. It was she who broke first, her eyes fleeing toward the walls. "I can't wait to see your work. You don't know how I've wondered about you. I kept looking in all the galleries, reading the art announcements."

"I couldn't get into the galleries. Not even as a janitor."

"Well, you got in here. And it's beautiful."

"Sure. But it's not a gallery."

She frowned. "What is it?"

"A whorehouse."

She looked startled, almost frightened. Was he aiming something at *her*? The last thing he had called her was a whore. Duvid saw her struggling with it, but some perversity, perhaps a small, lingering bitterness, kept him from rescuing her.

"Are you serious?"

"Very serious."

But he was smiling as he said it, so that she still could not be sure. She glanced about. Most of the guests, including the Karlinskys, had left, and those that remained offered no clues. Then she saw Annie watching them from the far end of the room, a small, high-breasted girl with a child's mouth and great, black eyes aimed as steadily as a pair of cannon.

"Is *she* one of the girls?"

Duvid knew whom she meant without looking. "Yes."

"Is she *your* girl?"

"Annie's a whore. She is anybody's who pays." True enough. But saying it like that somehow made him feel guilty, as if Annie would have been hurt hearing it. To right himself, he said, "But when I'm here, she's mine."

Rachel's tongue flicked between her lips, a mannerism that had once struck Duvid as deliberately sensual but which he had learned only meant she was puzzled. "I don't understand the whole thing. Why do you have to pay money for a woman?"

"I don't *have* to. It's more like I *want* to." He saw how much it bothered her. Even years later, she took it as a personal affront. Someone once hers degraded also degraded her, lowered *her* value. "It makes everything so much simpler."

"You don't really believe that."

The Artist

"Why else would I be here?"

"To punish *me*. To make *me* feel guilty. I was dirt. A whore. So you had to rub on a little dirt too. You had to show me. Isn't that why you invited me here tonight? I wondered about that. Four years and not a word. Then suddenly, an engraved invitation. *Now* I know."

He laughed. "You. Everything you. Doesn't *any* part of it have to do with me?"

"No. Not here. Not in this place. This is all mine. If it wasn't for me, you would never have walked in here in the first place." She shook her head in continuing wonder. "Someone like you. With all you have. My God! A place like this is for emotional *cripples!*"

And she, he thought, was an emotional queen. The depth of her feeling was her kingdom. She might have held a scepter. She took over every emotion around her as though by divine right. She could do more with them, so she just appropriated them. Aroused, she was majestic. There was no other word for it . . . her eyes so amazingly spirited, rich, or—he had to smile—like the chicken soup of her soul, hot and simmering.

She said, "Why are you smiling?"

"I'd forgotten how you could be."

"How am I?"

"Overwhelming!"

She laughed and took his arm. "Come, Duvid. Enough of this. Whorehouse . . . schmorehouse. Who cares? For God's sake, show me your paintings!"

His work, of course, was *also* hers. Had he forgotten this too? She was responsible for everything. All of it. Had she not pushed him to leave the cocoon . . . leave his father's furniture business . . . leave his parents' home? Who, but she, had given him direction? *You can only see and feel for yourself, from what you are. And what you happen to be, is a Russian-born, pogrom-driven Jew, raised in an East Side ghetto.* She did not have to remind him. His circle of Jews, his tenements, his collection of pushcarts, ghetto streets, sweatshops, all did it for her. What a testimonial! She had *birthed* him! Looking, moving from one painting, one drawing to the next, her face was radiant with creation. Motherhood by proxy. *Momma!* She held his arm through-

230

out, saying nothing, but letting the pressure of her fingers, clench-
ing and unclenching, react for her. Her nails dug through his sleeve,
probed, scraped, pried. Birth pangs. His flesh was hers. Squeeze,
Mommala! Push! Press! It's all yours. Without you, none of it. I'd still
be sanding cabinets at A. KARLINSKY & SON***FINE WOOD FURNITURE.
When the complete round was finished, his arm was sore, her eyes
moist.

"I'm so proud of you, Duvid." Whispered, it might have been a
trumpet.

Proud of *him,* or of herself? What difference? In this, at least,
they were one. But she *was* moved. It came off her in waves. *This*
was what he had needed, what he had missed. With whom else was
it possible? Who else had shared the beginning? She had known
about him, had seen what he wanted long before he had even suspected such things were there to want. Two separate hands had held
his brush. One had been hers.

"I'm glad," he said. "I'm glad you like what I've done."

She shook her head, her hair a pale gold under the lights. "I
don't *like* it. I'm eaten by it, swallowed, sucked deep into it. Whatever I once hoped for you, you've more than doubled. Duvid.
. . ." Light danced across her cheeks, caught the moisture on her
lashes. "Ah, Duvid . . ."

Then looking at her he thought, I must be careful, or I'll make
an absolute ass of myself. But the dream was still there, that confus-
ing and distrusted hope for some sort of completed circle. It
couldn't all be just a series of crazy accidents. There had to be an
order to things.

"I want to buy one," she said. "I've got to have that one-eyed
old peddler."

No surprise. He could have sworn this was the one she would
pick. Didn't she and the peddler both blaze with the same white
light? "You can't buy him. He's already yours. He was yours before
he was mine."

No protests. She accepted the gift as natural. He lifted the canvas
off the wall, massive in its gilded frame. "I'll help you get it home."
No protests here either. This, too, was natural.

Only a few scattered guests remained, men. And these were now

231

disappearing, one by one, with the girls. Time to get back to business. Before leaving, Duvid found Molly.

"You've forgiven me?" she asked as he kissed her.

He shrugged. "It's done. And I won't lie to you. Right now I'm glad. Which makes me worse than you. You're at least honest with yourself. I still keep thinking I'm better than I am." He took her hand. "Come on. I'll introduce you to a famous actress."

Molly was impressed. She had seen Rachel in several plays, remembered her ecstatically and told her so. Rachel was equally gracious. An overwhelming exhibition in a beautiful house. Ah, such *gemütlichkeit.* Annie was less impressed. Aside, she whispered meaningfully to Duvid, "She iss der *vun?*"

He grinned. "She iss der vun."

"I don't like her."

"No?"

"*Sie ist kein* . . . she iss not goot voman." Her voice and expression were grave, her opinion not offered lightly. "She has *kalte eigen.*"

"Cold eyes?"

Annie nodded. "*Sehr* cold. You take care, Duvidal. You vant make fuck vit her? . . . all right. But no marry. She not make you goot vife."

"So *who'll* make me a good wife?"

The smiling child's mouth oozed the pure honey of love. "You know who, Duvidal." Then she turned and went upstairs with a plump, perspiring gentleman who had been waiting patiently but with gradually swelling eagerness for the greater part of the evening.

So Annie thought her eyes were cold. Well, everyone saw differently. Maybe she did see them that way. Still, they were Rachel's eyes and he would not have wanted her to change them. Not even if she could.

The Artist

He lay beside her in the dark bed. The curtains were open and he could see the lights along the Jersey shore high above the wide shadow of the Hudson. Inside the room, a wash of moonlight softened the outlines of the bureaus, the vanity table, the chairs with their clothes thrown over them.

"You vant make fuck vit her? . . . all right." He'd had Annie's permission in advance. But what an ugly word for it. Maybe amusing, even innocent from the child's lips of an immigrant whore, but ugly in itself. And sweet Jehovah, it had not been ugly. It had been a soaring, knowing, passionate journey, a sensual milestone in his pilgrimage among women, a bursting flood that had swept away all the years apart, all the darkness, all memory of hurt and bitterness. All this had vanished here in the soft bed and the moonlit room.

His old teacher . . . He grinned and turned his head. Her hair tumbled in a fragrant mass on the pillow, Rachel was lying beside him, touching his flesh lightly with the tips of her fingers, her eyes hooded in the wavering light.

She smiled slowly. "See? See what you've been missing?"

They chuckled together. He moved his head and kissed her throat. Submerged in a pool of flesh and hair, he dove, swam, drowsily floated.

"There is something to be said," he whispered, "for all reunions."

Through the partially open window came the rhythmic clatter of horses and carriages along the Drive, stately and rich heard this way in an elegant boudoir through the perfumed strands of his lover's hair. The size and opulence of her apartment, the fine style in which she lived, had surprised him. The rewards of the theater, once tapped, were evidently greater than he knew. Hung over the living room mantel, his one-eyed peddler had glared distrustingly at such luxury. How lonely and forsaken he had looked, torn from his push-cart, exiled, without hope of reprieve, to the Elysian fields of Riverside Drive. Well, the old man would get used to it. Rachel had.

"I knew it would be like this," she said. "From the minute I got your invitation, I knew this was exactly the way it would be."

He'd had no such glorious visions. His thoughts had dared venture no further than the hope of seeing her. But then she had always had a far more sanguine view of things than he.

"Why did you wait so long?" she asked. "God! When I think of the time we've wasted. Why didn't you come to me sooner?"

"I'm a slow healer."

"Duvid, Duvid." She made a caress of his name, yet her voice, whispering softly in the darkened room, seemed remote. "I never wanted to hurt you. If only you understood."

"I understood. It had nothing to do with understanding. It was the way I *felt.*" He pulled back gently, turning, smiling up at the ceiling. "But I still saw every play you were in. Some, several times."

"I wondered if you did. Sometimes I'd try to look past the lights, hoping to see you in the audience. There were nights I could almost feel you out there, It was a little game I played. When I gave a really good performance, when everything seemed to go just right, that was when I hoped you were watching."

She waved her hand, as though to stop a contradiction he had no idea of voicing. "It was true. With all that was happening, all these wonderful things, some part of it was always spoiled by you. At the best moments, I'd think . . . ah, Duvid . . . and feel the air start leaking out of my pretty balloon." Her voice was suddenly empty, strained. "But I guess you can't have it all ways."

"You can try."

She laughed, a self-mocking, wry, womanly laugh. "No one can ever say I didn't do that. I *did* try. Duvidal." She kissed and held him. "And God knows, I'm trying still."

He had, it seemed, just drifted off, when he awoke with a start. The moon was a cold stone over the Palisades. The curtains at the window were silver. The bed was not his bed. Then he saw Rachel and remembered. She was asleep, face-up, in the moonlight. A touch of wetness glinted in the far corner of the far eye. What dreams, love? Propped on one elbow, he smiled through the dark. *His.* Her entirety. And loved. Her total length and breadth loved, her lower lip loved, and her knowing hands loved, and her soft, warm moistness loved, and that incredible prize of an ass loved and those delicately tipped breasts loved, and what all of these did to him, especially loved. Then he heard sounds outside the room and realized this was what had wakened him. He listened. There were

234

muffled footsteps, a door being opened and closed. He touched Rachel and felt her stir.

"Someone's out there," he whispered.

"What?" Her voice was heavy, clogged with sleep.

"Someone's in the apartment."

She sighed comfortably. "It's all right, darling. It's only Richard coming in."

He should have known. There *had* to be servants in a place like this. "Sorry. I never loved a lady with a butler before."

"I have no butler. Couldn't stand one around. A maid is bad enough."

"Then who's Richard?"

She giggled. "My husband, silly."

It seemed an unfunny kind of joke. But he went along with it. "Won't it get a bit crowded when he comes to bed?"

"We have a nice little working arrangement." Her lips were against his chest, the words half muffled. "I don't go into his room uninvited, and he doesn't come into mine. Privacy. A good solid foundation for any marriage. Don't you think?"

"Absolutely." It was his voice, except that it came from a long way off. He had just remembered. Cragan's first name was Richard.

"Should I tell you something, darling?"

The "darling" suddenly sounded very false, very theatrical. He wished she would stop using it. "What?"

"I lied to you before. I wasn't at all sure it would be like this. I was really very worried about tonight, about seeing you. I didn't know how you might feel."

"You mean," he said with great care, "about your being married?"

"Uh huh." She smiled sleepily. "You're really a very puritanical type, you know. Remember how I had to practically drag you into bed that first time?"

He was beginning to feel chilled, as if he were lying naked on cold stone. "I remember. Very puritanical."

"I had all sorts of arguments prepared for tonight. If you resisted, I was going to knock you over with the force of my logic."

"What logic?"

"That I loved you. That I never stopped. That whatever happened in between, didn't really matter now that we were together. That if I married Richard it was obviously for reasons that had nothing to do with what I felt for you."

"Obviously," Duvid said, suddenly glimpsing, in memory, the producer's cherubic face staring at him from the far side of Rachel's upended bottom. A cold, practical man, Cragan. And what lesson had *he* taught him? *Next time you'll knock before you walk into a room.* A force of logic there too. Two such logical people should do well together. "I've forgotten. Exactly how long have you been married?"

"It's nearly three years now."

He said nothing, but just held her for warmth.

"After the announcements came out, I kept expecting to hear from you. I guess it was stupid. What could you have said?"

He must have missed reading the newspaper that day. But he had seen her parents since. Why had they failed to mention it? Ah . . . she had married a Christian. She was dead to them. *Kaddish* had been said. "Congratulations."

Her laugh was flat. "Thanks. But I guess we both got pretty much what we asked for. At least I'll never have to worry about money, or getting the right parts again."

"And what did *he* get?"

"Richard?" The full lips murmured into a small smile. "Richard got the chance to feel like a man occasionally. It was getting harder and harder for him. And when he couldn't manage it at all, there was only me, his loyal wife, to know. Which was important to him."

Everybody, thought Duvid, had their problems. There was the sudden rush of a toilet being flushed, its roar swift and efficient between the solid Riverside Drive walls. Even the plumbing of the rich had a different sound. Poor old Cragan . . . in his solitary bedroom, jealously guarding his secret failures, squeezing his small remaining pleasures into a white, porcelain bowl. While in the next room, his lusty young wife was being happily serviced by her poor but energetic lover. Considering the nature of their single meeting four years ago, it was enough to renew Duvid's faith in a higher justice.

"Tell me, do we all have breakfast together in the morning?"

The Artist

"Richard's a late sleeper. You'll be gone long before he's up." She twisted over and kissed him. "My Duvid, my Duvid. I'd forgotten how it could be, loving you. Thank God you're back."

After a while, her breath came in an even, healthy rhythm. Duvid did not sleep. He lay uncomfortably, with growing rigidity, listening to her breathing. Outside, a passing automobile backfired. It sounded like gunshots in the still night, and not at all stately and rich. He turned his head a little and looked at Rachel. Even as she slept, there seemed to be a tiny, satisfied smile at the corners of the full, passionate mouth. Duvid Karlinsky . . . satisfier of unsatisfied wives. The pleasures of the past few hours began to drain. With mounting anger, he stared at the delicately lovely face on the pillow beside him. Three years married. And how many others before him in this soft, welcoming bed? He felt used, seduced, the eager victim of a carefully baited trap. She wanted everything, all ways, and she was managing to get it. Lying there, he hated her shrewd cleverness, hated the coldness with which she weighed her alternatives and made her plans, hated the certainty with which she carried them out. He thought of all the months and years of wanting her, of buying love, of chasing dreams, It was unjust for the cunning to always get what they wanted, to always know on which doors to knock and what to say when they were opened. She had done exactly as she chose to do, whatever she wanted. Then she had waited and he had finally come to her. He felt twice betrayed. Was the end to be Duvid Karlinsky, stud-at-large, sneaking in and out of a married woman's bed like some sort of night crawler? Was this all he had earned for himself in four years of waiting? Did she think that all she had to do to offer him love and happiness, the world, was open his goddamned fly?

Suddenly it was intolerable for him to remain in bed next to this woman who had used him so comfortably. He slid silently onto the floor and walked barefooted and naked over to the window. He stared out over the Drive, free now of all traffic, winding broadly away under the streetlights. Beyond it, the river caught pieces of moon, held them briefly, and tossed them back. One day, he thought irrelevantly, ghetto Jew or no ghetto Jew, I am going to paint the whole of the Hudson River.

Swiftly and soundlessly, Duvid dressed. Rachel stirred once, threw her arm out, and reached languidly toward the other side of the bed, but did not wake up. Her arm looked white and fragile stretched into the warm emptiness beside her. With his shoes in his hand, Duvid padded over to the door. Rachel was lying as he had left her, one arm extended in dreamlike invitation to her returned lover. On her face, Duvid imagined he saw a cool, sensual smile of satisfaction. Annie was right, he thought. Seen in certain lights, her eyes were clearly and unmistakably cold. Then he stepped through the door and closed it softly behind him.

He married Annie the following week. They were married by a rabbi in an East Side *shul,* with Hutchins as Duvid's best man and his mother and father and Aunt Tybie present, along with Molly and all her girls. Annie looked fifteen years old and beautiful as a bride, and Rifka Karlinsky and the other women wept, and Avrum Karlinsky looked dazed and a little confused throughout.

Earlier, Duvid had sent Rachel a note saying he was marrying a semiliterate, immigrant whore with the warmest eyes he had ever seen, and that if she and Richard happened to be free at that particular time, he would be happy to have them attend the wedding. He also said something to the effect that if his marriage seemed somewhat sudden and rushed, it was only because he had but recently discovered that the real and essential question was one of our useful employment by other human beings and their useful employment by us. Naturally, he didn't want to waste a single second before putting so marvelous a concept into practice. The Cragans, however, neither responded to his note nor attended his wedding.

ELEVEN

1945: Amagansett, Long Island

In the even, dependable print of the *Sunday Times,* which always reminded Duvid of the speech of elderly career diplomats, the war was still going on. The Japanese were dying by the thousands across the front page, but stubbornly continuing to fight: there were heavy air attacks by American fliers that left ten more of their cities in ruins; MacArthur was announcing the liberation of all the Philippine Islands; Truman, Stalin, and Churchill met at Potsdam for what was described as an historic conference, and Allied headquarters was declaring, for the third time that week, that total victory was imminent.

"Hoorah," said Duvid.

Laurie looked at him. "Hoorah what?"

"Total victory is imminent."

"That's great."

"It's all such crap."

"It's better than total defeat being imminent."

"I guess so." He stared off. "It's just when you're out there, when you're looking at what's suddenly left of the guy next to you, it's hard to remember it's better."

"I don't know how men face that, day after day, and stay sane."

"They develop a system. As long as they don't think about how bad it is, they can get through it. And it works the same way for countries. The last country to realize the whole thing is insane, wins the war." He shook his head. "It's all such crap, anyway. And the higher you go, the worse it gets. At the top, they think only in divisions and manpower. They're always squabbling for more men and all they do when they get them is kill them. The one that finally kills the most is hailed as a national hero and gets his portrait painted by Karlinsky for the cover of *Time.*"

Too bitter and cynical, he thought, not caring for the sound of it. But one of Richard's carefully censored V-mails had arrived the day before and he was still working it off. Instead of reassuring him, mail from his son always seemed to have exactly the opposite effect, personalizing the danger and reminding him, sadly, that Richard had no business being in the army at all. For his son was probably the only American combat infantryman in the Pacific Theater of Operations with active stomach ulcers. Of course the United States Army had no knowledge of this fact. Sergeant Karlinsky's ulcers were undoubtedly among the best-kept military secrets of the war. So that if the sergeant were ever to die quietly of internal bleeding in some jungle foxhole, only his father would suspect the truth. And if his mother were still alive to place blame, only his father would be blamed. "This is all yours," she had wept accusingly after Richard's enlistment. "If that boy dies out there, you can be proud of having killed him." Nice to hear. But he had kept control, kept his voice soft. "I never told him to do it."

"You didn't have to. He knew how you felt. He wanted to please you."

"He's past his majority. He makes his own decisions."

"How can you believe in killing?"

"You know I don't believe in killing."

"You believe in war."

"I believe in *this* war."

"They're all the same."

"This one is different."

"That's what they say about them all."

"I don't know about them all. But I do know about this one."

"War is war."

He sighed, "I'm sorry, I can't afford the luxury of that kind of humanity. I'm a Jew."

"What's that supposed to mean?"

"It means I remember what Russia was for us, and I see what Germany *is.* "

"America isn't fighting for the *Jews.* "

"No. But she's fighting, and that's enough. I like what this country's given me and I believe in paying for what I get."

"Then pay for it with *your* blood, not your son's."

"That's unfair."

"I *feel* like being unfair," she cried. "It's insane. A soldier with ulcers. What good will he be to them? I'll go down myself and tell those idiots they've taken an ulcer patient into their army."

"You can't do that to him."

"I can't save my own son's life?"

"It's his life. He has the right to do what he wants with it."

"Not if he's throwing it away."

"Even then. But I don't believe he's throwing it away."

"I know you don't. And *he* knows it, too."

She shook a fist at the ceiling. "Damn them! Why can't they get things right? Why," she wept, addressing the enlistment officers and the army doctors and the battalions in the field and the statesmen in all the capitals of the world, addressing the war and the times and all the anguish she saw ahead, "why can't they see when a man is sick and doesn't belong in their damned army?"

Duvid held her. "He'll be all right."

"He *won't* be all right. Do you think I'm a fool? If bullets don't finish him the army food will." She pulled away, her eyes flat. "I wonder . . ." she said slowly, "I wonder how you'd feel about this if he were your own flesh."

"Well," he said, and was surprised that he was not angry, that he should, in fact, actually be considering it a legitimate question, "we'll never know, will we?"

He had last seen his son in 1942 among the uniforms and the clasped couples of farewell in Pennsylvania Station. Richard was carrying his barracks bag because it was the end of his furlough and he was returning to camp to be shipped overseas. They had stood awkwardly in the gray light of the cavernous station, with the murmur of a thousand good-bys making a different music from the massed bugles and drums that traditionally marched men off to war.

Richard forced a grin. "Thanks for not letting Mom come down. That would have been too much."

"This hasn't been easy for her."

"I guess not. I'm sorry."

Duvid looked at him, at the still boyish face, so strange, suddenly, over the olive drab of the United States Army. The months of basic training had melted away what little spare flesh he had carried, and his bones were sharp. "Don't worry about it. She blames me more than she does you."

"Why?"

"Because she thinks you're doing it to please me."

"Hell. I'm a big boy now."

"That's what I told her." Duvid silently watched a soldier and his mother and two female relatives weeping together in a sodden mass. "But I know the kind of courage it took."

"It would have taken more courage to stay home and keep explaining why I *wasn't* in the army."

"Never mind. Just don't be a martyr. We've no need for martyrs in this family. If any bleeding starts, if you're ever feeling really sick, don't be a fool. Let them know what's going on and you'll be home in a month with a pension."

"Sure."

"I guess you don't know where you're being shipped."

"Probably the Pacific."

Duvid nodded. Then they just stood there, not quite knowing where to look.

"Listen," Richard said abruptly. "There's something I've got to tell you." His voice was rushed and uncertain and held, for Duvid, the same note of concern it used to hold when, as a child, he was about to confess some new transgression. But what now, at the age of twenty-two and leaving for a war?

"Yes?"

"I know about me." Something grave passed his eyes and darkened the blue. "I mean, I know I'm not your real son, that I'm just adopted."

All Duvid could do was stare at him.

"Grandma let something slip about a year ago. You know how

she's been getting lately, some of the wild things she says. Well, at first I figured this was just another of them. Then I started thinking and asking her questions." He smiled carefully. "Poor Grandma. I'm afraid I took terrible advantage of her."

Searching, Duvid found his voice somewhere near the bottom of his stomach. "That's crazy."

"No it's not. It's one of the few *un*crazy things I've ever discovered about myself. It was a real shocker at first. Jesus, after twenty-one years. Then it started to make sense. It explained so much I could never understand before. Like why I was so different from every other Karlinsky. Not only in looks, but in everything. Hell, I wasn't like *anybody*. And I'll tell you now. It used to really eat me."

Deny, deny, thought Duvid, recalling the emergency procedures he and his wife had planned for just this situation. If ever there were questions, if ever Richard were to hear anything to make him suspicious, it was all to be denied. Yet how foolish, now, to deny what he obviously knew. Instead, Duvid just gazed at that look of his, at that elite look of proud pain his son had carried in and out of trouble for so many years, and his heart ached angrily. The boy aged beyond his years. He grew ulcers in his stomach like a botanist grew flowers in a garden. He wasted himself in senseless schemes, in impractical projects that ended in disappointment and despair. And he was not like some, who, after a while, become blunted toward their own pain. No, his pain was still sharp, still continual. And Duvid again was pierced with anguish for this solitary young man whom he called his son.

"But mostly I used to wonder why I couldn't be more like you," Richard said, his voice soft and low and losing itself quickly in the murmur of the wartime station, "why my hands couldn't do what yours could do, why nothing about us was the same. Suddenly, I knew why. And it was like a ton load off me. Finally, I could stop trying to be what I wasn't."

"I never asked for that."

"I know. It wasn't your fault. You couldn't help being you, anymore than I could help being me. Except, I guess, I never really knew what being me meant." He looked down at his boots. "Do you know who my natural parents are?"

"No."

"Would you tell me if you did?"

Duvid shook his head, still slightly dazed by this whole bizarre conversation with a son to whom he was about to say good-by for years and, perhaps, forever. If there was a time for truth, this was surely it. Yet what possible benefit in knowing you had sprung from a Polish whore and any one of a dozen of her Saturday night regulars. He looked past Richard's shoulder to where the hands of the station clock were moving closer to train-time and experienced an instant of panic. With just minutes left, what could you *say?* In all this rolling-on world, he was probably the one who knew this boy best, yet even what he knew was very little. "We loved you," he said. "All of us. We've never felt any difference."

"Well, it would be hard for you to know. You've no way to compare. But *I* can. For twenty-one years, you and Mom and Grandma and Grandpa were my family, my blood. Then, for the last year, I've known the truth and looked for how I might feel different about you. I waited to feel the change. Only none came. Everybody was still what they were before. The only difference was in *me*, in how *I* felt about *myself.*"

"And that was good?"

"Yes."

Duvid breathed deeply and said nothing.

"But I don't think you should tell Mom."

"No."

"I just wanted you to know before I left."

"Why?"

"In case you ever felt any doubt, or worried about how I'd feel about you." He paused. "I didn't want you to have to worry."

This was said with something vaguely resembling a smile, and Duvid understood he was being ordered, as subtly as possible, not to embarrass them both by bogging down into any sirupy Yiddish sentiment. So that trying very hard to obey and behave like a properly cool Anglo-Saxon father, he almost succeeded in not putting his arms around his son and clutching him, wet-eyed, as he kissed him good-by.

Three years.

The war was nearing its end and Richard had gotten through it so far, but at what cost? Duvid could imagine, but would never know. His son's path had run steeply down into shadow and up into fear and he had walked it naked and alone. But at least he had chosen the way himself, and there weren't many who managed to do that. His son carried none of his blood, but sometimes acquired characteristics were accepted into the hospitality of children's souls through the imitations of love. In this, at least, Richard had found a way to follow him. And the guilt, never far removed, was brought still closer by each of his letters. The guilt was always the same, always carried alone, but this time he tried to share a small piece with Laurie.

He dropped the *Times* to the floor. "Did you ever hear about 'The Cripplers?' "

"No," she said.

"During the last century, in Russia, Jewish fathers often chose to have their sons maimed, rather than let them be drafted into the Czar's army. The men who cut off the fingers, punctured ears, and worse, were called 'The Cripplers.' "

"How ghastly."

"Yes. But not as ghastly as dying in one of the Czar's holy wars."

She was suddenly cautious. "Why are you telling me this?"

"Because I want you to know the kind of Jewish father you've picked for your child."

"What kind?"

"The kind that lets a boy with ulcers go into the army, instead of crippling him to keep him out." He looked at her. "Which is what I did with Richard."

"How could they take him in with ulcers?"

"They didn't know and he didn't tell them."

"You couldn't talk him out of it?"

"I didn't try."

"That doesn't sound like you."

"What do you know about what sounds like me?"

It came out more sharply than he intended, and she was startled. "It's just that you keep saying it's all such crap."

"It is. Only I think I sometimes get nostalgic for death and forget. Everyone waits for death, but Jews seem to wait for murder.

Six million of us waited this time, and we got it. I didn't want my son bargaining for his life with his ulcers, like those old Russian Jews bargained with their sons' chopped hands and blinded eyes."

She read his guilt as clearly as she could read the paper. "Then why do you beat yourself about it?"

"Because I'm a lousy Jewish father."

"But you did only what you believed."

"A good Jewish father spits on what he believes when it comes to his children. He spits on principles, on theories, on politics, on all questions of logic and national priority. The only question he asks is whether it's good for his child or bad for his child. *That's* a good Jewish father." His voice deepened, grew harsh at the edges. "Do you think *my* father would have let *me* march off to war with ulcers? In two *minutes* he would have reported me to the medics and dragged me home by the ear. My father never made noble gestures, or worked at building my character, or lectured me about patriotism and obligations to my country. All my father ever did was love me."

The dark mood lasted through the day and into the evening, when he finally carried it out for an airing to a small tavern they sometimes went to at the edge of town. The place smelled pleasantly beery and there was a juke box playing Helen O'Connell's recording of "Tangerine" as they came in. Three soldiers at the bar looked at Laurie with the hungry, lonely eyes of men far from home.

"Hi, Mr. Karlinsky . . . Miss Wallace."

The proprietor was behind the bar, a round, shiny-faced man whose deep respect for Duvid's reputation made it utterly impossible for him to accept a less formal, first-name relationship. "Two scotch-and-waters coming up," he said, and brought their drinks to a table.

The soldiers had swung around fully at the bar so that they wouldn't have to crane their necks to see Laurie. She wore a crisp white dress that set off her tan, and her hair was brushed and shining, and Duvid did not blame the soldiers for looking. Their uniforms only accentuated the expressions of loss and loneliness and dumb desire on their faces, and Duvid knew exactly what they must be feeling, seeing a middle-aged civilian sitting with a beautiful young girl. Probably, he thought, behind those lost stares, were visions of him happily drinking with one beautiful girl after another in the cool, comfortable taverns of his homeland, in bed with those girls between smooth civilian sheets, while they fought and sweated and hurt and died on distant alien shores. All three had on the blue combat-infantryman's badge and the European Theater ribbon, and two also wore bronze stars and purple hearts to show they were heroes and had bled.

Duvid drank quietly, enjoying Laurie across the table and the beat of the music, and nursing an insane desire to go over to the soldiers at the bar and assure them he understood perfectly how they felt, and that he had a son somewhere in the Pacific who was in a far less enviable position right now than any of them. He also wanted to offer assurances that he was not nearly so well off as they might think at first glance, with at least three-quarters of his time used up and few surprises left and many of those he had cared about gone and others going and each good-by getting a little harder than the one before. Fools, he thought, don't envy me. You've got the whole banquet ahead of you, all the courses, while here I am, somewhere near the end, nibbling at the dessert. I'd change with you in a minute. The days you've got ahead. The best days of America, with the war soon over. The hopeful, optimistic days, the killing done, the crisp invigorating mid-century weather opening the sky to undreamed-of wonders. You'll marry and sit down to dinner with many children in the same house for thirty uninterrupted years and tell your grandchildren endless stories of how bravely you fought for your country as young men, and you will have forgotten entirely this brief, lonely moment in a bar in the summer of 1945.

The propietor passed their table with fresh drinks. "Everything OK, Mr. Karlinsky?"

"Fine, Mr.. Hoyt."

The juke box began to blare "Deep In The Heart Of Texas" and one of the soldiers at the bar drawled loudly, "Yo' heah that, Frank? Mistuh Karlinsky heah says everthin's jus' fahn."

"I heard it all right, Corporal. Man, I sure wish *I* was a civilian Jew."

"There any *other* kind?" asked the third soldier.

"Well, Ralph, Ah once knew a Jewish soldier," said the corporal.

"When he got shot, Ah sweah to God they stuffed him and put him in a museum."

The other two soldiers laughed and Duvid laughed along with them. But Laurie said angrily. "How can you *laugh* at that?"

"It's funny."

"It's disgusting."

"They're just lonely and jealous."

But he gazed with fresh interest at those doing the talking. The southern corporal had the lean, tough, but agreeable look of a fighter who has won fifty fights and lost ten, and of those ten, four were on bad decisions, three were fixed, and for the other three he went in the tank. So it was a confident look, that of a man who knew what he could do. The other two had the smooth, flat bones and clam-colored eyes that might have followed behind some Christian knight's horse and been buried outside the walls of Acre. All good soldiers' faces that would take well to training and perform dependably under fire. And since they had fought Germans, they were to be forgiven a great deal.

"You can't blame the Jews for not fighting," said Ralph. "It's not their fault they're smarter than the rest of us. If I was that smart, I wouldn't be no doughfoot, either. I'd be sitting at home, too, watching the money roll in and grabbing all the beautiful blondes."

Laurie hissed, "Let's leave. I can't stand any more of that."

"Finish your drink," Duvid said. "They're harmless enough."

"Hey, Mistuh Karlinsky," said the corporal. "How yo' doin' with yo'r black market tires an' gasoline?"

Duvid looked at him and smiled vaguely, but did not say anything. He was glad Mr. Hoyt was in back and had not heard. He would have been upset.

"Yo' heah me, Mistuh Karlinsky?"

"I heard you, Corporal."

"Then why don't yo' answer?"

"Because I'm not in the black market business."

"Ah thought *all* Jews were black marketeers."

"No. Just some of us."

"What do the rest of you do?"

"We run all the banks and whorehouses in Paris and Berlin.

That's why Roosevelt had to declare war. To protect our money."
The soldiers laughed.

"Ah believe yo'," said the corporal. "Yo' Jews got us into this war, all raht. The least yo' could do is give us a little help fightin' it."

"Too dangerous," Duvid said. "They say people are getting killed out there."

"You can bet your ass they are," said Frank. "I don't mind your killing Christ, Karlinsky, but I'll never forgive you getting my poor buddy's head blown off on Omaha Beach."

"I'm sorry about that."

"Being sorry don't help him none."

"Will it help if I buy a round and we drink to him?"

"Well," Frank said, "I don't see how it could hurt any."

"Ah don't know," drawled the corporal. "Ah ain't never drunk no Jew whisky before."

"Whisky is whisky," said Ralph.

But it was finally too much for Laurie. "You apes! You don't deserve to bathe this man's *feet*, let alone *drink* with him."

They stared at her, as did Mr. Hoyt, who had come back behind the bar at that moment.

"Take it easy," Duvid told her.

"Don't tell me to take it easy. I've taken it easy long enough. I've sat here listening to these apes say things that should rot off their tongues." Her voice was loud and harsh and aimed like a weapon at the soldiers' heads. "They've just finished fighting the bloodiest war in history and what have they learned? Nothing! They're as stupid and full of hate as when they started. I look at them and want to weep. Is *this* what it was all for? So skunks like these can come home and foul the air with their stink?"

"Listen lady . . ." said the corporal. "Why don't yuh do like Karlinsky says an' jus' take it easy."

Laurie rose from the table, took two quick steps toward him, and spit squarely in his face. *"You* take it easy, you dumb cracker!"

The corporal stood looking at her, saliva running down his cheeks. Then he hit her twice with the flat of his hand, the sounds going off like small-caliber bullets in the suddenly quiet room. She stumbled and Duvid caught her and eased her into a chair. He studied her face closely.

"You all right?"

She nodded but seemed a little dazed.

"That was a silly thing to do. He might have hurt you."

"Tell her," the corporal said without malice. "Some women gotta be taught these things." He had wiped the saliva from his face and was drinking as though nothing had happened. The proprietor, the soldiers, and the bar's other patrons stood watching like figures in a tableau.

"Don't worry, Karlinsky," Ralph said, "She ain't hurt none. If you Jews gave your women a taste of knuckles once in a while, maybe they wouldn't crap on you so much."

"You might be right," Duvid told him.

"Now how about that whisky?" said Frank.

Duvid nodded to the barman. "A round for our brave boys in uniform, Mr. Hoyt."

The barman hurriedly set up the drinks. The other patrons lost interest and turned away, and someone fed the juke box a nickel for a jazzed-up version of "Loch Lomond."

Duvid lifted his glass. "To a buddy."

He and the soldiers solemnly drank. Laurie sat exactly as Duvid had placed her, looking eighteen years old and in water over her head. There was a male conspiracy here she knew nothing about, and would not understand if she did know. She sat in a cold silence that made her shiver, but there was nowhere else for her to go. When she picked up her glass, her hand was shaking and some of the drink splashed her cheek. She wiped it away as if it were blood.

At the bar with the three soldiers, Duvid looked at the corporal and a sweet smile came off him. "You're probably a damn good soldier, Corporal, and I appreciate any Germans you may have killed. It's just" . . . his smile was pleasant, true, unforced . . . "I don't know that I can let you get away with hitting her."

"Shee-it," said the corporal.

"Sorry," Duvid told him and felt his fists vanish, one in the region of the belly, the other below the throat. Making small, choking sounds, the corporal curled up and dropped, dry as a roach. The other two came at Duvid together, but got in each other's way, and

The Artist

Duvid caught Frank on the back of the neck as he went past, with a dead, cold chop that dropped him flat on his face. Ralph tried to stop coming, but a hard knee rammed his groin and sent him down, retching, his stomach emptying.

Duvid put a bill on the bar. "For the drinks and cleaning up, Mr. Hoyt."

He took Laurie's arm, led her out to the car, and drove away in silence. They were almost home before he spoke. "Don't ever push me into anything like that again."

"I just couldn't listen to it any more."

"If I could listen to it, so could you."

"I don't understand you. They're animals."

"They're not animals. They're American soldiers."

"They're bigots."

"Yes," he said. "But they've been shooting Nazis, not Jews."

"I'll bet they'd rather shoot Jews."

"Maybe. But in the meantime, they were out there when we needed them. They and a lot of other dumb redneck regulars aiming the guns and taking the hits while the rest of us smart civilians were running around trying to get ready. And I didn't enjoy one bit having to do that to them."

They reached the house and went in. "I'm sorry," she said. "I guess I didn't think past my own feelings."

He kissed her. "I know."

"I might have gotten you hurt. That was dumb of me. But my God! What you *did* to them!"

"Oh, I'm good enough at that, at hitting and hammering. Sometimes I'm sure I missed my calling."

"I can't imagine you as anything but an artist."

"I can. I don't believe there's only one job for a man."

"Still, what you are is an artist."

"Yes."

"Are you ever sorry?"

"Sometimes. Other times, I'm ashamed."

"Why?"

"Because art's gotten so self-indulgent, so pathetically useless. It changes nothing."

"What should it change?"

The Artist

"The state of the world."

"Can it do that?"

"Once, it could. Goya helped lift the heart of Spain, Daumier fought social injustice, Millet made humanism a part of daily living. Now it's mostly a sterile, pretentious toy that has nothing whatsoever to do with the way things are."

"Not *your* work."

"Of course not. I'm different."

"You *are.*"

"If I was really different, my son wouldn't be off in the Pacific tonight, fighting another war. Not after the one I saw end twenty-five years ago."

"How could you have stopped it?"

"I don't know. But I should have done more than I did. Ah," he said tiredly, "let's go to sleep."

But sleep did not come, and he lay staring through the silent dark. Some part of it *had* to be his, he thought. He had gone all through that first war, the one that was supposed to have ended them all, and knew what it was like and tried to show it to anyone willing to look, but maybe he hadn't taken his responsibility seriously enough. Maybe he should have put aside everything else and just concentrated on preventing his son from ever having to go to another war. He had worked hard and painted a lot of pictures, but he had been painting the wrong things. He should have concentrated solely on stopping this. He should have been absolutely single-minded about peace, a fanatic. There was nothing else in the world as important. All the rest was nonsense. He had been playing with toys. He and millions like him. This war had been in preparation for twenty years while they had ignored every sign. And if he couldn't stop it with his brush, he should have been out screaming in the streets, out grabbing people by the collar to make them listen. *Listen! War is no solution. We all want the same things. We're none of us different.* He should have traveled through every country in the world, walking the cities and towns, the back roads, using fists and clubs when necessary. Versailles, Manchuria, Ethiopia, Spain. Each one a battlefield. And he had stayed at home, painting pictures of other things because he had believed there was one war and it was over.

252

TWELVE

1914:Belgium

It was better now, but the road had been under heavy artillery fire for the past twelve hours and shells could still be heard screaming over and exploding in the distance. Earlier, some Belgian transports had been hit, and the dead horses were beginning to bloat and smell in the August sun. The odor mingled with the yellow smell of cordite and the brassy smell of burned rock and the old smell of broken trucks, burning rubber, and singed paint. The dead and wounded had been removed, but otherwise the remains of the convoy lay on both sides of the shell-pocked road, curving up the long hill like a ruptured snake.

Duvid and Hutchins went by it slowly, on foot, in a straggling stream of refugees and retreating soldiers. The wreckage of two ambulances lay among the overturned trucks and wagons, their sides sadly marked by the torn and useless red crosses that had done no good at all. Duvid looked at them with a mixture of anger and despair. Anger at the coldly efficient Germans who had loaded and fired their howitzers, miles away, at these truckloads of broken and dying men. Despair, because he felt that bad as it was so far, much worse was on the way. Those around him, he could see from their faces, did not share his anger. All they had left was the despair. They dragged slowly westward, their eyes dull and flat, moving like a dying beast, without reason or hope, toward the final sheltered place where they might lie down and die. Some of the refugees, through all the welter of retreat and death, still clung to a few prized possessions. One elderly man carried a violin case, nothing else, as though on his way to perform at a long-planned recital somewhere along the road ahead. A silver teapot jutted out of the top of another's bundle, mute, stubborn evidence of hope, even in this anguish, of a future that included moments of easy, gracious living.

Hutchins stumbled as he walked and Duvid grabbed his arm to keep him from falling. The reporter's face and hair were caked with dust, his eyes red-rimmed, his body shrunken inside his clothes. It was only a matter of weeks since the German invasion had swept across the Belgian frontier, but Duvid was beginning to feel there had never been a time when the war had not been part of the condition of his life. Guns and death and retreat had become the general weather of existence. Going back, going back, always exhausted, always with the smell of fire and the dead in his nostrils, always with German guns exploding behind him, their crews surely grinning because they were confident and safe from reprisal and they were killing hundreds of men, women, and children every hour. *Germans.* Less than two months before, Duvid had known little or nothing about them. But he knew now.

There had been no war when they came over in mid-July. Gavrilo Princip had fired his three pistol shots in Sarajevo in late June, and the Archduke had done his dying, but who had expected what was to follow? Hutchins! "Watch the Germans," he had said and persuaded his editor to send him over to do just that. Then he told Duvid, "Come with me. It's where things are going to happen. It's time you got away from New York for a while anyway. It'll do you good." *It would do him good.* The doctor prescribing for his patient. Take an ocean voyage to Europe in the summer of 1914 and cure your ills. What ills? He had no ills. Look again. All right. A few things here and there, but who was without them? It took him exactly three hours to decide to go. Standing before a half-finished study of a bearded Jew in *tallis* and *tfillin*, he squinted at the mournful, suddenly familiar face on the canvas and thought, *"My God, how many times have I painted him?"*

He told Annie at dinner that night. "the *Times* is sending Hutchins to Europe next week. He wants me to go with him."

She looked at him across the kitchen table.

The Artist

"He thinks things are going to happen there."

"Vot . . . what things?" She had worked hard to improve her speech, and had, but still slipped occasionally. "A war?"

"I doubt if it'll go that far."

"You doubt?" She had stopped eating.

"There may be some excitement for a while, but wars don't start because one schoolboy goes crazy with a pistol."

"So?"

"So I've decided to go."

She nodded slowly, still holding her fork, still looking at him. "Why?"

"I told you. Hutchins said . . ."

She cut him off. "I don't care what Hutchins said. I care what *you* say."

He saw how it was going to be. For a long time she had been on the edge of something, the wide eyes growing wider and darker, the small mouth stretching flat. A confused hurt had slipped over the smoothness of her face like a net. It added years, robbed her of innocence. "My work is going stale. I've been painting the same things too long. I'm repeating myself. I've got to get away from here for a while."

"You're sure Europe is far enough away? Maybe you should go to China."

He did not say anything.

She put down her fork very gently, very carefully. It made no sound as it touched her plate. "Why don't you tell the truth? Why don't you say the *real* reason you want to go?"

"And what's that?"

"To get away from *me.*"

He said tiredly, "Annie . . ."

"Don't Annie me. You think I don't know how you feel?"

Tears welled, clung to her lids and Duvid felt her anguish. I should never have married her, he thought. I should never have done this to her. She didn't deserve it. It was what she had wanted, but it was wrong from the beginning. And it was nothing she could help. She had given him everything she had. When this wasn't enough, she gave him more. She had a funny, greenhorn accent?

The Artist

She went to night school, practiced ten hours a day, and buried it. She had only a fifth-grade education? She read a book a week for two years. She was married to an artist and ignorant of art? She studied every painting in every museum and gallery in the city. What more? *What more?*

"It has nothing to do with you," he said. "I feel at a dead end. I don't know where to go. There used to be so much I wanted to paint, I'd wake up at night in a panic. I couldn't wait for morning. Now everything I do, I feel I've done before."

She didn't seem to have heard him. "Maybe . . ." she wept softly, "maybe if I could have had a baby it would have been different."

"Annie, for Christ's sake! I've told you, I don't give a damn about a baby." True enough, yet she refused to believe him. How could he not resent her barren state? She was almost biblical in her guilt. *The sons of Abraham to be forever without the sons of Duvid.* They had gone to a doctor, but he could find nothing wrong with either of them. He said sometimes these things happened. It was impossible to know why. Annie knew why. She was being punished. Retribution. Repayment for her past life. She had finally educated herself out of all innocence. The guilt she had not felt in five years as a whore, she felt now. Even her love-making was affected. All that clear, pure sensuality was drained, its dedication lost. Where now those lovely journeys into carnality? . . . those joyous, erotic romps? Abandoned forever among the sheets of a whore's bed. No more her flesh a precious vessel in which the spirit awaited pleasure. *Whores* made love for pleasure. *Wives* made love for babies.

"It *would* have been different," she said. "You wouldn't be leaving now if there were children. You would have found something to paint right here. This is just an excuse, this going across an ocean. At least be honest. You *want* to get away from me. If you've gone dry inside, it's because I've gone dry inside." She rubbed her eyes with a napkin. "I'll tell you something. I'm not surprised. I've been expecting it. I didn't know where or when you were going, but I knew that one day you'd walk in here and say good-by."

"I'm not saying good-by. The whole thing shouldn't take more than a month or two. As soon as the excitement dies, I'll be back."

"The excitement won't die in a month or two and you won't be

The Artist

back and you *are* saying good-by." She recited it in a high, sing-song, little girls' voice, but she had control now and was calm and no longer crying. She glanced about the kitchen where they sat, with its black iron stove and its washtubs and its cabinets in which she kept her dishes so neatly arranged, then looked past the cabinets to the parlor and its couch and upholstered chairs, and its tables and lamps that they had shopped for together and that had delighted her so much because they were the first pieces of furniture she had ever owned. Looking through the parlor, she could see the bed-spread she had embroidered herself, laid over the bed upon which she had tried so long and hard to produce, yet had produced noth-ing. She looked at it all, as if taking final inventory of her failures, then turned to Duvid. "I'm not blaming you. It's my own fault. I was stupid. I didn't really understand what I was when I married you. If I'd understood, I would have known it couldn't work. But I wasn't too stupid to know you were just marrying me to punish that bitch of yours. I did know that much. But I was happy to take you anyway. For whatever reason you wanted. I figured we'd have a family, I'd make a good life for you, make you forget her, and it would work out. Only I figured wrong. There's no family, I've bored you half to death, and you haven't forgotten that woman for a minute." She looked at him and her eyes were clear, unblinking. "Have you, Duvid?"

"Annie, listen to me . . ."

But she hadn't listened to him. Even as he was swearing denials, she rose from the table, tiny, yet tall with a carefully put together dignity, walked into the bedroom, and closed the door, not slam-ming it, but making the closing seem somehow final. When he sailed a few days later, he last saw her on the pier with his mother, father, and Aunt Tybie, everyone else waving and shouting and throwing confetti, but she just standing there and looking at him until she blurred in the distance. Good-by, Annie, he thought, although he had not said good-by to her in any true sense. No reason. He was sure he would be back soon.

Yet now, stumbling bleary-eyed along a shell-torn Belgian road, with a wagonload of wounded leaking blood in front of him, he was no longer sure of anything. There was a world coming to an end here, and any minute he might be ending with it. He was a civilian, an accredited correspondent of a neutral country, but that, he had discovered, meant nothing. Neither to the shells screaming overhead, nor to the Germans firing them. He had already borne witness to the German treatment of noncombatants. He had seen the mass graves outside Ardennes, the unburied bodies in Aerschot, the victims of the burning of Louvain. And in once-beautiful Saint-Trond, he and Hutchins had hidden in the cellar of a ruined house for a day and a night while the Germans systematically destroyed the town above them. The invaders had a name for their policy of deliberate murder and destruction. It was called *Schrecklichkeit* . . . frightfulness . . . and was meant to demoralize the enemy. A lovely people, the Germans, Duvid thought. But it worked. Everyone looked about as demoralized as they could get.

They had been heading for Brussels until word came of its fall. Now their only hope was to reach Antwerp. But there was no longer a stable front and the Germans were everywhere. If the road ahead was cut, they would have to take to the back country. They had picked up a military map of the area and had already laid out alternate routes. How quickly, Duvid thought, you adapt. If anyone had told him a month ago that he would soon become expert at survival in a country overrun by an army of murderers, he would have laughed. Yet that was precisely what had happened during the past weeks. Germany had declared war on Belgium on August 4th, and instantly sent six brigades against Liège, where, two days before, Hutchins had been interviewing the garrison commander and receiving his assurances that Germany would never violate Belgium's neutrality. Caught near the border by the first thrusts of the invasion, they had been fleeing the Germans ever since . . . sometimes alone, sometimes, as now, part of the long lines of soldiers and refugees clogging the roads everywhere. Where possible, Hutchins tried to get his dispatches off from towns along the way. But most of the wires had either been cut or were restricted to military use. Duvid thought ruefully of his own work, of the two notebooks of sketches he carried in his musette bag. The drawings were good. What a shame if they ended up unseen, scattered in scorched fragments across some dusty back road in Belgium.

The Artist

The artist at war. No. Not *at* war. He wasn't *at* war with anybody. He was just trying to keep out of its way. And obviously not doing too well at that. Although he was at least alive, where a lot of others were not. He wondered how Goya had felt when Napoleon's cut-throats were plying their trade about him. How had *he* responded to the sound of guns, to the sight of blood soaking the hard, rust clay of Spain? No need to wonder. He had seen Goya revealed, sliced open in the black violence of his *Disasters of War.* He had seen how he felt in the chilling *May 3, 1808,* with its shrieking, trembling citizens facing the French firing squads. It was all there, all in that terrible power of the brush, along with an irrepressible kind of joy. Not joy in the terror and the blood, but joy at having been able to rip some of that anguish out of the air and freeze it, make it seen. Duvid had already felt it in his own first sketches, in the stunned faces and doll-like awkwardness of the wounded, in the entire night-mare confusion of retreat. The clamor alone was overwhelming . . . the rattle of wheels, the throbbing of motors, the clatter of hoofs, the cracking of whips, the groans of the dying, the cries of women, the whimpering of children, threats, oaths, screams, imprecations, and always, above it all, the monotonous shuffle, shuffle of countless feet. And behind them the dead, with their gray-green flesh and all dignity gone. All that was left were suppurating corpses that still showed the horrors of dying and the terror of death. And this was how it was. Nothing remained to be hoped for but that the earth would cover them quickly, the surrounding darkness extinguish them. The final act of grace was oblivion.

Duvid blew his nose and spat to get rid of the smell and taste of the dead horses. The horses were well behind them by now, but the odor, or its memory, hung on, while around them, the countryside, in the full bloom of summer, with the fields a lush green, and the geraniums red along the farmers' walls, was shining and bright under an azure sky.

Hutchins grinned vaguely beneath his mask of dust. "Belgium in August. Lovely. We must remember to come again sometime."

"If it's still here."

"It'll be here. Belgians are very stubborn. They refuse to live anywhere else." There was a thin, tight edge to his voice that had been stretching a little tighter each day. "Or die anywhere else, either." He shook his head, the motion that of an old man no longer able to comprehend the behavior of the world about him. "They should have let the damned Germans through when they asked. In the end, it'll be the same anyway. Except for the dead. Except for everything laid waste. I could beat my head against a tree and weep. You know why I could weep? Because it's so useless. Germany will get what she wants no matter how many die. She wanted this war, she was prepared for it, and she's amoral, pragmatic, and contemptuous enough to win it. Very important ingredients in waging war. Especially this war. I can already see how this one's going to be. It's going to be different from the usual nice, simple, European-style war that everyone could understand and forgive because they'd all been fighting the same kind of war for a thousand years. One group of civilized gentlemen fighting another group of civilized gentlemen under the same set of rules."

Hutchins stared, gravel-eyed, at the back of a soldier, lurching along in front of him. "But this war," he said, "this war isn't going to be simple and understandable. It's going to be an attack of the animal world upon the house of humanity. Europe will be turned into a cemetery a thousand miles long and a thousand miles wide. Men, women, children . . . it won't make any difference. This is only the beginning, but the pattern has been set. I have nightmares about it. I close my eyes and see visions of Europe a few years from now. Ruins. Ruins everywhere. Ten-year-old children using knives to steal a crust of bread. No young men anywhere except those on crutches, because all the rest are dead or in prison camps. Old people stumbling around in rags and dropping dead of cold and hunger. No factories producing, because they've all been shelled to rubble. No laws or justice, only military rule laid out by the Germans. No homes, no schools, nothing . . ."

He paused and shuffled through the dust in silence, a spare, bookish man, looking curiously out of place in the winding column of soldiers and refugees. "Nothing," he repeated softly. "And America . . . I'm not sure yet about America. But if we're smart we'll . . ."

Then there was the sound, and Duvid automatically shoved Hutchins into a ditch beside the road and dived after him. The shell hit close by. Duvid saw a flash and felt the earth rise and himself being lifted with it, and he thought, it's not fair, I'm not even at war with anybody, it's not fair at all. Then there was a roar that started white and went red, and he felt the strange shock of iron tearing his arm and knew he was hurt, except that there was no pain. He sensed that he was going to go out and it was quite peaceful to relax into the spinning, painless chaos. He tried to breathe but his breath would not come, and he went out.

He opened his eyes. Something was weighing him down. He pushed against it and it rolled off. He saw the uniform and knew it must be one of the soldiers, but there was no longer a face above the uniform. There was just a pulpy, red-and-white mass. He turned away. The ground was torn up and there were cries and screams and the sound of more shells coming over and exploding in the distance. Duvid looked for Hutchins and saw him sitting close by, in the ditch. His face was black, the whites of his eyes enlarged. Duvid crawled over to him. "You all right?"

The eyes blinked dazedly, then focused. "I don't know."

"You hit?"

"I don't think so."

He started to get up, but Duvid pulled him flat. Hutchins was staring at his arm. "Jesus Christ!"

Duvid looked down, surprised, remembering all over again that he had been hit. His sleeve was sodden with blood, and the arm was numb. He shook his head. It still wasn't part of him. Then he thought, it's my left arm, I'm glad it's my left arm.

There were bodies all around. Some were crawling, or trying to crawl, but most lay still. Soldiers were going about picking up the wounded and loading them into wagons and trucks. The dead they just dragged to the side of the road. A Red Cross man examined Duvid's arm, put on some medication and a bandage, and said something to him in French. Hutchins translated. "He said you're lucky. It missed the bone. It went straight through."

Duvid nodded his thanks to the aid man, a short, deep-chested peasant with crossed eyes. He felt a sudden and deep affection for the little cockeyed Belgian. Strange, to feel so warmly toward someone he had never even seen until a few minutes ago. His name, Duvid learned, was Rougier and he had a small farm that was now overrun by the Germans. Karlinsky, out of a Russian *shtetl* by way of New York, and Rougier, out of a patch of land not far from Louvain, linked by a blood-soaked bandage somewhere near the reduced city of Malines, on a summer's day, with a *Times* correspondent named Hutchins crouched beside them as interpreter.

Then the shells again started reaching for their sector and they all went flat. And with the flash and the bump of the bursts and the smell, they heard the singing off of the shrapnel and the thump of falling earth. There were cries and swearing up and down the road and Duvid felt a common hatred, with those about him, for the impersonal killers, miles away, who had them helplessly cowering in holes, blasted and sought out by the machine age with great blocks of explosives hurled from an impregnable distance. God! You couldn't even see what was killing you. Everyone crouched together, as close to the ground as they could get, their legs and bodies touching, as shell after shell hit around them, deafening them, covering them with a pelting shower of earth, stones, and broken twigs.

"Oh, the bastards!" Hutchins was yelling. "Oh, the murdering bastards!"

The shelling stopped, and Duvid raised his head and peered over the ridge of the road. Out of a grove of trees, perhaps half a mile away, a long, moving line had appeared, the figures tiny, gray, curiously unreal in the distance. There they were. At least you could see them now. There was wild excitement among the refugees. Many abandoned their belongings and fled across the fields. Others struggled to carry their effects with them. But all who could ran, splitting apart from the main column singly and in small groups. Some of the soldiers, Duvid saw, ran with them, but most seemed to be taking defensive positions in the drainage ditch along the road. Officers on horseback galloped up and down the line shouting orders and waving pistols or swords and looking, Duvid thought, pathetically heroic and futile. In half an hour, they would be either dead or captured.

"I think," Hutchins sighed, "the time has come for us to get out of here."

The Artist

Duvid nodded. The initial shock of being hit had worn off and he was beginning to feel pain. They left the road and headed for a patch of woods on a hill off to the right. Reaching it, they stopped to look back. The wooded elevation offered a clear, protected view of the Belgian defensive positions and the fields across which the Germans were advancing. How beautiful and sad, Duvid thought, like a brightly colored carpet upon which a death was about to occur.

The Germans came shoulder to shoulder in long, even rows, as though parading down the streets of Berlin. Disdainfully erect, unhurried, they seemed to expect little resistance. And so far, the Belgians had not fired a shot. Duvid hoped they had decided to surrender. It would be more sensible than fighting and dying. One way or another, the Germans would get what they wanted. The most that could be bought here was a brief delay, paid for in blood. Duvid wondered where Rougier was in all this, and what the little, cross-eyed aid man was thinking as he lay behind the road, waiting for the big, gray machine to roll over him. Was he thinking of the farm he would probably never see again? . . . or perhaps a family to whom he had said good-by just a few weeks before and to whom he represented a major portion of the universe? Was this what soldiers thought about when they marched off to war, to the drums and the bugles and the fluttering of banners, down the clean, scrubbed streets of home? Did they realize then that all it would finally mean was lying in the dirt under a blue August sky, waiting to die?

When the Germans were halfway across the field, the Belgians opened fire. They apparently had no artillery, only rifles, pistols, and a single machine gun . . . and the firing, reaching back to where Duvid and Hutchins lay, sounded less like guns than small firecrackers. Nevertheless, scattered holes began to appear in the advancing lines. And in the sector opposite the machine gun, the holes quickly widened to great, wide gaps.

"My God," Duvid whispered, "Look what that machine gun is doing."

"One of the great scientific advances of our age," said Hutchins. "Adds a whole new dimension to the art of war. One soldier can now kill two hundred men a minute. Beautiful!"

The Artist

The back rows were stumbling and falling over the bodies of those in front, but kept coming, line after line, still erect and unhurried. Duvid fought a grim exaltation. They were Germans and he had learned to despise them, but how could he take pleasure at the sight of men dying? Yet watching the gray tide being ripped to pieces, seeing those spiked helmets go down and not get up, he *did* feel a wild kind of joy. He *wanted* those Germans to die. The more that died here, the fewer there would be to do their butchering elsewhere. And viewed from this distance, it hardly seemed real anyway. No screams heard, no blood or torn flesh seen. Only tiny, anonymous figures moving and falling. This, he imagined, must be how war seemed to the generals back at headquarters, sitting in elegant, pressed uniforms and matching wits with their counterparts a hundred miles away. How much more pleasant to sit back there moving colored pins on maps, than to have to look down at the queer, unattached leg lying beside your face in the mud and realize it's yours.

The battered German lines finally broke and retreated to the grove of trees. Behind them, the yellow-green field was spotted with clusters of gray. The Belgians cheered. Then the German artillery started again and the cheering stopped. The shells came in a closely spaced barrage that straddled the road and sent up geysers of earth. Before the last explosion died, a line of horsemen came out of the distant grove and started across the field at full gallop. "Christ!" said Hutchins. "Uhlans. They really want that road." Hoofs pounded, lances gleamed. Duvid stared. It was awesome, curiously anachronistic. Cavalry charges in a war with machine guns. The Germans. If the Valkyrie could somehow be mobilized, they would throw them in too. The Belgians kept up their fire until the lances were on them. Then it became a pigsticking.

Leaving, Duvid looked back once through the trees and saw, dimly, all that remained of the Belgians. It wasn't much. Good-by, he thought. Good-by, Rougier.

The Artist

Duvid woke up, listening to the rumble of the guns. He smelled the damp, loamy odor of the burned-out barn, and saw the stars and the lightning flash of artillery through the bones of the roof. The firing came from several different directions and, at times, seemed quite close. Hutchins was curled up close by, his face troubled even in sleep. They had made some progress toward Antwerp, but German patrols were out in force and there had been a few very bad moments. When they picked you up behind their lines, they asked no questions. Nor did they care what papers you carried. They just shot.

He lay rigid, too tired to move. His arm ached and he could feel the warm seepage of blood through Rougier's bandage. In a general, impersonal way, the German army had tried to kill him and failed. But it had not missed by much. A few inches to the right, and it would have been over. No more Duvid Karlinsky. The thought had not fully broken through before. It did now. He closed his eyes and tried to imagine his own death. The blow had fallen. The agony was over. He was dead and had entered the final blackness. If it *was* blackness. Maybe it was the final *light.* Anyway, he was there. And one by one the people in his life came to look at him. His mother, father, Aunt Tybie, Rachel, Annie. What did he have to say to them now? What did he feel for them? Now there was nothing to say but what he really felt and thought. And he couldn't say it to them because he was dead, but only to himself. Reality, not make-believe. Truth, not lies. Everything else was over.

He smiled vaguely in the darkness. His mother, father, and Aunt Tybie were simple. What he felt for them was clear. Alive or dead, he would say the same things. Rachel and Annie were something else. Not simple at all. It was his inclination as a poor human thing to lie and to live by lies. He probably lied even when he thought he was telling the truth, because there was no sure way for him to know the difference. The most important lies were for yourself anyway. Survival hung on them. If you had to face the cold, sharp edge of truth every morning, you'd soon slit your throat on it.

When it came to truth, Rachel was the only bona fide expert he had ever known. He had once seen a photograph of her, aged thirteen, in a ruffled birthday dress. She was posed in the photogra-

265

pher's studio beside some fake Grecian columns, a delicate, fair-haired girl with bony wrists and intense dark shadows under her eyes, premature signs of suffering. In virginal white, she had the cool, disdainful pride of the female child who knows it won't be long before she is nubile and has the power to get what she wants. She knew more about truth at thirteen than he did at twenty-five. Maybe more than he would ever know. Although she had been teaching him now for six years. Yet he had the feeling, increasingly, that he would never quite learn enough.

And she was smart . . . with that fine sense of timing that made her the actress she was. She had waited a full six months before coming to him after his marriage, had waited just long enough to make him anxious. He knew she would come, finally. But when? Then she appeared one morning at his studio, smiling, aglow, as bright as the spring sun lacing the tenement walls. No anger, no bitterness, no recrimination. She had come to see him and was delighted with what she saw. Not only him, but his work. He was up to his eyeballs in Jews. With Flemming's help, he was beginning to set a kind of minor vogue in *Yidischkeit*. It took her half an hour to get around to the subject of his marriage.

"I never did congratulate you," she said.

"An understandable oversight."

"It wasn't an oversight. It's just that I thought condolences were more in order. I didn't want to lie."

"God forbid!"

She smiled faintly. "That sounded like my mother. More and more, I find people are sounding like my mother."

Duvid remembered the Sunday visit to Bellevue. *My daughter prides herself on her honesty. She will tell you the truth if it tears your heart.* "Maybe you should try lying."

"Does your wife lie?"

"No."

"Of course not. I forgot. Whores are supposed never to lie. They're also supposed to have big, warm hearts, aren't they?"

"You tell *me.* Annie stopped being a whore the day I married her. When are *you* going to stop?"

She showed no change of expression. "You shouldn't have left

266

me like that. Asleep. In the middle of the night. You gave me some
bad moments until I figured it out. You didn't know I was married,
did you?"

He shook his head.

"Why didn't you at least stay and talk about it?"

"I had nothing to say."

"*I* did."

"You knew where to find me."

"I didn't want to find you. Not for a while, anyway." She looked
at him. "But did you really have to *marry* her?"

"I guess I did."

"It wasn't worthy of you."

That made him angry. "How the hell would *you* know what was
worthy of me?"

"I know everything about you. You forget. We go back a long
way."

He glared.

"All right. So you showed me. You married a whore. Is that
supposed to make us even?"

"Nothing can do that."

But the ritual fencing was over with the first visit. What needed
to be said had been said. When she next appeared, she brought only
a single, basic fact of truth and handed it to him like an apple. "I
love you, Duvid. I always have. Whatever else you think you know
about me, please . . . know that."

Of course he knew. How could he not? All sins, all existent
problems were *hers.* *He* was lovable. And along with her love, she
offered her usual devoutness toward the flesh. She had the religion
of all creative people, which was pleasure. Her skin was subtle,
white, silken, animate. Why should he deny himself? Why indeed?
Deep inside him, there was something that responded with a loud
bark to this woman's skin. *Woof! Woof!* A purely animal reflex that
had nothing to with age, intellect, experience, or history. In sickness
or health, in anger, joy, or sorrow there came the old woof-woof at
merely the sight of her. Forget fidelity. Forget the sacred vows of
marriage. *What* sacred vows? *What* marriage? Standing for two minutes under a marriage canopy with a whore? *Woof! Woof!*

The Artist

But now he was dead, his flesh unfeeling. All that was through. What would he say to her *now*? He didn't know. The whole idea was crazy. He *wasn't* dead. His flesh *did* feel. And what it felt was pain, a dull, throbbing ache that began in the upper part of his left arm and spread through his chest and stomach. That was the only truth he could swear to. The rest was a fake. He might think, I'm dead and from now on I'm going to speak the truth, but the truth would hear him and run away even before he was through thinking. And it would keep running. He knew. It was an old friend. He had been chasing it for years with his art. But it was no easier to catch with a brush. At least not for him. Maybe other artists found it easier. Most of the good ones seemed to burn with the kind of flame that plucked inspirational truths out of the air like bananas. They walked in a perpetual aura of color and design. They saw forests of jewels in rich settings. While he, Duvid Karlinsky, traveled through this same glut of wonders with a box over his head. Like a blind man stumbling through secret landscapes, he felt rather than saw. And all he felt were people. Not things. Never things. He had once read, "Man liveth not by Self alone but in his brother's face." He couldn't say it better. What didn't breathe didn't move him. What he couldn't find in his brother's face, he didn't want. And now, having left the East Side of New York, having broken free of his tenement walls, he found himself with a vastly expanded number of brothers. None of whom, (consider *this*) seemed even remotely Jewish.

When lying became too painful, he got up, moved quietly past Hutchins, and stepped outside. There was a low moon, looking pale and lost against the flash of the guns. Occasionally a flare went up in the distance and the rattle of small arms could be heard against the deeper rumblings of the howitzers. Even in the middle of the night, he thought. A twenty-four-hour-a-day, seven-day-a-week business. When were you supposed to sleep, rest, eat? Soldiers should organize, form unions. They should demonstrate. For what? Better *dying* conditions?

Hutchins had heard him get up and came out behind him. "What's wrong?"

"Nothing. I just couldn't sleep."

The reporter looked unhappily at Duvid's arm. "You must hurt like hell. Want me to put on another bandage?"

"It'll be all right."

"Jesus, that was a close one. I keep thinking about it."

"So do I."

"It's my fault. I never should have gotten you into this."

"I got in all by myself."

"It was my idea to come over. If it wasn't for me, you'd be home in bed with your wife right now."

"We'll be home soon enough. Once we reach Antwerp, there shouldn't be any trouble getting out."

Hutchins stared off at the gun flashes, at the distant line of a steeple, graceful and poignant in the broken dark. "If we reach Antwerp, I think I'm staying."

"Staying *where?*"

"Wherever it's happening. If the Belgians collapse, I'll tie onto the French. But as long as this goes on, I want to be around to write about it."

Duvid frowned. "You said yourself it's going to be a disaster. You're crazy to get involved."

"I *am* involved. I was involved the minute I saw what those butchers did at Ardennes." He shook his head. "Human beings."

"I know."

"Three weeks ago I wouldn't have believed it possible."

"Why not?"

Hutchins looked at him.

"I saw the same things twenty-two years ago in Russia. Except that Germans are more efficient than Russians. Neater too. At least they bury the dead."

"I forgot," said Hutchins.

"It's nothing new. If it doesn't break out in one place, it'll break out in another. And you won't change any part of it by staying around and getting killed."

"Maybe I won't. But I can't see myself sitting fat and safe in New York and reading what others write about it."

"Why not? What's so noble about being blown to bits? Haven't you seen enough corpses to know what it's like?" He was suddenly furious. "Goddamn Christian hero!"

The Artist

Hutchins grinned. "What's poor old Christ got to do with it?"

"It's a feeling all Jews carry in their stomachs. Every time a Christian starts acting chivalrous, we expect the worst. And we haven't been wrong in two thousand years."

"Am I acting chivalrous?"

"You're acting like a *schmuck!*"

"All right."

"It's not all right. It's all *wrong.*"

"Call it what you want." Hutchins's voice was soft, almost lost under the guns. "But whatever else I am, Duvid, I'm no hero. Christian or otherwise. I'm not even brave. In fact I've always considered myself a physical coward. Even as a kid, I ran from fights. The result of an overdeveloped imagination. I can picture much too clearly what happens to flesh when it's struck by a hard, solid object. And I have a very real and terrible dread of dying violently. So understand. If I ever consider putting my body in harm's way, it's not through any sense of chivalry. It's just that I can't help myself."

"Bullshit! You don't *want* to help yourself. You love the image of yourself gallantly braving shot and shell in the cause of truth. My God, look at you! You get positively beatific at just the thought. And how much better if you could get yourself killed. What a beautiful martyrdom. Saint Hutch! You'd like that, wouldn't you?"

"It does have a ring to it." Hutchins's smile was remote. "But why so angry? Jealous?"

"Why should I be jealous?"

"Because you've got an even greater need to stay with this thing than I do. Your art is thriving on it, growing fat, eager, excited. Every line you put down soars. Whatever the dangers and horrors, you *know* this is where it's all happening. You're getting a glimpse of the dark underside of the moon and it's moving you as you haven't been moved in years and you hate like hell to let it go."

Duvid said nothing. He *did* want to stay. And he was ashamed. It made no sense. He had a wife at home, a pleasant life, increasing acceptance of his work from critics and public. He had love, warmth, strong ties. He had safety. He could live in the same place for fifty peaceful, uninterrupted years, sit down to Friday night dinners with his family, and die comfortably in a soft bed, an old man surrounded

270

The Artist

by grieving relatives and friends. Fool, he thought. You have this waiting for you, but would risk it all. And for what? A short, terrible horror show with a possibly violent ending.

"You're sicker with it than I am," said Hutchins. "And you suffer more with it because you're a Jew and have an ingrown sense of tragedy running through your blood." He stared thoughtfully at the shadows thrown by the moon on Duvid's face. "But I envy you your Jewishness. It runs so beautifully deep and dark. It's so marvelously uncompromising. You *know* who you are. Not many Christians do. Mostly, we have to be told in Sunday sermons. We're told to love our neighbor as ourself and our enemy as our brother. Yet look at us. We live among our guns and their sound drowns out the soft voice of Christ, and only the screams of vengeance can be heard above the explosions. Then we get down on our knees on Sunday, and think our words fly straight up to God, after we've spent the week killing our neighbors and brothers."

Hutchins blinked and seemed to forget for a moment to whom he was talking. He looked around vaguely at the ruined barn, the silvered dark of abandoned fields. "Our good Christian governments," he said, his voice very tired. "Ah, I'm going back to sleep." He turned abruptly and shuffled in through a dark, jagged hole in the barn wall.

Duvid stayed outside. When he was upright or moving, the pain in his arm seemed lessened. He walked over to the remains of the farmhouse, its stones fire-gutted and black, and wondered about those who had lived there. Were they alive or dead? If they still lived, would they come back to rebuild? He hoped they would. Judging from what was left, it had been a fine place. I must remember where this is, he thought. Then later, after the war, maybe I can return and see it rebuilt and tell them of the night I spent here. There was a curious comfort in the thought, until he recalled a fragment of half-forgotten rhyme:

> They are all gone away
> The house is dead and still
> There is nothing more to say.
>
> Through crumbled walls and gray

The Artist

The night shows bleak and dark.
They are all gone away . . .

And he felt, sadly, that a small, lovely world had reached an end.

Later, he sat outside the barn and watched the sky slowly lighten and the flash of guns fade with the night. Then he must have dozed, because his next awareness was that of a trembling of the earth beneath him and the sound of horses' hoofs. He opened his eyes, blinking in the early light, and saw them coming. There were two of them and they rode out of the east, out of the place where the sun would come up, and Duvid saw the spiked helmets and the lances and thought, *Vay iz mir,* the fucking Cossacks. He quickly rose and ducked through the hole in the barn wall. But he knew they had seen him.

Hutchins had heard them also and was up. "What is it?"

"Uhlans. Two of them. And they saw me."

"Sonofabitch!"

"We can't run. They'd have us like stuck pigs in fifty yards."

Hutchins's face had turned gray under its layer of dust. "What do we do?"

"Go out and meet them. Show them our papers. Technically, they can't touch us."

"Technically?" Hutchins swallowed dryly. "Technically, I think I'm going to vomit."

Duvid stepped outside. "Come on. We can't let them think we're hiding. And for God's sake, don't act frightened."

"Jesus! How do I do *that?*"

"First, stop shaking."

"Well, I *told* you I was a coward."

"Just lean against the wall here. That should hold your knees. And let me do the talking."

"Since when do you speak German?"

"I don't. But Yiddish should be close enough. They'll understand me."

"I hope so."

Duvid saw them clearly now as they rode at a trot across the field, saw the sun-darkened faces of the men, the casually held lances, the sweated flanks of the horses. One of the Germans had a big, blond moustache and seemed young. The other held a cigarette between his teeth and was heavy-jawed and smooth-shaven. Then Duvid saw the bottle in the hand of the blond horseman and felt an old coldness crawl into his stomach like a lizard.

At twenty yards, the Uhlans reined to a walk. Duvid moved toward them, smiling. "Good morning!" he called in Yiddish.

"Halt!" came the command in German.

Duvid stopped where he was and waited as they approached. The top buttons of their tunics were open and a small collection of household silver was tied to their saddle rolls. There was something wildly incongruous about these Teutonic warriors, lances in hand, carrying off their loot like a pair of itinerant peddlers on their way to market. Bad for the Prussian image. They should be reported to higher authority. Except that higher authority was probably too busy carting off their own wagonloads of Belgian valuables to pay attention. A lance came to rest inches from Duvid's chest. Its tip was stained red. (The former owner of the silver?) The stain was long-dried and dark and Duvid had the feeling, looking at it, that the Uhlan had been very careful not to wipe it off, that it was carried proudly, as a mark of valor. He looked at the other lance and found it clean, its steel point shining and virginal. He filed these facts away, as though they were of particular significance and might have to be reckoned with in future dealings.

"Who are you?" demanded the German with the stained lance. His spiked helmet was tipped backward and slightly too large, giving him the look, with his smooth, young face and fair moustache, of a little boy masquerading as a soldier.

"American newsmen," said Duvid, relieved at being able to understand the German. "And we're just trying to get home without being blown up by either you or the Belgians."

The soldiers looked at one another. "Jews," said the older one, who had a fine, jagged dueling scar high on his left cheek, and dark, close-set eyes. He grinned, as though at a private joke.

"American," Duvid declared and started to reach into his pocket.

"Halt!" The lance plucked at Duvid's shirt buttons. "Hands in the air."

Duvid slowly raised his right arm. "I only wanted to show you my papers."

"We don't care about your papers. Everybody has papers. And spies have the best papers of all." The top of the lance moved to Duvid's throat. "Put up your other hand too."

"I can't. That arm is hurt."

The lance tapped the bloody bandage and Duvid gasped and knew, if he hadn't known before, that it was going to be bad. "Where did you get the wound, Jew spy?" It was the one with the moustache who was doing the questioning. His companion, still grinning, leaned sideways in his saddle, took the bottle from the other's hand, and drank from it.

"On the road. Your cannon didn't recognize me as an American."

"Are you saying German cannon are stupid?"

"No, no. They're very intelligent cannon. They just didn't see me."

"You!" The Uhlan nodded his oversized helmet at Hutchins. "Hands in the air!"

"He doesn't understand German," Duvid said. Then, in English, to his friend . . . "Put up your hands. The sons-of-bitches are half-drunk and playing with us. Just try to stay relaxed."

"Sure," said Hutchins, raising both hands. "If I can keep from fainting."

"Silence!" commanded the moustache. "What is he saying?"

"He says he's very happy to meet two such fine soldiers of the Kaiser and that I should interview you for our newspaper."

"The Jew is lying," said the dueling scar. "I think we should just kill them both."

"No," Duvid said. "That would be a big mistake. Your superiors would be very angry if you killed two citizens of the United States."

"Jews aren't citizens of anyplace. They're just Jews."

Everybody in the world, Duvid thought, loves us. "My friend isn't a Jew. He's a Protestant. A very good one." At this point he was just trying to keep them in good humor and talking. He couldn't think further than that.

The Uhlans studied Hutchins gravely. Not understanding what

274

was going on, he stood, hands in air, smiling nervously at first one, then the other.

"He looks like a Jew to me."

"Me too. Look at the eyes and nose. You can always tell from the eyes and nose."

"No, no," Duvid said. "I assure you. He's not Jewish."

Both Uhlans took a drink from the bottle. They grinned at each other. "Tell him to prove it," said the moustache. "Tell him to pull down his pants and show us he's not a Jew. Tell him if you're lying, we're going to cut it off and feed it to you."

Duvid half turned to Hutchins. "I told them you weren't a Jew. Now they want you to drop your pants and prove it. For both our sakes, you'd better not be circumcised."

"You don't mean it."

"I'm afraid I do. And so do they." Duvid moistened his lips. *"Are you circumcised?"*

"No."

"Thank God!"

A lance probed Hutchins's belt and he hurriedly undid his trousers and let them fall. Then he stood there, trembling with fear, anger, and humiliation as the Uhlans pointed and laughed. Poor Hutch. But let them have their little joke, Duvid thought. As long as they're laughing, we're all right. His eyes searched the landscape. For what? A miracle? Slowly, he lowered his right hand. The sun had broken through a line of poplars and the trees showed clear and graceful in the morning light, their trunks tapered and the road before them shiny with a wisp of mist over it. Then he turned and saw his friend weeping, making no sound but just standing there, exposed, the tears making small paths through the dust on his cheeks, and Duvid thought that of all the things he had ever wanted to do in his life, he had surely never wanted to do anything as badly as he wanted to hurt these two laughing soldiers.

Finally they tired of that part of the game and the laughter ended. "What have you got hidden in the barn, Jew spy?"

"Nothing," said Duvid. "Just our musette bags."

The moustached soldier dismounted, went inside, and came out

275

with the bags. He emptied them onto the ground and picked up Duvid's sketch pads.

"Who made these spy pictures?"

"They're not spy pictures," said Duvid. "They're sketches I drew for my newspaper. I'm an artist."

The moustache remounted and both Uhlans studied the drawings.

"You don't like German soldiers," said the dueling scar. "Do you, Jew spy?"

Duvid did not say anything.

"You were asked a question," said the moustache.

Now, thought Duvid, we're coming to it. "I've never really known any German soldiers."

"Then why do you draw pictures of us killing women and children? Why do you show us burning buildings?"

Again, Duvid did not answer, He was watching both soldiers closely. The moustache was the more aggressive, but didn't worry him as much as the dueling scar. He didn't like the close-set eyes. When something came from there, it would come fast and without warning.

A lance swung against his wound. "Answer the question."

"I only drew what I saw."

"You're a liar," said the moustache. Aren't you, Jew?"

Duvid glanced at Hutchins. The reporter had lifted his trousers, but there was a tight, frozen look to his face. When it came to it, there would be no help from there.

"Yes," he said. "I'm a liar."

"And you were going to put these lies in your American newspaper," said the moustache. "Weren't you?"

"Yes."

"Jew pig!"

The lance flatted the wound again, but harder this time and Duvid cried out.

"Please!" begged Hutchins.

They didn't hear him. They were too deep into Duvid now and feeding on it. The moustache was grinning, the little-boy-playing-grown-up-soldier-look soaring free. But it was still the dueling scar that Duvid watched, seeing the narrowing of the close-set eyes and the pressing together of the lips and hearing the blood shriek like eagles in his ears. And he thought, *he is going to put it into me now,* and moved even before he saw the steel come, moved just enough for it to go by and not in, and his hands on the shaft then and pulling with the forward momentum of the thrust. The pull caught the Uhlan off balance and he slid forward as Duvid twisted the lance free, not falling, but hanging there over the horse's withers and staring, with vague surprise, as his own steel came back to him. It went in where his tunic parted, went in through the pale flesh at the base of his throat, and although his mouth opened to scream, there was no sound other than that sometimes made by water rushing through a narrow place, a soft, not unpleasant *chunk-chunk-chunk,* which was the last sound he was ever going to hear.

Duvid spun to meet the other German, but the moustache was still struggling for position, his horse rearing, the long lance swinging as he fought to bring it down. Shock had melted his face into something it had not been before, a fast aging that spoke of ancient hatreds and dark fears.

"Jew!"

It was all packed into the single word. And hearing it, Duvid felt the pure certainty that comes with knowing that for one moment, at least, things were in perfect balance, exactly as they should be, and that he was about to ride them to the end.

He was grinning, although he did not know it, his mouth straining into a grimace that had nothing to do with what he felt. *Cossack!* Then the German's helmet fell off as his horse reared and Duvid saw the fair, close-cropped hair and the smooth, soft, mother-loved face which, freed of its martial covering, suddenly seemed less threatening than frightened and confused. My God, he thought, he's a boy. And the joy suddenly went out of him.

"Leave us alone," he said. "We're Americans. We're not at war!" He wanted no more of it. The flurry of action over, the lance was a ton load in his hands, his bad arm numb, almost useless. He wondered about Hutchins, but couldn't shift an eye to look for him. The Uhlan had his horse under control now, his lance level and in line with Duvid's chest. He glanced at his companion where he lay, face down, in the dirt and blood, his horse waiting a short distance away. Then he looked at Duvid and Duvid looked back into his eyes, the bluest he had ever seen, a pure, celestial blue that must have come from one of the original Huns in Attila's horned, hairy band. "Leave us alone," Duvid said again and saw the light fading in the German's eyes as it does in those who are dying, and he felt he had him then, saw it, in fact, in that great sweet, overspoiled young beauty of a German face, saw the fear and the not wanting to die. It was like a presence that had taken over the body that hosted it and that now wanted to run because it had had a clear, cold whiff of the grave and had decided it wanted no part of it. But the body and the uniform and the beautiful grown-up moustache would not let it run, but forced it, instead, to face the dark Jew eyes that had already killed once and might kill again, forced it to hold because to do less would be to die anyway. And Duvid, watching, saw this too and with it the returning light which was beautiful enough to paint and which he might have loved if he did not understand so well what it meant. Ah, he's coming, he thought, and knew that either way now it wasn't going to be good.

He came with the new sun lighting his hair, a Teutonic knight without armor, came with a hoarse cry they must have told him, on some remote regimental training ground, was guaranteed to chill the blood of any and all enemies of the Fatherland. Duvid gripped his lance and took a step toward him. He did not know what he was going to do, but it felt right to take that step because he felt a sudden lack of will in his legs and he had to be sure they would move when he needed them. By any reasonable judgment, he should be dead within the minute. On foot, hurt, untrained in the use of the curiously archaic weapon he held, he was no logical match for the mounted Uhlan. But he sensed an uncertainty, an emptiness in the German's mood which, if he did things right, he could enter. He waited then, watching the slender spear come, waited until it was almost on him, then dropped to his knees and felt it brush his hair going by, felt it even as his own lance went up, thrust hard by his good arm and guided by the bad. He felt a shock through the shaft and let go his grip as the charging horse carried it off, one end dragging the ground, the other held fast inside the rider.

Unguided, the horse stopped twenty yards away and Duvid slowly followed. The steel had gone in just under the heart and the Uhlan had died fast. Duvid pulled him from the saddle, lowered him to the ground, and carefully withdrew the lance. The German's head lay in a small, pale bed of pink flowers growing very close to the earth. His eyes were closed above his pale-fuzzed cheek, giving the upper part of his face a look of gentle youth. But below, the moustache remained fierce and warriorlike. Duvid stood staring at him. His brain seemed to be working with difficulty. I have just killed two men, he thought. No. One man and one boy.

When he turned, Hutchins was coming toward him. His earlier, frozen look had been replaced by an expression of thoughtful reserve, and he seemed to cling to it as a man clings to a very expensive possession. "Is he dead?"

"Yes," Duvid said.

Hutchins nodded slowly, consideringly. "I see. And you? You're all right?"

"I'm fine."

He said nothing more and they went back and collected their things. Duvid brushed the dirt from his sketch pads and put them away. His spy pictures. Then they left.

They walked in silence. The sun was still low in the sky and there were long paths of blue-purple shadow across the hills to the east. Duvid had a compass and they were following it almost due north toward Antwerp. They kept away from the roads. Sometimes they passed farmhouses, but saw no movement about them. The sound of gunfire, when they heard it, grew fainter and came mostly from the south and west.

About midday, they entered a forest and stopped to rest. Duvid sat with his back to a tree. Hutchins stared at him. He had hardly spoken all morning and the expression of thoughtful reserve he had worn earlier had remained. But now, as Duvid watched, his face trembled and the expression seemed to be sliding away, melting, exposing what was beneath.

"I just stood there," he whispered. "I just stood there and did nothing while they tried to kill you."

"There was nothing you could do."

279

The Artist

"I could have done *something!* Not a movement. Not a sound. I should have at least distracted them. But I didn't ever do that."

"Stop it. It's over."

"Hutchins, the inadequate man. Karlinsky kills two Germans and Hutchins can't even open his mouth to yell."

"All right," Duvid said flatly. "So I'm a better killer than you. What makes you think I'm so proud of *that?*"

"You better be. It's the only reason you're alive. It sure as hell isn't because of me. And you know what bothers me most? I didn't even *try* to help."

"You were frozen. It happens. When you're like that, you *can't* do anything."

Hutchins shook his head. "I didn't *want* to do anything. You think I cared what happened to you at that moment? All I was thinking about was me. Me! Me! Me! If I just stayed quiet, I thought, and didn't move, maybe they wouldn't notice me. Maybe they'd be satisfied enough killing a Jew, to leave a good Christian alone. Jesus, I was happy to be Christian then." He blinked rapidly at Duvid. "If it was me they were trying to kill, you wouldn't have just stood there. Would you?"

"Hutch . . ."

"Of course you wouldn't. You're not made that way. If you had to crawl, if you had to go at them with your teeth, you would have done it." Hutchins laughed, the sound bitter and lost among the sun-spotted leaves. "And I'm the one who wanted to stay and write about the war. What did you call me? A goddamn Christian hero? Some Christian. Some hero."

"You never claimed to be a fighter in this war."

"Of course not. Just a critic of it. Oh, I'm great at criticism. It's my life's work. I can tell you what's wrong with anything. Only don't ask me to *do* something about it. It's the nature of the profession. Writers. Look at us! A pack of poetic despairers, oversensitive resigners. We pick up a pen and resign from all action. We criticize books and poetry and social conditions and governments and wars and the policies of every nation in the world. But when we're asked to take a risk, when we're asked to really *do* something about what we've fought so bravely for on paper, what do we do? We freeze.

The Artist

We suffer instant and total paralysis." Hutchins stared piercingly at Duvid as though hunting down any trace of mockery or resentment of his failure in Duvid's face. "There comes a time when words just aren't enough. There comes a time for wild-eyed fighters, crazy with faith, oblivious of danger and death. There comes a time," he said coldly, "when you *do* charge a lance. Not because it makes sense. But because to do less would be unthinkable."

Hutchins sighed and shivered a little. "I watched you. I saw the things you did. You've earned the right to make your statement about this war. *I* haven't."

Duvid stared at the patch of ground between his legs.

"The next time," Hutchins said fiercely, ". . . the next time I won't freeze. I'll die first. Believe me."

Duvid believed him. Especially the part about dying.

He believed him all through the rest of that day of skirting roads and villages and German patrols, believed him halfway into the night when, somewhere along the Scheldt River, they ran into and joined another column of retreating Belgians, believed him even as they stumbled at last, dry-mouthed and exhausted, into the comparative safety of Antwerp. Just as he also believed, feeling the depth of his friend's anguish, that he was not about to sail home and leave him to do his dying alone. Dimly, he realized his personal declaration of war had already been made. It had been made on lunatic terms, on the threat of a pair of archaic Prussian lances and the killing of two Germans, on the memory of mass graves and dead women and children and senselessly reduced villages, all jumbled together with the equally insane image of a cock-eyed little Belgian putting a bandage on his arm and telling him he was lucky. But the declaration was real. And shuffling through the refugee-clogged streets of Antwerp, staring dazedly at this beautiful and gracious city that would soon be rubble, he knew that any hope of an armistice was a long way off.

THIRTEEN

1919: New York, N. Y.

The sighting of land came early in the morning and sent a flurry of excitement through the ship, as if the long, low smudge on the horizon was a great surprise and not something that had been expected at precisely this time and place ever since they had left Cherbourg. So that Duvid was drawn to the rail with the other passengers, where he had his first glimpse of America in four and a half years and felt himself moved so deeply, and by so many conflicting emotions, that he had to turn, slightly shamefaced, and climb away from the crowd to the forward boat-deck. Alone, he pulled his cap tight in the biting sea wind and squinted through the sun at the Atlantic Highlands. The purity of the air left him breathless, and there was no stain in the water, which stretched off, unbroken, except for an occasional whitecap. Its color was deep and clear, its smell pungent with life. A vast, unseen action was going on below. Yet, Duvid thought, death watched. So if you had a moment of joy, it was better to conceal it. And when your heart beat loudly with hope, you kept that as quiet as possible also.

But the war, the organized death and its threat, was over and he was going home. "I'm going home," he said aloud and the wind threw it back into his face, the same face with which he had left New York, except that it was older and bore a crescent-shaped ridge of scar across the left cheek. He lifted a hand to finger the welted curve ... a habit, a tic, a necessary touching to assure himself it was there.

The Artist

He bore other scars, but these were on his body and not that easily reached. His flesh had drawn shrapnel like a magnet. And this without even carrying a gun. He had fought through four years of war with an arsenal of hard and soft pencils. He had tried to enlist when the Americans came over, but the early wound in his shoulder had healed badly and kept him out. The United States Army, it seemed, had little use for any man who couldn't raise his left arm to an absolutely vertical position. Besides, his combat drawings, reproduced in the *Times* and syndicated across the country, had brought him a fair amount of fame by then, and the word had apparently come down. No guns for Karlinsky. Just pencils. For which he felt no true regret. It was more guilt than belief that had made him try to enlist anyway. After a certain number of years of watching men being blown apart in a variety of styles, uniforms, and places, of listening to the changing reasons they gave you for dying, even the strongest of convictions tended to fade. Finally, it was just more blood, more bodies, more wasted earth. Finally, too, you believed nothing.

The progression of feeling had shown in his work. How different, at the end, from those first angry indictments of German atrocities. The change had come slowly and with pain, but it had come. So that when the uniforms in his drawings were no longer distinguishable from one another, when both living and dead shared the same timeless anonymity, there remained only one enemy . . . the war. And it was everywhere, in everything . . . even, he found, in himself. After Verdun, he had felt it as a grieving, crazed beast, gnawing at his liver with bloodied teeth. He had long ago stopped hating the Germans. He had seen too many of them dead. He had stopped hating anyone. As had his drawings. They spoke neither of pride in killing nor of joy in victory. They spoke only of remorse. We're sorry, they said, that we have been forced to kill our enemy as he stood before us armed and dangerous. Had we been able, we would rather have made him our brother.

Four years, and he had held on till the finish. Hutchins had lasted less than nine months. At which point, for him, it was either home or madness. He had chosen to go home. "I'm sorry," he told Duvid. "I've tried. You know I've tried. But I can't. Not anymore." He held up a gaunt, trembling hand. "My God, look at me! I can't remember when I last slept through a night. Nightmares. I keep swimming in blood. I'm just not made for this." Who *was?* Duvid Karlinsky?

Once, Hutchins had half-accused him of thriving on it. Not true. Maybe his *art,* but not *him.* His friend had later apologized. Still, Nietzsche had claimed that deep pain was ennobling, pain that burned slow, like green wood. But Nietzsche was a German and a bit out of favor at that moment. Also, for this higher education in pain, survival was necessary. You had to be able to outlive the hurt. And this, at least, he had managed. He had not always thought he would. Often, he was sure he wouldn't. But he had done it. He had actually lived with the void. Not closing his eyes to any part of it, not soothing himself with lies about the ultimate triumph and beauty of the human soul, but staring into, through, and past the worst of its blackness. And what he saw there, he had tried to put down. The greater part of his work was done in the trenches, often in the most forward positions. He had it all . . . lice, rats, cold, heat, mud, bombardment, gas. His own particular brand of insanity. But how else could you find out?

Come home, begged his father's letters. *You're crazy,* joined in his mother. Didn't he know this wasn't *his* war? . . . that it was the sole property of the Christians? If they wanted to kill one another off, blow up and bury half the world, that was *their* business. They had been doing it for thousands of years. It had nothing to do with the Jews. No matter who won, the Jews would lose. They *always* lost. True, thought Duvid. Except that this time, everyone was going to lose.

His wife's letters were different. No mention here of his coming home. She knew better. She had known long before he did. Duvid read her letters with the unpleasant feeling that she already considered him dead and was merely fulfilling a vestigial sense of duty in writing at all. If not dead, at least gone. In either case, she clearly did not expect him back. What she was doing now was awaiting the final disposition of her case. In the meantime, she wrote polite, infrequent notes that asked little and told less. For his part, Duvid had found it increasingly difficult to even remember her face. She was a ghost whom he had married a long time ago in a moment of pique, and who had been sending him occasional letters for the past four and a half years. She made no claims upon him with her vague, impersonal accounts of life on the East Side of New York, with her tales of soaring prices and food shortages and the efforts of the young men to keep free of the draft. She made no professions of love, nor did he expect any. His own letters were equally generalized, with no details of the massive dying to which he was witness. Once, curiously, she had asked for a photograph, but he had never sent any. The agony of his face was no fit decoration for the bedside table of a pretty young woman who rolled bandages for the Red Cross and who had a special fondness for pink hair ribbons when she went to sleep at night. Nor had he sent her any notice of his intermittent stays at military hospitals. What point? If he died, she would find out soon enough. If not, it was better that no one at home knew. He did not feel close enough to his wife to tell her the truth of what he was enduring. Sometimes, when he sat down to write her a letter, he had the feeling that he was writing to a strange child, known briefly a long time ago, who had to be protected from the horrors of the grown-up world. Which, he knew, was an utterly senseless way to regard a woman who had traveled all through adolescence and into an early maturity as a working whore.

The wind on the boat deck cut deeply, and he struggled back down to the promenade, his bad leg aching from the cold and making him limp more than usual. On warm, clear days the leg felt better; on cold, damp days it felt worse, and after more than a year he no longer thought about it. It was just there and part of him and it was hard to remember a time when it had been different. An American doctor at a French military hospital had let him know pretty much what to expect from it. The doctor was a fat, middle-aged major from Boston, who seemed to find a perverse satisfaction in squeezing the pale, scarred flesh above Duvid's right knee until Duvid saw red-and-white spots. "Good enough," he grunted after the final examination. "It might not look so pretty, but it'll get you where you want to go. Just don't try to get there too fast for a while."

"I won't."

"What kind of work did you do before the war?" asked the doctor, assuming Duvid to be a soldier like the rest of his patients.

The Artist

"I was a painter. An artist."

"Well, you won't need two perfect legs for that anyway. If it hurts standing up, you can always paint sitting down. You're lucky. It might have been your eyes or hands."

It seemed every time he was chopped up, there was someone around to tell him how lucky he was. But the point could not be argued. He *was* lucky. And limping along the sun-splattered deck of a ship that was half a day out of New York harbor, a ship that was carrying him home alive and comparatively whole and not, like those several thousand others stacked in the cargo hold, laid out in one of the plain, pine boxes that was the final gift of the government for which they had crossed an ocean to die . . . he *felt* lucky.

In his cabin, he finished some last-minute packing, then looked at the single valise and the carton of paintings that held everything he was taking back with him. Not a hell of a lot to show for four and a half years, a less than perfect arm and leg, and multiple fragments of Bavarian iron. Or was it? There were exactly nine canvases in the carton, his total output for the period, other than the newspaper drawings. And just how much they were depended on how much or how little he had been able to get into them. But how did you squeeze nine million dead into nine pieces of canvas? A million per painting? And what about the twenty-one million maimed and wounded? . . . and the pulverized towns and cities? . . . and the oceans of ruined land? Where did you put *them?* Nine paintings that he had managed to eke out during his several convalescences, during those few scattered months of quiet in the backwash of the guns, when he had tried to blink the blood out of his eyes and add it all up. Those nine million dead held an important place in his life. He lived among their bones and their gray flesh and their silent voices. He saw them in the morning mists, in the yellow light of midday, in the green of evening settling in, when his eyes, turning from the shadows of grass and trees, looked up at the darkening clouds and found them there too. Everywhere, the dead. Except, as it turned out, in his paintings.

A curious fact. Nine million dead and not a single visible corpse in any one of his nine canvases. Yet thinking about it, it made sense. The war was over for the dead. Finished. It existed only in the faces of the living. And this was where he had looked for it, in the eyes and mouths of those in trouble, in the way flesh acted in grief and pain and shock. He had looked for it, too, in the wounded reaching for each other, or giving comfort with the terrible tenderness men can show in the darkest places. He had found it even in those odd moments of laughter, in the rare joy that is the underside of the deepest anguish. Yet the eyes did not alter very much. They held a strange sameness, regardless of what they were feeling. Weeping or smiling, they seemed little different. It was as though the creatures they represented were too far sunk in a tragedy which had moved off the plane of normal human reaction onto an animal level of despair, and the comparatively complicated expressions of sorrow and happiness had fled beyond their primitive grasp. Painting them, Duvid had thought he was able to tell what each of the separate pairs of eyes was saying. But afterward, he was no longer sure. Except for one particular pair of eyes. About these, there was never really any doubt.

He had painted them while convalescing at a large pink-and-white villa in the south of France. The villa had once been the vacation home of a prosperous Parisian underwear manufacturer, but had been converted to a hospital for some of the surgically interesting products of the fighting on the Western Front. Duvid shared a room with an English infantry captain, most of whose face had been shot away at Ypres, and who was in the process of having another one built for him by the French Medical Corps. The captain's head, when Duvid met him, was a smooth, white, featureless ball of bandages, with two holes through which eyes peered, and a third hole that brought forth occasional muffled sounds. At first Duvid could not understand the sounds, but gradually he learned, and they were able to have long conversations that often lasted far into the night. The captain's greatest worry was his wife's reaction to his face. He had written her that he had been wounded in the face and had received assurances that she loved him and that it would change nothing, but he was still worried. "They tell me," the muffled voice said, "that in a year they can build me a face I can take out in public without frightening people. Do you think I can believe them?"

"Of course," Duvid said, although he had seen some of the faces the surgeons had patched together on their tables and he was not hopeful. "They work miracles these days."

"My God, I hope so."

Duvid was in the room, two weeks later, when the bandages were removed. The captain asked for a mirror. "You must understand," explained the doctor, "that this is only the beginning. We have a long way to go. But for a beginning, I would say it is quite satisfactory."

"Please give me a mirror."

A nurse handed it to him.

"Oh, God . . . Oh, Jesus Christ . . . Oh, God!" said the captain.

He refused to eat or speak for three days. On the fourth day, he accepted food and said to Duvid, "I would like you to paint my picture."

Duvid looked at him. Even after three days of getting used to it, it was not easy.

"Please," said the captain.

"But why?"

"Because I believe a record should be kept."

Duvid did not say anything.

"I have been thinking about it," said the Captain, in the remains of once-perfect Oxonian accents. "And I have decided that this is the only way left for me to be of value."

"You're alive. You can be of value in other ways."

"Yes, I can take what they have given me for a face and parade it through the capitals of the world. I can walk up and down city streets for the remaining thirty or forty years of my life and frighten every man, woman, and child who sees me into remembering about war what they will otherwise soon forget. *That*, I admit, would be of value." He looked out through the high, elegant windows of the underwear manufacturer's villa at the sun on the Mediterranean. "But I'm afraid I wouldn't be nearly brave enough for that. What I would be more likely to do is crawl into a hole somewhere and just wait to die. So that lacking courage, I must depend upon you to perpetuate what will otherwise be lost. Unless, of course, looking at me would be too painful even for you."

The Artist

"No," said Duvid. "I'll do it."

They started the next day. The captain sat in full uniform, wearing all of his decorations, among which was the Victoria Cross. Duvid worked carefully and the captain studied the details after each pose. It was important to him that nothing be left out. The captain's spirits seemed to improve as the portrait progressed, as if just transferring his disfigurement to canvas served, in itself, to drain off some of the horror.

When the portrait was finished, he stood staring at the still-wet canvas. "You have it," he said. "It's just the way it is."

Before an azure, Mediterranean sky, a red, veined, pulpy mass sat upon the splendidly uniformed shoulders of a captain in His Majesty's Royal Fusileers. The head did not resemble anything human, but looked, rather, like a ripe, oversized peach that had been roughly and inaccurately broken down the middle. Only the pale gray eyes, oddly untouched and immutable amidst the ruins, reflected a core of life.

"We must give it a name," said the captain.

"It has a name."

"What?"

"Yours," Duvid told him.

The captain nodded slowly. "Of course. It *is* me, isn't it." There was a rearrangement of lines that might have been a smile. "I keep forgetting."

He studied his portrait for the rest of that day and into the night. The painting seemed to loosen hidden restraints and he spoke to Duvid at length, telling him in detail of his boyhood, of growing up in Sussex in a house surrounded by ancient oaks and green fields in which sheep grazed, and by clear, quiet streams crossed by stone bridges. "You're a good man," he told Duvid at one point. "You listen well. A good man can bear to listen to another talk about himself. You can't trust those who are bored by such talk."

When they were lying in parallel beds later, with the moon throwing its blue light on the underwear manufacturer's marble floor, the captain asked, "Do you believe there is a design, an overall pattern to things?"

"No."

The Artist

"I did, once. I was sure that everything happened for a reason. I must say it was a reassuring concept to live with. It didn't last long, of course. It can't if you think at all. Finally, you know everything is just a series of crazy accidents. It has to be. It would simply be too terrible to imagine anyone deliberately planning most of what takes place. Yet every so often something does happen to make you wonder. Was it really just an accident that of all the thousands who might have been placed in the bed next to mine, *you,* an artist, were placed there? It undoubtedly *was,* but I'd like to think there was something more to it. Call it an indulgence if you wish, but at this particular moment in my life I prefer to believe that you were put in this room specifically to do my portrait."

The voice faltered slightly, shook in the soft summer night. Then the captain made a sound that was probably intended as a laugh. "There is something so insanely tragic about the human condition, that civilized intelligence has to make fun of its own feelings. So I will tell you this as a great joke. From the moment you finished that portrait this morning, from the moment I looked at it and knew that you had faithfully and permanently recorded what had taken place, I have felt freer from hurt, felt a greater peace than I had ever expected to feel again. Because whatever remained for me to say, whatever screams I had left to scream, you have, with this painting, screamed for me. And I thank you for that."

When Duvid awoke the next morning, the captain was dead. He had died sometime during the night, his life having quietly and neatly flowed from his wrists into a large basin of water on the bed beside him. He lay with his eyes open, the covers shrouded over the frail, patrician body beneath. Gently, Duvid closed the captain's eyes. Then he went over to the painted ones, those still on the easel, feeling, as he stood looking at them, that he had finally, after four years, been graduated from a special university of the damned, whose every battered, blood-stained book he had memorized and sucked dry.

The Artist

Duvid did not really feel he was home until the taxi turned into Hester Street and he had his first glimpse of the pushcarts. It was late evening and dark, but the peddlers were still out hawking under the streetlights, their incredible mixture of English and Yiddish exploding like shrapnel in the frosty air. Nowhere, he thought, was there a sound quite like it. Yet hearing it, there were suddenly sharp beaks pecking at his bowels. He had not told Annie he was coming and it was beginning to worry him. It wasn't right to just ring a doorbell and appear like this. Not after four and a half years. People needed a warning, a decent interval to prepare themselves. Surprise could reveal too much. It was what he had thought he wanted, but was no longer sure. Perhaps he ought to stop somewhere and call. At least soften the shock. Then he knew it wasn't so much Annie he was worrying about as himself, and thought to hell with it and let the taxi take him directly to the front entrance of the building where he had once lived.

Face white, he stood on the sidewalk with his valise and his package of paintings and fought an impulse to leap back into the cab. And go where? It didn't matter. One place was as good as another. There was really nothing for him here anymore. Only a deeply embedded sense of duty and tradition had brought him back to this building at all. When you had gone away and left a wife behind, this was where you returned. Where you went from there was something else. But first, you came back. He had thought it all through. The marriage had been his mistake to begin with, and it was up to him to correct it. Annie, he was sure, would not object. From the time he had left, she had just about written him off anyway. More than likely, she had made plans of her own. She might even be involved with another man. Duvid had considered this possibility and had, he believed, accepted it. For his part, he had done what most men do who are away from their wives for long periods of time, and had a series of brief affairs. Some with nurses at the hospitals where he was treated; others, with girls he had met in Paris and Cherbourg. He had never felt guilty about any of the girls. His loyalty to the ghost who sent him those occasional impersonal notes, and whose face he could barely remember, was not in the least binding. Besides . . . in a four-year deluge of blood, it was hard

291

to take seriously a few random drops of semen.

Several passers-by stared curiously at him, a tall, scarred man in a khaki war correspondent's uniform. He stared back. Then he picked up his things and carried them into the building and up four flights of stairs to the door of apartment 5D. He pressed the bell and heard it ring inside, the same shrill sound he remembered, a little uncertain at the beginning because a connection was loose, then catching hold and screaming. He waited. Annie had always been slow to open doors. Whatever she was doing when a bell rang, she finished before going to answer it. Totally unlike him. A bell rang and he dropped everything and flew. A family characteristic. All the Karlinskys flew. You never knew. It might be the Messiah at the door. Could you keep *Mashiach* waiting while you finished drying a plate? Annie could. At last he heard her coming and the door opened.

"Yes?"

The hall light was behind him and she couldn't quite see his face. But Duvid saw hers, saw the round, dark eyes and small mouth, and all the rest that he had once known so well, but had forgotten. My God, how young she looks, he thought, not knowing what he had expected, but suddenly feeling a coldness on his cheeks and along his back.

"Hello, Annie."

She saw then and knew, yet she didn't know. She breathed deeply and said. "Duvid?"

"Yes."

Still, she stood there. It was not something to know all at once. It had to be taken in small pieces. She started at the top, with the visored garrison cap that added to the strangeness by making him look like a soldier, which he had never been, technically, although he had done most of the things that soldiers do. Then she came down and looked into his face, her eyes grown used to the light and seeing his face fully, with nothing left out, seeing it with a fright and feeling that made her stop there and go no farther. She tried twice to speak and could not.

"May I come in?"

She stepped back and made a small helpless gesture with her

hands. Duvid carried his things in and closed the door behind him. He tried to step carefully, but the effort betrayed him and only made his limp worse. He took off his cap and put it down on his valise. He felt her watching him and his face ached with the effort of constructing what he believed to be a pleasant expression.

"I'm sorry," he said. "I should have let you know. I should have given you warning."

Her fingers were clasped like spikes, her eyes stricken. "What have they *done* to you?"

"It's not that bad. I've really been lucky." By now he believed it. Unaccountably, he felt his left hand shaking and put it in his pocket. Something was wrong. Somehow it wasn't going as he had expected. I must take hold, he thought, and had a sudden dread of going wildly hysterical in front of her.

"I still can't believe it's you."

"It's me. Who else could it be?"

She came over and stood close in front of him and he smelled the clean, freshly bathed smell that had always been part of her, but that had fled his mind along with everything else. "I don't know who else it could be," she said, "But this wasn't the way you looked when you left here." Her fingers reached for and touched the scar, a gentle tracing, much as he did himself. The same need was there. You had to touch it to believe, to know for sure. "What happened to your leg?"

"It'll get better."

"And what else?" She searched his body behind the uniform. "What else'll get better?"

He shrugged. "At least I'm here."

"How thin you are, how bony."

"So I'm thin, I'm bony. I apologize. What do you want from me?"

She was fighting tears and losing, so she fled to anger. "Why did you do this to yourself? You didn't have to. *Why?*"

He turned away without answering, took off his coat, eased painfully into a chair. The room, he saw, was the same, the air faintly sweet with furniture polish, the drapes rigid and perfect at the windows, each lamp centered on its own table. He had crawled through Armageddon, and here, incredibly, not a detail had changed.

"Why didn't you just stay home and lie down in front of a trolley? You could have saved yourself a lot of trouble."

He sighed. "Annie, leave me alone."

"Leave you alone?" she said tonelessly. "I've left you alone for four and a half years. Wouldn't you say that was long enough? Wouldn't you say that qualifies me as an exemplary, patient, non-complaining wife?"

He thought, how beautifully she has learned to speak, how naturally she uses words like "qualify" and "exemplary." Things have happened to her too. Whatever she is, she's not what she once was. I must remember that. "In all this time," she said, "Have I ever written to question you? Have I ever grumbled or whined about a single thing?"

He was suddenly aware that she had not kissed him, that whatever else her reaction to his appearance had demonstrated, affection was not included. Well, so much the better. It would simplify the rest. "I'll write to Congress," he said. "I'll see if I can get you a medal."

"I don't want any medals."

"What *do* you want?"

She sat down facing him, the threat of tears controlled now but the effort showing in small, tight lines about her mouth. "I want to scream," she said softly. "I want to wail and beat my breasts. I want to swear with every foul word I ever knew in Russian, Yiddish, and English. I want to let go what I've been holding in since the day I watched you sail away on that cursed ship. But mostly, I think I just want to hate you for doing what you've done to us both."

"All right."

"It's *not* all right."

"Annie, I'm sorry."

"For what?"

"For everything."

"No you're not," she said. "You're not sorry at all. And if you had it to do over, you'd do the same thing again."

"When did you get so smart?" he said flatly.

The Artist

"I don't have to be smart to know that. I just have to look at you. It's all there. It shines out of your eyes, out of your scarred face, even out of the terrible way you walk. It screams and begs for attention. It has seen the absolute bottom, the worst, and it was worth everything it cost. *Wasn't* it, Duvid?"

He said nothing, but felt, listening to her, the full weight of the blood in his heart. This is where we left off, he thought. One of the last times we spoke she was pouring boiling kettles of truth over my head, and here she is, still pouring. In the meantime I've spent four years being shot at, stabbed at, and blown up, I've suffered freezing cold, wetness, filth, and lice, and she's still busy explaining the way I am.

"And I suppose in that one miserable bundle," she swept on, pointing accusingly at the package of paintings, "you've managed to carry home everything you've paid for, everything you've scraped together out of the blood and the dirt. Let me see them. I'm anxious to look at these valuable bits of canvas. I want to see for myself what's worth part of a face and a leg and God only knows what else. Show me."

"Not now, Annie."

"Yes," she said. "Now."

"This isn't the time."

"Yes it is. It's exactly the time."

He shook his head. "No."

She stared at him, then rose, wordlessly, went over to the carton and began to rip at the bindings. Duvid started from his chair to stop her, but changed his mind and settled back. Why not? Let her look. He watched her struggle with the heavy cardboard, her mouth grimly set, her cheeks flushed. Then she had one end of the carton open and reached in and pulled out a canvas. It came out reversed and she quickly righted it, leaned it against a wall, and stepped back to look at the portrait of the captain. She stared blankly. Her eyes were wide, without expression. She gasped a little. She tried to swallow, but couldn't.

"You imagined it," she whispered. "You made it up."

"No. Do you think *that* could be imagined?"

She bent, went to her knees on the floor. She stayed there,

swaying slightly, the rest of the paintings forgotten. "Who was he?"

"An Englishman. We were in the same hospital room. The portrait was his idea. He wanted a record kept. The night the painting was finished, he killed himself."

"Oh, Duvid."

"He was a very high-class Englishman. Educated. A don at Oxford University. He was also a great war hero. That's the Victoria Cross on his chest, Britain's highest military decoration. Does that impress you?"

Annie knelt silently.

"I told him the painting would carry his name, but I've changed my mind. I've decided to just call it *The Hero.* I think that would be better."

Annie's mouth fell open, the lips contorted. She wept.

"What are you crying for?"

"For him. For you. For me."

She was, as she wept, a small woman. How frail and sad, he thought, and felt himself moved.

After a while, she said, "I never expected you back. I never thought I'd see you walk in here again."

"Well, I'm here."

She wiped her eyes. "Are you staying?"

The question surprised him. "Why? Have you gotten yourself someone else?"

"Would it matter to you if I had?"

He looked at her and saw worlds whirl past and cloud her eyes. Four and a half years. What *had* she been doing, besides improving her speech, reading books, and taking night courses? "You're still my wife."

"And you're still my husband. But has that stopped you from doing whatever you've felt like doing?"

So there *was* someone. He stared past her at their framed wedding photograph still standing, polished, where he had last seen it . . . Annie with her fresh, smiling face and that unique innocence of a nineteen-year-old whore, and he beside her in his last incarnation, a hopeful young artist full of passionate protest. Abandoning himself to the warm, sirupy pull of nostalgia, he remembered them both, not as they had been under the marriage canopy, but before, at Molly's, when everything was new. *My name is Annie.* Her name had also been love. And he had managed to spoil even that.

"I may have been barren," she said, "but I was too young for the grave you'd put me in. I had to do something besides tear at my dry breasts and curse my empty womb. When you went away, I was sure it was me who had driven you. Later, I knew better. I had plenty of time to think, so I thought. And I stopped blaming myself. I'd had enough of that. No one drove you away. You drove yourself. You would have gone no matter what I was."

"Who is he?" Duvid asked.

She stared at him boldly, a dark gaze. She had changed. It hit Duvid. Change was betrayal. There was no other way. There was no getting somewhere without turning your back on someplace else. He felt curiously cut off, angry. What *right* had she? Every right, he thought.

"Why should it matter who he is? You don't really care about me. You haven't for years. Why should you be angry because I've filled a bit of the emptiness you left me?"

He had no answer to that. At least, not anything reasonable. And he was trying very hard to be reasonable. But he felt confused. Something was slipping away and he didn't know what. "Has he been living with you?"

She hesitated. "Yes."

"Here?"

"Yes."

How honest she was. He had always been blessed with honest women. Her answers had opened a hole in him, and he would not have expected this. He thought he had been prepared, yet he felt hurt and the hurt surprised him. He was hit by conflicting tides, a desire to know more, a fascination with the layers of betrayal possible, and a deep disgust with it. He yielded to the fascination. "Where is he now?"

"In the bedroom."

Duvid slowly pushed himself out of his chair. Emotion blinded him. My God, I've learned nothing. I can live a hundred years and I'll still be hurting, still be confused, still be making the same mistakes.

Annie said, "He's asleep."

The Artist

Duvid limped toward the bedroom door. His wife, his apartment, his bedroom, his bed. There was no bottom to it.

"Please don't wake him."

Duvid turned at the door. She was behind him. Hidden constraints had dropped over her face, pulling the skin tight. He almost had the feeling that she *wanted* him to go in. Were they *both* crazy? Then he opened the door, turned on a light, and stared at the empty double bed against the far wall and the child's crib beside it. A blond head, the tip of a nose, and a round cheek showed through the crib's slats, and all Duvid could do was stand there in a tangle of feeling.

"His name is Richard," Annie said. "He's fourteen months old."

"What in God's name are you trying to *do* to me?"

She saw his face. "I guess it wasn't much of a joke."

"Joke?"

"I'm sorry. But when you asked if I'd found someone else, when you were so sure I had, I couldn't resist. Though I didn't really think it would matter to you that much. It was probably just your pride."

His voice was flat. "Who's is he?"

"Mine."

"What do you mean, *yours?"*

"I've had him since he was a week old. That makes him as much mine as any child could be."

"What about his real mother and father?"

Her eyes went hard. "You mean his *natural* mother and father. *I'm* his real mother. Whoever acts the parent, *is* the parent."

"Call them what you want."

"His mother died having him. She was one of Molly's girls. The father could have been any one of a dozen customers."

Duvid looked at the sleeping child. A whore for a mother and God only knew what kind of father. Who said we're all born equal? He felt an urge to touch a pink, translucent ear, but held back, as though even so slight a contact might, in some way, commit him.

"Why didn't you ever write me about him?"

"I didn't think you'd be interested."

"That's not the reason."

"I didn't know how you'd feel about the idea."

"What's there to feel?"

The Artist

"Some people don't believe in adoption."

"I've never thought about it."

He limped out of the room. Annie followed, closing the door carefully behind her. "I also didn't tell you," she said, "because if you decided to come back, I didn't want it to be for any reason but me. Which was foolish, I suppose. I should have tried to get you back any way I could. But I, too, had some pride left." She looked away, then at him. "Only I can't really afford it anymore. It's gotten much too expensive for me. If pride is all I'm going to be left with, it's just not worth it. I want you too much. If I lose you, then I lose you, but I'm through playing games."

"Annie . . ."

"No. Let me finish. If I stop now, I'm afraid I'll never get started again." She breathed deeply and stood facing him on her fake Oriental rug, surrounded by a couch and chairs that looked as though no one had sat in them for years. "Whatever I made you believe before, there's been no one else. We both know there could have been, but there wasn't. It was no sacrifice. That part was easy. I wasn't even tempted. I'd rather just think of you than have the best of what I saw. You've always been able to do that for me. The hard part was not knowing if you were coming back. Your letters told me nothing, so mine told *you* nothing. I gave you only what you gave me, only what I thought you wanted. If you'd tossed me even one small bone of affection, I'd have smothered you with all I felt. But you didn't want that, so I didn't give it to you. When Richard came along it was like something from heaven, but even blessings bring their worries. What if you came back and didn't want him? I worried a lot about that. What if you called him a whore's bastard and refused to have him in the house?"

She cracked her knuckles against her chest. "Duvid, I couldn't love that baby more if I'd had him myself. But I'm telling you this. If it ever came to choosing, he wouldn't stand a chance against you."

"What do you think I am?" He spoke roughly. His mouth felt stiff, made of clay. "A baby's a baby. They all start the same. We can make him what we want."

Her eyes glistened. He shifted his weight to his good leg and touched her for the first time, lightly, the back of his hand against

299

her cheek. Soft. Something else he had forgotten.

Kissing her then, holding her, feeling a dry, helpless ache somewhere deep in his throat, feeling the frail, deprived body through the clumsy material of his uniform, he was filled with a bursting sense of relief, of unreasonable hope. We might still be all right, he thought confusedly, though he saw the captain's eyes over her shoulder, and found little enough to hope for there. If we've come this far and something has lasted, we might still have a chance.

Annie pulled back to look at him, top to bottom. A second inventory. "Take them off," she said fiercely. "Take off those damned clothes."

FOURTEEN

1945: Amagansett, Long Island

There was no advance planning to it. The painting simply evolved, bit by bit, over a period of weeks, and was finally a surprise even to Duvid. It sometimes happened that way. Maybe not so much during the early years, when he had to know exactly where he was going with each stroke, but later on, when he was better able to go along with a feeling or a mood and gamble on where it would take him.

At first it was little more than a mass of swirling color, all blues and greens, a dark abstraction from some hidden memory of the womb. Then he had seen that first floating eye (at least it *seemed* an eye) so clear and pale, so perfectly blue and evil and mad, it must have gone all the way back to the earliest stone god in a jungle clearing. He faltered for a long time before that stare, clear as ice in the moonlight and reminding him, too, of the eyes in that sweet, spoiled German face he had lanced in a Belgian field back in 1914. But it was, after all, an eye, and accepting it as such, he added another to make them a pair. Together, they gave a fine stain to the mood of the canvas, which was fear and funk and a sniff of the grave, and he and the emerging face were on their way, with a curving shadow for a nose and a burn of total blackness below that was the mouth. But what a special terror there, in that wide, screaming hole, in that silent howl of maniac speech.

He worked his brush with care, as if stroking the softest breast of the softest dove that ever flew, and he laid on blue blood and

301

green mud like medals of death pinned to the chest. Then a stab of darkness went in above the mouth and spread and sucked the face in backward, as though upon the gouge of a bullet. The look was that of an old man, toothless, sly, reminiscent of fear and pain, with a splash of something gray across the broken lips. An arm appeared, but only one, the other having been lost somewhere, or erased, or blown off, or eaten away. There were choices enough to offer the blue stump, but Duvid made none and simply abandoned the bereaved place to dig another cave somewhere toward the middle. *Whap!* went the brush and the new hole appeared where the heart should have been. The face above grinned with a clown's deep gloom, as if there were pleasure even in this. Shoot out the heart and pain was erased with the same bullet. Still, you could never be sure where you were going to hit. All you could do was hope you found the right place.

But was it all accident? . . . a blind groping, nothing more? Or were there moments when the blue thing spoke to him? At times, it seemed so, and he could almost feel something, some anguished hope in the deep of that emerging figure. Not that he understood, or even tried. It was enough that he could feel lights moving between them, driving his brush to charge as if that were their contract, as if the pale eyes were begging him to advance, to attack, to rend, to mutilate further. Until suddenly, he could no longer face the eyes, for they now contained all of it, the blood, the carnage, the dark screams that never sounded. And again he faltered and had no stomach for the rest. The clean sense of grace left him and he painted and missed. And painted again. And missed. And finally he could feel what was sure and good in him going away, going away perhaps forever, because you *knew* you were only as good as your last ten strokes. Thinking about it, he felt sickened in a way he had never been sick before. This illness was an extinction. It wiped him out, left nothing of value. Creatively, it left him dead. Never had he known such a sickening. The vengeance of those maniac eyes was complete, his suffocation total. Nothing productive or noble seemed to remain of him.

Then the stubborn part of his brain said, *You can't die yet, schmuck! You haven't finished your work.* And he pleaded to himself, *Let me be not all dead,* and went back to the painting to do what he had known all along had to be done.

He decided to show it to Laurie when it was almost finished. Or perhaps it *was* finished. It was always hard to know exactly when a painting was done. No warning bell ever rang, no curtain came down, no door closed. Maybe, he thought, every painting really needed two artists. One to paint it, the other to drag the first away when it was time. For there was always that terrible fear of letting go, that need to add, to take away, to change, to pat, to comfort, that dread of sending the infant thing forth, naked and vulnerable, into the cold places of judgment. Laurie was no cold place. Yet in any eyes but your own, there *was,* inescapably, judgment.

He showed it to her after dinner one evening, bringing her into the studio, sitting her in front of the canvas, and silently gazing with her at the big, blue nude. For this was what it had finally come to be, a life-size male nude painted almost entirely in tones of blue. The blue had nothing to do with the clear azure of summer skies or sunlit water, but was soiled and dirty and carried the stain of midnight swamps, of pestilence and rot, of frozen flesh in winter tombs. *This* was the blue. And a stench seemed to come off it, a scent like that some dark malignancy would carry, were it to invent its own perfume. The figure was rendered broadly, freely, yet no detail of its early promise had been lost. The mouth still howled its maniac speech, the demonic eyes still glared, the stump of a missing arm still flailed the heavens, and from the chest cavity, from that dark hole where a heart should have been, crawled things viscous and black.

But the worst of it lay not above the waist, but below. Here, in the blue orchards of the loins, minutely painted worms munched upon what remained of the wrinkled fruit. Little was left, only a few pitted fragments, disdained by even the maggots and left dangling forlornly between withered thighs. If a howling madness came from the mouth, it screamed doubly loud among these chewed-up roots. And down here, more than ever, you sensed the smell. It came in through blue nostrils, milled through blue blood, went into blue tissues, and was exuded by blue cells. You looked and breathed the stench as though it were real, but could breathe it only to the top of the lung and draw no further. You pinched it off in the windpipe, and after just two minutes of such breathing, you knew your lungs would ache for an hour afterward.

Then there was the background, dark, turgid, swollen with foul intent. If you believed in spirits and demons, in wizards and fiends and omens of evil, they would have dwelt in such a place as this. Beasts were hidden here. They shrieked in muted whispers, prowled beneath a hurricane sky, crept through cities of shattered stone and burned rubble. You knew they were there, but did not see them. All you saw were the ruins and suffering sky and a single, thick, snake-like vine, murderous and deadly, winding itself about the legs of the howling blue man.

Laurie sat staring for a long time, hands folded in her lap like an obedient child. Her face showed no emotion, but only because her skin kept it that way. The nerves beneath moved in separate broken bits. One bit wept, another was angry, a third trembled minutely.

"Well?" Duvid said at last.

"You're a great artist."

"Is that all?"

"What else is there?"

"What do you *think?*"

"I'm no art critic."

"I *know* you're no art critic."

She turned and faced him. "Shall I tell you how I *feel?*"

"Sure."

"Like killing myself."

He laughed.

"I'm not trying to be funny. I think if I believed what you've said here! I couldn't see much point to getting up in the morning. And if I thought you believed it yourself, I wouldn't feel much better."

"Don't you think I believe it?"

Something strangled in her, some wistful desire to change what was beyond alteration. "For *weeks*, I've been hoping you don't."

"You mean you've seen the painting before?"

"Every day since you started it. I've been taking it out of the bin and sneaking looks when you weren't around. I kept hoping it might

304

brighten up a little, but it just kept getting worse. And so did the way I felt."

"I didn't know."

"I was sure you'd notice some difference in me. I was sure it showed."

He *had* noticed. She *had* been different. But he had blamed it on other things. There'd been enough, lately, to blame it on, enough to make anyone different. The two bombs, a quarter-million radio-active dead, the sudden, terrible end to a terrible war. And all in a span of eight days. *Who* was the same as before? Looking at her now, he could actually pinpoint the changes, could actually sense the anxiety in her face. Even the smoothness of her skin seemed vexed, troubled by hidden disasters.

Without knowing why, he felt he should apologize. "I'm sorry you don't like the painting."

"I don't just not like it. I *hate* it. Why in God's name did you have to paint anything like that?"

"Why does an artist paint any picture?"

She stabbed an accusing finger at it, a dagger. *"That's* not any picture, that's an . . ." She groped for the word. "Abomination!"

"Call it what you want."

"I couldn't. I don't know enough ugly words."

It was fascinating to him to see her circling in, to watch her collecting the necessary anger for her attack. He fought a lover's wish to collaborate, to help make it easier for her to do what she so obviously needed to do. Still, her reaction puzzled him. It was much too strong.

"Why do you let it bother you so?"

"Hopelessness *always* bothers me. I despise it."

"I wasn't really trying to be hopeless."

"My God!" She stared at the silently howling mouth. "What *were* you trying to be?"

"Realistic."

She grimaced.

"It's true," he said and had to smile at her little-girl look of distaste. But she was no little girl, he thought, remembering her face asleep beside him that morning. She had slept as though she were keeping a secret, and he had wondered what she was hiding. That soft, sealed face on the pillow, that locked vault. What did she have cached away?

"Why are you smiling?" she said.

"Shouldn't I?"

"Not now. There's nothing to smile about now."

He made his face solemn. "How's that?"

"I don't think you're funny."

"I know. I've never had any great gift for comedy."

He turned and stared at the canvas, a mulling, discontented look, puzzling to pry something open, to get something out. "I *was* trying to be realistic, though. At least I thought I was. You never know for sure while you're working. Emotion clouds. Especially in something like this. Maybe I shouldn't have touched the whole idea right now. It might be too soon. I should have given myself more time to live with it."

"With what?"

"The Bomb."

She looked shocked, hurt, as if merely the use of the word was an insensitive breach of taste.

"It's too much," he said, "you can't soak it in all at once. From the instant that thing went off, the planet stopped being the same. We've finally gotten smart enough to finish it. Not just bits and pieces, but everything, everywhere. All of it. *Boom!* Just like that. It's enough to make you believe in God. Who else could have done it so beautifully? He looks down, sees our latest mess, realizes the species is insane, and hands us a fast way to clean it up. Then when He's rid of us, when we're all lying in the ruins giving off signals like radios, He can try out some new and, hopefully, better species."

"The war's over. We don't have to use it again."

"It'll be used," he said. "Finally, everything is used. And it'll be bigger and better by then. We're very inventive in our killing machines. Once, in Belgium, I watched what a machine gun did to a couple of hundred Germans. It was the first time I'd ever seen anything like it. The gun was too terrible to believe. Now it seems like a stone ax. Progress. Great brains. Too bad we haven't the souls to match."

The Artist

She kept her lips tight, made her voice harsh. "When did you get so scared? I've never seen you so scared before."

"Is that what I am?"

"Aren't you?"

He saw that she still needed to go after him, still needed some sort of abrasion. Since it was all hers, he couldn't even call it an argument. They'd never really had a fight, he thought. Maybe it was just time.

She said, "Or would you rather call it being realistic?"

"You might be right. They *could* be the same thing. Maybe it's impossible to be realistic anymore *without* being scared."

"Oh, damn it! Stop it!"

It came out a shrill shout that startled her as much as it did him. Grief burned her cheeks, singed her eyes, melted the line of her mouth. Duvid saw it all and understood none of it.

"What is it, Laurie?"

She shut her eyes as though the light had suddenly grown too bright.

"Laurie? . . ."

"Just don't say anymore. *Please?* I just don't want to hear anything more. All right?"

"But what's the *matter?*"

She opened her eyes and looked past him at the blue nude, her glance drawn, held, pulled deep inside the flat canvas as though there were true depth to it. *"That's* what's the matter," she said and ran out of the studio and out of the house.

Duvid found her in the darkness at the base of a dune. He sat down beside her, but neither of them spoke. A small, warm breath of salt came off the water, which heaved gently under the moon.

"I'm sorry," she said at last.

He took her hand and held it between his, feeling it moist and trembling and without warmth. "Just tell me what it is."

"It's us. We've done it. We've made the baby."

He waited for some sensation, but none came. "Are you sure?"

"I went to a doctor."

"When?"

"A few weeks ago."

"And you're telling me *now?*"

"I was afraid."

"Of *what*, for God's sake?"

"Of you. Of how you'd feel about it. I was afraid from the minute I saw that painting. I thought, how could you possibly paint something like this and still want a baby? How could you see such ghastly visions ahead and want a child of your own to have to face them? Can you blame me for hating that picture? It's a knife at my belly."

"It's only a painting."

"It's *not* only a painting. It's the way you *feel.*"

"That has nothing to do with the baby. I'm very happy about the baby."

"How *could* you be?"

"I don't know. I just am."

"But you're so *pessimistic* about everything."

"Not about everything. Just about the world."

"What else is there?"

"There's you and me," he said, smiling because there had always been this insane contrast between his world pessimism and personal hope. "And now the baby."

She went soft against him. "Do you meant it? Are you really happy?"

"Yes."

"Swear to God?"

"Whose? Yours or mine?"

"Anyone's."

"I swear to both."

"If you're lying, it's a double sin."

"I'm not worried."

"Oh, Duvid," She held him. "I was so miserable. You'll never know how miserable."

He stroked her hair where the moon caught it.

"I'll have a beautiful pregnancy, darling. You'll see. I won't cause any trouble. I won't bother you at all. I promise."

"Please," he said, "bother me."

"No. Men don't like to know too much. They just want it to happen. They like the mystery. Darling, I'm going to give you the most mysterious, most amazing baby you've ever seen."

"You're the one who's mysterious and amazing."

"No I'm not. But I love you to think so. Oh, Jesus!" she shouted. "I'm suddenly so happy I could die. Do you think I shouldn't be so happy? Do you think there's something wrong in it?"

"What could be wrong?"

"You know. The way the world is, and all."

He laughed. "You won't make the world any better by being miserable."

"I just hope they give us a little time before they blow it up."

"We'll have plenty of time."

"Wouldn't it be a shame if we didn't. I mean, wouldn't it be too bad if we hardly had any time left at all."

"That doesn't sound very happy."

"Oh, but it does," she said. "When I'm not happy, I don't care how much time there's left. But right now I want to live forever."

"I'll try to arrange it."

"But only with you. If you can't stay with me, I don't want it. Agreed?"

"Agreed."

"Kiss me on it."

He kissed her and she held him hard and touched him until he felt the magic of it begin. They lay back against the dune. *"Here?"* he asked.

She freed her lips briefly. "Where else, *schmuck?"*

Then she was at him again, smothering the laughter in his throat and pulling at his clothes, along with her own, until they were naked in the sand, feeling it give softly against flesh, the strangeness of it exciting to him, even remembering it was not nearly so strange for her. A strangeness, too, in knowing of the tiny, living thing inside, too fragile to believe. He must have held back, because she said, "Don't worry. You won't hurt him." Still, it was like three of them together there now instead of two, not better or worse than before, but different, and he could feel it begin to take him on, this new invisible thing he had helped produce, giving wisdom to his touch, and tenderness, and drawing fresh secrets from her flesh.

Afterward, she would not let him go, but held on against the final

309

slipping away. "I hate when it ends. Why does it always have to end?"

"It doesn't really. It's just getting ready for next time."

"That's lovely."

"I told you I'm no pessimist."

"Just about the world."

He moved his cheek against hers. "Maybe not even about that. Sometimes I feel like a superstitous old Jew, beating my breast and prophesying doom just to ward it off. I don't think there *is* any such thing as a pessimistic Jew. We're *always* sure tomorrow's going to be better. We *always* have hope. It comes with the faith. Even in a gas chamber, we're sure they're just going to give us a shower."

"I'm glad our son is going to be a Jew."

"There *are* inconveniences."

"He won't mind them."

"Maybe not," Duvid said, and really accepted the fact of it for the first time. "I guess we should think about getting married."

She laughed.

"What's so funny?"

"You. You and your proposal. So grave and sweet and proper." She traced the line of his nose with a finger. "Darling, I never expected you to marry me, and I still don't."

"Don't you *want* to get married?"

"I *am* married. I *feel* married. Aren't I a good wife to you?"

"You're a lovely wife."

"And you're a lovely husband. What more do we need?"

"A child might need more."

"Not if he has us."

"It's not that simple."

"But it *is* that simple. It's only people who make it complicated. And religion. But I have no religion. Only you. You're my religion, darling. And we've been married since the day we decided to make a baby. *That* was our wedding day."

"Well, we'll see."

"There's nothing to see," she said and rose to her knees so that her hair shone under the moon in much the same way as the water, "All I want is to be with you and love you and feel our son grow in me. I don't care about the rest."

The Artist

It wasn't news to her, but he had to say it. "I'm not young, Laurie."

"So?"

"So I don't know what I've got left."

"Neither do I. And neither did my mother and father and two sisters and two brothers. Darling, I'm not looking for lifetime guarantees. There aren't any. You of all people should know that. You couldn't have painted that blue man in there and *not* know."

He lay studying her as she knelt, still naked, in the sand. Then he leaned forward to pull her close, to press lips to flesh and let the wonder of this first stage of fatherhood draw him in. As he held her, this girl who looked like the century's dream of passion, this girl he'd plucked like a shell from the ocean's edge, Duvid felt suddenly warm and accounted for, felt that in its own way, on this late summer night, some mystic grace had deliberately put out its hand and smothered whatever remained of that bitter, blue threat in his studio.

"All right," he said. "We'll try it your way."

Then they dressed and walked back through the sand and found, when they reached the house, that they had visitors.

FIFTEEN

1921: New York, N. Y.

Making love, Duvid thought, was the wrong term for it. The mood of what they were doing was too cool for that, more as if they were two professional dancers come together in a series of long, slow, carefully rehearsed moves. There was no urgency, no great haste to give or take pleasure, and Duvid felt he could go on with it forever.

They were in Rachel's apartment, the draperies drawn against the afternoon sun, but a few pale, wavering rays still managing to break through. A bedside clock ticked softly. It was just past four o'clock. Was it the French, Duvid wondered, who said that only peasants made love at night? Probably. They were, after all, the world's acknowledged love experts. Still, for an American and a Jew who normally carried the Puritan work ethic across his back like a monstrous yoke, he felt he wasn't doing too badly. Imagine! Karlinsky cavorting in bed when he should be painting. Never mind the adultery involved. He had made a separate peace with that a long time ago. The thing was, what right had he to such pleasures at four o'clock in the afternoon, while unfinished canvases awaited his brush? But with Rachel's expert help, even this old problem had been overcome.

And she *was* expert. An acknowledged master, not only in bed, but in everything leading up to it. Reason, she believed, could make steady progress from disorder to harmony. And the conquest of chaos did not have to be begun all over again every morning. "You attack each new day, hour, minute," she told Duvid, "as though you'd never fought them before, as though you had to prove your worth all over again." Did she mean he *didn't* have to? She did. Look. He was thirty-two years old, had a decent body of work behind him, and should learn to relax and enjoy things more. *What things?* Her smile could be beatific. Why, *her,* of course. She had become a practicing philosopher. She had looked in the mirror and discovered that ruin comes to beauty, inevitably, that time took you away bit by bit and that all you faced was the void. Neither a great nor an original discovery, but true. Was there a faint odor of panic mixing with her perfume? If there was, Duvid could see no reason for it. Her face, her body, the firmness of her flesh was still, to him, undiminished. Or did love simply grow more myopic with the years?

Now, moving with her through that sweet, deep water below sex, Duvid felt aerated, weightless, intensely alive. All those cool, blond shadows. How familiar, how dear she had become. And how he had learned to exult in these moments. She was still his teacher, still opening new avenues to him, still showing him places he had never been. She said she understood his needs better than he, and she might be right. But most importantly, she loved and admired him. Or so she claimed. And why should he want to doubt her? It was very pleasant, very flattering being loved and admired by a beautiful, famous, rich woman. And she was all of these things. With her husband three years removed via a series of strokes, she had wealth without the original burden of its attainment, an established position in the theater, and was on a first-name basis with many of the country's most prestigious figures. She had a deft, clever way with people, and was always being invited to parties at famous town and country houses where garrulous men of high rank in industry and government seemed to reveal a great many secrets to her. Duvid had once gone with her to such a gathering at an old shipping tycoon's Fifth Avenue mansion, but spent the greater part of the evening staring at the faces of renowned guests and deciding he did not like them. They looked too much like the faces of small-town merchants, growing a little too fat, too sleek, too overcomfortable. Statesmen and captains of industry, he thought, should have better faces. That is, better for statesmen and captains of industry. They should be harder, stronger, more ruthless, gazing out coldly at the world through quick, narrow eyes. They should even have a vaguely haunted look to them, like the men in nineteenth-century Russian novels, with expressions of intense rapture and nameless terror. These faces looked as though they might easily sell you a pound of butter or a suit of underwear.

"What are you so busy looking at?" Rachel had asked.

"The faces of our nation's leaders," he said. "I don't like them."

She smiled. "The trouble with you is, you've been painting the dark underside of things for so long, you don't even know how the light at the top is supposed to look."

She was right. These were not the men and faces he chose to paint. Nor was upper Fifth Avenue the street on which he found his faces. Instead, he wandered the less exalted streets of the city . . . Broadway, heavy and blue in the dusk, with its honky-tonk, its lights, its high and low performers . . . Eighth Avenue, with its broken fighters, its gin mills and whores . . . the Bowery, and its derelicts in doorways, its flophouses and soup kitchens . . . MacDougal Street and its bohemians, its painted transvestites, its lesbians looking so male you had to see them from behind to know they were women . . . Union Square and the old people sitting on its benches, on hands and heads the marks of decay, the varicose legs of women and blotted eyes of men, sunken mouths and inky nostrils. Here were the signs and comments he wanted. Eyes that held metaphysical statements. Lips that tightened against trembling. Hands and fingers that reached. Proving what? Maybe nothing. Except perhaps that they were alive, that they were susceptible to pain, that they were not all of one piece, that they were hungry and afraid and did not know what they were hungry for or afraid of. If the war had served to free him from the ghetto, then it was the whole of New York, in concert, that now helped free him from the war. The healing was slow, the sound of guns still faintly lingering, but the shooting was over and you had to move on. In a moment of cynicism, he had thought, *if they smite you, O schmuck, turn the other face.* Which one? The hero's?

His eyes had been closed, but he opened them now and looked at Rachel in the soft half-light. She smiled faintly and he kissed her.

The Artist

She had a virtuoso's lips, full and alive and lightly fevered, that pressed endless promises into his, yet hinted of where they had been and where they might still be going. He rarely saw her more than two afternoons a week and knew little of what she did or whom she saw in between. With her, he could feel disturbed, tender, excited, and wary at the same time. What did she want? The question often skimmed the edges of his mind. What *could* she want? What could he give her other than the little she already had from him? Once, in a gallery full of people, she had said softly, "Don't go away from me. I couldn't bear it if you ever went away from me." She had been standing close, seemingly unaware of anyone else about them, looking up at him very seriously. With some wonder, he had thought, she means it . . . she actually does mean it. Yet moments later, in the same room, her face was not serious anymore, but curled into its usual slightly questioning smile, as if she believed only a small portion of what the world told her.

How naturally they had slipped back into it. Just three weeks out of France, he had answered his phone one day and heard the instantly recognized voice say, "You're home!" He met her that same afternoon, only vaguely guilty about his wife. Annie would hardly have approved, but of all the people he knew, she would probably be most likely to understand. One of the unadvertised advantages of being married to an ex-whore. They had few illusions. They might accept the idea, academically, that there were marriages in which both partners were faithful from beginning to end. They might read about them, see plays about them, or hear sermons from the pulpit that were crammed full of them. But among the hard realities of their own lives, they just never ran into any of them.

For Rachel, their first coming together after five years was like a private Resurrection. She experienced a real Easter. Her Duvid had risen from the dead. Still, when she saw his scarred face, the red, welted cross-hatching on his body, some of the joy went out of her holiday.

"Oh, Duvid."

He was embarrassed as she looked at him. "I'm sorry, I know it's ugly."

"No." She bent and kissed the torn places. "Thank God they at least left you what's important." Happily, she took possession. But later, she let her anger fly. "The stinking bastards!"

Sipping champagne between satin sheets, Duvid was angry at no one. "Who?"

"All of them. The generals, the profiteers, the politicians. All the damned war lovers," she said bitterly. "All those who got fat and rich and made glorious speeches while millions of poor fools like you were out getting shot up for God and country. Oh Jesus, how I hate those two words. They scare hell out of me. Any kind of faith does. Whether it's faith in a religion or faith in a land or government. Because sooner or later people are asked to die for it. Look back and it's always the same. Either it's the Jews killing the Philistines or the Christians killing the Jews, or the Moslems killing the Christians or the Romans killing the Egyptians, or the English killing the French or the Americans killing the Germans or the Germans killing everybody. Five thousand years and nothing different. Except that we do it better now. More efficiently. Sometimes I think our only hope is not to believe in *anything*. Not in any kind of gods or nationalities or even ideas. Don't believe in anything too strongly and there's no need to take offense, no need to feel it endangered, no need to fight and die for it."

"My God, I'm in the bed of a godless traitor." He grinned. "Or is it traitor*ess*?"

But she meant what she said. At least, while she was saying it. So that if a bitter, world-weary cynicism was her style at that particular time, it was hers completely. And in this case it extended even to her work in the theater. There had usually been a fair sprinkling of humor among her roles, but she now refused to appear in comedy of any form. "They're lies," she once told Duvid. "All comedy is a lie. It has to be, because there's always a happy ending. Everything turns out fine for the hero, good wins out over evil, and the audience goes home believing the world is better than it is. If public lying was ever made a criminal offense, every writer of comedy would be thrown in jail."

Duvid had shrugged it off. "An occasional fairy tale can be nice."

"Maybe for children, but not for adults. And never as an art form. I don't see you coming home from the war and drawing comic sketches. You're working closer to the truth than any artist painting today. Why should *I* climb on a stage and lie to audiences? Why should I tell them people are good at heart and that virtue must triumph? How can I do that when I see us tearing at each others' throats like animals and enjoying the blood? Yes, *enjoying* it. My God, we've turned death into our greatest amusement. How can there be the joy of victory if there's no victim? Then we indulge in the extra pleasure of pity to excite us even more. We look at the carnage, beat our breasts, and feel noble in our grief. Oh, we *are* lovely."

Hardly a warm or gentle judgment, but Duvid would not have expected anything different. Not from her. When had Rachel ever left room for sentiment? Yet for almost a year, she had tended a dying husband she had never loved, stubbornly refusing to exile him to what she called the final garbage heap of a hospital. While a man breathed, she felt, he was still a man, and nobody deserved to die alone in a puddle of urine. Even here, no sentiment. Just facts.

She was above him now, a sweet, flowing oil to his flesh, her warmth rosy in the perfumed air. Breathing hot images, she gave him a short lecture with her tongue on the bed habits of Jews and Christians in general and the French in particular. Maybe there was even a hint of Moslem or Hindu thrown in for luck. Duvid lay back, feeling like a sultan, and let her frolic. A rare greed shone in her eyes, pleasure came from her mouth, and she was happy. She had that special woman's look that the world and everything in it was hers, so clear, so graphic, that Duvid was sure he would be able to paint it from memory later.

The things she brought out in him, the way she pumped him alive. It never made sense, he thought, it was always a mystery. Yet she still teased, still called him a Puritan, still enjoyed reminding him of their first time together (had thirteen years really gone?) when it was *she* who had to do the seducing. She said he was a rarity in New York, where men seemed to develop all sorts of special tastes in bed. But she was eager to give him his pleasure in any way he cared to choose. He told her she would have a hard time turning an old *schmatlz* herring into a goldfish, but she was free to try. Although he often found it strange that she should put on so elaborate a performance between the sheets, when she was so direct and without trimming in all other areas. Even her preparations were tricky. There was all that perfuming and anointing, all that black lace and satin, all that careful arranging of draperies and lights. Duvid was sure everything would have been fine without it, but with it, it was superb, a total setting for her most luxurious jewel, her flesh. Sometimes he laughed at her efforts and sometimes she laughed along with him, but the desired effect was there. He was amused, but his body burned.

Oddly . . . the guilt, when it came, was in the degree of pleasure she gave him. Was not joy, unshared with his wife, joy stolen from her? Which made no sense, of course. What should he do? Invite Annie to join them? A wicked twisted thought, yet always darkly intriguing. How many levels you functioned on, how many levels there were. Come Annie, Join the party. Don't I love you both? Don't you both love me? You did worse as a whore. And with strangers. No, he thought, not Annie. Never Annie. If anyone was likely to go along with such a thing, it would be Rachel. A lover had none of a wife's claim to exclusiveness. But even if their roles were reversed, Duvid was sure it would be no different. There was probably nothing in the world Rachel would not be willing to try at least once. And if it pleased her, if it gave her pleasure or advanced some ulterior purpose, no further justification would be needed. Nor would any abstract concept of morality stand in her way. The ultimate pragmatist, she had more of the basic reasoning of a whore working for her than Annie had ever had. And he? In the middle of his workday, in the midst of facing a canvas on which he was struggling to set down some of life's more penetrating truths, what did he do? He dashed out of his studio and got laid.

Ah, but *what* a lay. The original coolness, the lack of urgency had gone. There was a rushing now, that wild blend of scent, sight, and movement that always made you begin. He was ready to go over the cliff, but he did not want it to end, not this one, not yet. Her greed and pleasure, mixed with his, rode through him, made him want more. What a hunger she had. It came off her tongue and he tasted it . . . strong, stubborn, private . . . a hunger sated only by getting what she wanted, and she always wanted something. It spoke of ghetto alleys and dark tenement rooms, and sweatshops, and years of casting calls and peddling her ass, finally, on a backstage couch. There was excitement in the taste and he savored it with the rest, with the champagne and furs and thousand-dollar bills that came after. But it was bitter too, turned sour with hatreds and betrayals and the cold, dirty scavenging of having to get along and make your way in the world. Yet it was all part of her and the place he was into and there was no need to separate it from the rest. It was all melted together now anyway.

Small cries came from her, and her face, that fluid, mercurial, know-the-cost-of-every-deal ghetto face, broke free of her and became its own master. She was still a minute away, but she had started the trip. All right, Duvid thought, and joined her, pushing a little to catch up, then holding the pace. Love was not a gift, but a vow, and he was making it. I swear this is . . . what? *Schmuck! What are you swearing to now?* He was no longer that young and had had a hint of this before with others, had it with Annie, had it with girls he had known for a night or a week and never knew again. Mostly, at the end, it had been the same. Love was love, and if you tried, you could manage to find some small part of it with almost anyone. It was just that you could never hold onto it for very long. Not at this level. Not unless you were willing to pay the cost. And that usually came high.

Then with a great and sudden urgency at his back, she had hold of him and he felt her dissolve, and himself with her as all hell broke loose.

"Oh, Christ," he breathed.

"No, darling," she whispered. "It's me. Rachel."

His face lay like a wounded soldier on the heart of her breast. Even now, he had to touch some part of her. She was the sea and he was floating off on a tide. Then a reproachful image of the unfinished canvas on his easel intruded and he sighed. "Ten minutes."

"What?"

"I have to leave in ten minutes."

It was warm in the room and they lay naked, the sheets thrown back. She moved her head to look at him. *"Have to?"*

"You know what I mean."

"Go ahead. Love and run."

"I've been here almost two hours."

"I'll write a note of apology to your conscience." She nipped his ear with her teeth, a bite so neat and small a pin might have pricked him. "It's all right. I have to start getting dressed myself. A gentleman is calling for me in an hour."

"Well," he said. "Busy day on lower Riverside Drive."

"Don't be nasty, darling."

"I don't know why you should bother dressing at all."

She smiled. "Oh, we *are* being nasty."

Duvid lay there, content to feel the tip of a breast against the stubble of a cheek.

"The gentleman who's calling for me," Rachel said, "is Greene."

"A *colored* gentleman?"

"William Greene."

"All right. I'm impressed."

"I'm not trying to impress you," she said, although she obviously was. A distinguished historian, recently appointed to a high State Department post, William Greene was generally regarded in Washington as one of the few things President Harding had so far managed to do right. "But William *does* happen to be a very impressive man."

Duvid grunted.

"Would you rather I saw only *un*impressive men?"

"Absolutely. The more unimpressive the better."

"I've been seeing him for about six months now. Off and on."

"I wouldn't expect you to be seeing him any other way."

This time she did not smile. "If you're finished with the bad jokes, I'd like to tell you something."

"That's exactly what I was afraid of."

"Why should you be afraid?"

The Artist

Duvid slowly sat up in bed. He stared off at her leg, at the inside of the thigh with its wealth of soft skin . . . sexually fragrant. "Because I have a feeling I'm not going to like what you're going to tell me."

"Last night," Rachel said, "William asked me to marry him."

Duvid was silent for a moment. "What did you say?"

"That I'd give him my answer today."

"Well," he said flatly, "it's today. Are you going to marry him?"

"It depends."

"On what?"

"On whether *you* want to marry me."

Duvid got out of bed, padded barefoot and naked to the liquor cabinet, and poured himself two inches of whisky. Now that he had heard it, he knew he had been expecting to hear it for a long time. Then he sat down on the edge of the bed and sipped his drink. He stared dimly at the pleasantly familiar room, at its elegant, antique lamps and period dressers, at its custom commodes and bed tables, all standing about like sentinels prepared to warn him, in his most secret moments, of any intrusion. The intrusion had finally come. As had the earlier warnings. He had simply chosen not to notice them.

"I think," Rachel said quietly, "I've just about used up the possibilities of my present life. I'm thirty-four and getting a little old for the role of perennial transient. I want a home that's more than just a place to sleep and make love. I want a husband I can respect . . . a husband that's my own, not somebody else's. And before it's too late, I want children." She smiled almost apologetically. "It's the nature of the sex. No woman has ever really learned the art of just passing through. We're all permanent settlers at heart. Finally, we have to put down roots. I've fought it longer than most, but I don't want to end up as one of those silly, aging women chasing younger men. And you have to know when to quit the theater too. I don't like *grande dame* roles and there's nothing more pathetic than a forty-year-old ingénue with sagging jowls and tits." She paused. "Well, there it is."

Then she lay still, staring up at the ceiling. She had spoken without emotion and made no claims. Now she let her exceptional

321

face and still-perfect body make their own claims. The quiet went on so long that Duvid could hear a ringing in the air. He saw his reflection in a dark mirror on the opposite wall. His shoulders slumped and he looked drowned, defeated, in the dim glass.

"What I don't understand," he said, at last, "is why you would want to pick a poor *schnook* like me over a big, important man like William Greene."

"I have my reasons."

"What reasons?"

"We both know them. Why are you stalling?"

"Because I happen to have a wife and a child. Remember?"

She made an impatient gesture. "A whore you married to spite *me,* and a son that's not even your own."

Duvid sipped his whisky, feeling a solid dread start small inside him and spread wide, the kind of sensation that comes from a nightmare where you're killing rats. One way or another, he thought, I'm going to lose something here this afternoon.

"I know the kind of loyalty, the kind of *Yiddishkeit* potato love you can grow," she said. "But don't be a fool. This is the rest of your life we're talking about. Don't throw it away because you think you owe it to your wife. You don't owe her a thing. You've already given her more than she deserves. And you don't have to worry about her either. She knows how to look out for herself. She's smart. Smart enough to have nailed you with that baby the minute you stepped off the boat from France. Leave, and she'll have another husband in a month. That was all she really wanted to begin with anyway, wasn't it? A husband?"

"I guess it was."

"Of course. And if it hadn't been you, it would have been some fat-bellied peddler supplied by Molly Adelman."

Rachel propped herself on an elbow, breasts lolling nicely. Gifts offered. But at the moment, Duvid wasn't taking. God, what you could do with facts. Everything she had said was true, yet in sum, it all added up to a lie. He had worked on paintings that turned out the same way, with each brush stroke, each tone and color, each line seeming as close to the truth as you could want it. Then you stepped back and saw that the whole was somehow different from its parts.

The Artist

Yet where did the changeover begin? At exactly what point did the placing of one clean fact upon another start getting muddy? When did it finally turn to dirt? In the case of his wife, Duvid thought, the very real fact of her love had been left out.

"And don't go telling me how much she loves you," Rachel said, as though plucking the thought full-blown from his brain. "Whether she does or not doesn't change anything. She's as wrong for you as a woman could be. Remember. You're no ordinary man. You're an artist. You have special needs. Your work requires special understanding. Yet you're chained hand and foot to an illiterate whore who doesn't know an oil painting from a cockamamy."

"I'm not chained to anyone."

"If you won't break loose, you're chained."

"And just to keep the record straight," he said, his voice gentle because he understood what she was trying to do, "Annie stopped being both illiterate and a whore a long time ago."

"You know what I mean."

He did. With all her reading and self-improvement, with all her going to museums and studying, his wife still had no true comprehension of what his work was all about. Although she tried, often desperately, to understand what he was attempting, what he hoped for and sought from each canvas, what his problems, frustrations, and triumphs were, the creative concept was simply beyond her power to grasp. Sometimes Duvid was sure she viewed the entire business of painting as a less than fitting enterprise for a grown man with a family, that she regarded this part of his life as a foolish addiction which she was willing to suffer because she loved him, but which she would have been very happy to see him give up for a more sensible occupation. And his absorption with his work often angered her, made her feel shut out, unloved. When they fought, it was usually over this. Because she was unable to share his creative mystique, she felt it a threat. Just as she felt Rachel a threat, a woman whom she rarely saw (except for an occasional exhibit or opening) but whose presence haunted her marriage like a darkly omniscient spirit who had first claim on her husband and who might one day reach down and pluck him away. Rachel, the moon-maiden . . . Rachel, of the evil eye. A faint whiff of Old Country superstition still

323

clung to Annie, a lingering feeling that there might possibly, just *possibly*, be those who held the power to lay a curse of sorts. And if there were, Rachel would wear the robes of high priestess. But Annie was a bit psychic herself and could somehow sniff out the times Duvid had come from his witch's playground. Not that she ever confronted him with it. She was too smart to force anything there. Yet some devil's spite was alerted and she would invariably push him to perform again, that same night, in his home arena. Oh, she could be spiteful, his Annie.

"I can give you children," Rachel said. "Your own. Duvid Karlinsky's flesh. Not someone else's. A man deserves that much from a wife."

"That's not fair."

"Who cares about being fair? Do you think this is some kind of athletic contest? I don't want any sportsmanship awards. All I want is you."

"Or William Greene."

"Exactly. But preferably you." She lay back and looked at him, unsmiling, flecks of light coming and going in her eyes as the draperies moved in a breeze and the sun's rays shifted. "I've thought it all through. Long and carefully. There are different times in people's lives for different things. What may be wrong at one time can be right at another. And I feel this is the right time for us."

"Strange," he said. "I always thought the right time for us was thirteen years ago."

Her expression did not change. "There were too many other things I wanted then."

"And now that you've had them, you've decided you're ready for me."

"Yes."

"And what if *I'm* not ready for *you?*"

"I think you are," she said. "If you weren't, you wouldn't be here now and you certainly wouldn't have looked as if I'd kicked you in the stomach when I mentioned William Greene. Darling, don't ever play poker for high stakes. With your face, you'd be broke in an hour."

Duvid finished his drink and started to put on his clothes. How confident she was, he thought, how certain of her appeal, of his doing precisely what she expected. A sharp, sad pain, almost pleasurable, thrust into him and he smiled, because if he didn't, she would have seen and known and she already knew too much.

"What's so funny?" she asked from her pillow.

"Nothing. It's just that I've known you all these years, yet somehow keep forgetting what a self-indulgent, coldly calculating bitch you really are."

"I love you too."

"You're the center of the universe, aren't you? . . . the absolute hub of the wheel, and everyone and everything else have to circle round. I swear, you're almost unbelievable."

She had been lying exposed, but reached down now and covered her nakedness with a sheet. A shadow touched her face, vaguely, then moved on, leaving a pink mottling behind.

"You decide it's time to get married," he said, "so what do you do? You pick your candidates, stick them in the right order for your needs, start applying pressure, then sit back and watch the machinery roll. You're not a woman. You're a goddamn army tank."

"You needn't work yourself up so, darling. All you have to do is say no."

A fire had begun in his stomach, and his lungs were dry as old leaves. Struggling into his trousers, he hopped awkwardly on one foot as the other became trapped in the cloth. Feeling foolish, he grew angrier. He stared hard at her. "What I don't understand is, did you *really* think I'd walk out on my wife and kid because *you* wiggled your finger at me?"

"I did hope you would. But not because of any finger wiggling. I just hoped you could be honest enough with yourself to admit you wanted me as much as I did you."

"And if I did admit it?"

"Then the only thing that could keep us apart would be your stupid sentiment."

"Why does it have to be stupid?"

"Because that's the only kind of sentiment there is . . . a sweet, gooey lie that can smother truth faster than anything I know." Her eyes went dark. "And it can smother us too."

The Artist

Duvid dressed in silence. Rays of sunlight filtered between the drapes and touched the walls and furniture. Splinters of yellow were all over the room, on perfume and makeup bottles, on the mirror, on the rugs, on the rumpled sheets of the bed. This room is going to be here, Duvid thought, and she'll be lying on that bed on other afternoons with the sunlight outside, and I won't be here with her. He combed his hair and arranged his tie under his collar. In the mirror, he looked unaffected, a still-youthful man with a wife and someone else's child waiting for him a few miles away in another room, a man who usually knew the right thing to do, but did not always manage to do it.

"I'm sorry," he said, when he was dressed and ready to go, knowing there would probably be moments in the weeks and months ahead when he was going to be even sorrier, "but I'm afraid I just happen to be an unalterably sentimental man."

He leaned over the bed and kissed her. She looked very pretty, lying there, blonde and mussed, her hair spread in a soft fan around her head. Her eyes, slightly puzzled, were suddenly those of a hurt child who has been punished without quite being able to understand why. Duvid had a powerful impulse to take her in his arms and say, "Rachel, Rachel," softly, and hold and comfort her. Then he turned and went out of the room, out of the apartment, and down in the elevator into the traffic noise and bright, spring sun of Riverside Drive.

He turned off the Drive on Seventy-fourth and walked slowly crosstown. He had his hands in his pockets and his head was bent and his shoulders seemed tired. Six months, he was thinking, he would give her just six months from the day she got married until the first time she called him again.

SIXTEEN

August, 1945: Amagansett, Long Island

There were two of them and they were sitting on the porch rail in the shadow of the house, but rose and came forward as Duvid and Laurie approached. In silhouette, one was tall and thin, the other of medium build. That was all Duvid could see with the lighted windows behind them. Then the taller man said, "Evenin', Mistuh Karlinsky. Evenin', Ma'am," and Duvid recognized the voice at the same time he was able to distinguish the caps and uniforms. But the voice tonight was soft, almost deferential, and the face behind it friendly. The other soldier, Duvid saw, was the one called Frank.

"Ah hope yuh don't mind our intruding like this, Mistuh Karlinsky. But we're fixin' to ship out soon and didn't want to leave without apologizin' for the other night."

Duvid stared.

"I guess we had a few too many," Frank said. He was wearing glasses tonight, the steel GI frames refining his features, giving them a mild, almost studious look. "Anyway, we didn't mean you and your lady any hurt."

"No hurt done," said Duvid.

The corporal grinned and rubbed his throat. "Maybe not to *you*, Suh, but Ah swear Ah couldn't swallow for a week. Man, you got a pair of *hands.*" He spoke to Laurie. "Yuh all right, Ma'am?"

She nodded stiffly, eyes cold, one hand tight on Duvid's arm.

"Ah don't usually hit ladies. Ah'm truly sorry."

327

Laurie said nothing and they just stood there in the dark, on the weathered deck. Frank moved his feet. "We didn't know who you were, Mr. Karlinsky. We're kind of dumb about art."

So that was it, thought Duvid. The barman had impressed them with his importance. He was no longer just a Jew. He was now a *famous* Jew. It made a difference. Like finding an ordinary-looking dog suddenly capable of dancing a tango.

"Ah got a lil' brother draws real good," said the corporal. "Leastways it looks good to *me*. Seems Jed was *born* scratchin' with a pencil."

Duvid waited.

"Me? Ah got ten thumbs. Couldn' draw a straight line if mah life hung on it. But that Jed, now. He's somethin' else again." The corporal abruptly fumbled some papers from a pocket, smoothed out the creases, and offered them to Duvid. "These here are some drawin's he sent me. If it ain't askin' too much, Ah'd be obliged to hear what you think."

Amused and relieved, Duvid took the papers. The relief surprised him. He hadn't known he was that tense. But he found this a lot better reason for their being here than any need to apologize. Laurie, he saw, didn't go along. Her face was blank, her fingers still gripping his arm.

"Jed's only ten, Mistuh Karlinsky. Seems to me these drawin's are real lifelike for someone that young." He laughed at himself. "Ah'm not tryin' to push, understand."

It was too dark to see the drawings, but Duvid suddenly found something oddly appealing about this redneck panther out pumping for his brother. He gave off the sharp, physical communion you usually get from an exciting woman, an awareness of him that Duvid could almost feel.

"Come inside," he said. "We'll see what they look like."

He led the way through the nearest door, the one opening directly into his studio, and was almost startled to see the blue man, still on his easel, facing him.

"Jesus Christ," Frank said.

Duvid watched their faces, watched Frank's stale, calm-colored eyes and the corporal's pale gray ones, seeing first the confusion, then something else, which came off them like smoke in a fog, or the mood that is near a man when he walks through a graveyard. Neither of them said anything, but the corporal turned, once, to look at Duvid with an even, raw gaze that stung the surface of the eyes. In the bright studio light his face was thin, bronzed, arrogant, a mask. It was even handsome, Duvid thought, in a curiously Southern way. Not with the bloom of magnolia and flowering fruit, but with the cool darkness of cypress swamps. The face also brought a few snakes from its tropical garden, along with a strong hint of wild boar. The other soldier's features, behind the crescents of light from his glasses, held the kind of confused shock you see in Midwestern newspaper pictures of newly arrested killers, who never miss a Sunday in church until they go beserk one Saturday night. There was a petulant, hurt look too, a dull resentment of whatever it was it couldn't quite understand. *What are they trying to do,* it wondered, *to a nice kid like me?*

"Jesus Christ," Frank said again, but softer this time, as if speaking Christ's name were an incantation against evil, a needed protection against this fearsome blue blasphemy. "What does the damn thing mean?"

"It means," the corporal told him, "that Mistuh Karlinsky, here, ain't got much hope."

"For who?"

"Us. Everybody."

Frank looked at Duvid. "That right?"

"In a way."

"Hell," Frank laughed. "I got hope. I got lots of hope."

"That's fine," said Duvid.

"How about you, Clay?" Frank asked the corporal. "How're you fixed for hope?"

"Yuh *know* Ah'm nothin' if not hopeful."

"And you, Ma'am?" the soldier said to Laurie.

She almost smiled. "I've got a bit."

Frank picked up and nuzzled Sammy, who was still busy sniffing him out. "How do *you* feel about things, dog?" Sammy licked his face and barked. Frank nodded. "Hear that, Mr. Karlinsky? *Everybody* got hope."

The Artist

But Duvid was only half listening. He was looking at the drawings, a cluster of smeared pencil sketches, showing assorted views of a single subject, an old, down-home, country church. And they were good. Though rough, even crude, they still had all they needed, still carried enough of the soul of the place to send a whole congregation of gray-haired Southern ladies, faces lined and white and with vertical wrinkles on upper lips, parading through Duvid's mind, offering glimpses of passion scarred by righteousness, of bigotry in rheumy eyes, of generations of hate blowing over empty graves. For a moment, with these drawings, he was alone with the boy. Things flowed from Jed (yes, that was his name) to him and then flowed back again. And there must have been some true art here, for he did not entirely despise those dried-up Baptist witches, though witches they were, knowing they had once had love for *somebody,* that they perhaps still kept old letters tied with ribbons and smelling of lavender, still stored the remembered warmth of romance in the icelocks of arthritic joints. All this Duvid thought, from some smeared pencil lines on a few scraps of paper. A fair amount to get from *anything.* Yet he saw it all in the brief period it took to scan the drawings; his sense of time, like that hesitation when you look down from a high place, was as long as the first deep breath you took as you felt the fall. It seemed a long instant indeed as he looked at those drawings, then looked up and saw the pistol in the corporal's hand.

The gun was German, its barrel oiled and sleek, its front sight pointed at his chest. He stared at it as if his reactions had been packed away in ice. "That's a nice Luger." His voice spoke out of that frozen calm.

"Ah took it off a German captain Ah shot in Aachen. Caught him twice in the head." He grinned. "Ah'll tell yuh, Mistuh Karlinsky, them pot helmets ain't worth a damn 'gainst a .30-caliber bullet."

"I don't know whether that thing is loaded or not," Duvid said, "but either way, I don't like it pointing at me."

The corporal slowly lowered the Luger until it was aimed at the floor. His grin widened, turned sweet. "Ah just thought yuh might be interested in pickin' up a lil' souvenir of the war. A hundred bucks and it's yours. Here . . ." He held out the pistol, butt forward. "Take a look."

The Artist

Something in Duvid's stomach began to flutter. A new wind was coming off this tall Southerner, a poisonous snake of a mood that entered his lungs like gas and burned all the way in. Duvid took the pistol, released the ammunition clip, and found it empty. He also found his hands shaking.

"That's right," said the corporal.

Duvid shoved back the empty clip and returned the weapon. "Very nice. But I'm not interested."

"Ah jus' thought, this bein' a German pistol an' all, it might be of special interest to yuh. Ah mean, seein' as how the Germans weren't exactly sweetness and light to the Jewish people, Ah thought it might be nice for yuh to have this piece as a kind of token of their defeat."

"I'd just as soon forget about guns."

"Maybe that's why yuh people are always in trouble. Yuh keep forgettin' 'bout guns while everybody else is busy rememberin'."

A significant insight into the Jewish problem, thought Duvid, from an acknowledged expert. He picked up the drawings from where he had placed them to examine the Luger. "Your brother's good," he told the corporal. "He shows more at the age of ten than a lot of artists *ever* show."

"No foolin'?"

"That church is *there*. I've never seen it, but these few sketches make me know it, make me feel every piece of it. And that's what it's all about. The rest is trimming."

Clay took the drawings and studied them in the fresh light of this pronouncement. "I'll be damned." His face showed pleasure. "Hear that, Frankie? Mistuh Karlinsky says m'ah brother's an honest t'God artist."

"Satisfied now?" asked Frank.

"Ah sure am."

"Good. I'm getting a little tired of all this sweet-assing."

Then having said this, Frank took two short, quick steps behind Duvid and chopped the back of his neck. There was only the single blow, but it came down at just the right angle and hit precisely the right spot, and Duvid went down with it, dropping slowly to his hands and knees, and remaining frozen in that position until a casual shove from Frank's foot rolled him onto his back. Dimly, he

331

The Artist

heard Laurie scream, along with Sammy's barking, and although his eyes remained open the entire time and he saw everything that was going on, it all seemed to be happening under water. He saw Frank's hands on Laurie, pinning her arms, saw Sammy jumping and scurrying to join the fun, saw the corporal remove the empty clip from the butt of the Luger, fill it with cartridges, snap it into place, and draw back and release the slide that would inject a bullet into the firing chamber. Then he saw the corporal point the gun at his head, and he closed his eyes and waited to die.

"Duvid!" Laurie shrieked.

"Open your eyes, Mistuh Karlinsky."

Duvid opened his eyes and he wasn't dead. Yet something had flown into him, silent as the shadow of a bat, and his body felt like a cold, empty cave where deaths were stored. He pushed to a sitting position and looked at Laurie. Her face was pale and her eyes had a washed-out look. He tried to smile for her, but knew it didn't come off and he had the feeling his face resembled one of those grimacing masks he had once seen in a German death camp.

He asked the corporal, "What do you want?"

Clay grinned behind the dark sheen of the Luger. "Ah don't know. Maybe jus' to pass some time in the house of a famous Jew. A coupl'a poor dogfaces like us don't much get this sort'a chance. Right, Frankie?"

"Right, Clay."

A damn vaudeville team, thought Duvid. *Frankie and Clay . . . songs, dances, fancy anti-Semitic patter.* They could take the act on the road, play to packed houses in the South and Midwest, leave audiences hysterical in the aisles. He felt a slight urge toward hysteria himself.

"All right," he said, speaking carefully because there was still some dizziness in him and he did not want to make any mistakes. A mistake, he knew, could be very bad at this point. "You want to get even? Is that it? You want to knock me around for the other night? Go ahead. You want money? I've got some in the bedroom. Take anything you want. Only don't hurt the girl. There's no reason to hurt the girl." Then in an insane afterthought, "She's not even *Jewish,* for Christ's sake!"

332

The Artist

"Got any whisky, Mistuh Karlinsky?"

"In that cabinet there."

"Good." Clay took off his cap and tossed it on a chair. "Now I'll tell yuh what we're gonna do. We're gonna sit nice and easy an' we're gonna drink and we're gonna talk and we're gonna see what comes out of it. But first, yuh better get up off that floor, Mistuh Karlinsky. Ah hate seein' an important man like you lookin' so undignified."

Duvid stood up, swaying slightly.

"That's fine. Now we ain't gonna tie yuh up. But try anythin', and we *will*. Understand?"

Duvid nodded. He was watching Laurie's face, which was calmer now as she seemed to settle into something. She even managed to smile at him, the loveliest smile she owned. It twinkled about her like a harbor light. It's not that bad, it said. Whatever else they are, they're not maniacs. They must want something. When we find out what it is, we'll give it to them and they'll go. The smile also said she loved him. But instead of helping, this somehow made it worse.

Frank went to the liquor cabinet and brought out some bottles and glasses. "You got a decent stock," he told Duvid. "I thought Jews weren't supposed to drink."

"We're learning."

Clay was busy. Like a stage director fussing over an opening scene, he arranged Frank and Laurie on the couch, placed Duvid on a painting stool to their left, and sat himself in a deep chair facing all three. Bourbon, scotch, water, and ice were on a table in front of him, and the Luger was stuck in his belt. Then about to settle back with half a glass of bourbon, he suddenly rose and swung the big studio easel so he had a clear view of the blue nude.

"Ah like yo'r blue friend, Mistuh Karlinsky. Ah find him real interestin'."

"Ah, come on," said Frank. "He's *gruesome.*"

"Yuh don't look at him right. Look at him right an' he'll tell ya' plenty."

"Like what?"

"Like yo're an evil, no-good bastard who is gonna get eat'n by worms."

"And what about you?"

"Me too."

Frank waved his glass at Laurie and Duvid. "And them?"

"Them, too. Damnation an' worms is our reward and ain't no one gonna 'scape." His eyes, still on the blue man, sank deeper into their sockets. "That ol' one-armed boy is tellin' yuh true. *Look* at him, yuh dumb hoosier."

"Hell. Lauries's prettier."

"But evil."

"I like evil women."

"Ain't no other kind. Only good creature in this room is that lil'ol dog there. Come heah, dog." He patted his lap and Sammy jumped up into it and licked his face. "Trouble is, he's stupid."

Duvid sat on his stool, watching and listening. Some new sport. But what were the rules, and for what stakes were they playing? He felt blind and dumb, yet sensed a stirring in the room, a feeling he was in some deepness of waters and had no choice but to keep swimming and not stop.

"Yuh got a name for this picture, Mistuh Karlinsky?"

"No."

The corporal considered the blue man with the air of a connoisseur. "The way he's sufferin' and screamin', he looks kind 'a Jewish to me. How 'bout callin' him The Blue Jew?"

"You've got Jews on the brain," Duvid told him.

"Ah guess Ah do." It was said slowly and in a voice so low his tongue and teeth were almost in the speech. "Least Ah got *you* on the brain. Which is all Ah got room for jus' now."

"I'm not really that special."

"Oh, but yuh *are* that special, Mistuh Karlinsky. Don't go bein' so modest. Ah been studyin' up on yuh. Ah mean, yuh are a *super*-Jew. Yuh think we'd be goin' to all this trouble if yuh were just an ordinary, garden-variety-type Jew?"

"What do you *want* from him?" Laurie asked.

"All in good time, Ma'am. No point in rushin' things. Yuh got somethin' yuh'd rather be doin'?"

She glared at him. To draw attention from her, Duvid asked, "What have you two got against the Jews, anyway?"

The Artist

"You kiddin'?" said Frank.

"I just want to know why you hate us."

"Hell! The whole world knows *that.*"

"I'm talking about *you.*"

Frank blinked, his yellow eyes pale behind their lenses. "I wouldn't even know where to begin."

"Ah'd know where to begin," said the corporal.

Duvid looked at him.

"Ah'd begin at the age of seven, when fat, ol' Mistuh Friedman, of Friedman's Department Store in Atlanta, had mah daddy put in jail the day befoah Christmas for stealin' a two-buck toy 'cause he was broke and out of work and didn't want his lil' boy goin' without a present. How about *that,* Mistuh Karlinsky? Yuh reckon that makes a fair beginnin' for Jew hatin'?"

Duvid said nothing.

"Ah know what yo're thinkin'," he went on quietly, reasonably. A teacher's voice. "Yo're thinking Mistuh Friedman could have been a fat ol' Baptist bastard as easy as a fat ol' Jew bastard, and that he was only one Jew anyway, not all of 'em. An' yo're right. Only at seven, yuh don't think that way. Yo're not that smart. All yuh know is, yo're daddy's in jail for Christmas and it's an ol' Jew put him there."

"You're not seven years old *now,*" said Duvid.

"No. But we were talkin' 'bout beginnin's. Ah've come on a bit since then. Ah've traveled up and Ah've traveled down, and Ah've seen nothin' along the way to make me think different. Listen. Ah got no use for niggers, but Ah'll take 'em over Jews anytime. Least they don't do yuh harm and they know what they are. But you Jews?" He was altogether calm as he spoke, but a vein in his forehead gave a jump and began to pulse. "You Jews are somethin' else again. Yuh talk 'bout bein' God chosen and act like yuh really believe it. Yuh think yo're the only good people walkin' this earth an' the rest of us is shit. Yuh even got a name for us. *Goy.* An' ah know what *that* means. *Abomination.*"

That much, at least, Duvid thought, was true. Literally translated, *goy* was not a happy word.

"Yo're always screamin' 'bout prejudice," the corporal went on,

The Artist

"but if a Jew dares marry a *goy,* he's cut off as dead. Why? Because
we ain't good enough. We ain't smart enough. Yuh and yo'r big
brains. A man works with his hands, sweats for a day's bread, and
yuh turn up yo'r noses at him. He's an ox, a dumb *goy.* If damn-
Yankee is one word to a Southerner, dumb-*goy* is one word to a Jew.
An' Ah'm not just sayin' things Ah've heard. Ah've *seen* it. Outside
the army and in. Look for the cushiest job around, the safest, the
one that keeps yo'r hands cleanest, and you can bet a Jew's got it.
Even in a war with the Germans choppin' yo'r own people like so
many hogs, yuh had to be drafted, had to be dragged, screamin' and
kickin' out of yo'r fat offices an' schools an' houses, 'stead of *beggin'*
to fight. What kind of people *are* yuh? Even animals fight to save
their own, to save themselves. Jesus Christ! All those millions sittin'
in their camps, singin' hymns an' waitin' to be butchered, waitin'
nice and peaceful to be shoved into the ovens. Ah'll tell you. Anyone
won't fight to live, don't deserve to live. Maybe that's why we been
choppin' yuh all these years. Maybe it's 'cause you're so damn easy
to chop."

Duvid lifted his glass carefully, with both hands. There must be
a giant radio transmitter somewhere, he thought, perhaps hidden
beyond the Himalayas, from which all of these half-truths, distor-
tions, and lies were beamed to the foolish and ignorant of the world.
But he was not amused, and as he lifted his drink to his mouth, the
scotch leaped up with a lurch of his elbow off his knee, and a splash
went on his cheek. It could have been blood, maybe some long-
dead, anonymous Jew's, even that of one of those hymn-singing
millions who had waited so peacefully before their final ovens. The
sensation of something wet on his face divided him from reason,
offered fresh premonitions he was unable to brush aside, as if there
would be a grim toll on his flesh if he failed to take them seriously
enough. This man was unpredictable, therefore dangerous. Every
moment, every sentence contained its possibility. And all Duvid
could do was listen and wait, and watch the butt end of the pistol,
which would, of course (and he wasn't even tempted to smile), turn
out to be German.

"Except you, Mistuh Karlinsky," the corporal said over the
golden lights of his bourbon. "Yo're no easy Jew to chop. Ah found

that out the other night. Which is why we're all sittin' heah now. 'Long with that poor *Blue Jew* up there." He smiled benevolently at the painting, and it was obvious how much he was enjoying himself. His voice, softened by the liquor, had rounded into humors, his manner had become embracing yet impersonal, as if he were the master of an enormous treat which would soon be offered up. Then he looked once more at Duvid and a hint of gray ice came out of the core of his humor. Yet his tone remained genial. "Yuh were beautiful back in that bar, Mistuh Karlinsky. Ah mean, the way yuh handled all *three* of us. Clean, neat, no fuss. A work of art by a truly fahn artist."

He paused and sat silent and unmoving, a cautious hunter in the midnight of a jungle. When he spoke again, it was to Laurie. "Yuh were pretty fair yo'self, Ma'am. Full 'a heat an' fire. Yo'r man was bein' insulted an' yuh weren't 'bout to sit still for it. Ah like that in a woman."

"Go to hell," she said.

"Jus' where Ah'm headed. Fact is, Ah'm lookin' forward to it. Wanna come along?"

He waited with deliberate politeness for Laurie to answer. When she didn't, he shrugged. "Ah'll meet yuh there, anyway. But in the meantime, Ma'am, Ah'd appreciate yo'r doin' me the small favor of takin' off yo'r clothes."

It was said in precisely the same soft, easy tone as the rest, so that Duvid did not absorb it all at once, but rather in small fragments, tiny shards, sharp-edged, cutting as they went in. Then half off the stool, he saw the Luger, no longer in the corporal's belt, but in his hand and pointing at him.

"Stay easy, Mistuh Karlinsky. Yo'r lady's not gonna be hurt. She's jus' gonna take off some clothes. Now, she can do it with yuh lyin' on the floor, or with yuh sittin' quiet on your stool. You can take yo'r pick. But either way, she's gonna do it."

Duvid held where he was, hanging there out of some instinct that the worst moment of any anguish must always be the first. Still, the temptation to move against the gun was strong enough to bring him close to nausea.

Laurie said, "Duvid. Please. Don't."

The Artist

"That's real sensible, Ma'am."

She looked at him and hatred came off her like a scent, dull and powerful, as though she carried the beginnings of a dead thing at her center rather than a living one. Then because she had so much it was spilling out of her, she passed some of it on to Frank, who was drinking quietly beside her, a dues-paying member of the club, waiting for the show to begin. "How do men *get* like you? What kind of sickness does it take?"

Frank smiled silently, without malice. "Ah don't know what all the fussin's 'bout," said the corporal. "Yuh been looked at by men before."

"Yes, but not by pigs."

The soldiers laughed, their humor broad and easy and floating higher by the minute.

Still on the edge of his stool, still leaning slightly toward the Luger, Duvid said. "Are you *really* prepared to shoot me over this?"

"Ah'm prepared to do anything Ah have to do, Mistuh Karlinsky. Only thing is, if Ah shoot *you*, Ah'll probably have to shoot yo'r lady too. And Ah *know* yuh wouldn't want that."

He *would* do it, Duvid decided, and felt the air go out of his lungs as he drifted back, away from the gun, felt, too, the scotch going bad in his stomach along with something in his brain. Maybe *he* was the senile one, not his mother, who, as age nudged her, was increasingly haunted by visions of pogroms, by imagined mobs outside her window. Sometimes, visiting, he would find her on her knees behind a chair. "Get down, Duvidal," she would plead. "Hide. They're coming." Then to her husband, Avrum, "Where's Tybie? We must warn Tybie." Aunt Tybie was ten years dead, but Avrum Karlinsky would pretend to seek her out, nodding sadly to his son. And he, Duvid, would say, "Don't worry, Momma. It's all right. We're in America now. They don't hurt Jews in America." Until, the spell passing, he would help his mother to her feet, this dying old woman whose failing mind might finally prove to have had a fairer knowledge of the truth than his own. *They'll shoot you, Duvid! They've got guns. Hide!* Where, Momma? Tell me. Where shall I hide?

Laurie had gotten up from the couch. Her eyes were blank. The two soldiers were silent, watching. But Clay was also watching

The Artist

Duvid, the Luger a dark extension of his hand. Sammy danced about Laurie's legs, wanting to play. Standing there, she remained blank some seconds. Then moving quickly, she stripped her dress over her head. She was wearing no bra and her breasts tugged upward with the movement, fell back, and stayed alive. She had on pink underpants and sandals and nothing more. She kicked off the sandals and without pausing, pulled the elastic down with two thumbs, wriggled, stepped out, and stood naked in the studio light.

No one spoke and there were just the small, nervous sounds of Sammy's paws on the bare floor. Laurie stared at the far wall, her face on the edge of dividing into two women . . . that queen of pride, that polished sex object grown certain of its powers, and a little girl forced into an immodest act. And the atmosphere in the room, which had quivered for an instant as she undressed, now slowly flared and went higher. Yet Duvid looked at her and was unable to feel a thing. Which was not to say that nothing was happening to him. Emotions passed like spirits through his body and he knew he would mourn this moment at some future time. But for now, he sat frozen in a block of ice.

"Mighty pretty, Ma'am," said Clay.

All Frank did was look. But the hand holding his glass began to tremble slightly, and the tip of his tongue flicked at his lips, trying to relieve the dryness that no amount of moisture would ever help.

"Now that you've had your big thrill," said Laurie, "may I put my clothes back on?"

"Not jus' yet, Ma'am." The corporal nodded to Duvid. "Now you, Mistuh Karlinsky. Let's see if yo're as pretty as yo'r lady."

Duvid had finally begun to understand. Debasement. *That* was the key. Humiliate the Jew. Rob him of all dignity. Demonstrate his helplessness. Demean his woman. Make him feel less than a man. It was a time-honored technique. He had underrated this cracker, hadn't credited him with this much style. But if this was indeed it, then it wasn't as bad as he had feared. Almost relieved, he slid off his stool and undressed, stripping off shirt, trousers, and underwear and dropping them to the floor.

They stared at his scars. "Jesus, you look like a damn roadmap," said Clay. "Who chopped yuh?"

The Artist

"Germans."

"Which war?"

"Both."

"Ah didn't know yuh were in the army."

"I wasn't. I was a combat artist."

"Ah see," Clay said. Then raising the Luger, he playfully squinted along its barrel at Duvid's genitals. "Well, Mistuh Combat Artist. Let's see yuh give us a lil' demonstration of artistic combat on the floor with yo'r lady."

Duvid looked at the corporal and a beast stared back at him. His teeth showed, the point of light in his eye was violent, and his open mouth was a cave where dark, crawling things lived. Listening, Duvid was sure he could hear a wind whistling up from the cellars of the earth. "No," he said.

"No, what?"

"I won't do it."

The corporal's eyes widened in mock surprise. He was an actor now and his face did a few quick turns. "Won't *do* it? Ah swear yuh shock me, Mistuh Karlinsky. What an ungentlemanly thing to say before yo're lady. And her waitin' there so nice and pretty. That's downright insultin'. Makes her feel un-dee-sirable."

At that moment Duvid was ready to risk a dive at the gun, felt death flail about him like echoes in a nightmare. Its guts clotted his lungs and he had to open his mouth to breathe.

The corporal must have felt it, too. "Don't try it, Mistuh Karlinsky. It ain't worth gettin' shot for." He spoke to Laurie as an ally. "Tell him, Ma'Am. Ah've a feelin' yuh got a better understandin' of what's important heah."

She touched Duvid's hand, but he refused to look at her. He would look only at the beast holding the gun, feeling his pulse, hearing his heart as if both were his own. The soldier's body gave off a raw, purple heat that gusted between them now in small fires.

"Duvid, it shouldn't matter that much."

He looked at her then.

"Please," she said. "Don't do anything crazy. It's not worth it. We'll just make believe they're not here."

"You could do that?"

The Artist

"They're no different to me than Sammy. Just two more animals in the room."

But it did not quite reach Duvid as she intended. He found something wrong with her voice, and her eyes suddenly seemed too bright, her skin too flushed, her breathing too deep. Of *course* she could do it. Hadn't she been doing it the first day he ever saw her? And how many times before that? And with what secret pleasures? Then having thought this, his belly became a pit of snakes and he forgot who she was.

Frank said, "Know what I think? I think the Jew can't cut it." He grinned at Duvid. "Want me to show you how, Karlinsky?"

"Never yuh mind, Mistuh Karlinsky. Ah got confidence in yuh. Yo're an artist and Ah know that artists are sensitive people. Yo're jus' a lil' bashful, is all. Yuh jus' need time to get used to the idea. Only don't go takin' too *much* time, or Frankie might get impatient and do it himself. And Ah'm sure none of us want that." He traveled Laurie's body with his eyes, top to bottom, them up again. "Or *do* we, Ma'am?"

She did not answer, but some tightly knurled pit of grief, some bitter hollow rose to her eyes and sparkled like tears.

"Maybe Ah've been neglectful," the corporal said. "Maybe yuh'd *welcome* a little change. How 'bout it, Ma'am? Interested in Frankie? He ain't had any rabbi's fancy trimmin', but he passed his last short-arm with flyin' colors and Ah personally guarantee him to be clean."

"Drop dead," she told him, then suddenly changed her tone and was not far from a child in her need for a quick answer. "Please. If we do what you want, will you leave us alone then?"

The gun in one hand, Clay carefully poured himself more bourbon with the other. "Well, that depends."

"On what?"

"On how good a job Mistuh Karkinsky does. Ah mean, we don't want one of them quick wham-bam-thank-yuh-ma'ams. What we do want is a true and proper demon-stray-shun of the art of forn-i-cay-shun." Fresh accents were beginning to fly in and out of his speech like birds and bats. He seemed to be making a strong effort to be amusing, even charming, as if his current role were only temporary, and he wanted to leave as good an impression as possible for future bookings. "Ah hear Jews got special sex-u-al powers from the devil, an' Ah'm anxious to find out if it's true. If Mistuh Karlinsky is *really* that great, Ah might be interested in signin' up with that ol' horned goat myself."

Duvid almost laughed. Suddenly the whole idea of the two of them standing there, naked as Adam and Eve, while this hambone Georgia cracker soliloquized on Jewish sexual powers and compacts with the devil, struck him as pure burlesque. Except for the Luger. There was never anything funny about a loaded gun. And he *knew* these two weren't comics. Still, the slight whiff of humor did help pull him from the edge. What, after all, was he being asked to do? Make love to a woman he loved? As always, it was Laurie who proved the more practical *We'll just make believe they're not here.* And she was right. Debasement couldn't be inflicted. It had to come from inside. The corporal would be disappointed.

"All right," he said.

Clay smiled. "Ah knew yuh'd come 'round, Mistuh Karlinsky. Ah jus' *knew* it." He pushed his chair back, cleared more space on the studio floor.

"Not on the floor," Duvid said. "On the couch."

"Yuh'll do it on the floor."

"No."

Frank rose from his place on the couch. "Hell, what difference does it make?"

"A lot of difference," said the corporal. "On the floor, Mistuh Karlinsky."

Duvid shook his head.

"For Christ's sake, Clay!" said Frank, anxious, now that it was this near.

Clay weighed it and shrugged. Having achieved this much, he could afford the small concession. He turned a pair of lamps so they shone on the couch, adjusted his chair to the new arrangement, and awaited his pleasure. And sitting there, holding his bourbon and his fine souvenir of Germany, a hunger came out of him that could be felt as hotly as that first sign of love a man feels in a woman who has until then given no love, a lust that had an awareness of even the studio air. He glanced once at the Blue Jew, as though to make sure he was still there, his message intact, then watched the naked Jew who had created him lead his equally naked lady to the couch.

SEVENTEEN

August, 1927: Boston, Mass.

The day of the funeral, a Sunday, broke gray and desolate and Duvid considered it only fitting that the sun should not appear.

Shall the cloud go over and the sun rise as before . . .
We shall not feel it again.
We shall die in darkness and be buried in the rain.

He did not normally believe in extended rituals for the dead, but today, for Sacco and Vanzetti, who lay with darkened faces in their open coffins, he believed in it.

Standing in a corner of the funeral parlor as part of the guard of honor, Duvid found it strange to look at those faces now. Langeone, the undertaker, had worked hard and long to repair the damage inflicted by the State of Massachusetts and had done a creditable job. But Duvid had known the faces of Nicola Sacco and Bartolomeo Vanzetti too well in life to accept these facsimiles as anything more than the embalmer's dummies they were. His own art had predated Langeone's by six years. He had first sketched them in the Dedham courtroom in June of 1921, partly for the *Times*, but mostly for himself. Nick, then, had been handsome and squarejawed, with dark, hurt eyes under even brows. Bart's thin face, jutting cheekbones, and great drooping moustache had made him seem ten years older than the thirty-two he was. There was a particular way each of them had sat, a watching and a listening, a struggle to understand a language to which they had not been born and which the threat of death was forcing them to hurriedly learn. *Listen, listen! These words can kill. Know it!* And they had known. They had listened and they had not believed it even as they heard, but they had known. Just as Duvid, too, must have known. Not consciously. To the end, his brain would not accept it. But he did not draw with his brain and Sacco had been quick to see it even in those early sketches. "Aieee, Karlinsky! You throw the first handful of dirt over us." Vanzetti had wryly agreed. "Bones without flesh. We must eat more." The primitive self-attachment of the human creature, that sweet, deep instinct for the self that makes us care, that makes us hang on no matter what. Duvid was to sketch them time and again, paint them twenty times more. A body of work in itself. Once begun, he seemed unable to stop. Karlinsky and the anarchists. Yet he had cared nothing for their political beliefs, for that nobly absurd anarchic conception of a governmentless future when, in Vanzetti's words, "Man would no longer be wolf to the man," and the workers would run factories cooperatively. All he had cared about were the two men themselves and that incredible tower of injustice that was slowly being toppled upon them.

Of course he had been called an anarchist himself. Guilt by association. You swung a brush in defense of anarchists, so you were an anarchist. Also, Karlinsky was a foreign-sounding name, which meant he had to be either an anarchist or a Red. It was the nature of the times.

For Duvid, there had been no warning. One moment he was asleep beside his wife . . . the next, he was facing blinding lights in the hands of hard-faced men armed with clubs and guns. They took him to the Manhattan offices of the Department of Justice on Park Row. Each time he asked a question, he was clubbed in the stomach. In a bare office they stood him facing a dun-colored wall. He heard screams from the next room, then silence. Then there were more screams and silence again. After a while he was turned around and pushed into a chair. A battery of lights hit him and he saw nothing.

"When did you become a Bolshevik?" a voice asked.

"I'm not a Bolshevik."

"Don't lie. If you lie, it'll be worse for you."

The Artist

"Go to hell!"

Something hit Duvid in the mouth. He started out of his chair, but hands held him.

"You're Russian, aren't you?" the voice asked.

"I'm an American."

"You were born in Russia."

"I'm an American citizen. Are *you?*" Duvid tensed, expecting to be hit again, but nothing came.

"This is your painting, isn't it?"

A sheet of paper was thrust in front of him. "I can't see!" The lights were swung out of his eyes and he saw a red handbill with a crude reproduction of *The Hero* printed over it in black. Below, was written *The Face of American Justice . . . 1920.* So *that* was it.

"Where did you have these printed?" asked the voice which, Duvid could now see belonged to a tall, heavily built man with eyes the color of lake ice.

"I never saw the thing before."

The tall man gave him five knuckles in the face. "I told you not to lie."

"I'm not lying."

"It's *your* painting."

"Anyone could have copied it." The portrait had been bought several months before by a museum in Rochester. The purchase had been exciting, but Duvid had half hated to let the captain go. Looking at the reproduction now, seeing the use to which it had been put, he found it curiously fitting. The captain would have enjoyed it.

"You Bolshevik son-of-a-bitch! *You* copied it! *You* had the handbills printed, and *you're* going to tell us where you had it done."

"I want a lawyer," Duvid said quietly.

They really went to work on him then, hitting in relays. He blacked out twice and twice they brought him back with a bucket of water in the face.

The big man said, "We know all about you, Karlinsky. We know the kind of dirty, Red paintings you turn out."

"What Red paintings?" Duvid mumbled through broken lips.

"All that pacifist, antiwar shit. All that un-American propaganda."

The Artist

"Since when is it un-American to be against killing?"

Duvid saw it coming this time and met it with his eyes open. I must remember his face, he was thinking. I must make sure I don't forget what he looks like.

They kept him in the Park Row offices for two days and nights. Later, he was to learn he was only one of thousands picked up in thirty-three cities that night. In Lynn, Massachusetts, forty-one Yiddish-speaking bakers were arrested as they allegedly gathered to plàn their part in the revolution. No one spoke enough English to explain to the police that what they were really doing was organizing a bakery.

Released, Duvid called Annie to let her know he was all right, but he did not go home. Instead, he checked into a small, downtown hotel to wait for his bruises to heal. He did not want his wife to see him that way. Also, he had some thinking to do. He thought of the big man's face, remembering the pale eyes, the broad, slightly twisted nose, the tight mouth. *The face of American justice, 1920.* An unimportant face and only one of many, but he found it less frustrating to personalize it. You had to start *somewhere.* He had been called a Bolshevik son-of-a-bitch and that in itself was startling. Didn't the *schmucks* know he was on his way to becoming a *capitalist* son-of-a-bitch? . . . a success, a walking advertisement for the American Dream? He had one painting in a small but bona fide museum, others were selling at good prices, and he was accumulating material goods at an almost frightening pace. Didn't they know he wanted *nothing* changed, that he thought America beautiful just as she was . . . gaudy whore's paint and all? He wanted no revolution. He wanted no Bolshevik takeover. He wanted no Bolshevik *anything.* The Reds were no better than anyone else. They were worse. Their hypocrisy went deeper. They told the world they were workingmen, that they were for the workingman, but they were liars. They were Vanderbilts and Rockerfellers in caps. Bismarcks without neckties. Everything was for effect. How many thousands had they already killed for disagreeing with them? How many more thousands would die? Their secret police could sit down to lunch with the agents of the United States Department of Justice, and if you changed their clothes nobody would be able to tell the difference.

347

The Artist

We know all about you, Karlinsky. In that, a genuine surprise. Yet, what could they know? That he was a man who despised killing and war, yet was curiously given to violence? That he painted more out of emotion than aesthetics? That with all his might . . . mind, heart, and brush, he tried to mourn pain and celebrate hope? That he frequently didn't understand, despaired of *ever* understanding the reasonless cruelties that humans performed upon one another? Although this last wasn't personal to him alone. It was the trouble with most people who spent their lives in the arts, and therefore imagined that once cruelty was described in books or shown in paintings, it was finished. Of course, he really did know better. He really did know that human beings wouldn't make a special effort to live so as to be understood by Duvid Karlinsky . . . artist.

He stayed in the hotel room for five days and nights, having his meals sent up. On the sixth day he went out and spent several hours watching the entrance to the Department of Justice, but did not see the big agent enter or leave. He returned the following day and the next with no better results. On the fourth day, toward evening, he saw the man come out of the building, get into a parked automobile, and drive off. Duvid waved down a passing cab and had the driver follow the car over the Brooklyn Bridge to a quiet, heavily treed section of Flatbush. When the car stopped in front of a row of small, attached houses, Duvid dismissed his cab and saw the agent go into a house no different from any of the others on the street, with their brick stoops and sun porches and lanterns over the doors. Lights shone through the ground-floor windows, and Duvid could see a fair-haired woman and two young girls. He watched the children greet their father with kisses and hand tugging, saw the pretty wife laughing at some private family joke. All right. So the bastard was a devoted husband and loving father. Good for him. So? So the human soul, Duvid thought, is an amphibian that lives in more elements than I will ever know. And what dark needs of my own would be satisfied by doing to him what he had done to me? Suddenly Duvid's intended violence, his patiently planned vengenace was turned into *theater,* into something ludicrous. His tightly held breath, released, came back to him. And how good it felt to breathe. You don't fight them that way, he thought. It had been worth the

348

trip to Brooklyn to find out. He walked away from the house, located a subway, and rode it home.

At ten o'clock, Langeone cut off the still-moving line of sympathizers, locked the doors to his funeral parlor, and closed the coffin lids forever on the remains of Sacco and Vanzetti. At one-thirty, a column of mounted police cantered over the cobbles of Scollay Square and formed a double line along Hanover Street, and the long funeral procession began its march.

Duvid was part of the honor guard for the procession, just as he had been for the lying in state. It was a coveted position and one that the committee had not awarded lightly. Duvid's work, they declared, was a lasting monument to the two martyrs and he therefore deserved the distinction. As if it mattered, Duvid thought, where he or anyone else walked. Besides, he had never thought of his paintings in such grand terms. They had simply been something he had to do, a way of siphoning off anger and frustration. Without them, he might have done something drastic and foolish. As it was, he had painted with a brush dipped in bile. No one important to the case was overlooked. He touched them all, stamping out faces and bodies in a strong, direct, almost primitive style. Outlines were stiffly drawn, colors strong and flat, and every distortion designed to imply that these people were puppets carried along in a drama over which they had little control.

Duvid had seen it fast, almost from the start. He had somehow been able to recognize the materials of a world issue in what appeared to others a routine matter. A socialist newspaperman spent a few days in Boston and returned to New York to report that there was no story in it . . . just a couple of wops in a jam. Not even the members of the Defense Committee formed immediately after the men's arrest suspected that the affair was anything larger than it seemed. It was Duvid, in his paintings and drawings, who rendered the case in broad, expressionistic strokes, embellished and retouched it, splashed it over a worldwide canvas. What did he do? He took two anarchist aliens, neither of whom really gave a damn about the organized labor movement, and helped turn them into a universal symbol of the workingman, of the class struggle. If he had not done so, Sacco and Vanzetti might have died with less of the comforts of martyrdom. And he? He might have spared his family and himself a lot of pain and trouble.

The worst of it started the day after the opening of the exhibition he called "The Persecution of Sacco and Vanzetti." The phone rang at home that evening and he picked it up.

"I want to speak to Duvid Karlinsky." It was a man's voice, rough and harsh.

"Speaking."

"You goddamn Commie, Jew son-of-a-bitch," the man said. "You better get the hell out of the country before you're carried out."

Duvid hung up. He stared thoughtfully at the telephone, then turned and looked at his wife.

"Who was it?" Annie asked.

"Wrong number."

"Was it another one of those calls?"

"Which calls?"

"They've been coming in all day," Annie said. "Men and women. They curse us both and make terrible threats."

"I'm afraid it was."

"I called the police this morning, but they said they can't do anything about it. They said they can't arrest everybody with nickels in their pockets."

"Just a bunch of cranks. They'll get tired of it."

"It's frightening. Right in your own home."

"If it continues, I'll have the phone disconnected. In the meantime, just make sure Richard doesn't pick up any calls. I don't want him getting involved."

It continued and Duvid had the phone disconnected. And two days later, a Saturday, his son *did* get involved.

"Mr. Karlinsky! Mr. Karlinsky!" The scream . . . high, childish, frightened, reached him in his studio along with a wailing doorbell.

The Artist

It was Freddy Levine, his potato nose running, his plump cheeks streaming tears and dirt.

"They got Ritchie!"

Duvid didn't waste time asking who it was that had Ritchie. He just followed his son's friend out of the building, across Riverside Drive, and into a thickly wooded area above the Hudson. A group of boys broke and ran as Duvid approached and he saw his son. Richard was bound to a tree, naked, muddied limbs and body shaped in a rough imitation of a cross. A piece of cardboard hung by a string from his meager nine-year-old penis, and on it, in red crayon, was scribbled, DIRTY COMMIE-JEW.

Duvid cut his son loose and ran anxious hands over him. "Where did they hurt you?"

"Dirty Irishers." Richard was trembling, but dry-eyed. "There were five of them. Bigger than me. Did you see?"

"Hold still." Duvid cut the sign free. No permanent damage. But what if he had come ten minutes later?

He covered his son with scraps of torn clothing and carried him back to the apartment. Grateful that Annie wasn't home to see, he put him a tub and cleaned him.

"What's a Commie, Dad?"

"It's short for Communist." Duvid lifted his son out of the soapy water and wrapped him in a towel.

"What's a Communist?"

"Someone who believes in everybody owning things together. Like they do in Russia."

"Are we Communists?"

"No."

"Then why did they call me a dirty Commie?"

"Because they're stupid and don't know any better." At least, Duvid thought, he didn't have to ask why he was called a dirty Jew. That much he had learned. Riverside Drive was a solidly middle-class Jewish neighborhood, but enough Irish toughs came down from Amsterdam Avenue to keep things normal.

"They didn't call Freddie a dirty Commie."

Duvid sprinkled baby powder on soft flesh and spread it with his palms. "It's because of me. A lot of people don't like the paintings

351

The Artist

I did about Sacco and Vanzetti, so they don't like me. And because you're my son, they don't like you either."

"Are Sacco and Vanzetti dirty Communists?"

"No. But some people call anybody they don't like a dirty Communist."

Richard thought about it. "What I don't like are dirty Irishers."

"There are good and bad Irish."

"I never saw any good ones."

"You will."

"I don't think so."

It stayed on his mind. There were things he wanted to know about the exhibition. The next day, Duvid took him to the gallery. It was the first time he had ever shown so specific an interest in Duvid's work. Until now, the idea of his father's being an artist had been accepted without question. Other fathers were plumbers, doctors, manufacturers, lawyers, salesmen. His own father painted pictures. It was all the same, all part of that same vaguely mysterious grown-up world that was out there somewhere, but had little to do with him. Now, suddenly, it did have something to do with him. Things had been done to him because of pictures his father had painted, and he needed to understand why.

Duvid watched him move from one canvas to another. He was frowning slightly and his eyes were puzzled. They were just pictures of people. Some were kind of funny-looking, some looked worried, others seemed happy, angry, or frightened. But they were still just pictures of people. What was there here to make those Irishers want to hurt him? What unseen power lay hidden inside the paint?

"Which ones are Sacco and Vanzetti?"

Duvid pointed them out.

"Tell me about them."

"I've already told you."

"Tell me again."

Duvid led him off to one side, away from several newly arrived groups of visitors. The attendance, so far, had been good, with each visitor representing another five dollars for the appeal fund. After a tour of a dozen cities, Duvid planned to have the paintings themselves auctioned off. "What part do you want to hear?"

The Artist

"All of it."

Some bedtime story, thought Duvid. "Well," he said, "Sacco worked in a shoe factory, Vanzetti was a fish peddler, and they both came to America from Italy. They were also both anarchists, which meant they didn't believe in governments or war. Then one day they were arrested for killing two men in a holdup. They said they didn't do it, but no one believed them and they were put on trial for murder. It was a very unfair trial and they were sentenced to die, mostly, I think, because the judge and jury and a lot of other people didn't like anarchists. Since then, those of us who don't believe they killed anybody have been trying to get them a new trial. We think it's a terrible thing for men to be punished for something they didn't do. Writers and poets have written stories and poems to tell how they feel about it. Because I'm an artist, I've painted these pictures to show how *I* feel."

Richard stared at a large painting of the two anarchists manacled to one another. "They're Italian?"

"Yes."

"I know some Italian kids. They carry knives."

"Not all Italians carry knives."

"These kids do." Richard turned away from the painting and looked thoughtfully at his father. "Next to Irishers, I think I mostly don't like Italians."

Two days later, he came home with a bleeding head. Annie screamed when she saw him. Duvid calmed her, cleaned the wound, showed her that the scalp cut was not a large one. "See? No stitches needed. It's nothing."

"*Nothing?*" She glared. "Are we supposed to be grateful they didn't *kill* him? How did it happen?"

"They threw rocks this time," said Richard.

"I'm calling the police," said Annie, and moved to pick up the phone before she remembered it was disconnected. She sat down wearily. "Why," she asked her husband, "can't you just paint sunsets and flowers like other artists?"

During the next few weeks, rocks were twice thrown through the plate-glass windows of the exhibition gallery, a group of women cursed and spat at Annie on the corner of Broadway and 157th

Street, and Richard was harrassed or assaulted on an almost daily basis. The boy took his punishment uncomplainingly and without tears, but in growing detachment and silence. Duvid watched him anxiously. "I don't like the way Ritchie looks," he told his wife. "Maybe you should take him to the beach or someplace until this blows over."

"When will it blow over?"

"Who knows."

"I'm not leaving you here alone."

"I don't mind."

"*I* mind."

Richard sat through dinner one night, staring at his plate, barely touching his food.

"Everything is getting cold," his mother said. "Why don't you eat?"

"I'm not hungry."

"What's the matter?" Duvid asked him.

"Nothing. I'm just not hungry."

"You haven't been hungry for a week," Duvid said. The boy stared at his plate.

"What is it?"

"I *hate* them."

"Who?"

"*Them.* Sacco and Vanzetti. It's all *their* fault."

"What's their fault?"

"Everything. Everything that's happened. And I hate the pictures you did about them, too. Why did you have to do them?"

"I told you."

"I don't *care* what you told me," Richard cried fiercely. "You didn't *have* to do them. Nobody *made* you, did they?"

"No. Nobody made me."

"See?" Richard glanced at his mother for approval and support, then attacked again. "They're just a couple of old Italians anyway. Why should you care what happens to some old Italians?"

"If I think it's wrong, I care what happens to *anybody.*"

"What about me? Don't you care what happens to me?"

"Of course. You more than anyone."

354

The Artist

"You *don't* care. If you did, you wouldn't have painted those pictures and got those Irishers after me every day."

"I'm sorry about that. I didn't know anything like that was going to happen."

"You know now. You can take away the paintings now and not let anybody else see them."

"I can't do that."

"Why?"

"Because I'm trying to help save two men's lives."

"I don't care," wailed Richard. "I don't want to get beat up anymore. Why do I have to get beat up for two dopey old Italians I don't even know?"

He got up and fled to his room. Annie shook her head. "It's too much to expect him to understand."

"I just hope he understands how much I do care about him."

"You can't pay attention to what he says. All children say things like that."

"It still bothers me. If I were his real father, maybe it wouldn't."

"You *are* his real father."

"I know."

But he didn't know. Not really. And all the little linguistic tricks that adoptive parents use to convince themselves they're no different from natural parents were useless. And logic, too, was useless, along with all those neat theories about the effect of environment on the young. Because Duvid felt he *was* different. Just as Richard, without even knowing he was adopted (Duvid had insisted he not be told), was different. A terrier pup raised from birth by wolfhounds will never be a wolfhound. It will still grow up a terrier, with all the looks and characteristics of the breed. And of what breed was this child he was raising as his son?

He had not thought much about it at the beginning. What was there to think? He had come home from the wars to the soft, plump arms of a beautiful little blond baby, who laughed often, cried rarely, and called him Daddy. What did it matter that he himself had not planted the seed? As he had told Annie when he first saw the child . . . a *baby is a baby. We can make him what we want.* But could they? And if they could, what *did* they want? Unendingly, Duvid's

355

parents hunted family features and traits for their sole grandchild. Ah, see the eyes. Tante Elke had such blue, Polish eyes. And Avrum Karlinsky's father, Duvid's grandfather, had exactly such a small, turned-up nose. Even the laugh, the instant friendliness were claimed for some branch of the Karlinsky family tree. Adoption was never mentioned. All use of the word was banned. If it wasn't spoken, it might go away.

But Richard would not let it go away. At least not for Duvid. His son was beautiful, but it was an alien, typically gentile beauty. It resembled nothing in either his wife or himself. Nor was he able to discover anything of them in the way he behaved. With a quick enough mind in most areas, Richard remained a dunce at school. He refused to read or study, came to class unprepared, and tried to escape the stigma of stupidity by pretending indifference. So what? So where did *this* come from? Wasn't a love of learning supposed to be as endemic to the Jewish male as circumcision? And why should he be the only Jewish student at P.S. 46 whose mother had to keep coming to school because of his behavior? This particular pleasure was reserved for the Irish, the Italians, and the colored. Never the Jews. Except, of course, for Richard Karlinsky.

Duvid had once gone so far as to see Molly Adelman. He felt ashamed, disloyal, a betrayer of his own, but went anyway. He had to know more. He tried to be subtle in his questions, tried to work around it, but should have known better. Molly had never been easy to fool. "You suddenly need credentials for your son?"

"I'd like to know who his mother was."

"She was a whore. And a good one. Just like your wife."

"Come on, Molly."

She looked at him, her flesh still holding up well through the years, still milk-fed and firm, her eyes still shooting old lights. The wages of sin, thought Duvid, were apparently youthfulness and good health. "What do you want me to tell you? That she was a queen in disguise? That your son is a prince?"

"I just want you to tell me the truth."

"What kind of truth? What difference could any of it make now?"

"No difference. That's why I can ask."

Molly's soft, powerful nostrils dilated with suspicion. They held knowledge. No question was innocent, nothing was what it seemed, no one was without hidden motives. "You think I remember?"

"Look in the book." Duvid was one of the few who knew about the book, a great, dog-eared ledger in which Molly had meticulously recorded the personal history of every girl who had ever worked for her. From arrival to departure, no detail of their lives was left out. "Or better still, let *me* look."

"You're sure it's what you want?"

He nodded. But waiting for Molly to get the ledger, he was less sure. Why breathe life into dead shadows? What possible good could it do? Yet, when she returned with the book, its pages open to the proper place, he took it eagerly.

ANULKA KOZINSKI, he read, and went no further. "This is the one? This Anulka?"

"Yes."

"What kind of name is that?"

"It's a name. A name is a name."

"It sounds Polish."

"So, it sounds Polish. So?"

"But I thought you only took Jewish girls?"

"You never heard of a Polish Jew?"

"Not with a name like Kozinski."

"Well, now you've heard of it."

But he did not quite believe her. And as he read on, he believed her less. The girl was described as having pale blue eyes, very white skin, and hair the color of straw. Her disposition was listed as even, her personality as pleasant, her intelligence as average, her health as good. Molly had acquired her from Ellis Island at the age of fifteen, and lost her three years later in childbirth after she refused to submit to an abortion. She had no known relatives, the child's father might have been any one of a dozen regulars, and Molly was relieved at being able to place the baby so quickly. Other details attested to Anulka's boundless energy and talent in bed, as well as to her single major professional problem . . . an unswerving refusal of all customer demands for oral sex. *Strong, cheerful, and steady,* Molly had written at one point, *but stubborn as hell. Won't suck.*

Duvid had found himself strangely moved by this brief, matter-

357

of-fact description of a long-dead girl, Anulka. He imagined her as she had been, young, fair-haired, with Richard's eyes and golden coloring, smiling and good-humored, yet standing firm in what she believed. Anulka, willing to sell all but that curiously held sanctity of her mouth, refusing to give up the tiny life within her and dying herself in its place. But unmistakably a Pole. Never mind what Molly said. Anulka had not been any kind of Jew. More likely, she had been of Polish peasant stock, one of those beautifully packaged products of a thousand years of inbreeding, whose favorite Saturday night sport was getting blind drunk and feeding a few old Jews to the pigs. The mother of his son, thought Duvid.

The sidewalks of Hanover Street were thronged with watchers as the two hearses rolled up the slope to Scollay Square. Duvid heard their muttering, a low growl, beneath the clatter of horseshoes on wet cobbles. The marchers behind him had linked arms, walking slowly, row after row, reaching all the way back to North End Park. He kept his head bent against the rain, but missed nothing . . . not the sleazy clothing shops and shoeshine parlors, nor the pasticcerias, poolrooms, and bowling alleys, nor the thousands of faces peering out of the second- and third-story windows above them. He soaked it all in along with the wetness, feeling it seep through him in a chill, dismal stream. He also watched the police. Their expressions were impassive, carefully controlled. So far, they seemed neutral. Then looking ahead, Duvid saw his son and stopped being aware of all else.

Richard stood about fifty feet away, at the edge of the crowd lining the curb. He was bareheaded, hair matted over his eyes, wet cheeks flushed pink. When he spied his father, he darted out between two mounted police. They tried to collar him, but were not quick enough and he grabbed Duvid's hand and held on.

"How did you get here?" Duvid asked.

"I took the train."

The Artist

"Did Momma know you were coming?"

"No. But I left her a note."

Then neither of them said anything and just marched in silence behind the hearses.

Duvid recalled one of his mother's sayings. Live long enough, you see everything. A strange boy, his son. With him, nothing was ever simple, or as it seemed. Nine years old and he carried nine centuries of confusion in his flesh. I love him, but don't really know what I'm loving. I call him my son and have the papers to prove it, but that doesn't even begin to make him mine. Then what does? Maybe nothing. Or maybe something like this, that he has done here, today.

It could not have been easy for him to come. Not with all that had gone before. Sacco and Vanzetti versus Richard Karlinsky. An abstract impersonal question of justice to most of the country, but a daily penance for him. He took blows and shed blood for these two strangers, until he came to despise them. "I hate those wops!" he screamed. "Oh, Jesus, I hate them." But who would believe him with his father's pictures there to prove him a liar? So he hated the pictures more than the two men . . . more, even, than the Irish who beat him. And the feeling grew. The pictures were to blame for everything. Without them, maybe he could live in peace. A month after the opening of the exhibition, he set fire to the gallery.

With the telephone still disconnected, a policeman brought the news. Duvid and Annie looked at the man as if he were mad. *Their* son? The policeman was kind, almost apologetic. "It could be a mistake," he told them. "But they said he was recognized running away. Has he come home?"

Duvid shook his head. "Was anyone hurt?"

"No. But there's been damage. You'd better come down."

The gallery was a shambles. At least half the paintings were singed, and three were completely destroyed. Duvid stared, unmoved, at the charred fragments of canvas. Just bits of colored cloth. Axiom. If it doesn't bleed, don't worry about it. He found the gallery attendant who had seen Richard and spoke to him alone. "Frederick," he said, "you were wrong. You may have thought you saw my son, but you didn't."

The Artist

Frederick was young, with the kind of delicate good looks that appear indigenous to bookstores, concert halls, and art galleries. He shook his head. "No, I . . ."

"I'll tell you why you were wrong. You were wrong because my son spent all day and evening with his grandparents on the Lower East Side and never left them them for a minute. And they'll swear to that. But you were also wrong because if it's handled right, this whole mess can not only double our receipts for the Defense Fund, but can point an angry finger at those who would stop at nothing, not even arson, to destroy our efforts." He swept an arm across the ravaged room. "Look at this place. It's perfect. We won't fix or change a thing. You know what effect this can have on people walking in here? It's like seeing Sacco and Vanzetti burned at the stake. A twentieth-century auto-da-fé. Which is exactly what it is. If we planned it ourselves, it couldn't have been better. Don't you see what I mean?"

Frederick nodded slowly, his eyes beginning to glaze with the vision.

"Besides," said Duvid, "Richard is only nine years old. He's having a hard enough time as it is. If he does deserve punishment, it would be better coming from me."

"Who's Richard?" grinned Frederick.

That was the simple part. It was much harder at home. Richard did not appear for two days and nights and the Karlinskys suffered. On the third day, watching from a corner of the living room window, Duvid saw his son peering from behind some trees on Riverside Drive. "He's waiting to see us leave," Duvid told Annie. "So let's leave."

They went out the front door, walked uptown for a few blocks on the Drive, then turned east on 160th Street. "Give me half an hour alone with him," Duvid said, and circled back along Broadway and up through the basement. He let himself into the apartment quietly and found his son eating in the kitchen. The boy's face and clothing were dirt-smeared, his eyes circled by darkness. He started to run, but his father blocked the doorway.

"Well, did you have a good time?"

Richard glared at him over a half-eaten apple. "I hate you."

The Artist

"All right."

"And I'm not sorry I burned all your paintings."

"You didn't burn them all. Just a few."

"I don't care. And I don't care what you do to me either. Even if you put me in jail."

Duvid watched him fighting tears, his lids holding like dikes against the rising water. I'm not very good at this, he thought. All I want to do is hug him.

"Go ahead," Richard shouted. "Put me in jail."

"You're too young to go to jail. But what you did was a bad thing. People could have been hurt. Even killed."

"I don't care."

"Well, you'd better care. And you'd better start learning there are others in this world beside yourself. You can't go around acting like a little animal."

The tears broke, "I'm *not* an animal. Don't you call me an animal."

"Then stop acting like one."

"If I'm an animal, you're a *bigger* one."

Duvid had to smile. It was a mistake.

"Fuck you." said Richard.

The smile went away. That's the way a son talks to his father? An old Yiddish joke, but who was laughing? In some crazy way this seemed worse to Duvid than setting fire to his paintings. It was not to be believed. Not in a Jewish home. What kind of home then? . . . a Polack one? He despised the thought, but there it was.

"What did you say to me?" As if he hadn't heard. Still, a chance for retraction had to be offered.

"Fuck you!"

Duvid slapped his son across the mouth, hard, the force of it spinning him against a wall. It was the first time he had ever hit him and they were both shocked.

Richard recovered first. "Fuck you."

Duvid's hand lashed out again. "Don't you ever talk to me like that. Do you hear? Not *ever!*" His voice had gone high, almost shrill. What was he so angry about? It was only a word. Kids always used it. He had used it himself. He still did. Yes, but not to his father.

361

The Artist

"Fuck you."

Duvid stared at his son through a red haze. The tears had left dirty paths on the boy's cheeks, but he had stopped crying now and his eyes were clear, with a coldness in the blue that Duvid had never seen there before. He started toward him again.

"Keep away!"

Richard stood with his back to the wall, crouched, teeth bared, a small animal at bay. His arms were raised against further blows and in one hand was a paring knife.

Duvid stopped and stared at the knife. Why not? Wasn't it the next step? After you burned your father's paintings and swore at him, what was left but to stab him?

"Give me that knife."

"No."

Duvid held out his hand. "Give it to me, I said."

"No."

"If you don't give it to me, I'm going to take it and beat you black and blue."

But Richard was too far into it. Exhausted, frightened, and near hysteria after two days and nights of nightmare, he was beyond reach. He screamed, "Leave me alone or I'll kill ya!"

I've raised a viper in my nest, Duvid thought dully, and went for the knife, which suddenly was not where it had been, but turned up an instant later, between his second and third ribs. Duvid removed it, stared curiously at the small, red-stained blade, then gave full attention to his son.

When Annie arrived, he had Richard locked in his room and was busy taping himself up over a blood-spattered sink.

"My God!" cried Annie. "What happened?"

Duvid looked at her. "What happened," he said, "is that that little Polack bastard we're raising just tried to kill me."

When the hearses and limousines crossed Scollay Square and turned left into Tremont Street, a convoy of state troopers in trucks suddenly cut between them and the massed marchers, who then swept over sidewalks and around subway entrances and tried to squeeze between the stalled vehicles. The jam became so great in Scollay Square that storefronts began caving in. Duvid pulled Richard away as a large pane of glass came crashing to the pavement. There were screams and some panic, but no one appeared hurt. The police now grew less neutral and arrested a few bystanders for jeering at them.

Duvid watched Richard's face. It showed interest and excitement, but no fear. Whatever the source, the boy did have courage. Lucky me, thought Duvid. How many fathers had kids with enough guts to stick a knife in them? And without apology. There had been no *I'm sorry, Daddy, I didn't mean it.* Why? Because he *wasn't* sorry and he *had* meant it. His son was no liar. He had been brought up to tell the truth. He had been raised on moral principles as young Victorian ladies were raised on pianoforte and needlepoint. It was all his father's fault, anyway. Whatever had happened . . . his being beaten by Irish toughs, his burning of the gallery, his swearing at and stabbing his father, had, in his judgment, been brought about by Duvid himself. If there was any apologizing to be done, his father was the one who should do it. Afterward, he had drawn into himself. He appeared for meals, answered when spoken to, but remained apart. Whatever he may have felt was not visible. He came and went in silence. "It's like having a boarder in the house," Duvid complained to his wife. "I think I'd rather he swore at me." Annie offered a solution. "Take him for a walk."

The walking was a Sunday morning ritual along the wooded paths above the Hudson. At the age of five, Richard had carried a cap pistol to protect his father from wolves, bears, and marauding Indians. Duvid had carried a cane with an amber handle. When he pointed it and went bang, the enemies of the Karlinskys fell. They had never talked much. Usually they just walked and climbed rocks and protected one another. There had never been a need to talk. Now, suddenly, there was. But Richard walked with his head down, studying the path beneath his feet, and Duvid stared off at the trees and no words came. They flowed in time. The trails, the rocks, the woods of Washington Heights gulped them down. Duvid's heart contracted with sadness for the boy beside him. He called him his son, but he was not really his son. A fake son to a fake father. Everything was fake. Even the walks. Because he had once walked the hills outside their *shtetl* with his own father, because the memory of those moments was still sweet within him, he had tried to force the feeling alive again. And until now, it had seemed to work. But it was still a fake. The silence made it more so.

"You should talk more," Duvid said at last. "It's not good to walk around like that."

"What should I say?"

"Whatever you feel like saying."

"I don't feel like saying anything."

"*Force* yourself."

A dialogue for a comic sketch, but not funny. "And maybe you can start off," Duvid said, "by forcing yourself to say you're sorry."

Richard's face tightened in the sunlight. He said nothing.

"Maybe *I* should say I'm sorry? Is that what you want?" It came in the form of mockery, yet it was generous. He would help his son expiate his guilt in a ritual of reprimand.

"I don't want anything. I just want to be left alone."

"Well, you won't be left alone. You're part of a family. And families may scream, kick, hit, and bite, but they don't leave each other alone. Don't you know that?"

"No."

"Then you'd better learn."

"I can't."

"Why not?"

"Because I'm dumb. I'm no genius like you."

He used the word genius as he had the paring knife. Duvid felt it enter his chest, accusing, bitter. Another surprise he could have done without. "I'm not a genius."

"You are so. You paint all those great pictures that everyone comes to see and they think are so wonderful." His voice went high, mimicking, a child's imitation of the gallery sycophant. "Oh, Mister Karlinsky, how smart you are. I just love your paintings, Mister Karlinsky. How did you ever get so marvelous, Mister Karlinsky? Blah . . . blah . . . blah . . . Mister Karlinsky."

All that, thought Duvid. How long had it been building? "I'm no genius. I just paint because that's what I want to do and that was what I was taught to do. And don't call yourself dumb. You're not dumb."

"I'm the dumbest kid in my class. Ask anyone."

"Why don't you study and do your homework like everyone else? That's all you have to do."

"I can't."

"What do you mean, you can't?"

"I don't like to study."

"No one said you had to like it. Just do it."

"I can't do what I don't like."

"Who said so?"

"Me."

"That's crazy."

"Then I guess I'm crazy, too."

The talking was finished. The silence returned. Duvid circled the territory like an explorer lost in snowy wastes. In July, there was a blizzard inside him. What kind of boy was he raising? He could not understand him. And what he could not understand made him angry. To hell with him, he decided, and denied the ache. But the pain was there. It remained, a growing lump. *If I am bereaved of my sons,* the first Jacob had said, *then I am bereaved.*

Yet, unaccountably, he had appeared here today, hundreds of miles from home, to join him at the funeral of the two men he judged most responsible for his trouble . . . those two unmet, hated *wops.* Why? Was the war over? Or was it just a brief cease-fire, a vague need to watch the final nails being driven into the two coffins? See? It's finished. No more Sacco and Vanzetti, no more beatings, no more daily penance. A visual rejoicing. But never mind reasons, Duvid thought. They changed from minute to minute. They were not to be trusted. Only flesh against flesh was to be believed. And with Richard's small, hard hand tight in his, he was willing, for the moment at least, to leave it at that.

The marchers had formed again on Tremont Street. Still numbering in the thousands, they were linked twenty-five abreast from curb to curb. Richard had picked up a red armband in Scollay Square and pulled it over his right sleeve like the rest of the marchers. The procession started to move once more, joined by some of the crowd lining Boston Common. A fleet of taxicabs followed the marchers, ready to pick up those who tired. In front of them, the gutters were littered with blossoms as floral pieces were torn up and strewn over the paving stones. The hearses were now a fair distance ahead, but still in view, and the rain kept falling in pale gray mists.

From Tremont Street through the slum miles of the South End and the Negro district, the police harassment intensified. At each intersection they directed traffic into the gradually thinning lines of marchers, breaking them, forcing them to stop and re-form, causing them to fall farther and farther behind the hearses. Scrambling to catch up, they broke ranks and ran after the hearses, suddenly a fragmented, rag-taggle force without order. More and more dropped out. Until this point the spectators along the route had been either silent or sympathetic, but now, in the Irish Catholic district of Forest Hills, they turned hostile. Angry faces lined the curbs and leaned from windows. There were shouts of "Dirty wops" and "Guineas, go home" and "Red pigs."

Duvid swore softly under his breath.

"Who are they?" Richard asked.

"Irish."

The boy faced them happily. "Dirty Irishers!"

They plodded under the dripping el structure on Washington Street, a few hundred left of all those thousands. Near the Forest Hills Terminal, just opposite the office of the Metropolitan Coal Company, the police charged them. Duvid had no idea why. One minute they were trudging along in the rain, the next the police were coming at them with flailing nightsticks. Duvid grabbed Richard's arm and ran with him. There were screams and shouts and patches of blood on the wet pavements. The police attacked wildly, furiously, without control, swinging at anyone wearing a red armband . . . men, women, children. *Cossack bastards!* Duvid caught a club in midair, wrenched it free, and used it to beat a path through the dark blue line. He pulled Richard after him. Drops of blood spotted the boy's cheeks like measles, but it was not his blood. It had erupted from the split scalp of a screaming girl beside him. Then the girl was hit again and the screaming stopped.

Duvid fought through to an alley which led to a back lot of the

The Artist

Gulf Refining Company. From here, he and Richard were able to join up with the others on the far side of the terminal. When they finally reached the crematory on Walk Hill Street, the hearse had already arrived, the coffins had been carried into the chapel, and the gates were locked.

They stood silently in the rain with the battered remnants of the procession. At 4:30 the coffins were placed in the retort chambers. Soon after, the gates were opened and the empty hearses rolled away. Watching, they saw a thin column of smoke rising from the crematory's central chimney. It hung there, black and unwavering against the leaden sky, then slowly faded. Duvid stared at the place in the sky where it had been. Nothing.

The others drifted away . . . singly, by twos, in small groups, but Duvid remained, shoes deep in the wet earth, his son, though close beside him, forgotten. Nothing. All those fine, brave, ringing words . . . *Never in our full life can we hope to do such work for tolerance, for justice, for man's understanding of man, as we now do by accident, by dying . . .* Bullshit. They were just dead. Disappeared into the sky. It was over. All of it. What was changed? Only a few more broken heads, a little more blood in wet gutters, a few more cries of "Dirty wops" and "Guineas go home" and "Red pigs," while all those holy puritans in high places would go on pretending they had upheld justice, proud of themselves because they had killed two poor, immigrant workmen. You had to beware of people in power, you had to beware of the rich. They were frightened of losing what they had. They struck out blindly, in all directions . . . at people passing in the streets, at children, at shadows, at two little Italians. *We shall die in darkness and be buried in the rain.* Nothing.

Duvid looked down. Richard stood watching him, drenched and shivering in the drizzle, a strange girl's blood staining his cheeks, his eyes wide with old hurts and new confusions. He has such sad, lonely eyes, thought Duvid, and I can't help him, I'm never going to be able to help him. But he smiled, because this much, at least, he could do, and embraced his son's shaking shoulders to show how he felt about his coming to stand beside him here today, wanting to say and do more, but afraid it would only prove an embarrassment to them both. Which was wrong, of course. But such knowledge comes late.

EIGHTEEN

1945: Amagansett, Long Island

At first he thought it might be better with his eyes closed, that shutting out all sight of the men might make it easier, but he was wrong. His senses were too alert and the darkness spilled over him like cold water over a wound. Thoughts scratched and scrambled through his brain and even breathing became difficult, an act of balance. Too little air strangled him; too much turned him dizzy. He touched, fumbled, struggled, and, not surprisingly, stayed soft.

"Darling?" Laurie whispered.

He opened his eyes and found hers.

I love you, they told him.

Yes, but what had love to do with it? Enough, it turned out. And a nourishment came off her. All rosy and scented, she fed him a sultan's feast and the mystic rising began.

The soldiers cheered.

"Ah knew yuh could make it, Mistuh Karlinsky!"

"That Jew is a *stud!*"

Fans at a sporting match.

But once charged, he barely heard them and went into her with all the deliverance of a man who has had to cross a desert to get there. And what a deliverance it was. And what a wisdom in it. And how sure a touch. And a grace, too, loose and free and clean, as though this was finally their natural act. Or else the Southerner had spoken truer than he knew and the devil's best gift had somehow been bargained for and received. How else this heightened sensing, this pure certainty of where the flesh was most alive, this fevered blending of scents into a single witch's brew?

The watchers were silent now. Had they been cats, their backs would have been arched and they would have been making high, nasal sounds. As it was, all that came out of them was their breathing, along with a thin, needling smell which reached Duvid's nose by way of a burnt-out *shtetl* a day's cart ride from Odessa and which could be mellowed only by gifts of blood. They were a midnight darkness, these two, but gliding free, Duvid felt an eye of each, one gray, one with its dirty yellow, leap into his own and double his vision. There was nothing he couldn't do. If a voice told him to leave the warmth below and fly, he was certain he could take off on some undiscovered nerve and fly.

Then he was back down, deep into the place where his child lay. And a loving place it was, its walls snug, its juices clean, a familiar sweetness in its touch. He waited for the full heat to rise and take him all the way, along with the gray eyes and the yellow, which were as much a part of it then as he. Then everything hit together and the explosion almost threw him across the room. But at the end, lying there, all he felt were cold waters washing over dead trees in a frozen pond.

"Ah'm real proud of yuh, Mistuh Karlinsky. Ah'd call that a truly fine performance." The voice was dry, thick, not quite as it had been. "Wouldn't yuh say, Frankie?"

"Not bad."

"Think yuh could do better?"

"Well," said Frank, "I could give it a try."

"Go ahead. She's all juiced and ready."

Duvid turned and sat up slowly. A very bad fear had broken loose in him and he was unable to hold it. His hands and knees trembled and he was incapable of speech. Like a terminal patient whose faculties were failing one at a time, his voice had left his throat. Just as at that moment he felt he had left his life behind him. All right, he thought, I guess I'm ready to die. And he understood the final moments of a man condemned to execution. Except that he had a certain envy for that man, who at least knew his death was part of an orderly process, that it might even carry a measure of justice. His own seemed so utterly senseless.

He heard Laurie speak behind him, "You promised to leave us alone if we did what you asked." Shock! A child stunned by her first encounter with adult deceit. *"You promised."*

"Yuh jus' *thought* Ah promised, Ma'am. Besides, yuh were such a joy to watch, Ah figured Mistuh Karlinsky might enjoy a lil' observin' himself."

Duvid went for him at that moment, packed so solid with anger and fear, he was seeing with his pores. He came off the couch in a flat dive, hands reaching, fingers wanting to pry this creature open because there had to be a soft spot where he could be split and killed. For an instant he sailed free. Then lightning went off somewhere behind his eyes and he caught a glimpse of a dark fall that opened like a crack in the earth.

He tried to move and couldn't. I'm dead, he thought. But he had not been shot, just hit over the head and tied, still naked, to a chair.

"Not a bad try, Mistuh Karlinsky. If Ah hadn't felt it comin', yuh might of made it."

Duvid had long had a vision of hell. Red walls and ceiling, a floor of hot coals, and a single, giant candle burning in the middle. Wrong. He saw now that it looked no different from his own studio, with an etched image of Laurie's face, turned to mist, staring at him from the couch, two American soldiers, in summer chinos, about to go on with their devil's circus, and the Blue Jew (he had apparently accepted the corporal's title) overseeing it all like a crippled ringmaster. If not hell, surely its antechamber.

Frank was getting undressed. "We were waiting for you. We didn't want you to miss anything." He took off his clothes and piled them neatly, but left on his shoes and socks. His suntan ended at his neck and his body flesh was white, pasty, the exact color, Duvid thought, of the maggots feeding on the Blue Jew. Naturally. He found himself settling into a curious calm. Just as a man in dying might have a moment when, though helpless, he knows he is already in death and so can wait for it without anger or fear. Not so Laurie. Crouched naked on the studio couch, she was like some sort of expensive animal, all fangs and claws, ready to spring.

"Come near me with that ugly thing," she told Frank, "and I swear I'll tear it off."

The soldier peered down at himself. He seemed hurt. *"Ugly?* My Momma always swore it was the prettiest sight in all Indiana."

"Then use it on *her."*

The corporal laughed. "Ma'am, yo' are *somethin'."*

"I mean it," she said. "If he comes near me, I'll cripple him."

"That's sure not bein' very friendly, Ma'am." Clay reached into his pocket and a switchblade came out of his palm like a snake's tongue. "Ah guess we'll jus' have to set up some ground rules. Behave proper and we'll all have a nice time of it. If yuh don't . . ." He drew the knife lightly across Duvid's chest, and a delicate line appeared, widened, let go a tiny red bead. "Understand, Ma'am?"

There was no pain in the touch of the blade, but the act itself was so careless, so impersonal and indifferent, that Duvid felt like a side of beef in a butcher shop. *Whose shop? His uncle's?* The image came up like a hurricane off a swamp and he remembered the meat that was his uncle, dripping from the hooks, and his aunt, naked on the dirt floor. Always naked. The first thing they seemed to do was take away your clothes, rob you of all cover. Russian, German, American . . . nationality meant nothing. The instinct was universal. Or was it a basic tenet of the Christian religion? Strip a Jew and be saved!

"Please, . . ." he said, willing to try begging. "Leave her alone." Then, insanely, . . . "She's going to have a baby."

Laurie looked at him with pity. "Do you think *that* means anything to them?"

"Why, Ma'am, we *love* babies. *And* small dogs." He picked up Sammy and crooned to him. "It's jus' *Jews* we hate."

Standing there in his glasses, in his GI shoes and socks, stiffening with excitement, Frank was beginning to squirm like a small boy in need of a bathroom. He edged toward the couch, but stopped as

371

The Artist

Laurie raked air with her nails. Their eyes locked and they were a man and a woman balancing on a high wire. There was a tiny froth in the corner of his mouth and a strain of red in the white of his eyes.

"I told you," Duvid said. "She's not even Jewish. Why do this to her?"

"Not to *her*, Mistuh Karlinsky. We're not doin' *anythin'* to *her*. We're doin' it all to *you*. Ah thought sure yuh understood that."

Of course. The final step in the debasement. To be rendered helpless and forced to watch your woman being used. What worse? A helpless man has lost an essential human dignity. It is impossible to respect him. All that can be felt is pity. And even this can't be felt for long if no sign of strength appears. Finally, there's just contempt. He had already seen Laurie look at him with pity. If he wasn't able to do anything, how long before the next stage? Still, it was for her that he pleaded, not himself. "Please. You've done enough. You've more than paid me back. Leave her alone and I'll give you money. As much as you want."

Frank shifted his glance from Laurie to Duvid. "How much you got?"

"Only a few hundred in the house. But about thirty thousand in the bank."

Clay grinned. "Frankie, yuh jus' got a real expensive insult. Imagine bein' willin' to pay that much green jus' to keep yuh from soilin' his woman."

"For thirty thousand," said Frank, "he can insult me all night." His eyes stayed on Duvid. "You got a bankbook?"

"In the bedroom. Top drawer of the bureau."

"What're yuh expect him to do?" Clay said. "Write yuh a goddamn check?"

But Frank was half out of the room by then, the dark crease between his buttocks twitching as he walked. When he returned with the passbook, Duvid saw that he had gone soft. No more itching between the legs. A significant insight into the sex drive of twentieth-century man. Against money, it was just no contest. Even without the Bomb, the species was doomed.

"He wasn't lying. He's got thirty-four thousand in the bank."

"Very nice," said Clay. "Ah'm happy to know Jewish artists are

372

doin' so well these days. Now put that thing down an' let's get on with it."

"It's a lot of money, Clay."

"We didn' come here for no money."

"That doesn't mean we got to throw it away if it drops in our laps."

"Nothin's droppin' in our laps," said the corporal. "That's jus' a lil' fancy bait Mistuh Karlinsky's danglin' to take yo'r mind off his lady." He grimaced at Frank's shriveled interest. "An' Ah see he's already done a job of it."

It was only a slight opening, but it was the first Duvid had seen and he pressed it. "You can have every cent there. One of you can come with me to the bank in the morning, while the other holds Laurie here."

"What's to keep you from callin' the cops after we got it and went?"

"I'll write a note. I'll say it's in payment of a gambling debt, that you won it in poker. I'll sign anything you want."

"It's not goin' to work, Mistuh Karlinsky. Yo're not suckin' us into anythin'."

But Duvid saw that the shaft had gone in. The soldier from Indiana had the appearance of a big fish just speared. Greed was hooked in both eyeballs. "Let's talk about it," Frank said.

Clay held his switchblade with the point up, looking down at it like a priest with a candle. "There's nothin' to talk about. Ah'm not interested in the Jew's money."

"Well, I am."

"Shee-it, boy!" There was utter contempt in it. "Yuh sure there's no Jew blood in yuh somewhere? Seems to me yo're lookin' more like that Blue Jew every minute." He lowered his knife to gaze broodingly at the big painting. "Maybe it's yo'r half-eaten nuts."

Reflectively, Frank's hands dropped to cover himself. But his face remained stubborn behind his glasses. "What's wrong with wanting money? The war's over. In a few weeks we'll be out grubbing for nickels. If we got a chance here for an easy touch, I say take it."

"This is no easy touch, yuh dumb bastard. What this is, is a shrewd Jew mind in operation. And if yuh think yuh can outsmart one of them, yo're even dumber than Ah thought."

Frank stood blinking his eyes. "You got no call talking to me like that."

"Forget it. We got things to do."

"I don't wanna forget it. And I don't wanna forget that money either."

"Ah'm no goddam *thief.* Ah didn't come here to steal no *money.*"

Indignation flowed from him like lava, filling the room, molten. Duvid could almost smell the sulphur, feeling himself sitting, trussed and naked, a plucked chicken in a volcano. *Unbelievable.* Honor at all levels. A little friendly rape and Jew-killing were not to be denigrated by acts of common thievery. The corporal's lips were tense, and long, bony fingers worked nervously on the handle of his knife. Forgotten for the moment, Duvid glanced at Laurie. Frowning, she seemed to float, motionless, above the couch. Yet she was as leaden as he, another bird without feathers. Duvid's heart felt hollow. Then she looked back at him and he was enclosed in a warmth so tender, that against all logic, he went soft with hope.

Frank clutched the bankbook like a talisman, a magical passport to Elysian fields. "I'm no bigger on Jews than you, Clay, but I'm not psycho on them, either. I mean, a little fun with a kike is okay, but Jesus Christ! It ain't worth no thirty *thousand.*"

"Yuh don't understand . . ."

"I understand fine. When it comes to money, I understand everything. I grew up understanding about dough. The first thing I remember my folks ever doing was fighting about it. Seems like that was all they ever did. Fight about money."

"Yeah, yeah . . ." said the corporal. "Well, listen . . ."

But glazed with liquor and self-pity, Frank was not listening to anything just then. "When I got old enough to figure what it was about," he said, "I used to blow air into my ears so I wouldn't hear. But I heard anyway. 'We never have no money,' Ma used to yell. 'What kind of man did I pick? What good is a man who can't make money? And look at your boy there. The way he sits around. Like he don't even hear us. He takes after you. Dumb as a stick. Why can't you ever get no money?' " Frank studied the passbook in his hand.

Reverently. It was now a sacred relic. "Poor Pa did the best he could, but there was never enough work and the Jews had all the dough. When he did work he got twelve bucks a week walking track for the railroad and would come home and sit in the yard, all pooped out. We had this wooden fence with a lot of boards missing and every year a few more would come off. Pop was always saying he was gonna fix it, but he never did. He just sat there, all pooped out, with the broken boards laying in the weeds and Ma yelling at him about money."

"Sure," said Clay. "It was the Jews caused the Depression too. That's where all the money went. We starved while *they* got all the dough."

"Well, here's our chance to get some of it back. *Man!* I never thought I'd see this much dough in my *life.*"

The corporal said nothing, but Duvid could almost feel his mind working with the intensity of a gambler who has lost every faculty, every part of his body but the nerve-end in his brain that tells him when to bet. His face looked red to Duvid, then green, then red again and Duvid wondered if he were close to fainting. His head still clanged from the pistol blow, he was going numb where he was tied, and he felt the sweet panic of an animal being tracked, a fox in a bog with hounds baying all around.

"Ah'll tell yuh what, Frankie," Clay said. "Do it m'ah way and yuh can have the dough *and* the girl."

"How? If I go near her, he won't get us the money."

"Mistuh Karlinsky will get us anything Ah *ask* him to get us."

"Touch that girl," said Duvid with more force than he felt, "and all you'll get is twenty years in Leavenworth."

Once more, the blade was erect in Clay's hand. He held it before Duvid's face, his eyes as blank as the threatened prison's walls. "Now don't yuh go talkin' tough with *me*, Mistuh Karlinsky. All *yo're* gonna do right now is sit an' watch the show. Then tomorra mornin', yo're gonna get Frankie the money jus' like yuh said, while Ah wait here with *this* knife an' *yo'r* lady. Now Ah think that's clear enough for everybody to follow. But if there's any questions, Ah'll be happy to answer them."

"I have a question," said Duvid. "But it's for Frank." He looked at the soldier from Indiana, standing confused and naked, bankbook in hand. "What I want to know, is whether you're really ready to kill two people just because Clay happens to be psycho on Jews?"

"What are you talking about? Nobody's killing *anybody*. Not unless you try something crazy."

"Then what do you expect to do?" asked Duvid. "Rape a woman, steal money, and then just walk away and leave me here to call the police? Because that's just what I'll do if you touch her."

The soldier stared at him. A blush appeared on his chest like a rash, and slowly spread.

"So far," said Duvid, "it's not that bad. You've had your few drinks and your dirty little fun and no one's really been hurt. No permanent damage done. And I'll even let you have the money clear. But go ahead with the rest of this, and you're going to have to do exactly what I think your buddy's been planning to do all along. And that's kill both of us."

"You're crazy. Clay never planned to kill *nobody.*" He turned to the corporal, his voice wheedling like a woman's, buttering over. "Ain't that right, Clay?"

"*Yuh* know it, Frankie." The corporal smiled, as if this particular problem had been settled to everyone's satisfaction and they could go on from there. "Now, yuh jus' forget all this crap and put yo'r mind to that dee-li-shuss lil' lady waitin' on yuh there."

"Ask him Frankie," said Duvid. "Ask him how he expects to go back to camp tomorrow or the next day and stand roll call after a rape job. Unless he's planning not to leave any witnesses."

Frank looked dumbly from one to the other, bending a little at the waist, as if dance music was playing somewhere and he wanted to choose a partner. "Yeah, Clay." The rash had spread from his body to his face, which seemed pained by the effort of thinking. "We never even thought of that."

"You mean *you* never thought of it. But Clay did. He's been planning this for a long time. It was *his* idea to come here, wasn't it?"

"Yeah. But there was no planning or anything like that. We were out having a few drinks before and he just came up with the idea then. I mean, he didn't think about it any more than me."

"Sure. And he just *happened* to have those drawings in his pocket. *And* the Luger. *And* the ammunition." Duvid gave him a moment, seeing it was all too deep inside for him to get out easily. He felt him digging, the liquor and the confusion and the sluggish brain burying it even deeper, but the yellow eyes sinking doggedly in after it. "Come on, Frankie. You might as well face it. You've been had. Your buddy's sucked you in way over your head."

Frank was staring at the corporal, his glasses catching and tossing small halos of light. If he was drunk before, he was sober now. "I guess I've been pretty stupid, huh?"

"Hell, yuh don't really *buy* that tricky Jew pitch."

"I don't wanta kill nobody, Clay."

"Ah promised yuh. Yuh won't haft'a."

"Of course you won't," said Duvid. "He's saving *that* pleasure for himself."

The corporal hit him across the mouth. "That's *enough*, Mistuh Karlinsky." Then he looked at Frank, who had dropped the bankbook and was pulling on his underwear. "Now what in hell are *you* doin'?"

"I'm getting out of here."

"Yuh *crazy?* What about all that money? Don't yuh *want* it?"

"Sure I want it. But I'm not murdering anyone to get it."

"Ah told yuh. Nobody's gettin' murdered."

Frank straightened, shoulders tucked back, an angry itch between his shoulder blades. "You're a damn liar. The Jew's right. You sucked me in and I was too drunk and stupid to even know what was going on."

"Come on, boy. Yuh knew, all right. Don't go turnin' all pure an' lily-white on *me*. Yuh weren't *that* drunk and stupid. Yuh were as hot to stick it to the Jew as me. An' if yuh didn't think 'bout the rest, it was 'cause yuh didn't *wanna* think about it." Clay stood glaring and a pestilence came up out of him, a ripple of the worm of hate trapped in its own ooze. Murder had already invaded and he gave off the essence of the disease. "*Jesus*, Ah never figured yuh for chicken. Ah thought sure yuh understood. Like *Ah* understood. Like the *Germans* understood. *They* had the right goddam idea 'bout the Jews. *They* knew they were nothin' but vermin. An' that's how they

The Artist

treated 'em. Cockroaches an' lice. Yuh don't *murder* a cockroach. Yuh ex-ter-min-ate it, by God! Ah went through one of those camps and it was just one big ex-ter-min-a-tor, one big, shiny can 'a roach powder. *Pouff!* One spray an' the roaches an' lice were gone. And Ah mean *gone.* Six million. Yuh know how many that is? *Six million!* Ah mean, those Germans are *eff-i-shent.* Ah'll tell yuh. Ah made a careful study of that camp, memorized everythin' Ah saw. If Ah had to build one here tomorra, Ah could do it. Ah admit it's still a ways off, but not as far off as some think. Americans are gettin' as fed up with vermin as the Germans. They shoved us into this war, then got fat an' rich watchin' us die. Ah been talkin' to a lotta boys. Ah see how they think, hear what they say. The talk, Frankie, is mostly 'bout not turnin' in rifles an' bayonets. They say take 'em home to use on the Jews."

"You sick, perverted son-of-a-bitch!" Laurie yelled. "You're *insane.*"

Bound and rigid in his chair, Duvid did no yelling. The corporal, unfortunately, was not insane. Perhaps a little sick and perverted, definitely a son-of-a-bitch, but not insane. No more insane, anyway, than the rest of the species. Unless anyone who had seen one of these camps *had* to end up a bit crazier. Duvid had seen, and had told people what was there, but knew they didn't believe him. It was too much to believe. The truth was simply too terrifying to gaze into, so they turned away. Just as Frank had turned away. And how many asleep in this pleasant beach resort tonight would believe what was happening among them right now? Why should they? The healthy never fully understood that they, too, were doomed. Or if they did understand, they pretended not to and blocked it out. The corporal, at least, pretended nothing. He had looked at the Blue Jew and cried out with recognition. Or else it was love at first sight.

Clay complained, "Everyone's gettin' much too serious. Even me. Ah swear, all the fun's bein' squeezed out 'a this party. Hey, Frankie boy. Yo're not *really* goin', are yuh?"

"Watch me."

"Ah don't think so." The Luger was out and pointing again. "Ah need yuh, Frankie."

Frank looked at the muzzle of the pistol. "What are you going to do? Shoot *me?*"

"Only if I have to. But yuh know Ah'll do it. Don't yuh, Frankie?"

"Yeah."

"Hell! Don't look so damn sad. Ah'm doin' yuh a favor. Ah'm gonna force yuh to do what yuh been dyin' for all night, but haven't the guts to do yo'rself. Then Ah'm gonna get yuh all that money. Now take off those GI drawers and show the lady how a fine Christian gentleman feels inside her."

"Don't make me, Clay."

"Ah *swear* Ah'll never figure people. Jus' look at that sweet lil' piece waitin' an' all yuh can do is whine. Frank, yo're embarrassin' me in front of Mistuh Karlinsky. Yo're makin' me ashamed for all good Christians."

The soldier stood visibly aching, the pain moving upward from his feet, through his groin and belly, to his eyes and out. A demon leaving. "Please, Clay."

"Frankie, if yuh don't start movin', Ah'm gonna shoot off that worthless peckuh an' *feed* it to yuh."

The olive-drab underwear, so newly put on, came off, and Frank slowly approached the couch. But he turned before he reached it. "What's so damn important about *this*. I don't understand it."

"Yuh don't have to understand it. Long as me an' Mistuh Karlinsky do." A conspiracy of perception. "Right, suh?"

Duvid said nothing, felt nothing. Everything seemed to have hemorrhaged out of him. As it had, he saw, from Laurie. She looked as blue, in places, as the Blue Jew. Women were strange, anyway. They contained this ancient craziness. Sometimes, holding them, it was like holding wind in your arms. Frank would find nothing waiting for him but cold gases bottled in caves.

But the corporal would not leave it alone. The moment was too big. He had to explain, share, formalize. "Ah'll tell yuh somethin', Frankie. This is no ordinary, run-a-the-mill lay yo're embarkin' on. This is a sacred ree-li-gious rite. Ah want yuh to 'preciate that fact an' be grateful for the important role Ah have conferred upon yuh. Ah want yuh to enter into it with the proper spirit of dedication and ex-al-ta-tion. Ah want yuh," Clay said, building up force and eloquence as he went, "to think of yo'r peckuh as a big spike, the Jew's lady as a wooden cross, and each stroke as drivin' another hole through Jew flesh. Yo're avengin' Jesus, boy. Yo're drivin' the

The Artist

moneychangers from the temple. Yo're a livin' flame that is purifyin' the Jews with its burnin'. Bless yuh an' amen," he finished with the soft reverence of a preacher. "Now let's get in there, boy, and drive that spike for ol' Jesus."

Frank approached Laurie like a man approaching the gallows. He took off his glasses, held them uncertainly for a moment, then placed them on his underwear. This time, he removed his shoes and socks. A gesture of respect. I'm different now, it said. See? I'm not what I was. "I'm sorry," he told her and waited for her nails to rip him. They didn't. They wouldn't. The knife was at the Jew's chest. "I'm sorry, I'm sorry," he whispered and lay down with her.

"Now watch real careful-like, Mistuh Karlinsky," said the corporal.

And Duvid watched. He had no intention of *not* watching. If this was what it was all about, if this was the ritual act for which he might be called upon to die for witnessing, he was going to see it all. It wasn't every day you got to observe someone you loved being sexually assaulted. That angel of a body. *His.* Another truth to observe. It would make him a better artist. And who had said *that?* Rachel? And how long ago? And what else was left to see? Pain rose in him out of a parched stomach, an aching head, singed eyes. Good. But it wasn't enough. He bit his lip until he tasted blood. Better. He strained against the cords so they cut his flesh. Nothing. Everything was nothing. Only dying was something. The final disaster, the waiting cliff. And they dangled love like a carrot to keep you walking toward it. They had even offered a child. *His.* One more soul. Three billion plus one. Only you'll probably never see light, kid. And you're well out of it. Listen to your old man, who's seen it all and knows. There's nothing to it, only disappointment and hurt and good-bys and struggle, struggle all the long days of your life. And there you are sleeping comfortably in your nice, warm nest and never knowing enough to regret any of it.

Then he saw that golden abundance of hair where it lay spread on the couch, and a small fragment of her face and thought, no. Don't listen to me, baby. I've been making it all up. I've left out all the good. You'll miss a lot. Don't let them cheat you out of a minute. Hang in there as long as you can. It's the only way.

The Artist

Thoughts on the observation of the rape of the mother of your expected child.
The thing was, the mind kept working. You couldn't stop it. *Note: Such observations are accompanied by neither fainting nor coma.* You remained lucid to the point of detachment, unless it only applied to this particular type of rape, which hardly seemed like rape at all. No screaming, no blood, no violence, no sign of forcible entry. Not in the least like the rape of Aunt Tybie. Now *that* was a rape. Of course, he had not actually *seen* that one. Still, Aunt Tybie's did have all the earmarks of a bona fide, classically tragic act of sexual violation, while this, if you wanted to be honest, was without any true mark of tragedy. In his prerape declamation, the corporal had described the forthcoming event as no ordinary run-of-the-mill lay, but that was precisely how it looked. And despite the unquestionably deep feelings of those taking part, there wasn't a single damn bit of visual tragedy or drama attached to watching two people screw. What it was, mostly, was ridiculous. *And* pathetic. *And* stripped of all human dignity. You looked at a pale, frantically waving ass, at spastic limbs and clutching hands, and felt yourself observing less an act of passion than the final symptoms of a terminal disease.

Note: There is a gradual rising concern about what the one you love (the rapee) may be feeling. You knew she'd had no choice, that if she resisted you'd have been sliced like an orange, but the basic fact remained . . . SHE WAS GETTING LAID. Was she repulsed? . . . sick inside? . . . a frozen wasteland? . . . a tomb? Or, accepting the inevitable, was she enjoying it? Look at all the men she'd had before he knew her. What possible difference could one more make? A lot of difference, he thought. She hadn't loved *him* then, hadn't been carrying *his* child. Yes, but the body had no memory or conscience. It might simply feel a man inside, neither know nor care that it wasn't him, and respond out of pure reflex. Hell! Would he rather she *suffered?* Yes, damn it! At least a *little.* He certainly didn't want her *enjoying* it, he thought, and searched for signs of pleasure in her the way a cancer patient searched for new tumors. An extra torment. But he couldn't stop, and held this new insanity as closely as an embrace he could not bear to leave. The smell of heat was loose in the room, a poisoned bouquet, and he sucked it in, feeling claws on his chest. Were her thighs cold, flaccid with disdain, or were they

warmly holding? And what were her arms doing? Nothing. Good.
And her face? Turned aside, averted. Fine. And her lips? Tightly
compressed, a battleline. Excellent. And her eyes? Steel darts aimed
at the ceiling. Wonderful. But these were all things he could see.
They were *outside*, measurable. What about what he *couldn't* see?
What was going on *inside*, in the lovely heated chapel where he
offered his regular devotions? How was *that* place responding to
another pilgrim's prayers? He didn't know. He could only remember its walls as snug, its incense green, its warmth of immeasurable
sweetness. At least this was how it had been an hour ago. And he
doubted that it had changed.

"Yuh payin' attention, Mistuh Karlinsky?" The corporal glanced
downward at Duvid and grinned. "Ah see yuh are."

Note: It is difficult to observe a rape in progress and not be aroused oneself.
He hadn't known until then, but there it was, and disgust rose in him
like the sewer-damp stink of a butcher's alley. What a treacherous,
two-faced monster he carried between his legs! It belonged on an
ape, not a man. No. A disservice to the apes. How *could* he? Was the
brain without any control at all down there? Or was this flowering
heat a diversion for its own protection? Maybe what the mind
couldn't handle without blowing, it switched down below. A built-in
safety device. If an explosion had to go off *some* place, better there
than on top, where the damage could be serious. That thing down
there was just *built* for explosions, right? A whole new concept.
Mental health through orgasm. Put enough eroticism to work, and
the nut-houses could be emptied in a week.

Looking at her, Duvid could see a little look of woe appear on
her face, a puckered, fearful little eleven-year-old, afraid of being
punished for what she cannot help, and he put aside any fear he may
have had that she would be touched or find pleasure here. He had
the sense she had traced a line across his eyes, a begging for him
not to see. Or if he did see, a hope he would understand. Or failing
even that, a pleading not to pass judgment. And how did you answer
that? Might as well ask, did you lift after death like a feather, rising
slowly.

Still, her eyes, the faint lift of a brow *were* trying to tell him
something. But whatever it was was lost in an oven of burgeonings.

The Artist

The room burned, and the look in Duvid's eye cracked the sad glitter in hers. He was ready to strike at anything. They were all part of it by then, the four of them and the Blue Jew, a bubbling stew of victims and oppressors, and this screaming portrait of the devil's own heir. Thieves, stealing one from the other, yet praying in the same rosy chapel. Behind his open eyes, Duvid saw one poor flower growing in a barren field, and all the love she felt for him might have been there.

This is what hell will be like for you, said the Blue Jew, and Duvid waited for smoke and flame to come through the floor, along with knives and guns and licking tongues. It held a promise like the smell of a bar when young whores are peddling ass inside. There was a new sound somewhere in his head and something violent was loose in him, but he held it with a delicate calm and made himself look at her face. He had never seen her more lovely. It was the truth. Her hair was alive, her skin aglow, and her eyes keyholes to a gate that opened into a palace. But most of all, she had splendor at a time when few could have managed it. And for that alone, he could have loved her.

He turned away to look at the corporal and saw the glazed eyes seeking their own jeweled cities. But the odor was that of a heated gallery in a zoo, and Duvid felt a high pinch of pain as if fangs had dug into him. He strained against the ropes, but nothing gave, and all he could do was watch Frank go into his final run, that wild lurching of a hot, humped-backed beast. But Laurie was no part of it, and the only sound that came out of her was a groan like the clanking of chains, and Duvid felt as though he had ripped loose a long-held promise to his soul and paid it over to the Blue Jew as ransom.

NINETEEN

1945: Ludenscheid, Germany

They moved silently through the German night, climbing single file up the long, wooded slope, Moskowitz at point, followed by Lieutenant Berger, Duvid, and the others, fifteen in all, faces and hands blacked out against the dark, but the whites of eyes still visible, still wide with alertness and a controlled, not unreasonable amount of fear. For only the stupid and the insane would not have been afraid of what lay ahead, and no one had been chosen from either of these categories. They had been chosen, rather, because they were intelligent, efficient with a variety of weapons, and had volunteered. They had also been picked because they were Jewish. If for no other reason, Duvid's sense of poetic justice *demanded* that this be a wholly Jewish operation. Sergeant Ellman had even named them accordingly. KARLINSKY'S KIKES. It had a ring to it, Duvid thought, a nice, wry, light touch. And a little lightness was needed. Because the place they were going into, and what they were planning to do there, was something quite different.

Duvid had first discovered the camp on an Intelligence battle map. Circled in red, it lay directly in the British path of advance, a bit north of the town of Ludenscheid and slightly west of their own battalion's position. It wasn't one of the big, famous camps like Auschwitz or Buchenwald. It was, in fact, rather small and unimportant, as such places went. Yet from the moment Duvid learned it was there, and so close, he could think of nothing but going in.

The Artist

With the German retreat fast becoming a rout, there were rumors of SS massacres all over the place, and the concentration camps were natural prime targets. The fewer survivors left, the fewer witnesses to testify afterward. To Duvid, it was obvious. This was not his first war. Nor was it his first experience with German thinking and morality. He *knew* what they would do. Anyone with half a brain would know. Anyone, apparently, but the battalion CO, an iron-assed West Pointer, who knew only what his orders *told* him to know. And his orders said absolutely nothing about leaving his assigned sector on any crazy, Yiddish missions of mercy. The kind of chickenshit *schmuck,* Duvid thought, who wouldn't go to the latrine without the proper directive from headquarters. So *what* if a few thousand more Jews were murdered? What did that have to do with him and the United States Army? These Jews weren't even *American,* for Christ's sake!

Climbing behind Berger, Duvid shifted his Schmeisser on its sling, feeling its weight solid and reassuring across his shoulder. He had taken the German machine pistol from a dead Pioneer sergeant two weeks before, and had been carrying it ever since. No other submachine gun could match it. When it came to efficient killing, you had to hand it to the Germans. They made the best, the most dependable instruments in the world for it. It was just that the Americans made more of them. Just as the Americans made more gasoline and more ham and eggs and more cigarettes. Which was the major reason the Americans were finally winning. How could you beat a country that had a practically inexhaustable supply of cigarettes?

The lieutenant turned, a dark blur in the landscape. "Close it up, close it up . . ." Coming in Berger's prim, teacher's voice, the whisper made Duvid grin. Fifteen men packing enough firepower to whipsaw a regiment, and Berger could somehow make it sound as if he were shepherding sixth-graders through a natural history tour. At forty-one, Berger was probably the oldest second lieutenant in the American army, a frail, scholarly-looking man whose uniform, helmet, and assorted weaponry could never quite manage to make him look like anything other than an old-maid teacher taking the part of a soldier in a faculty play. Yet Duvid knew of no one he would rather have in front of him at this moment. In the slightly more than two months that he had known Berger, Duvid had developed an enormous respect for the little Jewish lieutenant with his quiet, almost embarrassed manner. Slogging across France and into Germany, Duvid had come to realize that nothing in Berger's world was ever beyond repair. Not even the endless pain and despair which the Germans trailed behind them like the blood spasms of a dying beast, were, to Berger, anything more than unfortunate events that would, in time, pass or be remedied by energy, common sense, and the natural order of things. It was to him that Duvid had taken his plan after the battalion commander turned it down.

"You're crazy," was Berger's initial response.

"Why?"

Berger blinked through steel-rimmed glasses. "Well for one thing, you're supposed to be a noncombatant, an unarmed artist-correspondent. Under the terms of the Geneva Convention, you're . . ."

"Oh, come on, Marty. I've been shooting at Germans from the first day I got here."

"Yes, but quietly and unofficially. Not on this kind of scale."

"All right. What else?"

"Without Divisional authorization, it could only get me a court martial."

"General Harper is an old friend. I know him. He operates with one eye on *Life* and the other on *Time*. He might not okay this in advance, but when you pull it off, he'll be happy to give you a medal and take all credit for himself."

"And what makes you think fifteen men can do it?"

Duvid smiled. "I also have an old friend at Corps Counterintelligence. He tells me most of the camp guards have been pulled out for the defense of Berlin. With surprise going for us, and planning, we should be able to handle the rest." He showed Berger a diagram. "Here are the fences, gates, guard posts, barracks, and administration building. The place is militarily indefensible. Remember. It was built to keep people *in*, not *out*."

Berger studied the sketch for a long time.

"Can you get me thirteen tough, killer Yids?" Duvid asked.

The Artist

"I'm not even sure I can get *myself.*"

"About *you, I'm* sure."

"I'm no hero, Duvid."

"Who *is?* To tell you the truth, the thing scares hell out of me. But it's there and I can't just walk away from it." He stared at the lieutenant. "Listen. The sons-of-bitches have been sticking it to us for two thousand years, but this is the worst yet. They've finally reduced us to animals, pigs in a slaughterhouse. We're not even human to them. We're fertilizer. *Shit!* Every time I breathe, my *kishkas* stink with it. And I can't rise above it. I can't think broad, lofty, artistic thoughts and paint it out of me with a brush. If I get it out at all, it's going to have to be with a gun. And if I die doing it, then I die. But at least I won't feel as if I'll foul up the earth when they lower me into it."

Berger was silent. He took off his glasses and put them on again. Twice. "Maybe you're right," he said at last. "Maybe I've been fooling myself all along about why I'm really here. I wasn't drafted, you know. Too old." He smiled his embarrassed smile. "I even have asthma, though the army doesn't know. Would you believe it?"

"Yes."

"Actually, I hate the army. Not only the American army. I hate all armies. They're corrupt, cruel, and wasteful. Yet I couldn't stay out. I tried, but I couldn't. I finally had to volunteer."

"Why?"

"My own brand of guilt, I guess. Some kind of mystic idea that I owed a debt somewhere that had to be paid. Ever since the mid-thirties, ever since the Nazis, ever since the war in Spain, I've had this feeling of avoiding things I should be doing. Year after year I've had the feeling that somewhere, somehow I'd be asked to straighten out my accounts and pay up."

"Don't you think you've paid up by now?"

"Only partly." Berger laughed, which he did rarely. "Maybe this can help square the rest."

There were almost seven hundred men in the battalion, of whom eighty-three were Jewish. Of these, Berger eliminated thirty-one as lacking the necessary military skills, and another ten as emotionally unsuitable. Of the remaining forty-two, thirty-five volunteered.

The Artist

Berger and Duvid made their choice from these.

At the final briefing, Duvid looked at the thirteen grave, cork-blackened faces and thought, *vay iz mir . . .* kids going out trick-or-treating for Halloween. And *he,* their father? Except that he didn't even know who most of them were or where they came from. But they knew *him.* Everyone it seemed, knew him. Lately, he was surprised and amused to find he was taking on something of the dimensions of a legendary figure. And not only because of his work; although this, of course, lay at the heart of it. In the arts, you were either ignored or deified, and he just happened to be going through one of his more godlike periods. This year, at least, he was a genius.

But the Sunday supplements had also been busy developing his image as a kind of circumcised Lawrence of Arabia, an artistic adventurer who had somehow managed to turn up in the middle of every major war, rebellion, riot, and disaster of the past thirty years. Critics wrote long, esoteric pieces for *Harper's,* the *Atlantic Monthly,* and innumerable art quarterlies on the Karlinsky death wish, the Karlinsky obsession with violence, the Karlinsky need to prove his manhood. Symbols and recurrent themes were discovered in his work and hailed as the Karlinsky Mystique of Crisis, the belief that man truly reveals himself only in moments of extreme stress. Most of which was pure nonsense, of course. Still, the lieutenant had said it was mostly his name that had raised the necessary volunteers. If Duvid Karlinsky was going along, *they* would go along. It was a big responsibility and Duvid realized it. Until now, his needs had put only his own skin in jeopardy. This time he was taking along fourteen others.

"I want to be sure you've got this absolutely straight," he told them when Berger had finished his part of the briefing. "I want no mistakes about what you're getting into, or why."

They sat facing him in the light of a Coleman lantern in the cellar of a ruined German farm house. Thirteen warrior Jews, thought Duvid, far from home and Friday night dinners and the mystic blessings of chicken soup. They suddenly did not look so young to him in their blackface disguise, but rather like weary, aging minstrels, overburdened by the weight of weapons and ammunition and the effect of weeks without decent sleep. The victorious American troops. Winning made such pathetically little difference in their life-style. Victories were great for those back at headquarters, where they had fine, drunken celebrations every time an advance was reported. But to the soldier in the line, there was still the same bone-crushing tiredness, the same living in dirt, the same chance of dying tomorrow in the bright gardens of victory, as there was in the black caves of defeat.

"There's nothing that says we have to do this," Duvid told them. "The British should be in there in a couple of days and things may be no different then than they are now. But there's always the chance they *will* be different, and that's a chance I don't want to take. Not because I'm a great humanitarian, but because I'm a Jew. I admit it. If there were just *goyim* in that camp, I wouldn't be risking your necks and mine. I'd gladly leave it for the British. As it is, I feel this is all ours. The Germans have worked hard to teach us some valuable lessons, and if we're smart, we'll learn them. A Jew is a Jew, and what we don't do for ourselves, no one will do for us. They'll give us sympathy, and sermons from the pulpit, but not much else. They've also taught us that killing is an objective act and death a state beyond right and wrong. Which is why we're taking no prisoners. We're killing every German who moves. Tonight, for a change, the world's favorite sacrificial lambs are going to finally spill the blood of the priests."

Duvid gave them a moment. "When the war is over," he went on, "I'm afraid too much vengeance is going to be left in the hands of the Lord. I'm also afraid it's going to be impossible to find any Nazis. So while we have the chance, we're going to deal with as many as we can. We're all sane, reasonable men as well as Jews. But tonight we're going to break loose from both these restrictions and hit them on their own level. As a pack of madmen. And they *are* mad. Because only madmen would have known an empire could be won by turning the pogrom into a national religion. You really have to give them credit. Jews have been murdered for twenty centuries without anywhere near such important results." He looked at them. "If there's anyone here who feels he can't shoot an unarmed SS guard trying to surrender, you'd better tell us now."

There was some stirring, but no one spoke. "All right," he said. "You all know what to do." He grinned. "And *mazel tov.*"

The Artist

Cresting the hill, Moskowitz signaled and they all bunched up and lay flat. Duvid squinted through the tall grass and there it was, just as the CIC diagram had pictured it, a collection of barracklike buildings, surrounded by doubled, barbed-wire fences spaced with wooden guard towers. But what the diagram had failed to prepare them for was the smell. At a distance of a hundred yards, the smoke blew over from the crematorium and pressed down in a greasy, sweetish gas that made Duvid want to retch. The vapor of burning Jews. And you just lay flat and still in the grass, breathing it in with the night air and knowing that this, finally, was the bottom of the pit. You had read and heard, but the brain still built its own defenses to screen out the unthinkable. Now, suddenly, no more screens.

There were eight towers with attached floodlights, but only four were occupied. Duvid studied the guard on the nearest platform. You hardly ever saw them this close, he thought. Usually they were tiny, barely visible miniatures of men you saw running and dropping and running, and you tried to anticipate, take your lead and squeeze off your shots as best you could. Or else you poured it into a bush or a window not knowing whether you were hitting anything, but just trusting to luck and judgment. Rarely did you get a chance at them like this, with each figure clear and sharp and larger than life.

Gently, he pressed his cheek to the cool metal of the Schmeisser and let its front sight rest on the SS guard's chest. You, you Jew-burning bastard, are dead. And you, and you, and you, he thought, including those on the other towers and those sleeping in the barracks and those at the crematorium, and those in the administration building. All of you, he thought, feeling the rage spew out of him with the imagined rush of bullets, are dead in hell. And I damn you, every one, along with your fathers who did their butchering twenty years ago in Belgium and France, and your sons who will somehow manage a few of their own at some carefully chosen time and place. I damn you all the way from your Hun, Attila, up through your Hessian hounds, to your bloody Clausewitz, to your iron-assed Bismarck, to your crippled Kaiser, to your present frothing corporal. I damn you and your whole sentimental, *gemütlich* country and every Teutonic gangster in it, born and yet unborn. I damn you before and even after we die, I damn you for now and for the not-too-distant future, when everything but Beethoven, Goethe, and Wagner will probably be forgotten, and you will be hailed as friends and allies and allegedly sane people will be driving your automobiles and sitting comfortably on upholstery made from the hides of murdered Jews.

When the black, killing rage began to thin he heard Berger's voice softly dispatching his men, sending off those to cut the wire, those to silence the guards, those to set the charges that would blow the SS barrack. He watched them vanish through the grass, then appear moments later as shadows gliding up the towers, each tower being mounted precisely the same way, at precisely the same rate of speed, so that all four guards would be hit at once. Crazy Yiddish Indians, he thought, converted in a few short months from peaceful citizens into efficient killing machines. It didn't take long.

Berger checked his watch. "Let's go," he said and led Duvid and his remaining men toward the place where the wire had been cut. Moving low and fast, they stopped just outside the floodlit area. The lieutenant glanced up at the two nearest towers, saw that both guards were down, and ran his force through the open wire and into the camp.

They stopped in the shadow of the administration building, a Swiss-type chalet that also housed the commandant's quarters. There were lights on in the orderly room, and a duty officer could be seen reading, a heavy, balding man with a ring of beer fat over his collar. Berger motioned to Corporals Glazer, Ferber, and Sonking and an instant later Duvid saw the German die quietly at his desk. And you too, he thought. He could not see what happened in the commandant's quarters, but it was done just as quickly and quietly, because Glazer and the others were out in less than five minutes. Then they snaked across the compound, keeping to the shadows of buildings and passing through areas of light in quick rushes.

Their charges set, the demolition team was waiting at the north end of the SS barrack. A moment later, they were joined by the wirecutters, those who had taken out the remaining sentries, and Moskowitz, Friedman, and Leventhal, who had secured the crematorium. Duvid felt his breath tight now, as though a strand of wire bound his chest. No losses so far. They were all there. It was going so well it seemed almost dreamlike, a silent wandering through dark grottos. Germans were dying, but quietly and without fuss and without his having much to do with it. He was beginning to feel a little cheated.

Four charges had been placed, one on each side of the long, brick barrack. Sergeant Ellman, their demolition specialist, held the exploder. They moved into position and flattened out in a loose circle around the building and about fifty yards back from it. Duvid lay opposite the main entrance, with Berger on one side of him and Corporal Glazer on the other. He took a cluster of grenades from his pockets and arranged them in the dirt in front of him. Looking down at his hands on the machine pistol, he moved his fingers and found they responded slowly and weirdly, as if not entirely under his control. But when the time came, he knew they would be ready. Other things may have sometimes failed him, but never his hands.

No one made a sound and the silence stretched over the circle of Jews strung around the barrack like a necklace. Or a noose. Duvid heard the soft *pocketa . . . pocketa . . . pocketa* of a nearby generator, but that was all. What was Berger waiting for? He felt himself swallowing dryly and wondered what would go through the prisoner's minds when they heard the explosions and shooting. The poor bastards would probably be scared half to death. He hoped it went well and wished he believed in prayer, so he could throw some of that in too. This would be the time for it. He wondered if any of the others believed in it and hoped, for their sakes, they did. A little outside help would at least make the waiting easier.

Then he saw the lieutenant raise his arm to signal Ellman and an instant later there was a crackling roar and the middle and ends of the barrack seemed to lift slightly off the ground and he felt the blast from the four explosions roll back over him as he pressed into the dirt. His head was still down as the building settled where it had risen and the smoke rolled over him and it started to rain pieces of brick, wood, and steel. After things stopped falling, he raised his head and looked at the barrack. There were great gaps where the charges had been placed, and whole sections of roof had fallen in. The explosions had also started several fires and the flames could be seen through the broken walls. When the roar faded, the shouting and screaming could be heard. Duvid lifted his Schmeisser and waited.

Then the first of them came groping through the smoke and dust, through shattered doors, windows, and holes. They came in varying stages of dress and undress, in underwear, in partial uniforms, in pajamas, and in nothing at all, not yet knowing what had happened, but just running from the disaster within. You too, thought Duvid, and sighted at those coming through the remains of the entrance. He squeezed the trigger gently, felt the quick lurching of the submachine gun against his shoulder and saw the Germans start to fall. They looked surprised and hurt, some sitting down hard and comically on their buttocks, some grasping at chests and stomachs as though to scratch a sudden itch, some just falling forward on their faces. The men following behind them still did not seem to understand what was taking place, but staggered dumbly in all directions, unable to see the Americans lying fifty yards away and firing from the shadows. One man ran straight at Duvid, grasping his falling underpants with both hands. Suddenly he saw him and stopped. Duvid fired a short burst that caught him in the neck and exploded the right side of his face. Scraps of flesh flew at the cheeks of another man who had come up behind him. Running, he wiped at his face and shook his hand as though trying to shake off glue. Duvid swung the Schmeisser fractionally to the left and the man did a kind of quick dance, brushing at his arm, slapping his thighs, scratching his stomach, his hands everywhere on his body. There were six bullets in him when he fell.

Duvid stopped firing and reloaded. The smoke was so heavy that he could barely see Berger and Glazer on either side of him, but heard their guns going. The broken barrack was a gash that split open the world. Out of it tumbled bloody curls of flesh and splintered bones, the screams of dying men. Sounds roared and echoed through the night. Concussions swelled the ground like earthquakes as grenades were lobbed. The earth heaved like a sheet in the wind. And the Germans kept coming, scuttling about like mice looking for holes. They tripped and fell and got up and were shot and sprawled in the shaking dirt. It was impossible for them to run and impossible to stay still. Their feet moved and their mouths cried out and their bowels emptied and they died.

An officer had gotten a few men together and they came out firing. Duvid aimed at the officer and saw bubbly puffs stitch across his chest. The others broke and ran back, but were cut down before they reached the building. Firing came erratically from a few holes and windows until grenades were lobbed in and the return fire stopped. Here and there a man moved brokenly, like a squashed bug.

See the Germans, Duvid thought. The Germans have been shot by the Jews. The Jews have guns. The guns go bang. Fire comes from the guns. The fire kills. The fire burns away German lives. The Germans are bad. They deserve to die. They have killed Jews. The Jews are good. They are getting even with the bad Germans. See the Germans fall. See them squirm and wriggle in the dirt. See them die. See the Jews shoot the dead Germans. That is a stupid thing to do.

Duvid rose and held up his hand. "Cease firing!" he yelled and it was passed down the line and around to the far side of the barrack. The shooting stopped and there was only the sound of the wounded from inside.

"I'm taking some men in to finish them off," Duvid told Berger. "I'll do that."

"No," said Duvid. "This is mine."

He motioned to Glazer, Moskowitz, and Ellman, reloaded, and led them into the gutted building. Moving cautiously, they swung flashlights over the ruined interior, over the clusters of bodies in their stiffening death poses. Close-up, Duvid was surprised at how old they looked. Most had gray hair and sagging faces. One guard sat propped against a beam, his head almost severed by a piece of steel. He had an upper plate and it was half-hanging out of his mouth in an obscene leer. He had not shaved for several days and the stubble covering his cheeks and jaws was white. Here and there an arm moved or a groan could be heard. The Americans spread out and fired the necessary shots. A few patches of flame still glowed and there was the smell of singed wool and hair, and the smell of roasted flesh. Duvid came to a man who had been caught in the chest by a grenade, but who was still alive and conscious. He looked

The Artist

up silently into the beam of the flashlight, a thin, middle-aged man with that expression of sly stubborness and surface servility that was so typical of German faces. Duvid aimed, fired once and moved on.

"Kamerad! Nicht schiessen! . . . Bitte! . . . Bitte! . . .

Duvid swung the flashlight and the Schmeisser together. His finger was heavy on the trigger, but he did not fire. There were three of them and they were huddled in a wreckage of bunks and walls. Their hands were raised, their eyes were wide and pleading, and their flesh seemed to have been put together out of flaky cheese. My God, thought Duvid. They must be sixty years old.

"Don't shoot! . . . Please! . . . Please!" It came in a jumble of pleading German. "We surrender! . . . Prisoners of war!"

Duvid stood there. *Why were they so old?* Moskowitz, Glazer, and Ellman came up behind him. Ellman asked, "What are the bastards saying?"

Duvid translated.

"Shoot the SS murderers," Glazer said.

One of the Germans understood. "No, no please . . ." He was weeping. "We're not SS. We're *Volkssturm.* We're here just four days. We can't be blamed for this. It's unfair . . . unfair . . . They pulled out a whole SS company and stuck fifty of us here in their place. *Fifty! . . .*"

The others began to babble and Duvid felt something bad come into him. *Volkssturm.* No wonder they looked old. They *were* old. His hands shook. Instead of killing hard-core SS, they had butchered a bunch of Hitler's Home Guard, a pathetic collection of overaged misfits, pulled out of their bathrobes and slippers, given two weeks training, and shoved into secondhand uniforms at the heel end of a lost war.

"Nothing . . ." the old man cried in his cracked voice. "The SS left us with nothing. Not even enough food. They just told us to kill everybody here. Imagine. They wanted fifty of us to kill five thousand Jews. Crazy. They're all crazy. *Hitler's crazy.* Damn him! *He's* the one got us into this. Myself . . . I've got nothing against the Jews. I'm not to be blamed."

Duvid turned away. Not to be blamed. He had the feeling these were going to be the most popular words in postwar Germany. "Get

395

them out of here," he told Sergeant Ellman.

"Aren't we going to shoot them?" Moskowitz asked.

"No. They're not SS. They're pitiful. Just get them out of here."

They left the barracks. Duvid slowly followed, looking at the broken walls, the torn, overaged bodies, the still smoldering rubble, staring hard at the gray-haired *Volkssturm* with the false teeth hanging out, his head almost severed, his jellied eyes staring reproachfully back at him as though he, too, was surely not to be blamed.

The strangest thing was the silence. With the shooting ended, no sound came from anywhere in the camp. The prisoners' barracks were as quiet as if those locked inside had either died, or somehow failed to hear a shot being fired. Even those on the punishment fence were silent, five scarecrows in striped rags hanging with their hands tied behind their backs, their feet not quite touching the ground and their arms dislocated.

Duvid shot the locks off the first of the barracks and opened the doors. The stench clubbed them. Human senses could not accept it. They tied handkerchiefs across their noses and mouths and went in. A small bulb threw its murky, yellow light over stacks of bunks that reached from floor to ceiling and wall to wall and were separated by a single slime-covered aisle. The bunks consisted of boards that were either bare or covered with rotting straw. On each bunk lay four men. Or what had once been men. Now they were simply skeletons held together by a thin covering of flesh. Their eyes were open, but they did not move or speak. They just lay staring at the cluster of masked, helmeted soldiers, as though any demonstration of life on their part would be instantly punishable by death.

Duvid reached down somewhere and came up with a kind of voice. "It's all right," he said in Yiddish, "we're friends. We've come to help you."

Dark, cavernous eyes stared at him. There was a twisting of lips, a smothered cough. Nothing else. The faces were so gray they could have been bloodless Negroes.

The Artist

"We're Americans. We're going to take care of you. No more Germans. Nazis have gone away. It's all right." Duvid spoke to them as to children. But *what* was all right? This was the bottom of the universe. Here, nothing was all right, nothing could be believed, nothing remained living except the eyes, those last tiny centers of life into which death was already entering. There weren't even enough muscles left to show pain. The dim light veiled shaven, eggshaped skulls in yellow clouds. In the thick, pestilential air they looked as though they were steaming. Duvid watched a fly settle on the slate-colored eye of one of the skeletons. The man did not even blink his lids.

"*Wir sind Juden,*" he said. "We're Jews." He ripped off his helmet and mask and pointed to his face. "Jewish." He turned to those behind him. "For Christ's sake, show them your goddamned noses!"

Helmets and handkerchiefs were removed. Moskowitz tried to smile while gagging. Berger could only stand, wiping his glasses. Glazer and Ellman made half-hysterical noises. Laughing? Of course. They were still black with burnt cork. Duvid spit into his handkerchief and tried to wipe his face clean. The others did the same.

"*Juden?*" It came from one of the skeletons, but was like no sound Duvid had ever heard. A figure crawled out of a bunk, righted itself, and came toward him, slowly, a mechanical man crudely arranged for the act of walking. Wasted, without the normal, broadening cover of flesh, the skeleton seemed eight feet tall, out of perspective. He touched Duvid's cheek with an icy finger. "*Jude?*"

"*Jude,*" said Duvid.

He stood very still, letting the skeleton look and touch. Other skeletons struggled from their bunks, some naked, some in striped rags, all of them trying to squeeze into the narrow aisle and reach these fine, strong men from another planet who claimed to be their brothers. None spoke or tried to speak. They just seemed to want to touch things, guns, uniforms, helmets, noses (ah, those noses) as if only by actual feel could they believe what they were seeing and hearing. Most came with drooping heads, unable to hold them straight. A skull is heavy when the muscles of the neck have shrunk to threads. Those without strength to leave their bunks raised their

hands in an insanely ordinary gesture of greeting. From the movement of their lips, Duvid could tell they were trying to smile. But
all that showed was a twisted grimace.

Barrack after barrack was unlocked and entered. They were all
bad, but some were worse than others. In some, the dead had not
been removed for days. They had simply been piled in corners. To
Duvid, the worst of all was seeing occasional movement among the
stacked bodies, finding a raised hand, the lifting of lids, a mouth that
tried to speak. But this was unusual, it was explained. Such things
had begun to happen only since the *Volkssturm* were left in charge.
The SS had been far more efficient about everything.

By the time the last barracks had been opened, Duvid was moving numbly, his senses frozen. Almost trancelike, he stayed close
beside Berger as the lieutenant went about the business of establish-
ing order out of chaos. Setting up headquarters in the commandant's office, Berger picked a working committee and a leader out
of the stronger among the skeletons and explained that the British
would arrive shortly to feed and care for them. Then he sent a detail
to check existing food and medical supplies, and gave orders for
their distribution. Watching him function, Duvid heard his gentle,
girlish voice issue instructions with quiet authority, as though he
had spent the better part of his life taking charge of exactly such
disasters, as though this swampland of Hitler's dying millennium,
rather than a New Jersey schoolroom, was and always had been his
natural theater of operations. And through it all, his expression of
calm reserve did not change. Only once, when he had to walk past
the ulcerous remains of the dead and dying, removed from their
barracks and laid out in long lines under the soft night sky, and quite
beyond the reach of any possible liberation . . . only then did Duvid
see his face tremble, the calmness almost lost. But in a moment, he
was better, and once again looking cool and remote.

Out on the compound, the skeletons that were able walked about
in their new freedom. They moved cautiously, as though on wooden
legs, often swaying and having to hold onto one another. The dark,
shining holes no longer stared into the void. They were eyes again.
The front gate had been opened and some of them went there and
took a few tentative steps outside. It was a test. They were waiting

The Artist

to see if the machine guns would open up. When nothing happened, they came back and tried it again. It seemed childish, but was anything but childish. Something almost forgotten had begun to move in their brains. So they wandered about the camp, past the lines of their own dead and dying, past the exploded and burned guard barrack and the bodies of the *Volkssturm,* past the gas chamber and still-smoking crematorium, a spectral parade of skeletons in whom a faint breath of hope had somehow managed to survive.

The noise came just as the first streaks of gray were beginning to lighten the sky. It was only a murmur at first and Duvid did not know what it was until he went to a window of the commandant's office and saw a horde of prisoners gathering and converging on the building. They came singly and in groups, their strange, nontonal murmur growing louder as they approached across the roll-call ground. Some carried sticks, others clutched lengths of planking ripped from bunks, and their general mood, Duvid noted without joy, was clearly not one of celebration.

"What is it?" Berger asked.

"I'm afraid they've found out about our three *Volkssturm.*"

Berger joined him at the window. "Where have you got them?"

"In a back office."

"My God, they'll tear them to *pieces.*"

"Probably," said Duvid.

Berger's soft, Jewish eyes stared out at the advancing skeletons. They moved slowly, because they did not have the strength to move any other way, but the crowd kept swelling and coming. "It's so pointless. They're just three frightened old men."

"Excuse me . . ." It was the leader of the prisoners' working committee, a small, dried-out remnant of a man, with yellow, translucent skin and a curiously formal way of handling the English language. His name was Bronfman and he had once been a philosophy professor of some note at the University of Berlin. "I do not like

399

The Artist

to intrude, Lieutenant, but I must beg to correct you. They are not just three frightened old men. They happen to be three *German* men, who are wearing *German* military uniforms, and who have served in this camp as armed guards, which you must realize, is a very significant difference." He paused, consideringly. "I must also confess that it was I who discovered them and spread the word that they were here."

Berger said blankly, "But why?"

"Because after having spent five years in this place, it is my considered judgment that it was necessary." Enormous green eyes flamed under a high, ridged forehead. "Many thousands have died here, Lieutenant, and many more will die tomorrow, the next day, and the day after that. Nothing can be done for them. We all understand that. Evan those who are dying understand it. Thanks to you and your men, they are at least dying free, and there is some comfort in that. But there will be an even greater comfort in knowing some small reprisal has been taken."

Duvid watched the creeping, faltering tide edge closer to the building. Some fell, having used up what small reserves of strength they had gathered together for the march, and others struggled to lift and carry them along. What a sight, thought Duvid, this army of the damned and dying, coming to collect their first, small down payment on a debt that had no bottom.

"I can't understand," said Berger tiredly, "how three more human sacrifices are going to help anyone or anything."

"Of course you cannot understand," said the philosophy professor in rags. "Such understanding would be beyond the rationale of any normal, civilized human being. But you must realize that we, here, no longer fit into any such exalted category. We are no longer either normal or civilized. We have long ago been reduced to a level of subsistence that borders upon the animal, a level upon which survival can depend as much upon hate and lust for vengeance, as it does upon air and food."

The professor motioned toward the window with a translucent hand, a learned skeleton conducting an advanced seminar in the abominations. "What *they* feel out there, *you* can never feel or understand. No one who was not one of us can understand. In this, we

400

are separate from the rest of the world. Apart. As long as we live, we shall be apart. You cannot imagine. It is not possible for one human being to convey . . ." The professor sighed and shivered a little. His voice had grown weaker and his head drooped with the weight of his scarred, shaven skull. Then he lifted his eyes, blinked, and gazed abstractedly at the two American Jews in their alien uniforms, as though he had forgotten, in his pedantic, cluttered, absent-minded way, who they were and what they were doing there. "Christians . . ." he whispered. "What is it that they want of us? What have we ever done except present them with their God, except grace them with the ethics of love and learning? Is that *really* so heinous a crime? Is that why we must be punished in such a way as *this?*" He shook his head. "Sometimes I am hardly sure of what world I am in, whether I am speaking from the cradle or the grave. I gaze at those about me and see faces that have been dead for years and sometimes I even speak to them. Three frightened old men . . ." he said slowly, reflectively. "Well . . ."—he made an abortive attempt at a smile—"I suppose we shall just have to settle for what we can get."

Duvid and Berger left him sitting there. They went out and collected the others and waited in a thin line across the front of the building. The prisoners were less than forty yards away now, and Duvid could see how many had to be helped. Some of the more badly off had even been transported on crude stretchers made of boards. All who were conscious had apparently been brought along. Those who were unable to walk and who had no one to carry them, crept like giant crabs. As they drew closer, Duvid felt a thousand eyes focused on him. And they were hostile. Suddenly, he was the enemy.

"We're not going to be able to stop them, you know," he told Berger.

The lieutenant stood quietly, hands loose at his sides, and Duvid noticed he had not even brought his gun. He removed his glasses, wiped them on his sleeve, and put them back on. Otherwise he did not move.

The first of them stopped ten feet away, and it was only then that Duvid saw the guns. They had evidently been scrounged from the ruins of the guard barrack, a few pistols and rifles and one actual Schmeisser, all clutched with fierce pride by skeletal fingers. *Behold, O Jerusalem! The meek and the dead have risen!*

A tall scarecrow with an empty eye socket stepped forward. His pale skull leaned slightly to one side, as though weighted incorrectly. Speaking in Yiddish, he addressed the American lieutenant who had liberated him just a few hours before. "We've come for the German swine."

"They're our prisoners," said Berger.

"Yes. You captured them and we're grateful. But now they belong to us."

"I can't give them to you to be murdered."

"I beg your pardon, Lieutenant, but this is not the proper place to speak of murder."

Berger seemed to stare directly into the center of the eye socket. "Sanity must begin somewhere," he said slowly, "It might even be logical for it to start here."

"There are four thousand half-dead Jews behind me who don't care much about logic at this moment. If they live, you might be able to talk to them about it in five years. Maybe on some *Yom Kippur.* But right now, all they want are those Nazis." The one eye glowed dimly. "And I'm afraid if you don't hand them over, they'll just go in and take them."

Duvid saw Berger close his eyes briefly, as if the sights and trials of the past few hours had suddenly become too much to face even an instant longer. "I can't believe that."

"Take my word for it."

"I can't believe you haven't learned more than that."

"Learned?" said the one-eyed scarecrow. "We've learned all there is to know. That's why we want those Nazis."

The murmur had begun again. They were growing impatient. The murmur grew, rose to a chant, swelled to a high keening. Pilgrims at the Wailing Wall, Duvid thought. And they had reason to wail. He saw them press forward from the rear, saw the pressure build and spread down the line.

"Let's get out of here," he told Berger. "Let them do what they have to do."

The lieutenant did not seem to hear him. Calmly, concentrating solely on the one-eyed man before him, he might have been chatting with another teacher in the faculty lounge. "I understand how you feel," he said, "but we must still keep some sort of control. Human life must still be held precious. Even now. Maybe *especially* now. Human life . . ." he repeated, as if the two words were a mystical incantation against the special horrors about him, an impregnable line of defense against the indefensible. "Human life is still the only true miracle, the only . . ."

It was then that the shots went off. They came suddenly, in a wild, rattling, at first accidental, but then hysterically and badly aimed burst, and Duvid thought coldly, the Schmeisser, it's the one with the damned Schmeisser. But he saw neither the man nor the gun, only the one-eyed scarecrow popping like a skinny balloon, and Berger evaporating in lumps of brown smoke, his mouth still open in defense of his true miracle. Then a remnant of the same burst flicked off Duvid's ribs and spun him around to see Glazer and Ellman thump forward on their faces and Moskowitz somersaulting backwards, and the walls of the administration building dappled with something that looked like red sawdust.

"No!" he screamed as bullets sprayed like water from a berserk hose. *"No!"* as other guns swelled the deluge. *"No!"* as Leventhal's face flew to pieces. "Noooooooooo! . . ." as his own Schmeisser finally exploded with his scream.

Firing point blank, he saw them pop and blow apart. They did not fall. They were picked up and slammed into those behind. They shattered in tufts of smoke. They burst. Holes were punched through the solid ranks. But they just closed up the holes and wailed their toneless, catlike wail. The wail snuffed out the rattle of Duvid's gun in his ears. It blotted out the feel of the trigger. The gun was noiseless, a phantom. It wasn't fair, he thought distantly. They had come to lift off their shrouds, and were going to have to wear them in their place.

His gun emptied and he swung the barrel until a board hit him and he went down. Plumes of dust rose. Dirt oozed against his skin like dry fog. Feet pushed his face into the earth. He could not breathe. The cat-wail centered in his brain. The professor was right. *Animals!*

He lay half-conscious and unmoving as they brought out the

three *Volkssturm.* The Germans' mouths were open, but their screams were lost in the cat-wail. A jungle of hands reached for them. When the hands turned red, other hands appeared in their places. All had their turns. The weaker prisoners were helped forward by the stronger. They moved silently now, The cat-wail had died with the Nazis. At the end, their rites completed, they turned their backs on what was left and stumbled away.

"Yisgadal v' yiskadash, sh'meh rabbo . . ."
They were saying the mourners' *Kaddish* on the same ground upon which the dying had been done. Though thousands had died there during the past five years, it was the first prayer for the dead ever held in the camp. The service was being led by a former cantorial student, a wizened, bent skeleton whose voice had somehow retained a power and timbre that sent the ancient Hebrew words echoing through the spring twilight, sent it soaring over the laid-out bodies of the dead, over the army of prisoners and tiny cluster of Americans, sent it sweeping, too, over the tanks and men of the squadron of British armor that had reached the camp just a few hours before, and were now drawn up, at respectful attention, in front of the administration building.
". . . ba'agolo uvisman koriv, v'imru . . ."
Duvid silently followed the words. . . . *And may He speedily establish His kingdom of righteousness on earth . . .* With his head and side crudely bandaged, he stood with the five other surviving Americans and stared dully at Berger's face. How exposed and vulnerable he looked without his glasses. And how much younger. His eyes closed, the dark lashes shadowed his cheek and accented the old expression of calm remoteness. Moskowitz lay on one side of him, Ellman and Glazer on the other, and they all looked reasonably presentable. At least, Duvid decided, they looked better than those whose faces they'd had to cover.
"Yisborach v' yishtabach, v'yispoar, v'yisroman, v'yisnasseh . . ."

The Artist

He listened to the prayer, so resoundingly offered, and felt sorry for the little cantor. Where was his congregation? The dead were unable to hear, and those who lived had long ago stopped caring. They stood in silent rows, their faces not inspired, not comforted, not even angry, but tired and bored. The cantor was addressing a congregation that did not exist. He was chanting to ghosts. *"Our guide is He in life and our redeemer through all eternity."* A fine product, inspiringly packaged. But who was buying?

Certainly, thought Duvid, not Bronfman. The professor stood with his eyes closed and seemed to be sleeping. He deserved the rest. He and his committee had worked long and hard, cleaning up. By the time the British arrived, there was no sign, no visible evidence of what had taken place on the roll-call ground less than twelve hours before. The agreed-upon story was that the nine Americans had died liberating the camp. The fifty-two dead prisoners were also credited to the Germans. With so many murders already going for them, a few more would make little difference. The concept of Jews killing Jews, it was decided, had to be kept among themselves. It was simply too terrible to let out of the family. The *goyim* must not know.

Professor Bronfman had been very apologetic about the dead Americans. He hoped they understood how badly the prisoners all felt. Which was a lie, of course. The skeletons, Duvid knew, felt badly about nothing. They couldn't. And if they could, it wouldn't be over the swift, comparatively easy deaths of a few well-fed Americans, all in good condition, all with well-repaired boots and warm, clean clothing (no torture or starvation or rags for *them*) all with living, undefiled sweethearts, wives, sisters, mothers, all with homes they had left intact, in which no single wall had trembled, no single pane of glass been shattered. No, the skeletons did not feel badly about their dead liberators. If anything, they felt comforted, uplifted. *Look! It could happen even to Americans!* You felt superior to the weak, the sick, and the lame, but most of all you felt superior to the dead.

Except that standing here in the mild German dusk, Duvid listened to the Hebrew promise of the eternal (eternal *what?*) and was able to feel superior to no one. His head and side ached, he breathed with difficulty, and his mind seemed to slip in and out of focus like a faulty lens. He had tried to do what he believed was right, yet fifty-two prisoners, nine Americans, and half a company of overaged Germans were dead because of it. He had feared a massacre if he did not come, yet in coming had caused one. And how many of those dead were dead by *his* gun? How many of Berger's precious, true miracles?

Duvid looked again at the frail body of his friend and felt that something definitive should be said about Martin Berger. But what did you say about a middle-aged schoolteacher with asthma, who hated all armies, yet had died a soldier because he thought he owed a debt somewhere that had to be paid? What *could* you say? That the bookkeepers were either crazy, mistaken, or crooked, and that he had somehow been fooled into paying too much? That it had all been nothing but a dirty trick?

"May the Father of peace send peace to all who mourn," chanted the skeleton cantor, *"and comfort all the bereaved among us."*

And Duvid, along with those other few who were listening and could hear and cared enough to respond, said, *"Amen."*

The British were very good about lending them a lorry for their dead, and even sent along a lance corporal to drive. But Duvid refused to let the Englishman touch the wheel. He did the driving himself, because he knew he had to return Lieutenant Berger and his other Jews, living and dead, personally, to the victory-flushed American forces of liberation.

TWENTY

1945: Amagansett, Long Island

Now Duvid had nothing to do but wait until morning and watch time passing on the mantel clock. The time seemed to move slowly because there was only one lamp on, the clock was small, and he could not see the second hand from where he was tied. The corporal had angled the light so that it shone directly on the Blue Jew, leaving the rest of the room in shadow, a darkened wood through which fire had passed. The corporal was lying quietly on the couch, but Duvid could feel his eyes shifting between him and the painting. Equal time for each. Down the hall, Frank was asleep on a mattress he had pulled onto the floor, and Laurie was tied up in the bedroom. Duvid hoped she was asleep too. A good night's sleep was the most he could hope for her right then. In the morning, he would try to do better. But for now, he thought, sleep could be a very valuable offering.

His thoughts were controlled at this point, but he had not been so calm earlier. *Schmuck,* he had raged at himself. You goddamn, blasted idiot. You should have hit them the minute you saw them waiting out there on the porch. You should have *known.* You and that crap about heroic American soldiers. Laurie had known even back in that bar, but you, you *putz,* had to wrap them in Old Glory and carry them right into your home. You *asked* for it, and by God, you *got* it. Only *she* got it, too, you stupid, trusting crud. How long do you have to live before you learn? You *knew* he was a Southerner, that ultimate flowering of what background and tradition can produce. A festering harvest of malice, Christ, what a people they've been. What sons-of-bitches, from those earliest flesh peddlers on down. Still, it was said that Robert E. Lee had been a gentleman, and that Jackson had great integrity, and Jefferson Davis too. And probably a lot of others, although offhand you can't think of any of their names, you ignorant ass. But it should have been enough for you to know that this one came from the worst element in the country. You should have listened to his voice and known, and seen his eyes and known even more.

Then he told himself, now cut it out and take it easy. All Southerners aren't bad and you'd had no way of knowing it would come to this with him. Just keep your head and get the anger out and stop beating your breast like an old Jew at the Wailing Wall. What you did is past. The only thing you can do anything about now is tomorrow, so think about that.

Which was what he had tried to do. Until his rage had finally thinned with the thinking and stopped clouding his mind. All sorts of things would be possible tomorrow, and if he couldn't outmove these two, he deserved whatever happened to him. And what about *her?* Did *she* also deserve it? Cut that out, too, he told himself. Forget that whole business of deserving. That's not the way you think. That sort of thinking is for the old, the devout, and the ignorant. Whenever things get really bad they start trying to remember what they did wrong to deserve it, as if there were some grand system of moral retribution in force. Talk about idiocy. So half a million kids under the age of ten were murdered by the Germans because they forgot to brush their teeth one morning.

But was the only alternative really the final disaster represented by the Blue Jew?

Reluctantly, he looked at the painting, its flesh pale and rotten in the yellow light of the lamp. Some of Goya's last faces had carried much the same blight, and there were rumors of his mind's having finally been eroded by lead. Occupational hazard. Start painting things the way they really are, and you're sure to be labeled insane. Although at the end, Van Gogh hadn't been in any great shape. But which came first? Did he have to be crazy in order to see, or did the seeing make him that way? Duvid hadn't cared much for his work when he was younger, but was deeply moved by it now. Unless it was more the tragic Dutchman's life that touched him. Or did an artist and his art ultimately become one? And if they did, would the Blue Jew finally prove to be a self-portrait? A lovely image, he thought, for him to be leaving behind.

But what was he leaving? He wasn't going anyplace. He would handle tomorrow the way he had handled every other day in his life. One minute at a time. Still, you weren't supposed to live forever and there was a better-than-even chance he wouldn't make it past late morning. So why not at least accept the possibility? All right. But he would accept it only for himself, not for *her*. And certainly not for his child. The thought of the child was strange. There had not even been time to get used to the idea. The shortest fatherhood on record. No. In wars, there were even shorter ones. Some men became fathers and never even knew it. At least he'd had the chance to know it. For that much, he should be grateful.

And what about her? . . . he asked himself. Shouldn't you be grateful for *her*? Look at all she's given you. But it was such a short time, he thought, and was it really that much? No, you miserable *schmuck*, just everything she had. Now don't go crapping on it just because you're afraid you're going to lose it. What you've had with this girl in a few weeks, some people don't have in a lifetime. And whether it lasts as long as twenty years or only as far as tomorrow, it was still one of the most important things that ever happened to you. So remember it.

"Yuh okay, Mistuh Karlinsky?" It was Clay's voice coming from the couch.

"Great," said Duvid. With his clothes back on and the ropes less cutting, he could almost consider himself indulged.

"Yuh need the latrine, or anythin', let me know."

"Sure."

"Yuh should try gettin' some sleep. Yuh got a big day ahead."

"You're beginning to sound like my mother."

The corporal laughed. "Ah'm glad yuh ain't lost yo'r humor."

"Oh, I'm a barrel of laughs."

"Ah mean it. A man keeps his humor, he's *saved.*"

"I don't *feel* saved."

"Yo'll be all right. Jus' be nice an' smart in the mornin' an everybody'll be fine."

"Don't worry. I'll be smart."

"Then there's no sweat, Mistuh Karlinsky. An' yuh can believe that."

It was part of the new game they were playing. You believe my lies, and I'll believe yours. It seemed to make it easier all around.

"Ah'm glad things are workin' out," said the corporal. "Though Ah still feel bad 'bout the money."

"That doesn't bother me."

"It bothers *me*. It's not what Ah came here for. All the time Ah've been thinking, Ah never once thought'a money."

"Blame *me*. It was my idea."

"Well, yuh sure got to Frankie with it. He made things pretty sticky for a while back there."

But not sticky enough, thought Duvid. Frank had proven a big disappointment. With his forced felony behind him and the smell of money ahead, he had fallen straight back into line.

"Where yuh went wrong, was in yo'r reasonin'. Ah'm a lot of things, but Ah ain't no murderer. Ah don't have to be. Listen," Clay said, "Ah may not have much schoolin', but Ah'm real educated when it comes to people. Ah know more 'bout people than some college porfessors. An' I know 'bout *you*, Mistuh Karlinsky. Ah know yo're not the kind would ever run to the *po*-lice with somethin' like this. Yuh wouldn't want anyone to know. Yuh wouldn't want yo're lady's name all over the papers. If yuh did anythin', yuh'd come after me yo'self. *That*'s what yuh'd do. An' *that*'s why Ah didn't have to plan on no killin' to keep yuh quiet."

Sometimes, thought Duvid, he was sure there was a buried maniac somewhere who ran men's minds. Even the molecules in the air were a little crazy. "Why didn't you explain that to Frank when he wanted to walk out before?"

"The gun was faster and easier. He wouldn't have believed me then anyway."

"Does he believe you now?"

"He's got to now. He's had yo'r woman an' he wants yo'r money."

The Artist

Then neither of them said anything and the Blue Jew glowed through the silent dark, its presence as heavy as the last command of a dying pharaoh.

"Ah'm gonna tell you somethin', Mistuh Karlinsky." The words came evenly and flat, but they rode a wind. "Ah ain't got no lil' brother."

Duvid stared toward the couch.

"Ah did have a brother once, but he died. Anyway, he never did those drawings Ah showed yuh."

"Then who did them?"

"Ah did."

"*You?*"

"A real surprise, huh? Like visitin' a zoo an' findin' the ape sketchin' people."

Duvid said nothing.

"It surprises me too. Everytime Ah draw somethin', Ah can't believe it came from me. Ah mean, it's un-*natural.*"

"There's nothing unnatural about drawing."

"For *me*, it's un-*natural.* Listen, Mistuh Karlinsky. Where Ah come form that stuff's for kids, fags, an' lil' ol' ladies. No one even *knows* Ah do it, for Christ's sake. Not even Frankie."

Art as a secret vice in the Deep South. And what other terrible truths lurked beneath that happy facade of violence? But why the surprise? Hitler had been an artist too.

"Of course Ah've never tried paintin' with oils. Is it hard learnin'?"

"Nothing to it. Untie me and I'll show you."

The corporal laughed. "Yuh'd show me, all right." He rose from the couch and moved closer to the Blue Jew. "Ah gotta tell yuh, Mistuh Karlinsky. No paintin's ever hit me like this one. Ah swear, it is a kick in the *gut.* Ah can't stop lookin'. An' everytime ah look, Ah see somethin' new." He shook his head. "Jesus, Ah *know* Ah could never do nothin' like that. Ah can draw what Ah've seen, but how do yuh put down what yuh've *never* seen? That *no* one's seen? How do yuh do somethin' like *that?*"

"It's mostly accident. You close your eyes, and stumble around in the dark till you touch something."

"But how do you know it's right?"

411

"If it feels right, it's right."

"That's all?"

"That's all."

"But what about all the fancy stuff they write on it?"

"Bullshit."

"Then why do they write it?"

"It's their business. Also, people like reading it."

The corporal stared at the painting. "What sort of feelin's did yuh have doin' this?"

"Bad ones."

"Yeah, but *what?*" Something stirred his eyes. "What *kind* of bad things did yuh feel?"

"It's hard to know afterwards. It's all part of the painting by then."

"Know what *Ah* feel lookin' at it? What Ah once felt listenin' to a dogface screamin' half the night in the wire. It's *that* kind'a feelin'. We lost four men tryin' to bring that boy in. Ah finally had to go out and shoot him." Smiling dimly, he aimed his pistol at the painting. "Think it would help any if Ah shot this poor bastard?"

"No bullet can stop *his* kind of scream."

"Then what will?"

"Maybe our big, new bomb."

Clay stuck the pistol back in his belt. "Think we're all gonna get blown up?"

"Not you. Everyone but you. *You're* finally going to be left all alone in some Georgia swamp, the sole survivor of an insane suicidal species."

"Me an' the Blue Jew."

"You'll make a lovely couple."

"Maybe then Ah could really get to be an artist. Ah'll tell yuh, Mistuh Karlinsky, Ah swear Ah think Ah got the true callin'." He was looking at the painting again, peering deep down into it, as if the quivers of light in its flesh were the entrails of a sacrifice. "Sometimes Ah see an' feel things Ah've never told *anyone.* Like goin' to a place Ah've never been an' knowin' jus' what Ah'm gonna find there. Ah mean, Ah *see* it. And Ah also see lots 'a colors in people's faces that ain't really there and that no one else sees. It's like Ah'm drunk, with that good glow yuh get when it's jus' right and hasn't

412

started goin' sour yet. Or Ah could be out walkin' an' suddenly feel
a wind start up with a long screech, a crack in mah ear that makes
me want to bury mah head. Then Ah look at the trees an' there ain't
a leaf movin'. But Ah can *see* that wind as sharp an' shinin' as a row
'a pins. Once, Ah even had an' ol' hound that died, and Ah kept
seein' him in different things for years after. Or maybe *feelin'* him.
But whatever yuh want'a call it, there was ol' Josh comin' out'a some
winter-brown field, or the stump of a tree, or lookin' at me plain as
day from behind some bush. An' Ah could draw that dog as clear
as if he was really posin'. Sometimes, Ah could even smell him. Ah'd
get this whiff of somethin' comin' off a breeze, or risin' from a pile
'a weeds somewhere and Ah'd *know* it was Josh again. Once, Ah
tried to draw the smell, but couldn't do it with a pencil. Maybe with
oil paints Ah'd have a chance, if Ah really learned to use them
proper. You think that's crazy? Ah mean, to try an' paint a goddamn
smell?"

"No."

The corporal made a soft, dry sound that could have been a
laugh. " '*Course* it ain't crazy. Hell, you've *done* it. Ah mean, that ol'
Blue Jew does give off a stink, now don't he?"

So he's caught that too, Duvid thought, and felt a new stirring
in the room.

"Damn right he does. Ah breathed that stink the minute Ah
walked in here. An Ah recognized it right off. Ah *know* that smell,
Mistuh Karlinsky. Ah've lived with it all mah life. It came out'a mah
folks an' out'a mah lil' brother an' when Ah'm alone an' take a good
deep whiff, Ah can smell it comin' out'a *me.*"

"Funny. And you don't even *look* Jewish."

It had been a small attempt at a joke, but Clay was not amused.

"Yuh don't have to be Jewish to hurt. That's somethin' else 'bout
you people. Yo're so busy bleedin', yuh can't see blood on no one
else. An' if yuh do see it, yuh figure it's only a dumb *goy* anyway. An
animal."

"Well," Duvid sighed, "you did call *us* vermin, didn't you?"

"Yeah." The corporal was silent. "But Ah didn't mean it. Just as
Ah didn't mean most'a that other crap Ah been spoutin' 'bout
Jews."

His face looked drawn, its hollows deep. A barren landscape.

"Ah'm no idiot, Mistuh Karlinsky. Don't yuh think Ah *know* what Jews are? Listen, Ah've been envyin' you people for as long as Ah can remember. The way yuh live, yor' families, the things yuh learn an' do. Yo're a smart man, Mistuh Karlinsky. You should know yuh don't *hate* vermin. They ain't important enough. What yuh really hate are those yuh envy."

Duvid said nothing. At this point he would have preferred the Southerner a bit simpler, more predictable. Tomorrow was going to be one day he could do without surprises.

"Ah'm such a goddam liar, it's hard for me to know anymore what's true and what ain't. That heartbreakin' lil' Christmas story Ah told yuh before? Mostly lies. Mah Daddy stole all right, but he was roarin' drunk when he done it an' it wasn't no toy he took. It was junk jewelry for some whore he was cheatin' with. An' that ol' Mistuh Friedman let him go. Wouldn't even press charges. An' he *should*'a. Jail was where my ol' man belonged an' where he finally went an' died. But yuh think Ah hated Mistuh Friedman any less? Hell! Ah hated him *more*. Ah mean, how could yuh *not* hate a Jew that's all sweetness and light, when yo'r own Daddy's such a shit? Such a shit . . ." he repeated, as though the sound of the words brought a special pleasure to his ear. "No, Mistuh Karlinsky. Ah don't *really* believe Jews are vermin. But Ah'll bet *you* believe most crackers are. An' Ah'll also bet it wouldn't upset yuh too much if the whole damn South was exterminated right out'a the Union. How about *that*, Mistuh Karlinsky, *Suh*? Want'a be in charge of the ex-ter-min-a-tion camps? Think you'd be interested? Think your fine Jewish prejudice 'gainst redneck *goys* could carry yuh *that* far?"

"The plural of *goy* is *goyim*."

"Ah thank yuh." The corporal made a small bow with his head. "Ah'm afraid mah Jewish learnin's been neglected even more than mah English. But Ah'm sure there's a lot yuh don't know 'bout us either."

"I'm sure."

"Yuh can't learn 'bout the South by readin' Northern papers. Ah mean, sometimes we do a few other things beside lynch niggers an' beat up Jews."

"Like what? Burn Catholics?"

The Artist

"Oh, you are *one* prejudiced Jew, Mistuh Karlinsky."

"I'm sorry. My feelings are a little twisted right now. Try me again in a few months."

"Hell, yuh can't judge all Southerners by *me.*"

"I know. And I can't judge all Germans by Hitler."

"It ain't the same thing."

Of course not, thought Duvid. But was it really just an accident that one corporal happened to be a failed German artist, and the other a frustrated Southern one? Or was there something in the nature of the calling itself, some deeply buried pit of darkness, that transcended such things as national and state boundaries? And what of his own feeling for violence? No use denying it. He did have a rich taste for killing. Yes, but only under certain conditions. He had, after all, never killed anyone but Germans, and then only during a war. And if he had the chance to kill these two, here, now? Yes, he told himself, I'd kill them, too. But only because I believe they intend to kill Laurie and me tomorrow. And you wouldn't enjoy it? No. There's nothing to enjoy in killing. Don't kid yourself. Remember all those Germans you knocked off? There was true exhilaration in that, wasn't there? With enough hate jamming your gut, killing can be a sweet release. Yes, but I don't really hate these two men. Which was strange, he thought, considering all they had done. And he wondered about that, but knew that given the chance he would kill them just the same.

The corporal had picked up his drawings and was studying them with the quick, nervous eyes of a fighter who knows he's about to be hit, but isn't sure from which direction. "Yuh said these were good before, when yuh thought mah brother did them. Are they *still* good? Ah mean, for *me?*"

"The church is probably still the same church." But an odd thing there, too. Since there was no longer a Jed, what of that first fine flow of feeling between the artist and him? Could it really be shifted to *this* man, *now*, without change or damage? "Let me see the drawings again," he said.

Clay held the sketches for Duvid to see, and there it was, that same draft of sweetness coming off them again, with just a small distillate of sorrow mixed in for flavor. And it bothered him. He

415

couldn't say it didn't. If artist and work were truly one, then what did it make this redneck bastard? If anything, the drawings came over even better than before. They rode a gift of wings. They soared. They were just smudged lines on paper, and spoke with a little voice, but that little voice spoke with a pure, clean nerve. You'd never know it from looking at me, it said, but I believe in God, for who else could have put me here?

"Are you religious?" he asked.

"What do yuh mean, religious?"

"You keep drawing this church."

"It's as good as drawin' anythin' else."

"Yes, but it's *not* anything else. It's a church."

"Ma used to take me when I was a kid. It don't mean nothin' special. Ah jus' remember it pretty good. When Ah remember somethin' that way, it's easier for me to draw."

"You don't go to church any more?"

"Not since back then." He paused. "No, Ah did go once. It was over in England, jus' before D-day. Ah had a pass one Sunday an' hitched to this town on the Channel. When the fog burned off, yuh could see France from the cliffs. Ah was standin' there lookin', when the Germans lobbed a few over. Some smoke went up, some chimneys came down, an' that was it. But Ah'd never been this close before an' Ah was doin' some shakin'. When Ah passed this ol' church an' saw people goin' in, Ah suddenly went in too. The whole thing was kind'a crazy. There was an air-raid shelter out front an' barbed wire zig-zaggin' 'cross the lawn an' concrete pyramids to stop the German tanks when they came. Inside, the place was half-wrecked. Part of the roof was blown out an' pieces of wall, an' the wind came through the holes an' blew the ladies' veils an' ruffled the Bible pages an' the preacher's hair. The preacher was real old, with only a few white hairs on top an' they stood up kind'a funny in the breeze. He had a low, ol' man's voice that was hard to hear, but Ah wasn't really listenin' anyway. All Ah wanted was to sit there near those people, with the spring sun comin' through the broken roof an' walls an' shinin' from the few chunks 'a colored glass left in the windows."

Duvid said, "Did you draw that church too?"

The Artist

"Ah tried, but nothin' Ah did was any good. Ah got the buildin' down all right, but none 'a the rest of it was there. The thing was, there were these crazy English, sittin' calm an' peaceful in that wrecked place, listenin' to an' ol' man who could hardly talk, while outside, the smoke was still risin' from more shellin'. Ah couldn't get *that* down on no piece 'a paper." His eyes were off somewhere. "Anyway, that was the last church Ah was in. Ah'm no Jesus lover. Ah don't pray when Ah'm scared. What Ah do, mostly, is swear. Ah figure one's as good as the other."

He had been holding his sketches for Duvid to see, but put them down now. "Are they still okay? Ah mean, for *me?*"

"They're okay for anybody."

"Jesus, Ah *like* hearin' that. Ah swear, that makes me happier 'n a flea in a fuzzy dog's ear."

"Why? Would you really want to be an artist?"

Clay looked at him without answering and Duvid stared back. There were moments when the corporal's face fascinated him. The sun-bronzed, glinting luster of the skin, the something so sharp and spare in the bones, reflecting light at a dozen polished points. In comparison, most men's faces were soft, sleek blobs, unkneaded dough. There was a curious greased grace in his gestures, too, quick and watchful as a prowling animal's. His eyes, shadowed now, were cold, watery holes, so dark with sudden anger that Duvid would have liked to stick pins in them to teach him about *real* pain.

"Yuh think that's a pretty damn crazy idea for an ignorant cracker like me, don't yuh?"

"No. I didn't say that."

"Yuh didn't hafta say it. Don't yuh think Ah can read the signs? Shee-it. Ah been studyin' that *su-peer-e-ah* look 'a judgment a long time. Even in the army, a lot 'a officers turned up their noses at me like Ah smelled bad. Except when there was dyin' goin' on. Then, suddenly, Ah was as good as anyone. Ah was even as good as our fancy CO, an honest-to-God Harvard professor, who talked like a real doll. An' one day Ah was even *better* than him, 'cause an eighty-eight blew him clean in half and yuh *know* yo're always better than the dead."

And by sometime tomorrow, thought Duvid, using that same

417

simple paranoic rationale, he no doubt expects to be better than *me*. But he said, "If you wanted to be an artist, there's no reason why you couldn't be one."

"There's plenty 'a reason." A hand fumbled at his head, scratching, soothing, as if trying to calm an itch inside. "Ah never even went to *high school,* for Christ's sake."

"Neither did I. I quit school at fourteen to work with my father."

The corporal looked doubtful, his skull, beneath its close GI cut, as smooth as the bone handle of a knife. "Ah'd never figure yuh for uneducated."

"I'm *not* uneducated. I've lived fifty-six years. I've got eyes and ears and a brain. I've read books. You don't have to go to school to learn. It's all there waiting for you."

"Maybe for yuh it is. But Ah'm no Jew."

"What's that got to do with it?"

"Yuh people know 'bout learnin'. It's in yo'r blood. Know what's in mah blood? Shee-it. The droppin's of a thousan' years 'a hogs 'n chickens an' maybe, when we were real lucky, some mule dung. Ah come from a direct line 'a crackers, man. If we had tails, we'd be swingin' through our sweet Georgia pine right now. Think yuh can get rid'a *that* by readin' a few books?"

"Yes," said Duvid.

"Don't crap *me*, Mistuh Karlinsky."

"Know what your *real* trouble is?"

"Ah can't wait to hear."

"Self-pity. You're so busy feeling sorry for yourself, you're not even thinking straight. We all got here on the same dirty boat. You're not so special in that. But the big thing isn't where you come from, it's where you're going."

Then, watching that same spare, bronzed face, Duvid saw a smile come off it, the most innocent smile it possessed, along with a deep, sweet breath of something, as if this was exactly what the man had wanted him to discover, what he had spent the whole of this night in developing until Duvid could not possibly miss it. And for the first time, Duvid thought, we might have something more than just an outside chance tomorrow.

"Yuh might be right, Mistuh Karlinsky," said Clay. "But Ah'm too far into it now to ever scratch out."

The Artist

Duvid could almost feel the thought rise in the other man and drift over to him. But it was his own voice that said, "If you want me to help you, I will."

"Why would yuh do *that?*"

"Because you're so lovable."

"Yo're the funniest Jew Ah ever met."

"I'm not being funny, just practical. If you think I can be of use to you, I've got some insurance."

"But Ah *told* yuh. Yuh'll be all right anyway."

"I know."

"Yuh don't believe me?"

"A little while ago you said you were such a liar you didn't even know yourself when you were telling the truth."

"That was different."

"Sure."

Clay came over and brushed Duvid's hair back from his eyes. It was a curiously gentle gesture that caught Duvid by surprise and made him flinch as though from a blow. And with it, like a rainbow riding a summer shower, came that same innocent smile. "Ah'm not about to hurt you or yo'r lady, Mistuh Karlinsky. Ah'd like yuh to believe that."

"All right," said Duvid. "I believe it." Yet that simple act of lying carried with it a reverie of death, his own, with his spirit struggling to lift itself loose of the body that had died. Until that moment, he had believed in no such spirit, but evidently did now. It was a hard struggle, as if a balloon caught in water was reaching for a passing breeze to pull itself free. Then it lifted, shone briefly in the sun, and was gone.

The gray eyes had been watching him. "Yo're a lousy liar, Mistuh Karlinsky. But let's hear what yuh can do for me anyway."

"You want to be an artist?"

Even now there was hesitation, a clotting of doubts. "Yuh think Ah could?"

Duvid nodded.

The clot seemed to break like tears and blood. "Then Ah guess that's what Ah want."

"Okay," said Duvid. "Walk away clean from here tomorrow, get your discharge from the army, and I'll show you whatever I know."

419

The Artist

"Yuh'd *really* make me an artist?"

"I can't *make* you anything. All I can do is give you the tools and show you how to use them. But I'm sure you'll do fine."

Clay stared at him, then turned to look at the Blue Jew, as if expecting answers from the painting that Duvid, himself, was unable to offer. "What Ah don't understand is, how could yuh forget what Ah done to yuh?"

"I never said I could."

"Then how could yuh do somethin' like *this?*"

"It beats a bullet in the head."

This time Clay did not bother with the formality of a denial. "How do Ah know yuh wouldn't change yo'r mind once yo're loose?"

"The same way you know I wouldn't go to the police."

"It's not the same thing. Yo'r pride would be workin' *against* me here."

"Well," said Duvid, "you'd still have your Luger. You could always come back and shoot me later, couldnt you?"

Clay turned away from the painting and looked at him then. "Ah guess Ah could do that. An' maybe yo'r lady, too."

"Her too," said Duvid and felt his heart beating like a canary held in his hand. He had thought it, but hearing it said was infinitely different.

"Yuh got yo'self a real fine lady there, Mistuh Karlinsky. Ah guess Ah envy yuh that 'bout as much as anythin'. Ah've had a lot 'a women, but always whores. Ah always pay on the line." He paused. "Ah tried to figure it out once. Ah'm no beauty, but Ah ain't that bad-lookin' either. Ah could've had others if Ah tried. But with whores, nobody owes anybody, an' there's no fussin' afterward. That's what always worries me most 'bout the others. What yuh did with them afterward. Still," said the corporal, "when Ah see somethin' like you got, how it could be when it's good, Ah know Ah'm missin' somethin'. Even watchin' Frankie with her before couldn't spoil it. Ah hoped it would, but it didn't change a damn thing."

He was off somewhere and Duvid stared at the Luger in his belt. The sleeping snake. Oppression stirred again. The pistol was a weight on his will. When he looked at it, he could think of nothing else.

The Artist

Clay said, "What about the money tomorrow?"

"What about it?"

"Frankie's still gonna want it." He was back to considering Duvid's offer, searching for possible flaws. "Ah can try sittin' on him, but he can be real stubborn."

"You can have the money."

"Ah told yuh. Ah don't *want* yo'r damn money. That's Frankie's bug, not mine."

Amazing, thought Duvid. It actually made him angry. "I meant *Frank* can have the money."

"It might be better that way. For everyone. Least it'll hold Frank in line. Yuh won't miss the money anyway. Ah'm sure a rich an' famous artist like you got a lot more than that stashed away. Ah read how much they're payin' for yo'r stuff. Ah thought artists were supposed to starve?"

"Not the Jewish ones."

"Think yuh can make me a rich 'n famous artist too?"

"I guarantee it." Duvid could feel the pressure of his motive but could not name it. He seemed to be buying his offer, yet regardless of what he said, it was impossible to guess his intentions. Perhaps he didn't know himself. Which, if true, would make him even more dangerous. But either way, he was an obviously self-taught master in that great dialectic of uncertainty where lies could lead to truth, and truth spawns the beginnings of lies.

"Ah'll tell yuh somethin', Mistuh Karlinsky. If Ah could paint good Ah wouldn't care one bit 'bout that part. All Ah'd care 'bout would be paintin'. Ah wouldn't even care if *nobody* saw what Ah did."

"You'd care. If nobody saw, there'd soon be no point in doing it. It would be like talking to yourself."

"Maybe. But that's not how it is when Ah think 'bout it. Mostly, in mah thinkin', it's jus' puttin' down the paint and knowin' there ain't nobody ever done before what yo're doin' right that minute. Ah mean, *nobody ever*. Ah feel jus' knowin' that would be enough. If Ah got more, Ah wouldn't kick none, but neither would Ah kick if Ah didn't. Does that sound crazy?"

"No," said Duvid and thought, purity of motive didn't seem to care *whose* mouth it came out of.

"Didn't you ever feel that way?"

The Artist

"A long time ago. At the beginning."

"Then what happened?"

Duvid shrugged against his ropes. "You keep wanting more. When you paint something you really believe, you want others to believe it too. And not only a few. *Everybody*. Finally, you turn into a missionary and want to convert the world with every canvas."

As if on cue, Clay turned back to the Blue Jew. "Like with him?"

"I guess so."

"Anybody seen him yet?"

"Just Laurie."

"What did she think?"

"She hated him."

"Most folks will."

"But not you?"

"No, Suh. Not *me*. He's mah *brother*, Mistuh Karlinsky. Didn't it say in the Bible . . . 'The voice of thy brother's blood crieth unto me from the ground?' Yuh see? Ah ain't one to forget mah early acquaintance with the Book." He grinned. "Unless, of course, it happens to suit mah purpose. An' even then Ah remember mah favorite line from Genesis, chapter 8 . . . 'For the imagination of man's heart is evil from his youth.' It's reassurin'. Makes me feel more normal. Yuh do any readin' from the Bible, Mistuh Karlinsky?"

"Not lately."

"Yuh should. It can be comfortin' in time 'a trouble."

"I'm ready. Get me a copy."

Clay laughed. "Yuh got no trouble now, Suh. Yo're trouble's 'bout over. Ah've decided to accept yo'r offer. Ah'm gonna be yo' student an' disciple. Yo're gonna be mah Jewish Jesus, an' Ah'll be yo' Christian Paul."

And Duvid looked at that sweet, almost beatific innocence of face and thought . . . *Look not thou upon the wine when it is red, when it giveth his color in the cup, when it moveth itself aright. At the last it biteth like a serpent, and stingeth like an adder*. Proverbs. Chapter 23.

The thing was, the crazy bastard *did* have all the makings of a damn good artist.

TWENTY - ONE

1945: Beth Sholum Cemetery, N. Y.

Duvid parked his car outside the cemetery gate and went into the office, a long, cluttered room with a musty smell and walls lined with a hundred years of burial records. There was also a roll-top desk on which half a glass of tea, a partially eaten sandwich, and a newspaper lay abandoned. Duvid saw that the paper was the Yiddish-language *Forward,* and he nodded, as though affirming this as proper and in the natural order of things.

"Hello?" he called. "Anybody home?"

There was the sound of water flushing through ancient pipes and a moment later an elderly, bearded man, wearing a *yarmulka,* appeared. He looked reproachfully at Duvid. "The day is twenty-four hours long," he muttered in deep Yiddish, "and *you,* you *schlemiel,* have to pick just *this* minute to walk in here?"

"I'm sorry. Go back and finish. I can wait."

Duvid had answered in Yiddish and the old man was surprised and a little embarrassed at being understood. He shrugged. "At my age there is no such thing as finish. Sometimes, there is not even start. Mostly, what there is, is try." He smiled, a fresh arrangement of lines under the beard. "So that's why you came? To discuss my plumbing problems?"

"I'd like to know where Anna Karlinsky is buried."

The old man shuffled to a ledger. "Spell the last name, please."

Duvid spelled it.

"When was the deceased buried?"

"About three weeks ago."

"If I may ask. A relative?"

"My wife."

The old man looked at Duvid. "You don't know where your own wife, may she rest in peace, is buried?"

"No."

"You were not at the funeral?"

Duvid shook his head.

"What happened, you'll pardon my asking, that a man should not be at his own wife's funeral?"

Only a Jew, thought Duvid, would ask such questions of a stranger. Instant involvement. Or maybe it was just that there was no such thing as a strange *landsleit* to a Jew. At least not to an old Jew. Most of the younger ones didn't even know they were Jewish until the gentiles reminded them. "I was out of the country," he said.

"Ah. The war? You were away at the war?"

"Yes."

"In Germany, perhaps?"

Duvid nodded.

The old man considered it for a moment. "My deepest sympathy for your loss." He wrote section, path, and plot number on a piece of paper and handed it to Duvid. Then pointing him in the right direction, he went back to his lunch and paper.

The gravesite was a long way from the office and Duvid walked slowly, limping a bit more than usual under the warm midday sun. He was going, but felt in no particular hurry to get there. Annie would wait, he thought. She had spent time enough, alive, waiting for him. A few minutes more now shouldn't matter. He gazed across the forest of stones. The cemetery was old, crowded, and poorly tended, but for its purposes, probably as good as any other. With his usual talent for such things, he had neglected to buy a family plot, and his wife had been buried in one of his father's. Sorry, Annie. But that was just one more point to be listed against him, just one more of his famous truths. Well, he had them all now. Somewhere inside, he knew there was weeping going on, but he could not quite reach it. Pieces of him were breaking up, unseen, were melting, burning with pain, drifting away. So Annie was gone now. One more thing taken from him. He had been robbed of one more creature. One more reason to live drained out.

He lost his breath and stopped for a moment. Then he went on until he came to section 5, path R, plot 14, and looked at the patch of bare earth beneath which the old man's ledger claimed his wife had been buried. And he thought, why have I come here? And now that I'm here, what am I supposed to do?

Word had reached him in Berlin just the week before. He had been there for the signing of the surrender. Not in any official capacity. It had just seemed the right city for him to be in at that particular moment. It was Hutchins who had tracked him down, finally coming on him one day as he sat on a pile of rubble, sketching what little the Russians had left of Unter den Linden. He had stood up, grinning at the sight of his friend. *"Now* I believe it," he said. "If *you're* here, the war *must* be over."

"And if *you're* here, a new one must be about to start." The writer's face was more dour, more grim than usual. "Where the hell have you been? I've been looking for you for days."

"Where were you looking? In Nazi breeding camps?"

"You shouldn't drop out of sight like that. People should at least know where to find you."

"I'm better off when they *don't* know." But he stopped smiling then as something cold touched him. "What is it?"

Hutchins half-turned, avoiding his eyes. "I'm sorry . . ."

Like a reflex, the grin came back, grotesque and dark now, something dug out of the ground. It hurt his mouth, but he didn't dare turn it off. If he did, something terrible would come to take its place. "For Christ's sake! What *is* it?"

In the shadowed German ruins, Hutchins's color was bad. "I'm sorry, Duvid," he said in a cracked voice and again got no further.

"You don't have to tell me." Duvid felt every bit of air go out of him. "I know it all. It's Richard. He's been killed. My son is dead. You son-of-a-bitch! *That's* what you had to find me for? *That's* what couldn't wait?"

"No, no. It's not Richard. I've heard nothing about Richard. So far as I know, he's fine." Hutchins was startled out of his paralysis. "It's Annie."

Duvid looked at him, this ascetic, aging scarecrow in a wrinkled correspondent's uniform. He was no longer glad to see him. He wished he had never appeared. He wanted to be alone again with his lovely German ruins. *"What's* Annie? What the hell are you talking about? Is Annie sick? Is *that* what you're trying to tell me, you skinny *schmuck?"*

"She's dead, Duvid."

Duvid's first instinct was to hit him. He studied his friend's face with an eye to destruction. His fists were mallets. They would reduce him to dust and he would say nothing more. And what he had already said would be forgotten.

But Hutchins's cracked voice went on. Immutably. It was impossible to stop. "It happened almost two weeks ago. Didn't you even know she was *sick?"*

Duvid shook his head. The anger went away and left a deep sickness in its place, an oppressiveness, a ghostly pain in his stomach. No. In his heart, his lungs, everywhere. He watched a detachment of Russian troops go by, rifles slung, boots making a crackling sound in the dry Prussian air. "Nothing," he whispered to the passing boots. "I knew nothing." Then the sickness, too, subsided. It had felt like swallowing a mouthful of poison. But he had the floating suspicion that the poison rose from within. I went off in pursuit of a great moral crusade, he thought, and filled with my own inner nobility, exalted by my own importance, left her to die alone.

Hutchins took him to his billet in an old *Wehrmacht* command post, and kind and loving as a mother, fed him whisky to wash out the poison, and assurances to drain the guilt. "You can't blame yourself. If she'd wanted you there, she would have let you know."

"Nobody wants to die alone. I've been away from her for almost three *years,* for God's sake! Nobody forced me. I stayed away because I wanted to. What *right* did I have?"

The Artist

"The same right you had in 1914. And you were gone *four* years that time."

"That was different. We'd been married only a short while then. I didn't even know I loved her."

"And this time?" Hutchins said quietly, "How long had you been married when you left *this* time?"

"Thirty-one years."

"And there was no longer any doubt how you felt about her?"

"You know there wasn't."

"Sure I know. And don't you think she knew too?"

Duvid stared blindly at his whisky and felt the ache rise up out of him like a green thing from the earth. "I hope so."

Later, he had searched for hints and signs, rummaging through the past as through an old attic trunk and settling, finally, for their last night together. It had been early winter, but they were still out at the beach. They were spending more and more time there each year, enjoying the off-season pleasures of the house as much as those of the summer. It was a good place for Duvid to paint, with few distractions and no one appearing at the door except by invitation. The only intruder was the war, but there would have been no escape from that anywhere. Richard had left for the Pacific several months before, and they both knew it was only a matter of time before Duvid would be off also. But not for the Pacific. There were no Germans in the Pacific. Duvid's war began when the first Americans landed in North Africa.

His going was different from 1914. Annie offered no arguments this time, hurled no recriminations. This time, Duvid thought, she accepted his need to go in much the same way as a mother accepts her child's permanent disabilities. She probably considered him rather simple in his feelings about Jews and Germans and Jewish responsibility to America, believed that in a way, his feelings were actually childish, that at the age of fifty-three, he had somehow been spared the destruction of certain naive sentiments the way a pet duck is spared the ax. But she didn't fight it. And because she didn't, he had felt doubly guilty. Watching her gather his things that last night, seeing her pack his bags, he had wished she would rage at him instead of being so damned helpful.

427

The Artist

"I bought you extra socks and underwear," she said, arranging the pieces in neat rows. "This way you won't have to worry about laundry."

"You should have bought them for the whole army. The smell of soldiers is harder to face than bullets. That's why they fight wars outside, in the fresh air."

"You're no soldier. You're an artist."

It was a subtle reminder that he was not supposed to fight, that he was to be a good little painter and not get too close to the guns. Her first lapse. "I don't think you should stay out here at the beach too much longer," he said. "The winters can get pretty bleak."

"I'll see how it goes. I've been happy here. I've gotten to love this place."

"So have I." She had stopped to study him and he spoke with a great deal of caution, taking pains to give an impression of complete normalcy. Still, it must be noticeable, he thought, that he was not in a normal state. Surely his eyes must be dilated with excitement, maybe even the speed of his pulses visible in the large irises. How *could* he be so eager to leave this place and this woman? And he looked at her face, at one of the most deeply familiar and longest-loved of all human faces, looked at her in a way that could not be mistaken and thought . . . socks and underwear, look how she touches even my goddamn socks and underwear. "It's funny. I never thought a house, a *place,* could seem so important. It's never been things that mattered to me."

"I know. Not to me either." She went back to her packing.

With what restraint she's learned to conduct herself, he thought, and what a lot she had to hold down. The rage was still there, of course, but the explosions had become implosions. And where fire once showed, the darkness came, bit by bit. Where was it hiding, the wrath of Annie Karlinsky? Under a curtain of poise and quiet humor, part acceptance and part slavery? Come on, Annie. Shout, scream. Make me explain, justify. Make me tell how I am what I am and you can't teach old dogs, how I'm this and that and will always be this and that. So why fight it? If you have only one instrument, that's the instrument you must play, right? Or was that just the easy way? Well, it didn't really matter, did it? One way or another he would still go and she would still be left alone. One way or another he would still walk out of the place in the morning and, through actual choice, not necessity, perhaps never see it or her again.

He stood helplessly.

"Duvid, please bring me the rest of those undershirts in your drawer."

He did as she asked. She had always done the packing for their trips and it was no different now. Not that he had ever taken that much time off. There was always something that had to be finished, some self-imposed deadline to be met. I should have taken her on more vacations, he thought. I've cheated her. The state of the world would have been no worse had I taken off one additional week each year and done absolutely nothing but be with her and love her.

He wandered into the bathroom, dumped his toilet articles into a leather kit, and handed it to her as his contribution.

"Won't you have to shave in the morning?" she asked.

He returned his kit to the bathroom. Then he stretched out on the bed to watch her pack, finding something intensely touching in just the way she moved. What an extraordinary woman. She struggled, she fought, yet made do with what was finally handed her. Courage was needed to hold such poise. She had it in large amounts, but at times it was unsteady. At times it trembled. Now, as she bent her head to look for something in a corner of a bag, Duvid saw her cheek quiver. He closed his eyes. He did not have to watch that. His heart gushed pain and love like an hysterical pump, and it made him angry. Cheap sentiment. The expensive part was the act. It was what you *did* that came high. There was no charge for feelings. It didn't even *show*. If he looked in the mirror he would see only head, body, legs, arms, this strange arrangement of parts, nothing more. And he knew these would die. Yet inside . . . *something*. Surely some hearts put out more intensity, more love than others. As some trees produced more leaves. And didn't this feeling mean anything at *all*? Life on this earth couldn't simply be a *picture*.

"Where's your muffler?" she asked.

He opened his eyes. "What muffler?"

"That brown one I knit you."

"In my drawer, I guess."

"No. It's not."

"Maybe it's in the hall closet."

She went to look, but came back without it. "It's not there. Where else would you have put it?"

"I don't remember wearing it this year."

"Well, where could it *be*?"

"Forget it. I won't need any muffler in North Africa."

"Of course you'll need one. The nights get very cold in the desert." She went through more drawers and closets but without success. "That's infuriating," she said and the quiver spread from her cheek to her lower lip like a traveling ague.

Duvid rose from the bed. "Annie . . ."

"Mufflers don't just get up and walk away. It's got to be here *someplace.*"

"Don't worry. We'll find it."

There was an intense, distant expression on her face and she did not seem to hear him. She went into a storeroom and he followed and helped her rummage about. But he watched her all the while, seeing her movements grow more urgent and abrupt. When they left the storeroom there were small beads of moisture on her face and still no sign of the missing muffler.

"It's gone," she whispered, her voice curiously low and childish and hard to understand. "It's disappeared. We'll never see it again."

He wanted to reach for her, but was afraid she might crumble, melt, like one of those kids' snow dams with the water pushing through.

"I've been reading about desert temperatures," she said. "It can drop forty, even fifty degrees at night. You can freeze if you're not prepared."

"I'll prepare," he promised. "I'll buy another muffler. I'll buy *two.* I'll wrap myself till they think I'm a mummy."

She did not smile. Here and there the cracks began to show. All that poise, he thought with regret, all that lovely restraint. His insides felt suspended, as before some dangerous action. She touched her cheeks in a young gesture and he remembered her as a girl. Then she let her hands hang heavy beside her hips and tumbled into middle-age . . . hair beginning to gray, an all-over

The Artist

thickening, a sad uncertainty of line. When had she gotten so *old?* Surprise. *He* was no boy. But wasn't this all part of it? You shimmered briefly and at odd moments with a fine flame. Then it went out. As the graveyards and the madhouse windows told us.

"You think it's funny, don't you?" she said. "You think it's something to make jokes about."

"No. I don't think it's funny."

"Yes you do. You think I'm being silly and stupid to make such a fuss about a muffler. Admit it."

He said nothing.

"*Admit* it!" she wailed.

Her brow was vexed and she had slid into that state where the pain was coming right through her skin. So that looking at her, it enclosed Duvid too, and against all thought and wish, he said, "Do you have any idea how much I love you?"

She looked as though he had clubbed her. It was unfair, he thought. You don't say things like that to a woman you've lived with for thirty-three years. And surely not when you're about to leave her.

"Yes." She sounded tired. "I know how much you love me. Only sometimes I wish you didn't love me so damn much. Sometimes I wish you'd love me less and consider me a little more."

Then she got back her restraint and went on with the packing. But in bed later, with the dark soft all around and the moon patchy as quicksilver, they made love for the last time, although not knowing then, that it would be the last, and she said, "I didn't mean that before. About wishing you didn't love me so much. I lied."

"I know."

She sighed. "The things I can get my mouth to say."

"You don't have to explain."

"Yes I do. That's such a cheap, wife's trick. Trying to load you with guilt. I'm ashamed of it." She held him. "I'm glad you love me as you do. I wouldn't have had it any different. Not for a minute."

He looked down at the drawn, wounded, beloved face, pale and a little misty in the moonlight. If I come back to her all right, he swore, I'll never do anything to hurt her again. Never.

"Duvid?" She whispered as he was drifting off.

The Artist

"Mmmm?"

"I lied about the desert, too. It gets cold at night but not *that* cold." She giggled, the sound sweet and girlish in the purple night. "You don't *really* need a muffler there at all."

He sat on a cracked headstone, staring at the place where they had put her. At least the old man had *said* they had put her there. But mistakes *were* sometimes made and he might very well be looking at the dirt above someone else's wife. Not that it would have mattered. Dirt was dirt and there was no stone to mark it one way or the other. Nor, according to Hebraic law, could there be one for at least a year. An ancient, Orthodox idiocy. Give the wound a full twelve months to heal, so you can enjoy the added pain of ripping it open all over again with a properly delayed unveiling.

He was almost glad he had not been at the funeral. All that foolishness, all that theater. When I die, he thought, maybe I'll be cremated. Privately. Without anyone's knowing. Let them toss my ashes wherever they like. Or they can scatter them where I've been most happy . . . on a hill outside a tiny *shtetl* in Russia where a six-year-old boy sat with his father on Sabbath afternoons; on East Side streets where greenhorn kids played Follow the Leader; in the first bed where I knew about love and the other beds that added to my knowing; in the places where I've managed to paint well and truly what may not have been painted quite that way before; in a railroad station where my soldier-son left me a going-away-present of love; in the remembered heart of my wife which, in the midst of continuing change, remained constant.

The rabbi who officiated at the funeral had stopped by to see him at his hotel room the night before. The visit was a surprise. Duvid had never met or heard of the cleric until he opened the door and saw him standing there, a slight, delicately made man, a reed in dark clothes and silver-rimmed spectacles. He had a thin, suffering mouth in a sallow face and his voice, as he introduced himself, was

432

unprofessionally shy. "I'm Martin Tannenbaum, Mr. Karlinsky. I had the sad duty of conducting the burial services for your wife. I hope I'm not intruding. Perhaps I should have called first."

"No, no." Duvid welcomed him with little grunts of civility. "Please come in." He motioned him to a chair and sat down himself, a courteous expression arranged on his face. Professional condolences, he thought, and waited.

"I take it your wife never mentioned my name in any of her letters, Mr. Karlinsky."

Duvid shook his head.

"I didn't think so. It was not her way."

Duvid wondered what this man, this stranger, could possibly know of his wife's way. He had assumed his father had simply picked a local rabbi to handle the required ceremony. Apparently he was wrong. "You knew Annie?"

"For more than two years. Since she enrolled in a class I teach at the Theological Seminary. It was right after her first operation."

"What first operation?"

"Ah. Forgive me. I assumed you had been told Anna's medical history. I knew she had kept it from you, but thought perhaps you had spoken to the hospital, to her doctors. They are so precise about details these days. Too precise, I have found. They spare you nothing."

"I know my wife died of cancer. That's all."

"Perhaps that is enough."

"Maybe before you came in here, but not now, not anymore." Duvid's voice was flat, his eyes remote.

The suffering mouth suffered. "I'm sorry."

"What was the operation?"

"A mastectomy."

Duvid looked at the rabbi. An intelligent and sensitive man, he thought, with a deeply feeling, expressive face. And at this moment, I despise him. Old images flew, hovered, attacked in waves. That familiar body, that beloved flesh. *Langsam und zeuss, Duvidal. Slow and sweet.* "I see," he said and wept someplace where no one would ever see the tears.

"Please. I didn't come here to add to your grief. Just the opposite. I had hoped I might be able to bring you some small comfort."

"Thank you, Rabbi. But with all due respect, I'm no temple-goer."

Tannenbaum made a small, impatient gesture. "I know that. I wouldn't presume to preach to you. I wouldn't presume to preach to *anybody*. I'm not very good at it. My last three congregations threw me out, I was such a terrible preacher. Now I teach at the seminary and leave the preaching to those with deeper, more resonant voices. I'm a man who knows his limitations, Mr. Karlinsky. I was worthless in the pulpit. Try as I might, I could never quite turn God into a two syllable Gah-ahd."

Duvid said nothing, but suddenly began to like the man.

"All I have come for," said Tannenbaum, "is to tell you some things about Anna during these past two years that you might want to know, to fill in the gaps, so to speak. She had many questions and came to the seminary to see if our course in Theories of Religious Experience might offer her some answers. We had none for her, of course. Not about death. Not really. All we have are theories. Some are quite lovely, but are still only theories. Our Christian friends have one of the best. Each Easter they gather in lily-lined churches to celebrate the life and death of an itinerant Jewish rabbi who dared to say, 'I am the resurrection and the life. Whosoever believeth in me shall never die.' Yet few truly believe Jesus is powerful enough to raise them from the dead. For most, the deathbed shrug of Rabelais seems to be more acceptable. 'I am going away to the Great Perhaps.' "

The sad mouth smiled gently. "I found your wife to be a most remarkable woman, Mr. Karlinsky. A well of courage. And humor. Which is quite rare in such cases. Once it was established that we had nothing but theories to offer, she said to me one day, 'Martin, I've come to an important conclusion about the whole problem of human mortality.' 'Yes?' I said. 'Yes,' she told me. 'When you're dead, you're dead.' "

"She knew she was going to die?"

"The doctors kept saying no, but she knew."

"For two *years?*"

"Yes."

The Artist

Duvid looked at his hands. "Not a word. She never even let me know she was *sick.*"

"She talked about that a great deal. It used to bother her. She knew she was being unfair to you, but it was how she wanted it."

"We'd been married for thirty-three years, for God's sake. Didn't she even want to see me again?"

"Very much. But she didn't want *you* to see *her.* Not the way she was. Not with what was happening to her. And she felt you were where you wanted to be. She understood your needs very well."

"And what about *her* needs?"

"She believed she was serving them best in this way."

"But she was *alone.*"

"No," said Tannenbaum. "She was not alone." There were desperate, surface shadows under his eyes, but the eyes themselves were calm. *"I* was with her."

Duvid turned his head as if to hear better, listen more intently. His hands were folded in his lap, his shoulders drooped with fatigue (he had come all the way from Berlin), his feet were turned inward. The barren hotel room with its production-line furnishings, and his canvas flight bag dumped, half-emptied, on a chair, grated his nerves, made shrill noises in his brain. True things in surprising, grotesque form, he thought in growing wonder. Was it possible that this rabbi, this sad, curiously gentle reed, has loved my wife?

"I was not you, of course," said Tannenbaum. "As you said, you had been married thirty-three years. You were Anna's life. There is no replacing that. But it was not for living that she came to me. It was for dying. And our needs are different for each." Stiff in his chair, he put it to Duvid with a complicated helpless gesture. I lay it all before you, was what it said. "Please understand. She had her bad moments, but mostly, she had control. *And* a sense of responsibility. Not only to those she cared about, but to everyone she touched. Which is a very special kind of love. Perhaps the most important of all. In the final analysis, responsibility may be the only thing that prevents total violence and nihilism in the world. It's the connective tissue between the individual and the tribe. It's the way people stay sane, when they do stay sane. Responsibility to others keeps us from spinning off into insanity, which is, after all, total loneliness, total disconnection from others. That's why people use drugs and alcohol. To transcend the loneliness, the separateness. Only they invoke an irrational means of doing it."

"What *less* irrational means do *you* use, Rabbi? Religion?" It was not a friendly question, nor was it asked in a friendly way. "Is that how *you* connect with others?"

Tannenbaum shrugged. "I'm sure it is. Just as you use painting. And I don't mean that in a derogatory way. Although I know *you* did. As a matter of fact I'm a long-time admirer of your work. You're one of the few artists painting today who seems to care deeply about relating to the world and those in it. The rest just portray the superficial ironies of existence. To them, it's all a kind of mindless confusion, an hysterical study in black humor. And I reject that. A human being *does* have an earthly career. We are *not* a bunch of comic-strip characters endlessly slipping on banana peels and falling on our faces. I am constantly awed by what an individual is, by the possibilities in him for good and evil, by his unpredictability, by his capability for any betrayal, any cruelty, as well as any sacrifice, any altruism. There is genuine tragedy in this world, not just a black, hollow laugh. We're filling the graveyards and asylums at an incredible rate, faster than any time in history. Even our suicides are at an all-time high." The sad face turned inward, went dryly bitter. "I don't know. Maybe at this point of civilization, this point of the world, the only satisfactory companion we can imagine is death."

Sitting there in his wrinkled suit, his face pale and sallow, the rabbi measured Duvid with flat eyes. "I must admit I've been looking forward to meeting you, Mr. Karlinsky. Anna talked so much about 'her Duvid.' Sometimes I had the feeling she made you up, the way a lonely child makes up an imaginary friend endowed with limitless virtues. And I must also admit that I've resented you."

"Why?"

"Because as you've probably guessed by now, I loved Anna and found her image of you too much to compete with." It was said with no change of tone or facial expression, but Duvid noticed a small tic, a slight circular rubbing of thumb and forefinger, begin on Tannenbaum's right hand. "Not that there was ever any true possibility of competition. At least not in the accepted sense. I happen to have a wife of my own whom I have loved faithfully and without reservation for twenty-six years. Nor does one compete for the love of a dying woman under any circumstances. If you love her, you do it without expectation of return. Which I did." He paused, but the movement of thumb and forefinger went on, self-powered. "Does all this shock you very much, Mr. Karlinsky?"

"I don't know."

The rabbi's skin was moist, suddenly mottled-looking. "I'll tell you something. I didn't come here easily this evening. I almost didn't come at all. I couldn't decide whether it would be better or worse for you to know. And at the end, I don't think I really cared. I came simply because I *wanted* to come." He sighed. "So you can forget that nonsense about my being here to bring you comfort, Mr. Karlinsky. To be honest, what I'm here for is to bring comfort to *myself*, to soothe *my* loss."

"*Your* loss?" With some surprise, Duvid heard himself shouting. "You never had anything of Annie to *lose*. You never even *knew* her."

The rabbi smiled. A beggar's grin. "Oh, I knew her. She didn't hide anything from me. There was no reason. Mine was the last face she was ever going to see. There is something special in that." The smile went away. "I don't mean to steal anything from you, from your life together, from your thirty-three years. But don't think you can steal from me, either. I *did* have something of Anna to lose. It was different from what you had, but that doesn't make it less. Even the small failures of a dying body carry their own endearment. Shared pain can make as strong a claim as shared rapture. And it was *my* hand she held when she had to hold *some*thing, *my* voice she heard when there were only her own cries. Do you think that counts for *nothing?*"

The tic had spread, and Tannenbaum was now losing control over the nerves of his face. His cheeks had gone soft with the pain he felt. His mouth looked chapped, with small, black lines. His body seemed to shrink inside his clothes. His eyes, dark, severe, gripped Duvid, identifying him thoroughly, deeply, as his accuser. "Understand," he ordered, his voice hoarse. "I am no stranger to loss. I have had a great schooling in grief. I am familiar with the cries of the soul. I know them. They lie in the breast and in the throat and can be heard even when the mouth is unable to set them loose. I would have imagined myself to be accustomed to bereavement by now, to have developed an immunity, if you will." He shook his head. "Not so. It is as though this were my first exposure, as though the entire experience of loss was unique with me, was invented for me alone. And it should not be. As a man and as a rabbi, I know this. And especially now, with what happened during this war, with what took place in Germany. All claims to exceptional suffering should be abolished, or at least adjusted. We are on a larger, more brutal standard now, one that is indifferent to individuals. It makes me ashamed of what I feel. So many millions, multitudes, to have gone down in senseless anguish, and what do I do? I wail in the night over my loss of another man's wife."

Duvid looked away from the clutching eyes. With mind and heart, he tried to find something for the suffering rabbi. But what? How? He pressed himself, but could come up with nothing for Martin Tannenbaum. He felt only his own hurt, his own guilt. If he had anything at all for the other man, it was still, probably, anger.

"Ah, what's the use, what's the use?" mourned Tannenbaum. "Who am I fooling? Not myself. And surely not you. I am a wolf in spiritual clothing. I raise my eyes piously and hunger for what is not mine. Whatever has happened to me, I deserve. Given a heart, a trust, I betrayed it. I had only to write a letter, I had only to let you know and you would have been with her. Yet I chose to do nothing."

"But you said Annie wanted it that way."

"Never mind what Anna wanted. I knew *better* what she wanted. But I was careful *not* to know. Do you think I wanted *you* there at the end? You were away so long, you could stay away a little longer. There was room for only one hand in hers, and I wanted it to be mine, not yours."

The rabbi stood up and Duvid rose with him, as though connected. He felt stifled and there was an acid fluid in his mouth that had to be swallowed. Then getting down the loathsome taste, he said, "I'd like to break your neck."

Tannenbaum leaned forward, dramatically offered his throat. "Do it. Please. I would welcome it. I would consider it a favor. Do

438

The Artist

you think I am happy with myself? The only reason I am here is for punishment. I cannot even get myself to pray anymore. What shall I pray for? Justice? Mercy? Or shall I try to pray away the monstrousness of life, the evil dream it is?"

"Get out of here," Duvid said.

"Yes. I am going. Immediately." Tannenbaum shuffled toward the door, body bent. He turned. "I think you should know. Near the end, when she was almost gone, she started calling me Duvid." Then he left.

Now Duvid sat beside the freshly turned clay and thought, I lived with her for thirty-three years and there was so much I didn't know. I never even asked her the name of the town in which she was born.

And what of Tannenbaum? In retrospect, he was able to regard the mournful rabbi more charitably than he had the night before. What, after all, had the man taken from him? Surely not a lifetime of love. In a sense, Tannenbaum had performed an almost ritual act of grace. Never mind what his motives may have been. He had still played the surrogate husband when a husband of any sort was desperately needed. With all of a husband's privileges? Perhaps that, too. But even that seemed sadly unimportant beside a fresh grave.

"Excuse me. Would you like me to recite a prayer for the dead?"

Duvid gazed up at the old man from the cemetery office. His *yarmulka* had been replaced by a black felt hat and he was carrying a prayer book. In the bright spring sun, his face was a maze of lines and liver marks, his beard a forest of white vines. He looks a thousand years old, thought Duvid. About to shake his head, he changed his mind. Why not? Whom would it hurt? And the old man had walked a long distance to earn his few pennies. "All right," he said, and stood up, tall among the dead and near dead.

"Her name was Anna Karlinsky?"

"Yes," said Duvid, then stood listening to the same, *"Yisgadal v'*

439

yiskadash sh'meh rabbo . . . " he had listened to not many weeks before in a camp in Germany. Curiously, he wondered what Tannenbaum had said about Annie at the funeral, wondered too, what he himself, given the chance, would have said. That she had never hurt anybody? That she had a foolish belief that people were good? That she had loved her husband and her son? That she had been the purest, most innocent of whores? The foolishness of eulogies. He must remember to put a codicil in his will. A privately held cremation at which no one would be permitted to say a word.

The old man finished his prayer and Duvid offered him a bill. He refused it. "Do you think I would walk my legs off out here for just money?"

"Why else?"

"For a man who has been away, fighting Germans, I am happy to walk."

"Thank you. I appreciate it."

"No," said the old man in his deep, formal Yiddish. "It is I who give thanks. It is I who appreciate. I had family in Poland. In Germany, too. They are soap now. I am old and weak, but even in my grave, I will find strength enough to hate Germans. I will never stop." He peered at Duvid with red-veined eyes. "Tell me. You, yourself. You killed some?"

"Yes."

"Many?"

Duvid nodded.

"Wonderful, wonderful. A Jew who has killed Germans. Never before have I met one. I will remember this day. A small coming of the Messiah. No rising of the dead, perhaps, but all will rest easier. That is the only true way to control death, you know. Kill before you are killed. Maybe, at last, we are learning." He smiled somewhere behind his beard. "A terrible way for an old man to talk, eh? No doubt I shock you. I shock all those not old themselves. I fill them with wonder. Why should an old man be so hard, so bloodthirsty, so unforgiving? Where is the gentle philosophy, the softness, the charity of old age? I will tell you where it is. No place. It does not exist. It is a fairy tale invented by the young. There is not a thing gentle, soft, or charitable about growing old. It is a time of fear and pain, of bitterness and failing senses, of anger and selfishness. If we could, we would have everyone in the world old along with us. Dying, we would take the rest of you, sliding in the same basket."

Suddenly remembering why Duvid was there, he looked down at the new grave. "She must have been a young woman, your wife."

"Too young for *that.*"

"I am sorry for your loss. Good-bys are always hard. But only for those who remain behind. For those who go, it is something else. I have spent a lifetime here, among the departed, and never heard one of them weep, never heard one complain." The old man shrugged. "A poor joke. But if you choose to deal in truth, not really a joke at all. There is no tragedy in dying. It is something we all must do. The moment we are born, we sign a contract to die. Birth is a terminal disease. There is no cure. If there is any tragedy in death, it is in the aging that leads to it, in the sad things that happen to us along the way. Ugly, rusting machines, slowly breaking down. The most we can pray for is to be able to leave with some small dignity and as little pain as possible. And the younger we go, the better our chances."

Duvid stood in the sun and said nothing.

"Are you a believer in prayer, Mr. Karlinsky?"

"Not really."

"Too bad. It can be a comfort. Whenever I am in trouble, I pray. And since I am always in trouble, there is not a day when I do not pray, when I do not say at least a few words to God."

"Does He ever answer you?"

"Not in so many words. He is a silent God. He talks in deeds, in events, and we have to learn this language. But to me, belief in Him is as necessary as breathing. Whatever you may call Him, whether it be Almighty or Nature or Higher Power, doesn't matter. The force that takes care of things, of you and me and the farthest star, is God." He considered the scar, high on Duvid's cheek. "What did *you* feel took care of you while you were fighting Germans?"

"My Schmeisser."

"*Schmeisser?*"

"A German submachine gun."

"Ah." The old man's eyes caught the light, sparkled. "You shot Germans with a *German* gun?"

"Yes."

The Artist

"A blessing on your sweet head. You are a Jew out of the Bible, a Samson with short hair. Truly, God moves in mysterious ways."

Very mysterious, thought Duvid. But he saw no point in telling the old man that his gun had also succeeded in killing Jews. Nor that while he was off doing all that blessed killing, his wife lay deserted and dying and driven to take comfort from a love-hungry rabbi.

But the old man was no fool. And Duvid's face wore no mask. The wrinkled, hooded eyes went soft. "I must tell you, Mr. Karlinsky. My wife, too, died young. Fifty-two years ago. More than half a century. She was twenty-five. Bright as a flower. Here. Look." He took out an old, tattered leather wallet, flipped it open, and showed it to Duvid. There was a faded picture of a girl under the yellowed celluloid cover. Her features were blurred, but a glimpse of fair hair and dark eyes were still visible, along with the straight, serious mouth she had presented to the photographer that day.

"Very pretty," said Duvid.

The old man breathed deeply and put the wallet away. "We were living in northern Poland when the peasants came Jew-hunting one Sunday, came looking for a little amusement. We were hidden in a cellar, but she suddenly remembered her pet hen and ran out to get it. One of those *momzers* caught her in the neck with a pitchfork. Imagine. A *pitchfork*. For a lovely twenty-five-year-old girl. My brother hit me over the head with a shovel to keep me from going after her. When we went out later, she was lying in the gutter with her skirt over her face. She was wearing her best dress. Pink, with white lace cuffs and buttons down the front." He began to cry. The tears ran into his beard and moustache and he swallowed them wetly. "Fifty-two years and I still remember exactly what she wore and I still cry. The heart is an elephant. It forgets nothing."

He took out the wallet again and pressed the faded, celluloid-covered face to his lips. "I had her for six years. Then a pitchfork in the neck. The Germans and the Russians are bad, but the Poles are inconceivable. Animals. The worst kind. If satisfactory coats could be made of their skins, this would be their sole useful contribution to the human race."

"I'm sorry," said Duvid.

The old man shook his head. "I am not telling you this for

sympathy. This is too old a grief for that. You have a newer reason for tears. I am telling you because I thought hearing it might help you to remember why you were not with your wife when she died. From what I see in your eyes, you are already forgetting. Please. As God is my witness, you had good cause to be away. During these past years, there has been no single more important thing for any Jew to be doing than killing Germans. Gas chambers may not be as primitive and bestial a weapon as pitchforks, but they have left a lot more of us dead."

He looked once more at the photograph in his wallet. "Her name was Sarah," he said, "but I called her Little Flower. She was that delicate, that bright. I know it sounds silly for an old man to be saying such things, but I do not feel like an old man when I think of her. It is a curious thing. Here I stand, withered as an ancient, rotting oak, and she remains forever a lovely twenty-five. I sometimes wonder what she will think when the Messiah comes and she sees me." He stood in silence, stroking the wallet absently, suddenly lost somewhere back in northern Poland. "Imagine. For a pet hen," he said. Still stroking the wallet, he moved off down the cemetery path, vaguely, past the crowded gravestones, moved off without saying good-by.

Duvid looked after him, feeling his face rigid and aching. Then with a final glance at the mound of freshly turned earth that covered his wife, he slowly followed.

TWENTY - TWO

1945: Amagansett, Long Island

Duvid drove carefully, the wheel sluggish to his touch. Frank was silent beside him, the streets were wet and deserted, and the car felt like a hearse. It had started to drizzle sometime before dawn and there were few things drearier, he thought, than a beach resort in the rain. Weather had never played much of a role in his life, but he wondered now what effect the wet skies might have on what lay ahead. Primitive feathers of doubt stirred in his brain and he had some savage notion that the rain was a bad sign. Still, the air smelled salty and clean and the night's demons were burning off in the mists. If there was evil in the heavens, it would find him just as easily under azure skies. Yet given his choice for the day, he would have picked a high, bright sun.

He felt Frank's glance, but when he looked, the soldier turned quickly away, as if embarrassed. Earlier, using Duvid's razor, he had cut himself shaving, and the dried blood pocked his cheeks. He appeared very young in the daylight, and with his glasses shining, his face scrubbed pink, and his uniform neatly pressed and buttoned, he might have been a kid, thought Duvid, being driven home from military school by his father. The daylight seemed strange all around. It belonged to no part of the past night. Without the cover of darkness, it was like having fallen asleep in a room with a fire and awakened from a long nightmare to find yourself burning. Through empty streets, he drove past familiar houses, while the steering

444

wheel quivered like a dowsing rod in his hands, as if here, to the left, he had just gone by some terrible evil, and there to the right a nameless terror, caskets of gloom on either side, neighbors, while some hidden sense of direction went wild in his brain. He had the sensation of traveling through a tunnel rather than residential streets, with something vital waiting at both ends. Ahead, the bank. Behind him, Laurie. Then he had a moment of panic. What if I never see her again? he thought, and fought an impulse to turn around and go back. His stomach, if it *was* his stomach, felt severed from him, as in those nights before he knew her. He opened the window and a woe came riding the mist of rain against his cheeks. *Wait, love,* he told her, and breathed deeply, and in a moment was able to put the feeling down.

Before leaving, he had asked for and gotten a few minutes alone with her, but with the corporal watching through a window. She had kissed him then pressed her cheek hard against his. "Tell me," she said.

"I love you."

"Again."

He told her again.

"Swear?"

"To both Gods."

"The baby too?"

"Him, too. Or her. Equally."

She sighed. "I was afraid you'd hate us both."

"Not ever."

"It's all my fault. If I'd kept out of it that night, if I hadn't forced you to hit him, none of it would have happened."

He pulled back to look at her face. It was twisted, as a child's contorts before it cries. "Don't say that. Don't even think it."

"But it's *true.*"

"Stop it."

"All right." But tears slid out from between her lids and her face broke. "Duvid, what's going to happen to us?"

"Nothing. I'll get them the money and it'll be over." He couldn't bring himself to tell her about the contract, about the corporal as burgeoning artist. It didn't hold up well enough by daylight. Some

445

things, he thought, belonged only to the night.

"I hope so." She looked at Clay through the window. "But God, how I hate having to be alone with him."

"Don't be afraid. He won't hurt you now."

"I'm not afraid. I just hate it."

"There's no other way," he said miserably.

"I know. I don't mean to make it worse for you, darling. Just do what you have to do and don't take any foolish chances."

"Don't worry. I won't. Not while you're off somewhere with *him.*"

"Where is he taking me?"

"Only Frank knows. After we pick up the money, he'll take me to you."

She touched his face. "Poor darling. Look what I've gotten you into."

"I told you not to say that."

"You're such a big boss," she said and was able to smile.

"I'm no boss."

"Yes you are. You're the boss over me. Anything you want me to do, I'll do." She was silent and her face looked tired in the early light, with deep, green marks under her eyes.

"Did you sleep?" he asked.

"Not much. When I did, I kept dreaming about dying."

"Nobody is going to die."

"I'm not afraid of dying, darling. There were times I've wanted to. But not now. Not when I have you and the baby."

He didn't like the way she was talking. It was making him nervous. Sammy nosed around and he picked the dog up and let him lick his chin. "I've decided something," he said. "We're going to get married."

"Why?"

"Because I'm old-fashioned and sentimental and don't want my kid starting out a bastard."

"I might make a terrible wife."

"You'll make a lovely wife."

"Is that what you really want?"

"Yes," he said.

"Then I guess I want it too."

"Even though I'll be a middle-aged husband?"

"You'll never be a middle-aged anything. You're the youngest man who ever lived."

"Only lately. Only since you."

She started to cry again, but silently and without changing expression. "We did have fine times, didn't we, darling?"

"Yes, and we'll have more."

"Even if we don't, we had a lot anyway. And they can't touch those. No one can ever touch those, can they?"

"No," he said. "They can't."

"We were alone so much. And you never minded being alone with me, did you?"

"I wanted it that way."

"So did I. Though sometimes I was afraid you might be bored with me."

"I never was."

"Shall we have friends after we're married?"

"If we want them."

"I think we should have a few," she said. "But they'll have to be your friends. I don't really have any."

"All right."

"Do you think they'll like me?"

"They'll be crazy about you."

"They won't think I'm too young?"

"Only the women."

"I'll make myself look older. I can look *really* old if I try."

"Please. Not too old."

"And the baby will make me older, too." She hugged Duvid and Sammy in a single embrace. The weeping seemed to be over. "Darling, I *know* we'll have a lovely life together."

"All four of us," he said, including Sammy.

"Will you love me as much with a big belly?" The look of a child touched by angels came into her face. "When I'm fat and funny-looking and full of strange appetites?"

"Probably not."

"That's *not* what you're supposed to say."

447

"I'm sorry. I've never played this before."

"Neither have I," she said and gave him a final kiss for good-by as Clay left his station at the window and came back into the room.

It was Duvid who set out first with Frank, and his last glimpse of her as they drove off was of this tall, glittering, pale-haired girl, standing in grace and promise between his house and the sea.

Now, nearing the town's business district, Frank shifted nervously at his side and spoke for the first time. "How much farther is it?"

"Not very far. We're early anyway. The bank doesn't open until ten."

"Think there'll be any trouble?" Frank's voice, unattached to his face, sounded higher and less certain than Duvid remembered it. "I mean, will they just give you all that dough without questions?"

"Why not? It's *my* money."

"Yeah."

He was silent again and the car's motor seemed quieter than its tires swishing through the puddles along Montauk Highway, past the scrub oak and pine, and the shingled houses with their doors locked against the rain and imagined disasters. The corporal had given him his switchblade before they left, and he now held the knife tensely on the seat beside him, its blade open and pointing at Duvid. But when he glanced at it from time to time, it appeared to offer him less assurance than fear, until he finally stopped looking at it altogether and just gripped it with white-knuckled fingers and stared through the windshield at the road ahead.

"I'm sorry about last night," he said. "But you saw. I didn't *wanna* do it. I *had* to. You don't know that guy. He would'a blasted me if I didn't."

Duvid drove and said nothing.

"You shouldn't hold that against *me*. I wanted to leave before it even happened. It wasn't *my* fault."

"I know. You're a real hero."

"I didn't say I was any hero. But I'm no animal either. And I never meant for anyone to really get hurt."

"That's very nice. But unfortunately people *are* going to really get hurt." Duvid let several seconds pass. "And one of them is going to be you."

The soldier frowned behind his twin circles of glass. "What do you mean?"

"I mean the same thing I meant last night. Only now *you're* going to take a bullet along with Laurie and me."

"You're crazy. Nobody's taking any bullets. Don't go trying any of *that* on me."

Duvid swung the car to the side of the road and parked.

"What the hell are you doing?" Frank yelled.

"It's time we had a little talk."

"I don't wanna talk. I just wanna get to that bank." He raised the knife to Duvid's ribs. "Now *drive.*"

"Put that thing away. You know you're not going to use it."

"Yeah? Don't push me, Karlinsky." The tone was properly threatening, but there were suddenly small beads of sweat on his upper lip and the point of the knife had begun to tremble.

"Come on, Frankie. Whatever else you are, you're no killer. And you said yourself, you're not psycho on Jews like Clay. All you want now is the money and the chance to enjoy it, right?"

Frank blinked and moistened his lips.

"Well, if you listen to me, you'll get it," Duvid said. "But you're not going to get it the way you've been planning. Try it that way, and the only one who's going to enjoy that money is Clay. He had Laurie and me marked off from the beginning, but you bought it the minute you chickened out on him last night. Tell me. Do you really think he's going to trust you after *that?*"

Frank had the look of a man with several conflicting worries, worrying over which to worry about first. "You're just trying to scare me."

"Sure I'm trying to scare you. It's the only way I can get you to use your head before you lose it."

"If he wanted to shoot us," Frank said slowly, struggling with it,

449

"Why couldn't he have done it during the night? Why should he have waited until now?"

"Because he needed us to go to the bank."

"But he didn't even *want* that dough."

"Not at first. But the more he thought about it, the better it looked. He's not stupid. Why should he pass up that kind of loot?" Duvid was improvising as he went along, yet sensed the prodding of some still-amorphous area of logic. There was a dislocation somewhere. Had the corporal, perhaps, protested too strongly about the money? Had he really been that angry at the implication he might be sharing in it? If it had seemed hard to believe last night, it was doubly so now. Or, Duvid wondered, was he just trying to twist the facts to fit the theory? And if so, why? He didn't have to convince *himself* of anything. Just Frank. Still, the thought nagged. If Clay *didn't* want the money, and *did* intend to do away with them, why *wouldn't* he have done it last night and avoided further risk and complication? Unless . . . and a kind of sweet madness was attached to the possibility . . . unless everything Clay had said was true, and he *did* intend the money solely for Frank, and *did* intend Laurie and him no harm, and *did* intend to honor their agreement. What a beautifully fanatic image. But he wouldn't have risked a five-dollar bet on it, let alone their lives.

"Listen," Duvid pressed. "He's lied to you from the beginning. He even lied about those drawings. His brother didn't do them. His brother is dead. He did them himself."

"Where'd you get *that?*"

"We talked while you were asleep. It was important for him to know if he could draw. He wants to be an artist."

"Bullshit."

"Think about it. Did he ever mention his brother or the drawings before tonight?"

Frank looked at him.

"Of course not," Duvid said. "If his brother did do them and he was as proud of the kid as he made out, why didn't he ever say anything about it? And didn't you ever see him using a pencil himself?"

Frank stared down at his knife. "A couple of times I guess I did notice him fooling with a pencil. Only he never let me see what he was doing."

"It doesn't matter. I just brought it up to show you he's been lying right along and still is. But listen to me carefully now, because I'm going to tell you how we can *all* get out of this clean. I want . . ."

"I don't give a damn *what* you want. You're just getting me all screwed up." Frank raised the knife again, pressed its point to Duvid's shirt. "Now let's get to that bank or you're going to *bleed.*"

Duvid ignored the knife. "What I want you to do," he continued evenly, "is to tell me where we're supposed to meet Clay. Do that, and I'll be able to handle it from there. And you *are* going to do it. Because even if you don't believe what I've just told you, it's the only way you're ever going to see that money you're after."

"I swear, Karlinsky, I'll cut you in *two.*" Frank's voice had gone shrill.

"How is *that* going to get you the money? Now stop being an ass. Tell me where they are and you can be on your way back to camp in half an hour with thirty-four thousand dollars in your pocket. Otherwise, you're just going to end up with a bullet."

There was one instant in which the blade came so close to breaking flesh that Duvid felt a wave of frustration fly out of Frank's hand and move across his face like a hot breeze. Then the moment passed and the soldier sat there, his body quivering. "Jesus," he groaned, "I'm not made for this."

Duvid waited, measuring the damage he had done, sensing some new stretch of void in the silence.

"If I pull something like this on Clay," Frank said, "he'll *really* blast me."

"Don't worry about Clay. Just tell me where he is and he won't hurt *anybody.*"

Clutching his knife, Frank rocked unhappily on the front seat of the car. He closed his eyes as though in pain. "Aaah, what's the use. I should have known. I screw up everything I touch. I'm just like my old man. I can't do *nothing* right."

"You'll do *this* right. I promise you."

Frank opened his eyes, "You promise me," he said flatly. "What

451

the hell can you promise me except *more* trouble? All I did was start out for a couple of beers last night and *look* at me."

"Where are they, Frankie?"

"What are you gonna do? Call the cops?"

"Not with Laurie there. I wouldn't take the chance. I'll go myself."

"What can you do yourself? He's still got that gun, for Christ's sake."

"That's my problem."

"Like hell it is. The minute you go after him, it's my problem too. What do you think's gonna happen to *me* if he creams *you?*"

"I've got a gun back at the house. If I take him by surprise, I'll handle him all right."

"And if you *don't* take him by surprise?"

"I'll take him. I'm not new at this."

"Yeah." Frank nodded gravely, consideringly, a man making a life judgment. "I remember what you can do." He sat as though listening to voices. "And what about me? You say you'll get me the money?"

"The minute you tell me where they are."

"No. I want the money *first.*"

"How do I know you won't just take it and run?"

"Because I'm not that dumb. You could blow the whistle on me in a minute. Besides, I'm depending on you to put Clay away. You think I want *him* on my back?"

Duvid started the motor and shifted into gear. "Okay."

He drove on toward the bank. Another devil's contract. But he did not allow himself to dwell on it. There were too many other things to consider. Time, also, was suddenly important. Some instinct gave warning that if he wasted moments, even seconds from here in, disaster would strike. It made no sense. He knew Laurie would be safe at least until they appeared with the money. Still, the instinct was there and it needed no more supporting logic than could be carried on a sparrow's wing.

It was just past ten when they reached the bank, white-columned, brick, buttressed with dignity, a solid statement of faith, thought Duvid, in the sanctity of the American dollar. Bless it. What would he have done now without it?

The Artist

"Don't stop in front," Frank said, and slouched in his seat. "I don't want anyone seeing me with you."

The car windows were misted over, impenetrable, but Duvid drove twenty yards farther. Then he parked and started out. "This may take a while, so don't get nervous. Thirty-four thousand is a lot of cash to count."

"Wait." Frank gripped his arm. "I've been thinking. I don't want all that. Just get me five thousand. That'll be enough."

Duvid had the car door open. He closed it. "Are you serious?"

"Yeah."

"I don't understand."

"Thirty-four thousand is too much. I could never get away with it. I *know* I couldn't. Maybe another guy could, but not me. Something would happen."

"What would happen?"

"I don't know. But *something.* Maybe you'd start thinking about all that dough and decide to come after me. Maybe you'd call the cops. Maybe the bank would get worried at so much cash going out." He shrugged. "Who knows? In the end, taking five thousand might be as bad as taking the whole thing. But at least I feel I got a chance this way."

"If it's what you want."

Frank smiled weakly, a loser's grin. "It's not what I want. It's what I think I might be able to get away with." It took an effort, but he managed to look directly at Duvid. "Also, I guess I just don't want you to think I'm such a shit. I know that's crazy after last night and all, but I swear I'm not always this bad."

Eventually, thought Duvid, everybody wants to be loved.

"Listen," the soldier pleaded through some private sorrow, "I started shining shoes when I was eight, smelling the stink of people's feet, smelling the stink of shoe polish, getting laughed at in school because the smell was always on me. Sometimes I still put my fingers to my nose and sniff. You don't get rid of it that easy. Not that. And you don't get rid of washing dishes for eleven bucks a week either, or pumping gas for twelve, or knowing you're probably never going to do much better at anything as long as you live. That stuff sticks with you. It's *there.* It shakes around in your belly till you either have to puke, or start screaming, or . . ."

453

He stopped and Duvid finished, "or go out and pick on some lousy Jew?"

"I guess sometimes that too."

Duvid sat with his hand on the door handle. They all had their reasons, long lists, everything carefully documented. But the self-pitiers were the worst. Feel sorry enough for yourself and *anything* was justified. And given the choice, each laid claim to an essential goodness. *But I swear I'm not always this bad.* Of course not. Who *was?*

"Five thousand dollars," said Frank, intoning the sum like a prayer. "I could never squeeze that much together in my whole life. None of us could. Not in a hundred years." He looked tired, suddenly shrunken, diminished, sitting in the car, his body slack in its summer uniform, his voice weary, his face sorrowful in the misty light. "The war was the only good thing ever happened to me. Everything else was a joke. *I'm* a joke. I look in the mirror in the morning and see a twenty-four-year-old joke. Only I don't laugh."

Duvid pushed open the door. Some other day he might weep a few tears with him, but not right now. "I'll get you your money," he said and left him slouched down in the front of the car.

An elderly guard greeted him as he entered the bank. "Morning, Mr. Karlinsky. Wet enough for you?"

"Hello, Tom. How're you doing?"

"Not bad for an old man. Though this rain don't help my arthritis none."

Duvid nodded sympathetically, filled out a withdrawal slip, and took it to the teller's window. There were four people ahead of him and he stood stiffly on the polished bank floor, at war with an impulse to rush to the head of the line, yelling, EMERGENCY. LIVES ARE AT STAKE. LET ME THROUGH. Easy, he thought. A few minutes aren't going to make one damn bit of difference. But the line moved slowly and the dread came back like a recurring disease.

"How's the painting going, Mr. Karlinsky?"

The guard had come over to keep him company on line. A simple, friendly gesture, and a certain pride, too, in knowing a celebrity. At sixty-seven, you picked up points where you could.

"Okay, thanks, Tom."

"Another masterpiece for a museum?" Tom asked loudly, in

case anyone in the vicinity had failed to make immediate identification. Several of those on line did turn around.

"Well, I keep trying."

"I got a grandson draws like a whiz. I don't know where he picked it up. No one ever taught him."

"Don't worry. With luck he'll outgrow it. Like pimples."

The old man laughed longer and louder than the joke deserved. He shifted his gun belt more comfortably under his bulging middle, and Duvid studied the police special in its worn holster. He had considered and rejected any idea of police help, but thought wistfully of it again now. There would be less danger for *him*, of course, as well as the extra assurance of getting Clay. But he was afraid for Laurie. With each additional man involved, the chance of a mistake, of *someone* doing something stupid would be that much greater. And Clay was too much of a fanatic to ever play it safe. Once trapped, he was sure to go all the way and take Laurie right along with him. No, Duvid thought. For better or worse, this had to be all his.

The guard chatted on, but Duvid was watching the teller, mentally trying to hurry him along, increasingly irritated by his leisurely pace, by the small pleasantries exchanged with each depositor. Come on, come on. Christ, he was slow!

Then he was in front of the cage.

"Morning, Mr. Karlinsky. Wet enough for you?"

Duvid nodded and handed over his passbook and withdrawal slip.

The teller smiled, a round-faced man with pink cheeks and sunny eyes. "I guess the light's pretty bad for painting on a day like this."

"Pretty bad."

"Heck. Take the day off and enjoy it. I wish they'd close down banks on account of the light." He was looking at Duvid's slip. "I guess you want a check for this."

"No. Cash."

"A bank check is as good as cash and a lot safer to handle. It also gives you a record of your transaction."

"I know. But I'd like this in cash, please."

The teller shrugged. "You're the doctor. How do you want it?"

"Hundreds."

The Artist

The teller checked his drawer, found it short, and went in back to get what he needed. Returning, he counted out fifty bills, then counted them again. They made a sizable pile.

Duvid stuffed the money into two pockets and started for the door. The guard trailed along. He had seen the pile of hundreds. "You parked nearby, Mr. Karlinsky?"

"Just down the block."

"I'd better walk you to your car."

"Don't trouble yourself, Tom."

"No trouble, Mr. Karlinsky." He pulled in his stomach and walked a trifle straighter, layers of police fat trembling. "That's a lot of money to be carrying loose."

Duvid stopped at the door. It was just as well he hadn't asked for the full thirty-four thousand. The entire bank would have been in an uproar. All he needed now was for Frank to see him approaching with an armed guard. "I'll be okay. It's summer. All the good heist men are on vacation." He touched the old man's arm. "You'd better keep your arthritis out of this rain, anyway," he said and was through the door and headed for his car as the guard stood worriedly considering the weather.

He slid in beside Frank and handed him the money. The soldier sat looking at the pile of bills. His mouth twitched. "That's five thousand?"

"You want to count it?"

"No." He peered back through the rear window, as if expecting to see armed guards running.

"All right," Duvid said. "Where are they?"

Frank's body was quivering like a sea-jelly disturbed in its ooze. "Jesus, Clay'll kill me for this."

"Clay's not going to touch you. Now where *are* they?"

Tires swished by through puddles in the road, rain hammered the roof, and they sat there, the car holding a concentration of fears. Duvid could smell it like an early morning breath after a bad night. A contest was going on in some distant sewer. It took long minutes, but the money finally won.

"Go out towards Montauk on Route 27 for about three miles," Frank said, "to Ferris Road. You know where it is?"

The Artist

"Yes."

"Take it into that wooded area there for about a mile. Till you come to a dirt road without a sign. A few hundred yards in, to the right, is what's left of an old cemetery. They'll be right there. In Clay's car." He sighed. "You got it?"

Duvid had it. Yet, with it came a new horror, that of possible failure. He started the car and said, "Where do you want me to drop you?"

"There's a bus stop at the edge of town. Near Casey's Inn. I can get a lift to camp from there."

They rode without speaking, side by side, shared fears heavy between them. Also, in a very specific way, a shared woman. Though Duvid was careful to avoid mining in that particular cavern. Enough that he was sending off those myopic, clam-colored eyes with five thousand of his dollars and assorted worries. Which didn't especially bother him. Just let it turn out right, he thought, and all debts would be canceled.

He stopped the car in front of Casey's, a wood-shingled tavern with a neon sign in the window. The flickering red tubes advertised a popular draft beer, but their true effect in the continuing rain was sorrowful and foreboding, as though passing travelers were being offered a blood-colored glimpse, through the mists, of their final chance at sanctuary. Frank had been clutching the five thousand dollars with both hands, but now squeezed the money into his pockets. "How'll I know what's happened?"

"You'll know."

"Maybe I better not go back to camp right away. Maybe I better just hang around till I hear something."

"Suit yourself."

"Jesus, I'm scared."

Duvid said nothing. The Judas dilemma. Though Clay was hardly any latter-day Christ. Still, there were all kinds of betrayal, and who could say the anguish was any less at the bottom? Frank looked at him, and for a moment Duvid thought he was about to offer his hand. Then he blinked and ducked his head quickly, as though avoiding a blow, and got out. In the rear-view mirror, he looked oddly right in his summer uniform, in front of the flickering

457

beer sign. A solitary soldier from Indiana, standing empty-handed in the rain.

He had left the house less than an hour before, but coming back now was like returning after a long trip. The place suddenly had an abandoned look. Time, the invader. You opened the door a crack and it took over.

He went in through the kitchen and was met by a frenetic Sammy. Joy and love in black fur. Then he went to the cabinet where he kept the Schmeisser. The machine pistol lay behind stacks of pots and a loose board, its blue steel swaddled in oiled rags. Another German souvenir. The world was full of Lugers and Schmeissers, he thought. Even in defeat, the Master Race was still busily contributing its lion's share of the planet's disaster. And how many other American homes had machine guns hidden in their kitchens? Or was his the only one? And if it was, why was he so unique? Besides its being against the law to own an automatic weapon, why had he felt compelled to smuggle the thing back with him? It surely wasn't nostalgia. If anything, the Schmeisser only revived what he wished most to forget. Nor was he one of those gun nuts in whom the sight of anything lethal produced instant heat. Which left just one explanation. He had brought the piece back because he thought he might need it someday.

Yet why would he need it at *home*, for God's sake? . . . in *America?* The idea was insane. Yes? Then what was he doing now, squatting on his kitchen floor, mopping oil and loading clips? *Get down behind your chair, Momma. Keep away from the windows. Here they come.* The Jew as paranoic, in mid-twentieth-century America. Or was that really their only sane approach to survival? Machine guns and *yarmulkas.* Get the grenades out of your *tallisim,* boys, the *goyim* are coming. It's all they understand, the single thing they respect. So don't drop your guard, don't be lulled by foolish notions of acceptance. Because finally, when you least expect it, they'll come in the night.

The Artist

They've been coming for two millennia, *landsleit.* They may be delayed here and there, they may be diverted by one thing or another, but in the end, you can be sure they'll come.

Having loaded two clips, he slid one into the gun, the other into his pocket, and slowly stood up. Suddenly, he was no longer in a hurry. With the loaded Schmeisser in his hands, he felt almost lethargic, as if the proper delay at this point would miraculously change everything that lay ahead. Then he knew exactly how afraid he was, because he was hoping, against all conviction, that he had been wrong in every judgment, that he had totally misread Clay, that his own fears and prejudices had somehow blinded him to all but the worst. Wasn't there at least a *chance* the man may have been speaking the truth at the end? Wasn't it at least *possible?* Of course, he thought. Everything was possible. But even as he thought it, he knew some compass of direction was being forced out of line in his mind and he was not to trust any part of it.

Still, a molecule of hope must have remained, because he did not leave the house at once. Instead, with Sammy trailing, he stalled a bit longer, moving out of the kitchen, into the hall, and toward his studio. All bases had to be touched, said a voice in his brain, or the runs wouldn't count. But what was he looking for? A sign? A burning bush? He was ready, then, to believe in demons. And what about *God?* Him, too.

That was damned big of him, said the voice, but he couldn't just conjure *Him* up by rubbing a lamp. *Or* a Schmeisser.

Then how?

Perhaps a deal. Hadn't he been making them all over the place lately? Why not one more?

Duvid considered it. Yet what kind of terms?

It depended on what he was asking.

He just wanted Laurie to be safe. He just wanted to have figured Clay all wrong. That shouldn't be too much. He had been wrong about so many things so often. It shouldn't be very hard to make him wrong one more time, now, about *this.*

And what would he be offering in return?

Duvid stopped in the hall. He didn't know. He doubted if he had anything worth offering.

Wrong. He had plenty. He had the Blue Jew.

Why should God want *that?*

Idiot! . . . said the voice. If God had truly created man in *His* own image, and that painting inside was Duvid Karlinsky's sworn vision of man, then that was one hell of a looking Lord to be shown around. And God would hardly be happy about that.

Duvid hadn't thought about it that way before, but did now. Which meant that if he promised to burn that ugly, blue blasphemy, he might just grab himself a deal.

Then a chill passed by him like the beat of a dying heart, and he thought, what have I got to lose? Your sanity, he told himself. But he was hooked and he knew it. For he had to escape from that precise state of reason which allowed him no help other than that of his own hands and brain and the firing chamber of a Schmeisser. At this moment and for this girl, he was ready to stop being a rational man, free of magic and dread of the Lord.

Go ahead and promise, said the voice.

Duvid stood in the hall, chilled yet sweating, feeling a hard contemptuous self-disgust. Every lousy cockroach, he thought, lives with the memory of its one moment of greatest idiocy. This would be his. Nevertheless, he did it. He promised that if he was proven wrong about Clay, that if Laurie came safely out of this, he would burn the painting.

The voice asked for one thing more. There had to be no repeats. Once the Blue Jew was gone, it had to be gone for good.

Duvid agreed.

And would he further agree it had been a lie from the beginning?

How could he say that? He had honestly believed it to be true when he did it.

And what about now?

If he was proven wrong about Clay, then he could have been wrong about that too. But that still remained to be seen, didn't it?

Yes it did, said the voice, and left it at that.

Then Duvid went out of the windowless dark of the hall and into the studio light. He stood blinking for a moment because the eye is quicker than the brain in such things and time was needed to close the gap. Even so, he took longer than necessary. There was the taste

of pennies in his mouth and a breath of the tomb came off the easel
where the Blue Jew had stood. The painting was no longer there,
only the empty rectangle of its stretcher. The canvas itself had been
cut out, leaving a two-inch border of blue background. The cut had
been carefully drawn with a sharp blade and the edge of the canvas
was clean. Duvid walked over and touched it with the tip of a finger.
Of course, he thought, and sat down quickly as he felt his legs start
to go.

The immediate horror was of having to get up. If he just stayed
this way, maybe everything would be all right. No. He had already
tried that and *nothing* was all right. It was as bad as it could get. Oh
my God, it was bad. Never mind your God. *He's* out of it now. Never
mind anything. It was just bad. "Oh, God," he said aloud and
looked at Sammy and without having to see any more, wept.

He found her in the bedroom. She was lying on their bed, her
face a bit pale, but otherwise fine. Her eyes were closed and the
long, blond-tipped lashes curled over her cheeks, giving her a vulnerable expression of girlishness and youth. Had it not been for the
deep red stain on the pillow beneath her head, Duvid might have
convinced himself she was asleep. Ah, love . . . he thought, and
thought it again and kept thinking it because there was nothing else.
Then he lay down beside her, carefully, so as not to shake the bed,
and studied her face as he had done on mornings when he was the
first to waken and was trying to will her out of sleep so he would
not have to be awake alone. And sometimes, through her sleep, she
would feel it and smile, her eyes still closed. Once, smiling just that
way, she had said, "Good morning, darling."

"How did you know I was up?" he asked.

"I felt you."

"But I didn't even move. I was so careful to be quiet."

"I felt you inside."

"Did you *really?*"

"If I were *dead,* I would feel you."

He looked at her, this golden girl capable of such miracles.

"We had a lovely night, didn't we, darling?"

"We always do."

"And lovely days too," she said with her eyes still closed.

461

"That too."

"Which do you like better with me? Days or nights?"

"I like both."

"Equally?"

"They're both lovely."

"I think I should be insulted," she said. "Shouldn't I have more to offer you awake?"

"You do. But I love sleeping with you and sometimes nights are as important as days. When they're bad, they can be even more important."

"Were they ever bad for you?"

"Before I met you they were very bad. I think they were starting to make me crazy."

"Just a little crazy. But you're not crazy anymore, are you?"

"Not with you in my bed."

"I guess I was a little crazy too, at first." She opened her eyes then and looked at him. "We *are* good for each other, aren't we, darling?"

"It was a good *schiddach.*"

"What's a *schiddach?*"

"A love match, you dumb *schiksa.*"

"You don't mind my being a dumb *schiksa,* do you?"

"I wouldn't have it any other way."

"I'm not really dumb, you know. I was smart enough to make you love me, wasn't I?"

He smiled. *"That's* probably about the dumbest thing you ever did."

"And every day I'm going to make you love me more."

"Please," he said. "I love you enough now. What do you want to do? Destroy me?"

"Yes. *That* way, I want to destroy you."

"Good. That's what I want, too," he said and held her then, that morning, with the early sun splashing that sweetness of flesh, so warm with love and sleep.

But not now. He did not hold, or so much as touch her now. He couldn't. He was barely able to look at her. And after a while, when the necessary sanity had returned and he quite realized that despite what she had once said, there were *not* going to be any miracles, he left Sammy to stay with her and carried the Schmeisser out to his car.

But once behind the wheel, he stared dumbly through the windshield and was unable to think of where he was supposed to go. He sat there, his mind an empty sack, watching a streak of sunlight break the overcast. It's stopped raining, he thought irrelevantly. Then he glanced down at the machine pistol on the seat beside him and suddenly remembered every detail of Frank's instructions.

He reached Route 27 quickly and turned right, toward Montauk. The sun was out fully now and there were long paths of purple shadow across the road. He passed some houses on the ocean side, but saw no movement in any of them. They slept, neat, weathered, lifeless in the brightening sun. On the other side of the road was forest, mostly scrub pine and oak, dark, twisted trunks looking almost black against the white of occasional dunes. Groups of young people in bathing suits were walking toward the beach. They wore gaily colored hats and were laughing and talking loudly to one another, and Duvid thought, how safe they feel, how at home in America, how immortal, as though no notion that anyone in the world would dare to do them harm had ever crossed their minds.

He made his left turn onto Ferris Road, a rutted blacktop that wound through scrub growth toward the bay. The sun flickered in small, bright stains among the leaves, and the air was piney and aromatic after the rain. Overhead, he saw a squadron of fighter planes from a nearby base, low in the newly clear sky, headed for their firing range to practice for the next war. That's it, he said to them. Keep in shape. Don't let your guns get rusty. You're going to need them sooner than you think. He was moving very slowly now, watching for a dirt trail to the right. When he spotted it a short distance ahead, he swung the car off the road and parked in the brush. Then he picked up the Schmeisser from the seat beside him, switched off the safety, pushed the fire-control lever from semiautomatic to automatic, and slid quietly out of the car.

He stood very still, listening to the forest sounds, the summer hum of insects, the call of birds in the upper branches, the slight rustling of leaves in the wind. The air was cool, but he was sweating.

And it was not, he knew, from anguish, fear, or exertion, but because he was going to kill a man. It was always that way with him, he thought. *What* always? He made it sound like his line of work. And it wasn't. Because it was never anything he could do coldly, as that murdering bastard out there could. With him, *there had* to be heat. Or was he lying to himself even about *that?* If he wasn't, why didn't he just call the police and let *them* handle it. With Laurie gone, he no longer had any excuse not to. Hell, he told himself. Stop lying. Even with her alive, there was no sane reason not to have called them. You just had to do it yourself. Nothing else would have satisfied you. At least admit that much. But he admitted nothing, and with his shirt wet against his back, he slung the Scmeisser and started through the brush.

Ah, he thought, maybe I really am going to enjoy this one. *Enjoy.* There was a forest of nerves in his gut and he could feel them wriggling like a nest of worms. Only that was some Clay. Jesus, that was a Clay. And he'd had him figured so right. Except for one thing. Timing. You always missed one thing. But who'd have expected him to do that to her *first?* Oh, that Southern bastard. You figured and planned and thought you had it right, but who could have expected *that?* He had thought of everything but that. And if he *had* thought of it? There was no reason to. Yes, but if he *had?* It wouldn't have made any difference. There was nothing he could have done. Hell, there's *always* something you can do. That's lovely thinking, he told himself. Just keep thinking that way and if Clay doesn't put a bullet in your head, you'll put one there yourself.

Then circling through the brush, stepping carefully and lightly, with the green close above and thick all around, he tried to think only of what lay immediately ahead. More figuring and planning. And what would he miss *this* time? Nothing. What was there to miss? He would simply come up behind him where he was waiting in the car and blow him apart with one good burst. Exactly. In the *back?* Why not? Because, *schmuck,* you couldn't do it. *He* did it to her. Yes, but you're not him. Don't be so damn superior. What do you expect to do? Challenge him to a goddamn duel? No. But at least give him a chance to drop his gun. And then? Then turn him over to the police. Is that what you really want? You know it isn't, but it's what's going to have to be done.

The Artist

There was a flicker in the branches ahead and Duvid stopped where he was and swiftly unslung his Schmeisser. But it was only a bird swinging on a branch tip, and he continued on. He could feel his heart going very fast, and he kept yawning nervously. Frank had said the car would be parked a few hundred yards in from the dirt road, and he was trying to estimate distance. He was also watching for signs of an old cemetery. His finger was on the trigger guard now and he walked crouched over, stopping often, behind the trunks of trees, to listen. Why was he so edgy? Clay was expecting him to arrive by car with Frank. From here on, it was all his. Relax, he thought, or you'll end up shooting at a bird, and blow it all.

But just the thought of Clay had him spooked and he had visions of snakes and demons setting off delicate warning systems in his path. A sullen, poisonous fire seemed to be burning somewhere, oil on flame, which gave heated promise of the devil. All Southerners hunted with the spirits, and this one had the Blue Jew besides. Which meant what? That he had now been granted a special grace, been gifted with the devil's own powers? Hardly. All he had was a large piece of still-wet canvas, cut free of its stretcher. A portable cloud of foul intent, but no wizards and fiends. A few maggots, but no incubi and succubi. It was odd, thought Duvid, but he had to remind himself of that. Odd too, Clay's instant feeling for the painting. For he was sure the corporal did not see things as others saw them. No, out of the swirl of pigment on canvas, out of the rent of oil and turp odor, Clay clearly drew a mood, his own spirit in the grove. Just as he probably did not see this forest as others saw it. No sunlight and cool, aromatic green here for him, but a dark cavern spiced with damp and rot, circling in on itself, fenced with gargoyle's horns.

His foot hit against something hard, solid in the high grass. It was part of a tombstone. He was at the cemetery. True Southern Gothic. The only false note was the hour. It should have been midnight. He started to cut back toward the road, picking his way among scattered stones. His shoes made a crunching noise on the crisp, dead leaves underfoot and he was annoyed at himself for his clumsiness. Easy, easy. Don't be such a bloody *klutz*. That means an awkward clod, darling, he told her, and had more, but held back. He did not want to fall into that particular trap. Not now, anyway. He

needed his brain very clear for now. There would be time enough
later for that other. Yes, but why *her?* Now that's a bright question,
he thought. That's *really* a brilliant question. All right, but *why?* Shut
up, he told himself, because his eyes were blurring. Yes, but we'd
had something awfully lovely there, didn't we? Didn't we have
something awfully good going? No one's arguing that, but don't
think about it now. When? Later. I could be dead later. Fine. Then
you'll have no more problems.

He stopped to clear his eyes. Oh, you're a beauty, he thought.
I'm sorry. I can't help it. You can help *anything.* Where's that iron
discipline you're so famous for? To hell with it. All right. But Jesus,
you're disgusting. Talk about self-pity! You're the worst yet. It's not
her you're bleeding for, you gutless wonder. It's yourself. Now get
on with it before you make me sick, he said, and he started to move
once more.

The wind had died and the forest was very still. It gave him a
feeling that no human beings had been here for years. Not since the
last of the dead had been removed. Or were the old bones still there,
abandoned and forgotten beneath their scattered markers? No difference. The earth was the same, the air was aromatic, the silence
as complete. He wondered how the two soldiers had ever found the
place. He had lived in the area for years and never had been here.
Nor had he ever heard a word about an old burial ground hidden
in the forest. But leave it to Clay, the conjurer, he thought, and
would not have been too surprised either, right then, to come upon
a parade of crippled animals, a joyous hunter's bag of small, slowly
expiring creatures, of squirrels with exquisite faces, loving as a doe
in their dying swoon, of chipmunks with all joy going out of their
eyes, of white rabbits with blasted hindquarters and deep red stains
soiling their fur. The gentle, dying things of the forest, offering fun
and games to men with guns. And perhaps leading them all, a tall,
pale-haired girl with a small hole in the back of her head and a
mouth that could absolutely break your heart.

Suddenly the air was altogether sinister and Duvid thought, what
if he's not here? Don't be stupid. He *has* to be here. He has to kill
you. Yes, but what if Frank lied? What if he became frightened and
told you the wrong place? He wouldn't have done that. He'd know
I'd come after him. All right, but he might have been more afraid

of Clay than of you. And remember. He wouldn't have known about
Laurie. He'd have had no way at all of finding out about that. It's
possible, he thought. In which case Frank would be as good as dead
and Clay would have to come looking for *him.* Which meant going
back to the house. But Duvid still did not truly believe any of it, and
advancing cautiously through the trees, watched for his first sighting
of a black sedan.

It came a moment later. The car was parked on a dirt trail about
a hundred yards distant, and he was approaching it from the side
and front. The undergrowth was heavy here and he could see little
more than a dark, metallic body and a glint of windshield. But it was
enough to recognize Clay's car. For the second time, he checked the
Schmeisser's safety and fire-control lever, then started circling to
the left so as to come up on the car from behind. He moved quickly
now, trying to think only of what he had to do. The rest was shut
out, he told himself. The rest was gone. There was no rest. Like hell
there wasn't, he thought, and was able to shut out nothing. Instead,
he felt everything right there, all jumbled together and running
through him, all of it, each detail clear as the veins on the closest
leaf, all that had been, and was, and might have been, and would
now never be. And the reason, just sitting there in an old black
sedan, waiting.

No, he was not cool. His hands on the Schmeisser were not cool.
Nor were any parts of the fingers on the hands. If there had ever
been a killing heat in him, it was there now. Between clumps of
brush, he caught a glimpse of silhouette, head and shoulders,
through a rear window, and it came like a quiver of jeweled cities.
Lovely. Minarets and lights shining in the glow of a warm dusk, and
a black-biled lust building in him. As he moved closer, the pressure
grew and his mind cried out, easy . . . easy. But he was not ready
to listen, and listened instead to something else that told him, *do as
you feel,* and he knew there were dimensions of darkness in him that
light would never reach.

"Stand right there, Mistuh Karlinsky."

The voice came from behind him and slightly to the right and
was soft as the call of a thrush. Duvid stopped. Incredibly, he heard
himself laugh.

"What's so funny?"

The Artist

"I keep forgetting. Never underestimate your enemy."

"Ah'm not your enemy, Mistuh Karlinsky. Ah'm the greatest admirer yuh got in this world."

Duvid stood gripping the submachine gun, weighing his chances of whirling and getting off a burst before he was hit. The odds weren't good. But it was the only game in town and better than simply standing here and taking it in the back. Still, if Clay had just wanted to finish him, he'd be on his face right now. He obviously needed to talk first.

"Where'd yuh get the Schmeisser?"

"The same place you got the Luger."

"Drop it."

Duvid hesitated.

"Now, Mistuh Karlinsky."

He let the machine gun fall. But carefully, so as not to get dirt in the muzzle.

"Ah guess yuh went home."

Duvid said nothing.

"Ah'm sorry 'bout yo'r lady, but there was nothin' else Ah could do."

The insane thing was, thought Duvid, that he probably *was* sorry, and *did* believe himself without choice.

"Ah'm also sorry 'bout not holdin' to our deal. You could'a taught me a lot. But Ah knew yuh'd get to Frankie and Ah didn't want to be no pigeon. Ah hope yuh understand that."

Duvid stared off at the silhouette in the car, seeing now that it was rigged, some sort of dummy. Very clever. Trying to figure distance, he guessed Clay to be about fifteen feet behind him and perhaps a yard to his right. To keep him talking he asked, "What did you do with the Blue Jew?"

"He's all laid out nice and neat in mah car."

"What do you want him for?"

"Yuh kiddin'? He's gonna be mah teacher. If Ah study him real careful, Mistuh Karlinsky, Ah figure Ah'll know as much as you."

He must be down low, thought Duvid, deciding the voice was coming from below ear level, and probably from behind a bush. It was shady where he was standing, but shafts of sunlight struck down through the trees in oblique gold, catching leaves and branches, and he wondered if this would be the last sight he was ever to see.

"What about Frank?" he said.

"Ah ain't worried none 'bout Frankie. Not while he's got all that green."

Duvid edged his feet very slightly to the right. "He didn't take the money. He was too frightened."

"Yo're lyin'."

"You should know I'm not."

Clay swore softly. "Ah knew he had no guts, but Ah figured the money would prop him up."

"I guess you'll just have to shoot *him*, too."

"If Ah do, Mistuh Karlinsky, it ain't gonna hurt *you* none."

A spasm of illness lifted from Duvid's stomach and touched his brain. He said quietly, "If I don't meet Frank in an hour, he's going to the police." It was a quick and not especially good lie, but could still buy a bit of time. In the silence that followed, he turned slightly more to the right.

"Ah don't believe that. He'd be too scared to go to the cops."

"He might be. If he wasn't even more scared of *you*. And if I don't meet him, he's *got* to know he's next on your list."

There was silence once more and Duvid could feel the hesitation behind him as clearly as if it were an attachment on his own nerves. *Now,* he thought, I've got to do it *now.* And he had a moment when he remembered the two Germans with the lances and his legs were all but gone. Which is to say he looked deep into that glitter of past death and could hear its song. *Come on,* it was saying, and its appeal was as strong as it had been on that morning when he was out swimming alone and Laurie had called him back. Only this time she would not be there to call, and he could think of nothing important or attractive enough to want to go back to. Then the rational part of his mind said angrily, *Schmuck! You're not letting him get away with this.* And in one movement he dropped, grabbed the Scheisser, and rolled with it, hearing the explosions behind him as a single sound, and feeling that now-familiar burn, that fine hurt make entrance, but feeling also the quick, spastic lurching of his own gun, spraying low, spraying the green curtain where the voice had been, in a long burst

469

that ripped and tore like a wind. Duvid wasn't sure, but he thought, with the noise of the explosions still in his ears, that he had heard a scream.

There was a soft fluttering sound as torn branches and leaves twisted down, then no sound at all.

Breathing heavily, Duvid lay flat behind a tree. The rain-soaked ground had wet him and the forest floor was soft and he felt the cushion of fallen pine needles under his elbows. He had been hit twice. One bullet had entered behind his left shoulder, the other through the upper part of the same arm. His sleeve and arm were covered with blood, but he felt little pain. That, he knew, would come later. If there *was* a later, he thought, and wondered if he had been on target at all with his burst, or whether Clay was off somewhere right now, circling for another shot. He peered through the surrounding brush, trying to gauge which way Clay might have gone, but it was impossible to see more than twenty feet in any direction. I've got to move, he decided. I'm a sitting duck here. But when he tried to crawl, his arm and shoulder refused to hold and he thought, to hell with it. If it comes, I'll take it where I am.

A frightened squirrel chattered from a branch directly ahead, then came down the tree trunk, stopping on the way to look at him. He saw the squirrel's eyes, dark and bright, and the bushy tail, jerking with excitement. Better beat it, he told the eyes, it's getting dangerous around here. Then he watched the squirrel bound across the ground and out of sight, and he just lay quietly behind the tree with the submachine gun across his left forearm. What I ought to do, he thought, is change the clip. That was a long burst and I might run dry on the next. But with his left hand not working well, it was easier to think than to act, and he was hurting a great deal by the time he had ejected the used clip, gotten a fresh one out of his pocket, and inserted it in the magazine.

He closed his eyes against the pain, but this just made him dizzy and he opened them at once. For God's sake, he told himself, don't faint. All you need is to pass out now. Don't worry, he said, no one's fainting. When have I ever fainted, you idiot? Never. But when have you ever been fifty-six years old with two nice, fresh German bullets in you? Dripping sweat, he grinned at the surrounding brush. Two

The Artist

more holes for his aging flesh. Maybe it was some kind of record
. . . if they kept records of such things. Hell, they kept records of
everything these days, from sporting events, to weather, to stock
prices, to war dead. Just name the event, and someone had the
statistics. And he was still going strong. With luck, he might even
pick up some *more* holes in the next few minutes.

Come on, Clay, he thought. Where the hell *are* you? Let's not
drag this thing out. That was some Clay. *Jesus,* that was a Clay. He
and the Blue Jew. Who'd have imagined a love affair like that?
Funny, how he only thought of the painting now as the Blue Jew.
Names meant nothing, but it was strange how that one had taken
hold. *If Ah study him real careful, Mistuh Karlinsky, Ah figure Ah'll know
as much as you.* And did that poor, blue thing really represent the sum
total of Duvid Karlinsky, of everything he had learned in a lifetime
of living? Evidently Clay believed it did. Christ! If it were true, that
would probably be the saddest thing of all. No. The *second* saddest.
Laurie was the first. No, he thought again, *he* and Laurie. *Together.*
To have killed *that,* with all they had going, had to be the saddest.
Momma, that was sad. Nothing could be sadder than that. In the
whole, bloody world, with all they'd had in front of them, what could
be sadder?

Oh, stop whining, he told himself. How do you know how much
the two of you would have had? Maybe you'd already had the best
of it. Maybe from here on it would have been coming apart. Use
your head. You had a thirty-year age gap going there, for God's
sake, not to mention background and religion. All very exciting and
unique for a few months, but a lot different for long-term living.
And don't forget. There are more good love affairs ruined by marriage and time than by anything else.

Very clever, he thought. You're really bursting with these precious little witticisms, aren't you? All bright and cynical and absolutely guaranteed to render the beautiful ugly. Only don't do it.
Please don't get cynical. You don't know how much time you have
left and it would be foolish to spoil it with that kind of thinking. At
least hold on to the good. You can't do anything for her anymore,
but maybe you can do something for yourself. Remembering may
not be that much, but it's all you've got right now.

The Artist

The pain had become very bad lying down, and he shifted to a sitting position. Then he probed the wounds with the fingers of his right hand and found the blood clotted in the webbing of his shirt. He had always been a fast clotter. Doctors loved his clotting. Karlinsky, they said, you're a great little clotter. Maybe that was why his flesh had been punctured so often. Nature's law on the full utilization of talent. Whatever else he had produced would be forgotten. He would be remembered solely as Karlinsky the Clotter.

Clay, for Christ's sake!

Duvid's eyes searched bushes and trees, but found no movement. He listened, but heard only birds and insects and the rustle of leaves. And for the first time he thought, maybe I hit him. Maybe I really got lucky back there and caught him with one. Or was that just what he *wants* me to think? With the Schmeisser having the greater range and fire power, he'd be smart enough to want me to come to *him*, to want to get a shot at me up close. Still, there *was* something that could have been a scream before, and I might be waiting here for a dead man. I'm also getting weaker and less alert. If he doesn't make some sort of move very soon, Duvid thought, I'll have to make it myself.

Yet having decided this, he felt little confidence in the resolution, felt almost as though he had been pushed into it against his better judgment. He had a sudden horror of being forced, against his will, to do exactly what Clay wanted him to do, as if the mood of the wood itself, even the air, were enemies joined in the contest on the wrong side. And it was a mood he did not dare to break, for fear of an even greater penalty than that of walking toward a final bullet. *What* greater penalty? He didn't know. He knew only that he was in some black, all but inextricable situation in which Clay was managing to push him further, and then further again, like a chess master tracking his victory. Come out from behind your tree, hidden voices were calling. We have already taken your queen and we will soon checkmate your king, old friend. And Duvid could feel himself slipping, as in a fever, off the lip of all sanity. All right, he told the voices, I'm coming.

He crawled slowly, painfully, using his knees and one good arm, the Schmeisser dangling in front of him, hung there, from his neck,

The Artist

by its sling. Keeping tight cover, he moved in a wide, closing arc that would, if he had figured correctly, bring him to his target area from the rear. In his mind, he had marked the rambling cluster of foliage he wanted, as being slightly to the right of a tall pine, and he used the top of this tree as his guide. Crawling, he breathed as though there were hardly any air left in the wood, and what was left carried some god-awful stench. In his mind, he was passing through the blackest of swamps, with no choice but to keep crawling and never stop. Disaster would be on his body if he came to rest. If he so much as closed his eyes, he would go up in smoke. Then this suffocation passed and was replaced, on the beat of the silence, by some icy majesty of intelligence, and he was scored with a vision of Clay sitting quietly in his hidden lair, waiting, the Luger aimed at the precise point at which his, Duvid's, head would soon appear. And with that picture, dread came in and his own death passed by like a vagrant breeze. Or was it some other Jew being murdered some-where else at this instant, in some other wood, or back alley, or city street, or *shtetl* lane? The image in his mind was blurred with shock. Did he feel a saber go slicing into flesh, a bullet chasing a heart, a club start beating a brain? Was another Jew expiring, his cry un-heard in the summer air, but carrying across trackless miles to *him*, in *this* wood? And was one more murderer walking devoutly into his church for absolution, and, of course, getting it?

Then the vision passed and he wanted nothing more than to escape from that magic which let him know of unseen killings in one direction and his own death in another. He wanted to be free of wizardy, free of the Schmeisser weighted about his neck like some deadly steel albatross, free of any further violence. He wanted things to be as they had been twenty-four hours before and would never be again. He wanted to turn away from what was awaiting him somewhere in the brush, and just keep going without looking back. He wanted to say to hell with Clay and leave his payment to sources other than himself. Yet what he did was continue to crawl forward, two knees and one elbow at a time and the blood clotting beautifully in the fabric of his shirt.

But the pain and the exertion and the loss of blood were adding up, and these, mixed with the pestilence of mood drifting out of the wood, were suddenly too much. For a true sickness seemed to be rising from the green, something broken and dead, stale, used-up, and it collected as nausea in Duvid's throat and came rushing out. There it goes, he thought, and sent it off with the downrushing sounds of a stream reaching for its river, all of it, all the bile of anguish and the horror of loss and the stink of old fears, an army of deserters, saying good-by to his body. Good-by, he said, and with his eyes closed, hung there, drained, but feeling a rare moment of balm along with the sorrow. Then he opened his eyes and through a veil of the palest, most verdant green, saw the face of the Blue Jew looking at him.

I'm twice mad, he thought. Yet the staring eyes carried the same clear glint of ice, the mouth, the same silent scream, the broken cheek, its matching gouge of a bullet, the overall stain of its mood the same fear and funk and sniff of the grave. The bloodied mouth worked, struggled, came up with a garbled croak. "What . . . what took yuh . . . so long . . . Mistuh Karlinsky?"

Part of the burst had caught him in the chest, and his ribs were shattered and sticking in red-and-white splinters among the blood-soaked rags of his shirt. But he had somehow managed to prop himself against a tree, and in this half-reclining posture, seemed almost casual, a picnicker, taking his ease after a satisfying basket lunch. The pistol was still in his hand but not pointing anywhere, and Duvid thought, he could have *shot* me, why didn't he *shoot* me? He felt the weight of the Schmeisser about his neck, but it was hopelessly tangled in its sling and he knew that even now his one good hand would never be able to get it straightened in time, that even now he was dead if Clay chose it that way. He remained on his knees, unmoving.

"Ah . . . was afraid . . . Ah . . . had . . ." The words made a strange bubbling sound and came from a long way off. "Finished yuh . . ."

Duvid moistened his lips and tasted his own sickness. He looked at the maniac eyes and felt old lights moving between them. He saw the blood and carnage and wanted to look away. But he didn't.

"Jesus . . ." bubbled the voice, "Ah didn't want . . . *both* of us . . . dead. Not *both* of us." The Luger came up in a beckoning motion. "Come . . . closer, Ah can't talk . . . so . . . good."

The Artist

Duvid crawled through the fragment of green that separated them. Up close, the broken face grinned with that clown's deep gloom and Duvid thought, he's all mine, he's always been mine. I conjured him up out of paint and canvas and my own sickness and there's no one left to blame but myself. I dared the devil, spit in the face of God, and *he's* my payment. *He* didn't kill Laurie, *I* did. Then a small part of the large fear that is saved for eternity clotted in his brain, madnesses formed and were consumed, and he waited for whatever was to come next. But what, really, was left? *More* frozen flesh in winter tombs? Were they all, finally, dead?

Clay gave partial answer. "Ah'm dead . . . Mistuh Karlinsky. How . . . are . . . you?"

"Not yet dead."

"Good." It was all there in the eyes, perhaps more gray than blue, but the anguish still going back to that earliest of stone gods. "One . . . of us . . . gotta . . . stay . . ."

Or course, thought Duvid. They were of the same blood. At the least, father and son.

The broken grin held, but the light was beginning to go out of his eyes. "Ah swear . . . Mistuh Karlinsky . . ." Bubbles damaged the words. Or was it some final laughter? "Ah'm beginnin' to feel more . . . Jewish . . . every minute," he said, and letting go the Luger, gave a slow look of surprise and died.

Duvid rocked gently on his knees on the wet ground. Were they *both* crazy? There was plenty of evidence. But if they were, so was the rest of the species.

He stayed there until he heard the wail of sirens. That should be Frank with the police, he thought without surprise, and rose to meet them.

Riding back, the soldier said, "I had to tell them. I kept thinking about it and I finally couldn't have it no other way."

Duvid nodded.

"You can have your money back," Frank said.

"Keep it. You've earned it."

"But I didn't do anything. I came too late."

"At least you came," Duvid said and ended it there.

The police wanted to take him directly to the hospital, but he told them about Laurie and said they had better stop at his house first. There were things to be done there.

On the way, he sat holding himself together in the patrol car. Well, love . . . he thought. Then because all his usual disciplines were suddenly air, and he had nothing else to offer and no one else left to offer it to, he thought, all right, God, one last deal. Take her gently God, this girl known as Laurie Wallace, who was born a Christian and lived as one in the best sense of the word, but who was also, through the act of love, a Jew, and who, in the brief time allotted her, carried her pain without complaint or self-pity and offered joy without keeping account. Treat her kindly, God, because I loved her and I have not loved many. Which is perhaps no great recommendation in itself, but which must, I believe, be noted here, as part of any true record of agreement.

Then although his earlier try had turned out badly, and he knew there was even less chance of ensuring the success of this one, he had an obliging policeman get the Blue Jew out of Clay's car, lay him neatly in his studio fireplace, and, with the puzzled officer displaying the same unquestioning tolerance he might have shown for the young, the senile, or the insane, had him put a match to the canvas and let the poor, silently screaming thing seek its final peace in a shroud of smoke.

He didn't go into the bedroom with them. Feeling himself near to blacking out, he sat waiting for it in front of the fireplace.

One of the policemen came hurrying back. "I think you had better come in," he said.

Duvid looked up at him and saw three spinning heads.

"The shot must have grazed the bone. She's unconscious, but she's alive."

Duvid pushed himself out of the chair, took two steps, and fell forward.

The Artist

His arm and shoulder bandaged, he sat in her hospital room, waiting for her to come out of it. The afternoon light filtered in and splinters of sun fell on her face, on that incredible tip of of nose, the pale lashes, on the full, curving lips, still loving and without hint of bitterness. When she opened her eyes, she saw a nurse, two doctors, then him.

"Duvid?" It came out low and confused.

With his good hand he reached for hers, feeling himself grinning and nodding insanely, a mute, maniac clown.

"I'm not dead?"

He shook his head.

"I was sure I'd be dead," she whispered.

All he could do was hold her hand, feeling dry, helpless tears somewhere deep in his throat.

"Why didn't Clay kill me?"

Duvid found a kind of voice. "He tried. He thought he had."

"Then why aren't I dead?"

"I made a deal."

"With Clay?"

He gave her his crazy grin. "With God."

She smiled. Then suddenly remembering, she put a hand to her belly. "What about the baby?"

"The baby is fine."

She sighed and closed her eyes.

After the doctors had gone, Duvid watched her sleep.

All right . . . he thought. So he hadn't actually felt for a pulse or listened for a heartbeat. But neither had he noticed her breathing or seen any other sign of life. Looking at it logically, his extreme emotionalism at that moment could easily have clouded his judgment. Since he had expected to find her dead, he must have simply *assumed* her to be dead. Still, he was not unfamiliar with the look of death, and when had he ever made such a mistake before? And what, after all, had logic to do with the events of the past twenty hours?

He smiled. For him to even give thought to such a thing with any real seriousness would have been just too much, but he allowed himself to say, in the faintest of mental whispers . . . "Thank you."